LEGENDS OF ANTARES:

THE SKORATH
PROPHECY

SK⊙RATH THE PROPHECY

LEGENDS OF ANTARES
BOOK ONE

BENJAMIN BOEKWEG

To request permission, contact the author at
contact@benjaminboekweg.com

Paperback ISBN-13: 9798986144252
E-Book ISBN-13: 9798986144269

Library of Congress Control Number: 2023901750

First paperback edition April 2023

Cover design by: MiblArt
Illustrations by: Apartwork on Fiverr

Published by Heralds of Life in Provo, Utah

benjaminboekweg.com

To Grace, for giving me the idea to write a proper romance in space

Contents

ACKNOWLEDGMENTS

I want to thank my brother Richard who dreamt up this universe with me when we were children. The rich world-building we did together created such a unique environment that allowed creativity to flourish.

And to my precious Annie, thank you for your tireless work proof-reading my drafts and encouraging me to continue writing. Thank you for the space you created for me to unfold these stories to the world.

Thank you, Peter, for your invaluable insights and encouragement. Your willingness to assist me creatively in solving my little plot predicaments has been pure gold. Thank you also for beta reading and giving me early reader insight.

To my other brother Buck, remember that little story you helped me transcribe from a written notebook onto a computer file? Well, that has since become this book. Thank you for your help.

I wish to also thank my early fans, Grace, Alan, Layton, and Ann. Your enthusiasm has been such a blessing.

DRACONIS MUNDI

VARESH

Gamma Lepordis
53rd Fleet

CRYSTALLINE

CRYSTALLUS

CHANTELL PRIME

XANDRAX

CHANTELL

HG Arizona   TRKZPIZKS

ARKALAN

SCORPII

HG Chicago

ARKALAN

Able Station →

Frigate

Gama Station

SECUNDA
SCORPII

TUMNE

Bravo Station

HG Moscow

HG Washington

HG Warsaw

HG Shanghi

CALDEZE

ANTARES?

TUMNEI

Emerald Heart Nebula

← Anon's
Nebula

EUROSIA

EUROO

HG London

EUROSIA

EARTH

QUEL'SITAHR

PROLOGUE

Elyin'Adar stood with his back to the shiny metal door. Twenty years ago, he never would have left his back exposed to an entrance. But things were different now. Gone were the days of internal bickering and backstabbing. That all evaporated when the Draconians arrived. Those savage-minded brutes callously attacked anything that didn't bow down to them. Elyin'Adar had never seen anything like them. Their appearance was that of reptiles. And their starships resembled rough-hewn rocks flying through space.

The door opened behind him. It was his second-in-command, Tol'Kinas. "General," he said. "I have news from Quel'Sitahr." Tol'Kinas was a tall and skinny officer, with a sharp wit. But these last twenty years of the war had all but dispelled his sense of humor.

Elyin'Adar turned around. "Please tell me you have good news."

Tol'Kinas lowered his head. "I'm afraid the Draconians have overwhelmed our staging post."

Elyin'Adar sank into a chair beside a large conference table. "Then...it is finished."

"No! We can still regroup. The Skorath—"

"The Skorath have already taken way too many casualties. If we ask any more of them, both races will die instead of just one."

Tol'Kinas's breathing grew shallow. "You cannot be giving up! It's not like you!"

Elyin'Adar held up a hand, signaling to Tol'Kinas to calm himself. Elyin'Adar stood and paced around the room. "My dear friend, I will never give up so long as there is still breath in me. I have spent the last two years laying the foundation of our counter-strike."

"Then let us use this counter-strike, and regain Quel'Sitahr!"

"Tol'Kinas, you know as well as I do, that the Draconians outnumber us a hundred to one. And even with our technological advances, their superior numbers simply outlast us."

"General, why can't we simply use the Skorath to reclaim Quel'Sitahr?"

Elyin'Adar took in a deep breath. "We have the luxury of welding on metal plating to repair our ships. The Skorath are not so lucky. Even if we could retake Quel'Sitahr, it would be an uphill battle to regain the star systems we've lost to them."

Tol'Kinas dropped to one knee. "I beg of you, please let me take the rest of our starship reserves and make one final push on Quel'Sitahr."

Elyin'Adar closed his eyes a moment. He knew what the outcome would be. He had run the computer simulations a thousand times over. But then again, was there really any point in prolonging the inevitable? His preparations for the worst-case scenario had all been put in place. Why then was he hesitant to meet the end? He placed his hand on Tol'Kinas's shoulder. "Let it be done."

Tol'Kinas stood and bowed. "Thank you, General. I shall not fail you."

"My friend, failure is beyond our control now. But go with my blessing."

Tol'Kinas bowed again and turned to leave.

"Before you go," he said. "Send for the Seeress."

Tol'Kinas nodded and departed.

Elyin'Adar sat again and swiveled his chair to face the window. He stared out at the starry sky beyond. He studied each star. *There was a time,* he thought, *when they were all colonized. Each one with a name and a culture. Now they serve only to remind us of what we have lost.*

The door opened again and the Seeress entered. Bent over with age, she walked slowly. "You sent for me, my General?" she said in her old, hacking voice.

He turned to her. "The nightmare we feared, is now upon us. Are you still certain of what you say will come to pass?"

She nodded. "When the sentence of death is cast upon us, the long night will begin. And four thousand years shall not pass before a new light will arise from an uninteresting corner of space. They will rise up with ingenuity under their wings. They will frighten the star of Draconia. Even the very heart of Draconia shall tremble before them. But the tide of their rebellion shall only last a season, and Draconia shall swallow them up after a time."

He grinned in contemplation.

She studied his reaction with confusion. "That face you make. You do not seem troubled by the prophecy."

Elyin'Adar shook his head. "I am not. If I laid my preparations down correctly—and I think I have—I will change the ending of your prophecy. The new race that will rise up shall succeed."

She stared in dismay. "You? Change a prophecy?"

He nodded. "I need only to aid them at the critical time. It will be a tricky business to time it correctly, and I will be long gone by the time my assistance is needed. But by The Maker, I shall speak to them as if from beyond the grave. I will empower them to do the impossible. They shall succeed where we could not."

She glared at him. "You speak heresy!"

"Call it what you will, Seeress. But, though we die, through them, we will rise again." He stared into her aged eyes with a hint of victory within his own. "Antares will return."

Chapter 1

THE CHASE

War comes in many shapes and sizes. Today, it came in the form of a small poisonous dart. Lieutenant Colonel Fox Jagger had waited months for something to happen, only now that it was here, he wasn't sure he wanted it anymore. Leaning over the body of the ambassador, he felt for a pulse. It was weak, but it was there. He was alive...so far. The pungent bitter-sour stench of the poison filled the air.

The overhead klaxon blared its five-note fanfare. "General Quarters, General Quarters! All hands man your battle stations! Intruder on Sierra deck section 12. General Quarters!"

The Colonel, who knelt on the other side of the ambassador's body, quickly stood and brushed everything off the nearby table with one sweeping motion of his arm. Glass cups and plates crashed to the floor. The metal utensils clanked and clattered beside them.

"Help me lift him," the Colonel said, barely audible over the whining alarm.

Fox helped the Colonel hoist the ambassador's body onto the table. The ambassador's legs dangled off the end of the table. A dinner table wasn't the ideal size, but it would have to do. The Colonel loosened the clothing around the ambassador's neck; it should help with his breathing. Fox watched the Colonel as he worked. His name was Colonel Jonathan Terynn, but to Fox, he was The Colonel. He wasn't just any colonel in the Earth military, he was *The* Colonel. The hero of Mesa Sol.

Fox had waited years for the chance to serve under him and as of two months ago, that wish had been fulfilled. And although the Colonel had given him permission to call him by his first name, Jonathan, it still sounded wrong. To call a hero "Jonathan" just seemed like it would diminish the grandeur of the man's accomplishments. Maybe, given some time, it wouldn't sound so weird. But for now, Jonathan was the Colonel.

The Colonel tapped a button on the comm-band around his wrist. "Medbay Charlie, I have a medical emergency in the Wardroom!"

"En route," a voice replied from his comm-band.

A voice spoke from Fox's comm-band. "Assailant fleeing to Romeo deck is." It was the voice of Master Sergeant Grrrah'Kah. He was a Chantell. A race of nine-foot-tall locusts. Grrrah'Kah was the only bug assigned to the space station's security teams. But he was practically a squad all by himself.

The Colonel glanced over to Fox with stern eyes. "Get him!"

Fox nodded, noting the stern resolve on the Colonel's face. Fox pressed a button on his comm-band. "Grrrah'Kah, cut around to Romeo deck section 14. I'll see if I can drive him toward you."

He bolted into the hallway and joined up with one of the marine squads combing the decks. The marines were dressed in their black riot armor and carrying E.M. rifles. Electro-Magnetic rifles were the latest in firearms innovation. They fired aluminum rounds at incredible speeds. But the two marines bringing up the rear were armed with cannon-sized variants, called railguns. The railguns were so heavy that they were mounted to the marines' chest plate with a swivel mount. Their ammunition was powerful enough to punch through walls and floors.

Fox and the marines descended a stairwell and burst through the door into Romeo deck. Fox glanced up and saw the sign for section 5. Almost there. It was time to play cat and mouse yet again. Fox didn't mind the chase; it was his job after all. What he hated was that it always came at the cost of another human life. Fox glanced up at the wall again and saw the sign for section 12. Sergeant Greely shoved Fox against the sidewall. Fox hit the wall and fell to the ground. A little metal dart struck Greely's chest plate below the neckline. It tumbled in the air and clattered to the ground. Greely was taller than Fox. If he hadn't pushed him out of the way it would have struck Fox in the neck.

The marines fired their E.M. rifles in retaliation, peppering the walls with holes. Greely helped Fox to his feet. "Sorry for the push, sir."

"I owe you one," Fox said, cringing at the bitter-sour smell that now filled the hallway. He picked up the dart and handed it to Greely. "Get this to Med Bay Charlie. The Doc will need it to identify the poison."

"Yes, sir."

Fox turned to the remaining marines. "Colten, take point. Move out."

The marines advanced with quick short steps, keeping their rifles poised to strike. Fox took deep breaths to calm himself. Adrenaline surged through him and his heart pounded in his chest. This was not like combat in the field. This was an enemy that liked to hide in the shadows and strike from a distance. It was almost like being stalked by a sniper. But his opponent wasn't a sniper. He did not use a gun. As far as he could tell, this assassin used some sort of dart gun with poison darts. *Poison,* he thought. *Why use poison when a pistol could reach farther and penetrate better?*

There were a lot of unanswered questions. The only reason to use poison would be for stealth. But that bitter-sour stench was far from stealthy. No, this assassin was not trying to be covert; it was more like he was trying to announce himself. But that didn't make any sense. Why bother trying to remain hidden if he was going to announce to the world that he had just killed someone?

A dark figure in a black hooded cloak dashed down the hallway and rounded a corner. The marines fired again, peppering the walls with more holes. The two railguns fired, punching large holes straight through the corner of the wall. The assassin would be dead if he didn't move past the corner fast enough. A part of Fox hoped it would be that easy; another part of him wanted to catch the assassin alive. Alive was better for extracting information. And he wanted information. How had he gotten on board the space station in the first place? What was the poison he was using? And who had sent him?

These were all questions that needed answers. He felt a bead of sweat running down his bald head. He wanted to ignore it, but it tickled as it ran down his head, causing significant annoyance. He ran his hand back over his shaven head, wiping away the perspiration. Then, out of habit, he stroked his goatee. Well, as much of a goatee as the military regulations would allow. Clean-shaven was the preference in the regulations. Rank seniority only opened up a few extra options. Why did he even keep facial hair? It wasn't practical. But then it did remind him of his theater days before joining the military.

Fox followed Colten and the other marines as they rounded the corner. No body and no blood. The assassin was quick. Fox sighed with a mixed sense of relief and apprehension. He still had a chance to catch him alive, yet he was still loose on the station. Colton motioned for the marines to continue forward with a wave of his fingers. With cautious steps, they all proceeded down the hallway. Colton's hand left his rifle and swatted his neck. He had been hit with a poison dart.

Once more, the hallway filled with the bitter-sour odor. Colton collapsed to the ground. The other marines retaliated, blaring their E.M. rifles. Fox pulled Colton back behind the line of fire and checked his pulse. It was rapidly diminishing. Fox glanced down the hallway. Where had the shot come from? Shouldn't this have been a game of cat and mouse? Instead, they were being picked off one at a time. Fox's heart raced. He had to get the assassin off his rhythm.

"Kowalski, get Colton to a med bay as best you can!" Fox ordered.

"Yes, sir!"

"Jones, Peterson, Chaves, it's time we put that gozark on the defensive!"

"Orders sir?" Peterson asked.

"Just like Terynn's run. On three."

The three marines each nodded.

"One, two...three!" Fox charged down the hallway with the others close behind. Fox yelled as he ran, firing off a few shots from his E.M. pistol. The marines followed, yelling while placing a few wild shots of their own. Without aiming, their shots needed blind luck to hit the assassin. They were more for a show of bravado. One thing he had learned from his theater days was that *what* he did mattered less than *how* he did it. And right now, theatrics is what would drive the assassin to Master Sergeant Grrrah'Kah.

The assassin peeked around the corner, watching them. He spun on his heel and fled. Fox tapped a button on his comm-band. "Grrrah'Kah, he's coming your way!"

Fox and the marines continued yelling, rounding the corner in pursuit. Fox noticed a sign on the wall. Romeo Deck, Section 14. They charged around the next bend and skided to a halt. Grrrah'Kah stood before them holding the assassin by the neck. The assassin's legs dangled a few feet above the floor, his body dwarfed by the nine-foot-tall locust. Grrrah'Kah's hands were not really hands, nor were they pincers. They were a combination of the two. He stared at the assassin with his twin compound eyes that were as black as space. The assassin struggled for breath and then passed out.

Grrrah'Kah turned to Fox. "Assailant apprehended is."

Fox lowered his E.M. pistol. "Good work, Master Sergeant. Take him to the detention center."

"Sir, yes," he said.

Grrrah'Kah's English was rough at best, but Fox tried never to complain. It was refreshing to have a bug trying to speak English instead of just clicking his native language. Though Fox did correct him on a

few points, such as his rank. Grrrah'Kah had the unfortunate habit of calling him, colonel lieutenant. Fox made sure to correct *those* slips. Grrrah'Kah walked away. His four powerful legs, which supported his 800-pound frame, pounded the floor with each step.

Jones walked up to Fox. "Lt. Colonel Jagger, I'd like to continue the sweep of Romeo deck in case we missed anything."

Fox nodded. "Take the rest of Master Sergeant Grrrah'Kah's squad with you."

"Yes, sir."

Fox turned to Chavez. "Contact maintenance, and schedule repairs of the walls."

"Yes, sir," he replied. He turned back to Fox. "Sir, shall I update Colonel Terynn on the pursuit?"

Fox shook his head. "No, I'll take care of that personally."

A simple radio call over his comm-band would suffice, but this time was different. The ambassador had been hit. *The ambassador!* Fox thought. He tapped a button on his wrist-mounted comm-band. The small black screen turned on and displayed a video image of Dr. Jacob Mallory in Med Bay Charlie. "Doc, how is the ambassador?"

Dr. Mallory lowered his head in grief. "Not good."

olonel Jonathan Terynn slammed his fist onto the smooth surface of the conference table. "I have had enough!" His fist lingered on the table. Regret over the outburst trickled into him like a sponge soaking in water. He was not a drill sergeant and neither was he addressing recruits. Trying to keep professionalism within the ranks began at the top, so Jonathan had always tried to maintain the best decorum. Worry had fueled this outburst. Among all the worries he juggled aboard a space station, this was number thirty-seven on his list.

Jonathan straightened his uniform jacket and turned to the two officers in the room. "Please excuse the unprofessional tone."

Lt. Colonel Fox Jagger and Commander Isabeau Alexi, his two closest officers, stood across from him. Fox nodded. "Of course, sir." He cleared his throat. "We still don't know how they're getting on board."

Jonathan sighed. "How is the ambassador?"

Isabeau brushed aside some stray strands of her straight black hair. "He's not expected to survive the night."

Jonathan closed his eyes in exasperation and turned back to the conference table. He leaned his hand on the table, resting his mind more than his body. Paler skin around one of his fingers marked where his military academy signet ring once was. He took a deep breath.

"Colonel Terynn," Fox said, "I'm sorry, I...I was so sure..."

Although he wanted a professional decorum, he encouraged the use of first names among his close officers. Not only did it help with unity, but it was also the only perk to commanding a lonely space station so far away from Earth. Heaven forbid he should have to call his two closest officers Lt. Colonel Jagger and Commander Alexi until the end of time.

Jonathan turned back to Fox and put a comforting hand on his shoulder. "Fox, we're in private; you can call me Jonathan. And there was no way you could have known who the target was. We knew it was a gamble. The ambassador's condition aside, you did a fine job. We got him."

Fox took in a sharp breath and nodded appreciatively.

"Contact the Chantell medical center on the planet below. I don't know how good bug medicine will be for a human, but right now we are looking for miracles."

Fox nodded once. "Right away, sir." He turned to Isabeau, nodding farewell before leaving the room. "Isabel."

Jonathan raised an eyebrow. Before Fox left, he had called her Isabel, not Isabeau. Fox had been assigned to *Gamma Station* for six months now. That should have been plenty of time to learn her name. "Isabel?" he asked.

Isabeau rolled her emerald eyes. "I've told him a hundred times how to pronounce my name." Her slight French accent crept into her voice.

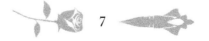

7

"Maybe the French pronunciation is complicated?"

"Is-u-bo," she enunciated. "How complicated is that?"

Jonathan grinned. "Point taken." He cleared his throat. "So, you've caught the eye of the new Lt. Colonel."

She returned a bashful smile. "I hope that isn't a problem."

Jonathan shook his head. "No, I checked the regulations. Your Naval rank is equal to his Marine rank. So, as long as your commanding officer approves it, you're okay."

She aimed a hopeful smile at him.

"Yes," he said with a chuckle. "Has he asked you out yet?"

She shook her head. "It's not progressing as I'd hoped."

"Well, he seems playfully defiant in calling you by the English variant of your name. That's progress."

"Yeah, but that's the *only* progress I've made in the last six months. At this rate, our first date will be at a retirement settlement."

They both laughed.

She looked into his hazel eyes. "I'm glad I can still make you laugh."

He grinned. "Izzy, ever since we were kids, there hasn't been a time that you *couldn't* make me laugh. Laughing with you always seemed to clear my mind."

It was true. They grew up together on the Ter-Alta colony and she always knew how to brighten his mood. She had also gone to the naval academy with him. And even though a twist of fate had transferred him to the Marine branch, they had always been close. She was like a sister to him, and in return, he became the brother she was never allowed to have.

Isabeau relaxed her stance. "You know that man looks up to you."

Jonathan huffed, turning partway around. "I hope he sees something worthwhile."

"He refers to you as the modern Sun-Tzu."

He snickered. "He's been reading my war stories about Cobra Squad."

"And Masa Sol, and the Ursar—Jonathan, they even teach it at the academy these days."

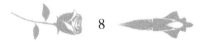

Jonathan rolled his eyes. The last thing he needed was a bunch of new recruits being trained to idolize the great Jonathan Terynn. Why did everyone have to make such a big deal of it? It's not like he reinvented the wheel.

She smiled and snickered.

He eyed her curiously. "What?"

She shook her head, recomposing herself. "Nothing, sir."

Jonathan gave her a playful scowl. "Don't you 'nothing, sir' me. What is so funny?"

She grinned and bit her lower lip. "Did uh, you read his report on the chase?"

He shook his head, picked up a handheld reader device, and scrolled through the text. "No, I hadn't." He appreciated written reports; they helped with the paperwork he had to fill out. He not only ran a space station, but he also had to oversee the four thousand men and women aboard. But when it came down to it, he preferred listening to his officers giving their reports in person. It was easier to read between the lines if he could see their expressions.

He stopped scrolling as one paragraph caught his attention. It was a part Fox had left out of his verbal report. It described how Fox had led the charge that spooked the assassin into Grrrah'kah's ambush. Jonathan lowered the reader and glanced at Isabeau. "Terynn's run?"

Isabeau giggled. "It's from your charge at—"

"At Masa Sol, yes, I remember the engagement. But since when is it called 'Terynn's run'?"

"Wouldn't the bigger question be how the other marines knew what he meant by saying that?"

She was right. A fancy name was one thing. But if the men knew what to do based on referencing that name, that was something else entirely. That was the gray area where fact and legend intersected. Were his stories becoming legends now? How? Or worse yet, was he becoming a legend? 34 years old was not old enough to be a legend. Legends were famous dead people, and last he checked, he was still breathing.

"Terynn's run," Jonathan said, glancing heavenward. "Now they are naming maneuvers after me."

She smiled. "When it comes to strategy, you have a brilliant mind."

Jonathan fingered his other hand, caressing where his missing signet ring had been. "If only my strategic mind translated into other parts of my life. Sometimes I tire of the uphill battles."

"Some might say that uphill battles are what you excel at."

Chapter 2

ELLYRA EL'ALLEL

Ellyra stood under a fruit tree. She wore her light blue hair down. She liked it down. She had had enough of official meetings and formal dress. Right now, she wanted to be comfortable. She took a few steps across the low-cut blue grass. She stopped and stared at it. She had never noticed it before. But since getting to know Jonathan, she had started noticing little things. When he visited last year, he had thought it strange to see grass and trees that were blue. He insisted their rightful color was green. *Who has ever heard of green plants?* She wondered.

But then again, Eurosia was her home and she had not seen any other worlds yet. She had only recently earned her Ascendency and was now in command of a starship. It was a girlhood dream of hers to captain a ship and zoom across the stars. But it was not until she met that Earthian man that she had any real drive to accomplish that dream. She wanted to see him again.

Her hand went to her necklace. The simple silver chain she wore held another treasure. A signet ring dangled on the end. She caressed the ring, recalling what it was like to stare into his alien eyes. They were so foreign and majestic. A gorgeous brown with amber gems against a white canvas. Her own Eurosian eyes were the boring blue within blue. Nothing as wondrous as his. Her contented light blue locks of hair slowly transitioned to a deep shade of romantic pink. It was an involuntary reaction to her emotions. Her father would not approve of her lack of control. Her father's reprimand was already echoing in her head. Do not display your feeling in public, he would always say. Then he would drone on about the need to conceal what she was actually thinking. Inter-house politics were a necessary nuisance. Which was another reason she enjoyed retiring to this spot in the garden. It was her sanctuary away from all the politicking and duties of belonging to a great house.

A scrawny woman in a light blue gown strolled up. It was Rana, her personal aid. "Ellyra, your father is delayed. He asks that you postpone your trip another week."

Ellyra turned away, her scarlet gown blowing in the breeze. Her hair color darkened into a regretful indigo. "I have waited for so long."

"Your Earthian man?" she asked.

Ellyra nodded. "I have longed to see him again. My memories of him are not as clear as they once were. I fear they are fading with each passing year."

She looked confused. "It's only been one year."

Ellyra shook her head. "Not for him. His solar cycles are a fifth of ours. For him, it has been five years."

Rana rolled her aqua within blue eyes. "You make it sound so dramatic."

Ellyra glanced at her. "You sound like my mother."

"That is probably why she chose me."

Ellyra smiled. She was most likely right. Her mother had the final say on who was assigned to be Ellyra's personal Eltashee. Rana was supposed to be at Ellyra's beck and call. But there were times when it seemed Rana was, instead, her mother's tool to keep tabs on her. Regardless of how much truth was in that, Ellyra and Rana had grown close. Rana was nearly the same age and had similar interests.

"Shall I have Brigadain Diahlus stand down from launch?" Rana asked, her long dangly earrings swaying as she spoke.

That was the one thing Ellyra envied about Rana; her dangly earrings were a symbol of her married status. It was the only thing still beyond Ellyra's reach. Which, for the daughter of the largest great house on Eurosia, was frustrating.

"That will not be necessary," Ellyra finally said.

Rana cocked her head in confusion. "But if we do not send word to stand down, he shall still be expecting to leave."

Ellyra took a few steps away. "I shall keep that in mind."

Her eyes narrowed. "You intend to disobey your father's wishes."

Ellyra grinned and looked at Rana. "You make it sound so dramatic."

Rana opened her mouth to protest but thought better of it when she noticed a man approaching. It was Xer Cora'Del. Xer was Ellyra's parliamentarian officer. He was in charge of verifying that rules and regulations were being followed aboard the ship. Xer, like all officers, was a member of the aristocracy. He was Ellyra's cousin and next in line to lead their great house if her father could not produce an heir.

Xer bowed to Ellyra. "My lady, I have somewhat to report."

She nodded. "Then let it be spoken."

"My lady, I regret to inform you that due to the imminent weather, Brigadain Diahlus has requested that we depart within the hour."

She eyed him a moment and suppressed a grin. The unfortunate change in weather was a boon to her more-immediate plight with her father. Her hair color brightened up to a thoughtful violet. "Brigadain Xer, what is weather to a starship? Are not our deflectors sufficient?"

Xer's eyes widened. "Forgive me, my lady. But electrical storms can interfere with guidance and other critical systems."

"Am I to understand the weather threatens the safety of the ship?"

Xer nodded. "Yes, my lady."

Ellyra looked at Rana while speaking to Xer. "Far be it for me to interfere in the safety of the ship by not launching when recommended."

Xer bowed and left.

Rana pursed her lips. "And to think your father ever worried about you grasping politics."

She grinned. "If you haven't already, have your things loaded onto the *Calmao* in the next three-quarters an hour."

Rana hesitantly curtsied and left.

Despite the victory, it meant she would have to cut her walk in the garden short. She sauntered over to a tree and touched the trunk. It was smooth to the touch. The gardeners made sure the bark would not spoil the hem of a dress. She lingered. *Am I ready for this?* She asked herself. Leaving her homeworld behind to galivant across the cosmos was intimidating. More so than going off to finishing school, or even the Stellar Academy. She fingered her simple chain necklace and Jonathan's signet ring that it held. Her hair transitioned to a contented blond as memories of Jonathan flooded her mind. She stood there for a long while, soaking in the memories. Ready or not, she *had* to do this. She needed to see him again. She straightened up and strode across the grounds. She made her way to the large building in the distance.

Ascending the many steps into the Great Hall, servants and guards each bowed to her as she made her way inside. She ignored any servants trying to get her attention. It was on purpose. If her mother sent any of them, they would be trying to delay her departure. It was best not to make eye contact and pretend she didn't notice. She lengthened her stride. The quicker she could reach the hangar, the sooner she could evade her parents. Why were they trying to keep her home for another week anyway? She was only scheduled to be away for three weeks. She wasn't a little girl any longer. She was a Sune; in command of a starship.

Her hand instantly touched the ring on her necklace. That had to be the reason. Her father was under pressure to produce an heir—a son. Her mother had not managed to bear one, so he had turned his attention to Ellyra's courtships with keen interest. Whom she married would greatly impact the future of House El'Allel.

She burst through the double doors as gracefully as she could, stepping into the hangar. Several servants stopped their work to see the commotion. They hadn't seen this much excitement in weeks. Ellyra's dance instructor would not be pleased with her. He often reminded her that doors were not to make any sound when using them. But there was no time for propriety; her window of opportunity was now.

She briskly ascended the ramp as two elegantly dressed men entered the hangar. The house guards were guards in name only. They were used to officially summon a guest or even a member of the household. *Mother must be getting desperate,* she thought. She stepped across the threshold into the ship and promptly pressed a red button beside the door. Small red lights on the boarding ramp pulsed and a low-toned alarm buzzed. Servants and officers on the ground dropped what they were doing and sprang into action. Some uncoupled the fuel lines while others dashed up the ramp. One servant carrying two suitcases sprinted up the ramp. Both house guards ran, their elaborate long overcoats swaying in their stride. They stopped short as the ramp retracted from before them and folded into the ship.

Ellyra made her way to the Center of Workmanship, the command center of the ship. She walked slower now. Once the hatches had closed, only an order from the Sune, the ship's commander, could open them again. But she wasn't safe yet; her mother would try to call her over the ship's transmissions. Ellyra held her head high as she strode down the crimson-carpeted corridors of the *Calmao*. She smiled as she passed several ornate tapestries hanging on the walls. She had hand-picked most of them. One of the many perks of captaining a ship was picking out the décor. And her mother had trained her well in color coordination and the use of space.

She halted in front of a door and glanced at a painting that hung on the wall. Her favorite of all the artwork on the ship was this portrait. It was a depiction of the famous iron-willed philosopher of long ago. She smiled at it. "Guide me, Kalmeedes."

The double door parted, allowing Ellyra to enter the Center of Workmanship. This circular room was designed with all the control consoles around the outer edge. They all faced the center of the room, toward the holographic viewing stage. Ellyra took her seat next to an older, portly man. Diahlus Melquinn was her First Dommicon, her most trusted bridge officer.

He glanced at her. "I take it our abrupt departure has something to do with the sudden bombardment of transmissions from Lady Elony?"

Ellyra's formal white hair burned into an embarrassed burgundy. "You can tell my mother that I shall read each message in the order they were received."

"Shall I cancel the launch then?"

She shook her head, sending her curly locks of hair swaying. "If I find a reason to cancel the launch from reading my mother's missives, I shall endeavor to inform you." She gave him a conspiratorial smirk. "My mother shall just have to hope I am fast enough."

Diahlus grinned. "As you wish, Sune Ellyra."

The large domed roof of the hangar spiraled open. It revealed a scarlet and pink sky with white chubby clouds. Ellyra's ship, the *Calmao,* flashed colorful lights all across its frosted-glass-looking hull. It floated up through the open ceiling and into the windy sky. The egg-shaped starship drifted forward. At one-third the size of the palace, it moved with the grace of a butterfly.

Ellyra held a reader device, scrolling through her mother's messages. She turned to Diahlus. "It would appear my mother wishes us to cancel the launch."

He grinned. "If only we had known sooner."

"My thoughts precisely."

A tall thin man, who wore his hair a formal white, walked up to Ellyra. There was something familiar about him. She looked closer. Where had she seen him before? He was a Dommicon with the rank of Shel Brigadain, that much was obvious by his uniform. He definitely wasn't one of the suitors her father had sent to meet her. Yet she knew him from somewhere.

He bowed to her. "Sune Ellyra, I was instructed to report to you when I came on board."

Something in his voice was also familiar. The tantalizing revelation teased her brain. Then the man smiled. It was a smile she had known in her youth. Arkamenos Arauri stood before her with all the boyish charm she grew up with.

Ellyra's eyes lit up. "Arkamenos!"

His smile broadened.

She leaped up and hugged him. "How has your father been?"

"Most productive, Sune Ellyra. My father's investment has proven fortuitous. I was able to afford to attend the Stellar Academy, and have studied security ever since."

"Splendid!" she said. "I do hope you will be on my security staff."

He nodded. "I most certainly am."

Diahlus motioned toward Arkamenos. "Sune Ellyra, may I present to you Shel Brigadain Arkamenos, your Master of Security."

She hugged him again. "I cannot think of anyone better suited for the position." She looked him in his green within blue eyes. "And I shall entrust you with your first task. Please encode a transmission to the Earthian outpost, *Gamma Station*. Please announce our visit and provide our hyperspace telemetry."

He bowed. "As you wish, Sune."

A woman in an emerald gown walked up to Diahlus. "Brigadain, we are in position to open the hyperspace portal."

Diahlus nodded and pressed a button on the arm of his chair. Gentle chimes sounded from the overhead speakers and everyone took their seats. "Astrogator, open the hyper-portal."

"As you wish," a male voice replied from behind.

"On stage please," Ellyra ordered.

A golden metal ring in the center of the floor lit up and projected a three-dimensional hologram. The hologram showed their ship, the *Calmao*, and the surrounding space. In front of the *Calmao*, a spark of light twinkled and opened into a hyper-portal. It resembled a fountain in reverse, sucking sparkling particles into a blue tunnel of light.

"Let it be done," she ordered.

The *Calmao* moved into the hyper-portal and vanished. The hyper-portal collapsed and dissipated.

Chapter 3
GAMMA STATION

D r. Mallory stood over the body of Ambassador Lucas Cale. He had known the ambassador for many years. They had been friends for the better part of two decades. While their careers had gone separate ways, their friendship had not. That is why it was unnerving to look down upon his degenerating body. Losing patients was nothing new—that came with the territory. But Dr. Mallory had never lost a friend before. That is what made this patient more than just a patient. That is why his failure to save him was more than just a simple failure.

A thin strand of hair fell across his forehead. At first, he ignored the impertinence, but in the end, he straightened up and move his hair back into position. He straightened his blue and green scrubs and glanced over to one of his automated "nurses". His nurses were a series of machines that took over the mundane and routine tasks that he didn't have time for.

"Time?" he asked.

A computerized voice moaned a reply. "The time is twenty-three hundred fourteen hours."

Dr. Mallory sighed and hung his head in defeat.

The silence broke when he heard a faint humming from down the hallway. He walked over to the door and pressed the button. The door opened by sliding up. *Gamma Station* was built by the Chantell. And those nine-foot-tall bugs sure knew how to make large hallways. To most human standards it was a waste of space. But, to the Chantell, it was efficiency. Humans didn't design hallways wide enough or tall enough for monster-sized insects to fly down, but the Chantell did. Three Chantell flew down the hallway toward Med Bay Charlie.

Med Bays Able and Bravo took the majority of minor injury cases. That left Med Bay Charlie with enough time to focus on the most difficult and severe cases. The bug doctors were from Terks, the planet that Gamma Station orbited. Two of them carried medical equipment. They landed and entered. Dr. Mallory guided them over to Ambassador Cale's body. "I'm glad you're here, and I hope you can help."

The foremost Chantell doctor looked at Dr. Mallory. His large compound eyes were each as black as space. He moved his head with sharp jerking motions. "Different is your smell."

"That's because I'm not in the military. I'm a civilian from *Bravo Station*," Dr. Mallory explained.

"Brav on *Gamma Station*?"

Dr. Mallory shook his head. "No, I'm sort of 'on loan' to the Gamms."

"No fear?"

Dr. Mallory smiled. "I may be a Brav but I've been around you bugs long enough for the shock to wear off."

"I vision."

Dr. Mallory chuckled. "The expression is, I see."

The bug doctor cocked his head in a sharp motion. "Forgive. I see."

The other two Chantell completed assembling their medical devices. Each resembled asymmetrical bundles of orange-tinted metal with dials and buttons. They approached Ambassador Cale's body.

"Also Brav?" one of them asked.

Dr. Mallory shook his head again. "No, Lucas just loves fancy clothes. Probably picked it up from all the years he spent as ambassador to the Euroo. The more buttons, sashes, and layers the better."

"Euroo, much art mastery, much to impress."

"Poison is what type?" another one asked.

"Teterophalezine," Dr. Mallory replied. "It's a neurotoxin that attacks the brain. We don't see much of it because most people consider it useless as poison. The strong, unmistakable odor gives it away."

"Much sense it not makes," the third Chantell doctor said.

The other one nodded his head in agreement. Well, it wasn't so much a nod as it was jerking his head up and down, trying to mimic a nod. "Much time we not have," he said as they went to work.

The Chantell spoke to each other in their native "clicking" language. They only broke into the Earthian language when they needed to update Dr. Mallory.

Fox paced across the dull green metal floor of the detention center, stroking his goatee. The steady clicking sounds of his footsteps faded into the ambient noise around him. Fox glanced back to the transparent wall. It separated him from the prison cell where the assassin sat. The interrogation went well, and yet it didn't. He did get some information out of the man but nothing he needed. What was he hiding?

Was there an angle he hadn't yet tried? Interrogations, after all, were simply performances. Whoever gave the better performance usually got what they wanted. And Fox was a good performer. Before his military career, he had been a stage actor. Fox could play any part, but his

passion was for Shakespeare. And it seemed Shakespeare always followed him around whatever career he chose. As a Marine in the Earth Military, he found his acting skills played a very useful role in security.

Yet this time was different. That assassin seemed to be playing a part in a well-orchestrated play. If only he could figure out what the play was about or how many actors were involved. Time, he hoped, would bring him the answers.

The door to the detention center slid up and Jonathan entered. "You know, it's a good thing the Chantell didn't know what carpet was when they built this space station. You'd have worn it out by now."

Fox glanced down to his feet, noticing his pacing.

"Has the prisoner talked yet?" Jonathan asked.

Fox shook his head. "Not much, I'm afraid." He strolled over to Jonathan. "I've interrogated him several times. He still won't say who he is or how he got on board the station."

"Have you run a DNA scan on him yet?"

"His DNA doesn't match anyone on file. And that is not the worst part."

"What's the worst part?"

"He has alluded to getting on board with the help of an Abe spy on the station."

Jonathan's brow wrinkled. "Is that possible?"

"I've run every DNA record we have against *Able Station*. Every member of our crew checks out. If there were an Abe spy aboard, I would have known by now. Besides, Grrrah'Kah has a knack for sniffing out Abes."

It was literally true. Grrrah'Kah, the sole bug on *Gamma Station* was able to smell which space station humans came from. He said they each had their own scent. He even said that Dr. Mallory, who had been living on *Gamma Station* for several years, still smelled like a Brav.

Jonathan stared at the assassin through the transparent wall. "And yet somehow an Abe assassin got aboard. He didn't trip any alarms or raise any suspicions."

22

"For months we've been trying to figure out how they've been getting aboard. A mole would certainly answer that elusive question." Fox scratched the side of his head. It often itched on the side when he was troubled.

Jonathan noticed. "So what's the problem?"

"Problem is..." Fox turned to also stare at the assassin behind the transparent wall. "Problem is...he's lying."

"Wait, but you said his story was the most plausible."

Fox threw up his hands. "I know, I know. But his eye contact, hand movements, and speech patterns all tell me he is lying. The confusing part is that it's almost as if he is lying about something he has not yet told me...if that makes any sense."

"Unless..."

Fox turned to Jonathan. "Unless what?"

Jonathan faced him. "Unless Ambassador Cale was only incidental."

"You think the ambassador was not his primary intended target?"

"Look at this man," Jonathan said, pointing to the assassin. "Who wears a black hooded cloak? His appearance is conspicuous. He uses a poison that has an unmistakable smell. Everything about this man screams audacity. Yet, now that we've caught him, he refuses to boast or tell us his name. Fox, audacious men crave recognition. He's not through with us yet."

Fox stroked his goatee. "Time shall unfold what plighted cunning hides; Who cover faults, at last shame them derides," he quoted.

"Hamlet?"

Fox shook his head. "King Lear."

Chapter 4

THE EUROO

Jonathan stepped into a lift tube followed by Isabeau and Fox. They wore their formal dress-black uniforms with white trims. They didn't often get to don their dress blacks. So, he was thrilled when he received word that a Euroo delegation was visiting. Even though the message was rather vague and didn't specify who was visiting or why, it was still exciting.

"Hey, Colonel, is it true the Euroo all have blue eyes?" Fox asked.

He shook his head. "Not exactly. They have blue eyes and green eyes, but the white of their eyes is also blue. The vernacular is, blue within blue."

"Or green within blue," Isabeau added.

"But they change colors when their mood changes right?"

She shook her head. "It's their hair color that changes."

Fox rolled his eyes. "This is getting complicated."

"Welcome to my world," Jonathan said with a sigh.

"I don't know what all the colors mean yet," Isabeau added. "But a lot of the time, their hair will be white."

"Anything else I should know?" Fox asked.

She nodded. "Don't be surprised if they call you Lt. Colonel Fox instead of Lt. Colonel Jagger."

Fox glanced back with a confused look. "What? Why? What's with the first name?"

Before she could reply, Jonathan glanced up in thought, reciting the greeting under his breath. Then he turned to Isabeau. "What am I missing? 'We express our gratitude for the Euroo presence here this day'. It sounds like I'm forgetting something."

"...for *the honor of* the Euroo presence here this day."

He nodded appreciatively. Isabeau was always very thorough in her research. And for that he was lucky. He had met with dignitaries of seven races so far. Isabeau had helped him avoid miscommunication with each one. Having English as her second language was an advantage in understanding alien languages. For as long as he had known her, she had loved languages. If only the Draconians had made an exception for her, she could have become a linguist on *Bravo Station*. But as far as he knew, the Draconians had never made an exception to their rules.

The lift stopped at their floor and they exited. Jonathan led the small procession toward docking bay six. He glanced back at Isabeau. "Remind me which ones I bow to?"

Isabeau shook her head. "You bow to anyone you show respect to. What you're probably asking about is arm clasps for men and hugs for women."

"You have to hug?" Fox asked, raising his eyebrows.

Isabeau nodded. "In Euroo culture, you greet a woman with a hug. Men clasp forearms."

"Wait," Fox said. "But if one is a man and the other is a woman, which one would they do?"

Isabeau rolled her eyes. "Think of it this way, if a woman is involved, you hug."

Jonathan smiled. "What would I ever do without you, Izzy?"

25

They rounded the corner and Isabeau stopped short of entering the docking port bay. She hesitated with anxiety in her eyes. After doing all that research on Euroo culture, she should have been the most comfortable. Something else had to be bothering her. Jonathan turned to her. "What's the matter?"

"I can't go in; you'll have to do this without me."

He put his hands on her shoulders. "Izzy, what's wrong?"

She lowered he voice. "Our uniforms don't include a skirt."

"That's never been a problem before, why should it now?"

She pursed her lips. "You can't curtsy in slacks. It looks ridiculous."

Jonathan ran a mental picture of what that might look like. She was right. Not the desired outcome when trying to impress an impressive people. The Euroo were very decorative and ornate in nearly everything they did. Even when they spoke the standard Earthian language, they expressed themselves ornately. Her hesitation suddenly made a lot of sense.

"Maybe you can bow with us then," he offered.

Her eyes widened. "In their culture, bowing is for men. The women all curtsy."

He sighed. Again, she was right. The Euroo had a strong sense of differentiation between how their men and women dressed. It wasn't like on Earth where a shirt, slacks, and a jacket were acceptable for either. The Euroo women wore dresses—rather, they wore elaborate gowns. The men all wore five-piece suits. Isabeau's predicament was more than just the curtsy, her whole uniform was out of place.

"I think I understand now," he said, considering options. "I don't suppose living on a military base you had any reason to ever own a dress?"

She shook her head.

Fox snapped his finger in conclusion to a thought. "Isabel, if you can't bow and you can't curtsy, just do something else. Like a head nod or something."

She looked at him for a few silent moments. The gears were turning in her head but she still had apprehension in her eyes.

"I'll do it with you instead of bowing," Fox offered. "They'll probably just assume it's a human custom."

After a moment of thought, she smiled with an air of relief about her.

It was a good thing that Fox's sentiment on formality could be measured in a teaspoon. It was a charming quirk that Jonathan was grateful for. He put a hand on Fox's shoulder. "Thank you, Fox. If I had to do this without Isabeau, it would be like marching into battle unarmed."

"Any time, sir."

The bay doors opened before them and they strolled in. The long, wide docking port bay was used mostly for loading and unloading supplies. The Chantell had built the ceiling incredibly tall so they could fly while unloading. Master Sergeant Grrrah'Kah was already in the bay with two squads of marines in dress uniform. They formed a single line, perfectly spaced apart. Grrrah'Kah was always efficient and very precise. He drilled his men until they expected precision from themselves. Jonathan, Isabeau, and Fox stood at the head of the line. Fox was on Jonathan's left, while Isabeau was on his right.

Several dock workers shuffled about, finishing last-minute preparations to complete the docking sequence. They were instructed to leave once the docking connection was established. Visiting dignitaries required a level of security in the form of isolation. That meant clearing out all unnecessary personnel from the bay.

"Euroo vessel, *Calmao*, approaching docking port," the overhead speaker announced. "Stand by for docking sequence."

Through the transpara-steel wall, they watched the luminescent ship. It moved alongside the space station. The beautiful lights shone through the luminescent hull. Even their ships were works of art. As far as he knew, no two Euroo ships were exactly alike. Small differences and decorative taste seemed to differentiate each ship.

Isabeau muttered something in French.

Jonathan glanced at her. "Impressive, isn't it?"

"I had seen pictures, but seeing it in person..."

"To the Euroo, a job worth doing is worth doing spectacularly."

"Hey Colonel," Fox asked. "Is it true they don't have a word in their language for dull?"

Jonathan nodded. "That's the rumor. Let's just hope their visit doesn't inspire them to invent one."

"Docking sequence initiated," the overhead speaker announced.

A long tube extended from the docking port hatch over to the Euroo ship. Once air pressure had been established, the port hatch would automatically unlock. Now it was a nervous waiting game.

Fox tugged at his collar.

"Something the matter with your dress uniform?" Jonathan asked.

"They're so...stiff."

"Just think of it as a costume that you can change out of when this performance is over," Jonathan offered.

"Atmosphere established," the overhead speaker said.

Jonathan turned to Fox. "Mr. Jagger, please clear the bay."

Fox walked into the center of the bay. "Okay, let's clear the room! If you are not in dress uniform, you are now to exit the bay!"

Dock workers hustled about.

Fox clapped his hands together a few times. "Come on, let's go, let's go!"

The last of the straggling dock workers jogged out of the bay. Fox returned to his position as a loud clanking sound echoed in the bay. The hatch door had unlocked. Jonathan nervously tapped his leg reciting his short speech under his breath. The door opened. Three men stepped into the bay. Their black crimson-lined capes fluttered as they walked. Their knee-high black boots over ivory slacks pattered against the floor of the bay. Their navy-blue jackets sported tails and double-breasted brass buttons. Each button had the crest of their great house engraved.

Two of the Euroo men stood to the side of the door. The third offered a white-gloved hand to a scrawny woman. He ceremonially assisted her through the hatch door. Her sparkling white gown glittered many colors as the fabric swayed. Her white sparkling gloves reached up to her elbows. Her high heels clicked against the metal floor as she took her place in line. The Euroo man then held out his hand for the last woman. She took his hand with a scarlet elbow-length gloved hand and stepped into the bay. Her scarlet gown shimmered with a metallic sheen. The curly locks of her formal-white hair draped across her shoulders. Jonathan's eyes lit up. It was Ellyra. She took her place at the head of the line of Euroo personnel.

When all the Euroo were lined up they uniformly took several steps toward Jonathan's crewmen. They floated closer like a well-coordinated ballet line. The Euroo were not demonstrating precision, they were displaying grace and flair.

Jonathan stood, nervous. He hadn't practiced for, nor expected, this kind of reception. He suddenly felt unprepared. He glanced over to Isabeau. She shook her head. It was not yet time for him to speak. He took a deep breath and waited. Ellyra's line of crewmen halted a few feet away.

Ellyra curtsied, floating down to the ground and rising back to her feet in one fluid motion. "Hail, Colonel Jonathan Terynn of *Gamma Station*."

He nervously glanced at Isabeau who nodded. He looked back at Ellyra. "Hail, Ellyra...of the Euroo."

Ellyra raised an eyebrow.

Isabeau cringed.

Jonathan cleared his throat. "On behalf of the humans—I mean Earthians, and crew of *Gamma Station*, we express our gratitude for the honor of the Euroo presence here this day. May your visit be a beautiful one."

Ellyra nodded, her curly locks swaying. "On behalf of the Euroo and the crew of the *Calmao*, we are honored by the magnificence of your salutation. May your grandeur increase."

Jonathan motioned to Fox. "May I present to you and your crew my first officer, Lt. Colonel Fox Jagger?" He turned to Isabeau. "And—"

Isabeau nudged him, mouthing the words "who is also".

He motioned back to Fox. "Who is also my 90."

Ellyra smiled.

29

Jonathan motioned to Isabeau. "And my second officer, Commander Isabeau Alexi."

Fox and Isabeau gave a head nod.

Ellyra curtsied.

Jonathan motioned to Grrrah'Kah. "And my security chief, Master Sergeant Grrrah'Kah."

Grrrah'Kah lowered his insectoid head and fanned out his four large wings. It was the Chantell equivalent of a bow.

Ellyra curtsied again. "A most gratifying pleasure." Then she motioned toward the portly gentleman beside her. "May I present to you and your crew my first Dommicon, Brigadain Diahlus Melquinn, who is also my 90."

Diahlus bowed.

She motioned to the next man. "My second and parliamentarian Dommicon, Brigadain Xer Cora'Del."

Xer bowed.

She motioned to the third man. "Shel Brigadain Arkamenos Arauri handles my security."

Arkamenos bowed.

Then she motioned to the scrawny woman at the end. "And this is my personal Eltashee, Rana Arauri."

Rana floated to the floor like a leaf in a flamboyant curtsy.

Jonathan bowed. "I bid you all welcome."

He couldn't remember any more of the formalities and glanced at Isabeau.

She whispered. "We're all done."

Jonathan took in a deep breath and turned to Grrrah'Kah. "Master Sergeant, you may dismiss your men."

"Company dismissed is!" Grrrah'Kah ordered in his poorly constructed Earthian language.

The marines turned on their heels and marched out in a tight formation, Grrrah'Kah in the lead.

Jonathan turned back to Ellyra, motioning to Fox. "Please coordinate with Lt. Colonel Jagger for any resupply needs for your ship."

Ellyra nodded, smiling.

Jonathan motioned again to Isabeau. "Commander Alexi will escort your officers, uh...Dommicons to their quarters. If their accommodations are lacking in any respect, please let her know."

Ellyra nodded again.

"And in the meantime, how about I take you on a tour of *Gamma Station* personally?" he said, offering her his arm.

Ellyra accepted by placing her hand on his forearm. Then she turned, looking behind her, and motioned for Rana to join them.

Jonathan motioned toward Rana. "She wants the tour as well?"

Ellyra smiled shaking her head. "It's not that. It just isn't proper to be seen without a chaperone."

"Are you sure that's necessary here? The only ones that will see us are my crew. And they surely won't think two people walking together would be scandalous."

Rana took her place beside Ellyra. "Propriety is always necessary," she said with an air of authority.

Jonathan walked with Ellyra's hand on his forearm, Rana trailing a few paces behind. They walked along a hallway bordering a roadway. Vehicles passed by and overhead automated machines carried supplies around the station. The walkway was enclosed by transpara-steel walls and ceiling. It provided a scenic and quiet commute on foot.

Ellyra reached out and touched the transpara-steel wall. "Remarkable," she said in amazement. "It's like a moving mural."

Jonathan smiled. "The transpara-steel walls are insulated from sound."

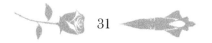

She turned to him. "And I thought you said your people were not very artistic?"

He chuckled. "I guess we do have a few peculiarities that could be classified as artistic. The main reason I brought you here is because of how quiet it is. I often come here to think."

"Ah, and what is it you are thinking of now?"

He smiled. "Actually, I'm thinking I messed up the beginning of that formal greeting. How was I supposed to address you?"

"Since I am a ship's captain, you would call my title, Sune. So, you would have said, Hail Sune Ellyra El'Allel of the *Calmao.*"

He smiled, repeating it under his breath. "Oh, and what does the phrase 'who is also my 90' mean?"

She smiled. "It means of great importance or worth. But it can mean a variety of things depending on how you use it."

"Can you give me an example?"

"Well," she began. "My first Dommicon is someone I trust very much and can rely on. So, I say he is my 90."

"So, that would be like me saying, my right-hand man?"

She stopped abruptly, trying to conceal her giggling behind her hands. "I have never heard that phrase before. And I have heard a *lot* of phrases from you."

He laughed. "Are there other uses for the 90 expression?"

She nodded and gazed at him. "I admire the beauty of your eyes. The remarkable tapestry of colors amazes me. So, I would say that your eyes are of my 90."

He looked into her blue within blue eyes. "Then I guess it's safe for me to admit that your eyes are of *my* 90."

She smirked and they continued walking. After a few silent moments, her smile fell. "Jonathan, I have somewhat I need to ask of you, regarding the time we shared together on Eurosia."

"I'm all ears," he replied.

"I beg your pardon?" she said with a confused expression.

Jonathan rolled his eyes. "Sorry, that's another human expression. It means you have my complete attention."

She nodded. "Five of your years is perhaps a long time to keep such a hasty promise. I, of course, understand if you have since...moved on."

Jonathan's hand went to his barren finger, where his academy signet ring used to be. Had it really been five years? His mind raced back to that summer he had spent on Eurosia. It was a rarity that, in vain, he had tried to repeat. Space travel for humans was very restricted and, looking back on it, he shouldn't have been able to go in the first place. So, it was either very good luck or galactic providence that had allowed him to travel to the Euroo homeworld. It was there that he had met Ellyra. Those three weeks had tormented him for the five years that followed.

"The first year was the hardest," Jonathan admitted. "Every year after that got a little easier." He stopped walking and looked directly into her blue within blue eyes. "I have missed you for the past one thousand eight hundred and twenty-seven days."

Her eyes glistened and she took a deep breath. "Your words describe one who has suffered greatly. To have chronicled each day that you have been without surely speaks of great misfortune."

"The greater misfortune would have been if I had stopped counting."

She smiled as if a great weight had been lifted. Then, as if a sudden realization struck, her smile faded. "Are you sure you wish to remain bound? The Draconian restrictions on your people will make it difficult."

He looked past her, up into the distance. "You do have a point. The high and mighty Draconians sure make things difficult for humans." He looked back into her blue within blue eyes. "But I've never been one to back down just because the course is difficult."

She smiled again. "You are a fascinating man, Colonel Jonathan. Perhaps with your persistence, the Draconian restrictions may not last too long."

Jonathan shrugged. "Perhaps if they get bored with studying us."

"They study you?"

"Not directly. They divide us among three of the five elder races. Most of us get to stay on Earth. The rest of us are hauled off to serve aboard one of three space stations. And the blasted Draconians never care if it splits up families. Poor Isabeau hasn't seen her family in over a decade. She has only met her brother once, about five years ago."

"Were you separated from your family too?" she asked.

He shook his head. "I was fortunate enough to have kept my immediate family. But it did come with a price; I have never been allowed to see Earth."

She brought a hand to her face in shock. "You mean, you have never seen your own homeworld?"

"I've seen pictures. And some combat missions took us very near our solar system. So close that I used to lay awake at night wishing upon every star I could count. The wish to see Earth never came true."

Her hair color muddied into a brown.

Jonathan blinked, breaking himself out of his reminiscing. "Sorry, I digress. Your question was what the great races study about us. Are you familiar with the three space stations?"

She nodded. *"Able Station, Bravo Station, and Gamma Station."*

"Interesting side note, by the way," Jonathan said. "Whoever named the space stations didn't do their homework. The first two are named after the first two letters in the joint-military alphabet, Able and Bravo. The third space station was named after the third letter in the Greek alphabet, Gamma. They probably got the two mixed up. This space station should have been called Charlie Station."

Ellyra snickered and held her hands to her face. "Please forgive my impertinence, Jonathan. But it is a good thing this station did not receive that name. It is a rather silly-sounding name."

Jonathan smiled. "Who knows, maybe cosmic fate needed the name to be different."

They began walking again. "Anyway, the Greys on *Bravo Station* study human intellect. The Bugs here study our military strategy. And the vile Scorpii on *Able Station* study human cunning—which has proven to be just a euphemism for our evil nature."

They walked for a few moments in silence. Ellyra's hair brightened to a violet. "Is it terrible then, that I am making my own study of you?"

He smiled. "Oh?"

"I have been endeavoring to decipher all your Earthian expressions."

He chuckled. "And how well is this study going?"

"Not as easy as one would have thought," she admitted. "I do, however, have my favorites memorized."

"Such as?"

She smirked. "Such as curve ball."

On the last night that he was with Ellyra, on Eurosia, he had given her his academy signet ring as an excuse to meet again. He had told her it was in case life threw them a curve ball.

He chuckled. "You even asked me if that was another human sport."

She glanced ahead, watching where they were walking. "Well, your people are rather fond of that shape."

"And life sure did throw us plenty of curve balls," he said, staring straight ahead.

"Your words proved prophetic," she said, stopping. "Draconian law has kept us apart for five of your years." She took off her necklace and removed Jonathan's signet ring, handing it to him. "Which reminds me that I am finally able to return your jewelry to you."

Jonathan slipped his ring over his right ring finger, fitting it back into place. It felt comfortable. It felt whole and intact. His hand had felt the ring's absence for so long, that it almost felt foreign to have the ring back in place. But it did look proper. It looked how he remembered it.

She smiled. "It is complete again."

They stepped aside to allow a uniformed man to walk past.

He took her hand. "Whenever—"

Rana audibly cleared her throat. Ellyra quickly withdrew her hand, her hair changing into an embarrassed burgundy. Jonathan's stomach muscles tensed in annoyance. What was so inappropriate about holding her hand? He took a deep breath to clear his emotions. The ridiculous irony was that he would have to thank her for ruining the mood.

He turned to Rana. "Thank you for the correction."

"My pleasure," she replied.

35

It probably is pleasurable for her to disrupt, he thought. He turned back to Ellyra, attempting to reengage the conversation. "Whenever I am with you, I *am* complete."

She narrowed her eyes. "Do you mean that or is it another expression?"

He sighed, glancing down. "I can see how it might be hard to tell when I'm being literal."

"It would be much easier if your hair wasn't always the same color; I can never tell how you're feeling."

"Well," he said, smiling. "Maybe it's to keep you guessing."

She giggled. "That sounds like something you would do."

He smiled. "Hopefully that doesn't hinder your studies too much."

"It's...an ongoing study," she said with hesitation in her voice. "One might even say, it would take a lifetime to complete."

The air grew heavy. He heard his heart beating. "With such a lengthy project, I would wonder if one could manage it all alone."

"Now that you mention it," she said, staring into his hazel eyes. "Such an undertaking might only be possible...if I had the appropriate company."

He reached to take her hand but refrained, glancing back at Rana. He put his hands behind his back instead and smiled at Ellyra. "Where do I enlist?"

She turned away, her hair dulling into a troubled gray. "Do not make this decision lightly; it will not be easy. Not a simple walk in the woods, as you would say."

A part of Jonathan wanted to correct her, that the expression was, a walk in the *park.* But he was proud that she was trying to use human expressions. It was best not to interrupt her train of thought.

She walked a few steps away from him in contemplation. "I am only here for a few short weeks. And with our duties, yours and mine, we would be under pressure to make the best possible use of this time." As she reasoned, her hands became more animated. "These things are only done a certain way, so we would need to do this properly. And then there is my father..."

Jonathan caught her by the shoulders and turned her to face him.

"Colonel Jonathan," Rana called out sternly.

He quickly removed his hands from Ellyra's shoulders and straightened up. Once again, he felt a volcano trying to erupt within the pit of his stomach and took a few breaths to calm his annoyance.

He glanced at Rana. "Sorry. Thank you again for the reminder," he said, feigning appreciation. He turned back to Ellyra. "Sune Ellyra, I have been fighting uphill battles for most of my military career. Making the best use of what I have been given comes naturally to me."

She gave a tentative smile. "Then you are resigned to move forward?"

"I am."

"Upon your honor?" she asked.

"Upon my honor."

She smiled, her hair brightening into an enamored pink. "There are conventions to follow, but before we can get to that, you will first need to formally announce your intentions to my Eltashee, Rana."

Jonathan glanced back at Rana.

"Oh, but not now," Ellyra cautioned. "It must be done privily."

"Consider it done," he said, with an air of inevitability.

She stared at him with a confused expression.

Jonathan chuckled. "Sorry, another human expression. It means I will get right on it."

She smiled warmly. "With all these expressions, it's a wonder your people can understand each other."

The comm-band on Jonathan's wrist beeped. It was a message from Med Bay Charlie. He had asked Dr. Mallory to let him know if Ambassador Cale's condition changed. He tapped a button and the little black screen flashed and showed Dr. Mallory's face. "Doc, the ambassador's condition has changed?"

"Yes, but...not for the better. The bug doctors were able to neutralize the poison, but I'm afraid the neurological damage is far too great. He has lapsed into a coma."

"Is there anything..."

Dr. Mallory shook his head. "I'm sorry. This is now beyond my abilities."

Jonathan tried to nod. He wasn't sure how effective he was. "I'm sorry for your loss, Doc."

He glanced down. "And I'm sorry for yours."

Jonathan tapped his comm-band to end the transmission.

"Ambassador Cale?" she asked with a shocked expression.

He nodded.

"He spent a lot of time on Eurosia as liaison with Earth. He was an artist, that one. He would weave logic into a tapestry of reason."

He turned away from her. "That is probably why *Able Station* assassinated him."

She pursed her lips. "Jonathan, you have to fight back."

"How?" he asked in exasperation. "How do I fight *Able Station*? I can't even keep their assassins from getting aboard."

She walked around to look into his eyes. "I apologize, Jonathan. This is apparently a very troubling subject."

He took a deep breath and looked down. "Please forgive the unprofessional tone."

She touched his cheek with her gloved hand, soliciting his gaze. "All is forgiven, Jonathan. I only ask that you forgive me as well. I was perhaps too forward in offering my opinion."

Rana pretended to cough. Ellyra immediately withdrew her hand.

"No, that's all right. I, uh. I actually would appreciate your insight. You have a lot more experience in these matters; you come from an important political family."

She nodded. "The largest of the great houses."

"How would you recommend I fight back?"

"They have already telegraphed their fears by assassinating Ambassador Cale. They fear your influence in the Draco Senate. Therefore, the place you can most hurt them is in the Senate."

Jonathan dismissed her comments with a wave of his hand. "This mockery of a Senate the Draconians have us all in? It isn't a real senate. The Draconians hold a two-thirds majority all by themselves. It's nothing more than a contest to see who can upset the Draconians against someone else."

"I don't think anyone pretends to live in a perfect galaxy," she replied. "Did you not just say that in fighting uphill, using the resources at hand has become second nature to you?"

He nodded.

"Then, if you would take my advice, take hold of whatever advantage you have and fight with it."

Something in her words rang true. He had heard similar words before. They had come from his own lips a decade earlier. His mind caught hold of the memory where he had spoken them. It was when he led the impossible charge at Mesa Sol and carried the day. The event that Fox called Terynn's Run. "We have not..." He concentrated, plucking the words from his memory. "We may not have chosen the field nor the day, but what we *can* choose is how we fight..."

Ellyra looked at him with renewed interest. "Well spoken."

"It was part of a rallying speech I gave to my men years back." He glanced back into her eyes. "Ellyra, I'm a commander, not a politician."

"The only difference between the two," she said, "is the weapon and the battlefield."

His comm-band beeped again. It was Fox in Command and Control. "Go ahead."

"Sorry to interrupt your tour, sir," Fox said. "But we have an urgent message on the Alpha Channel."

"Well, who is it?"

Fox shook his head. "Can't tell. The message is encoded for you only."

"Somebody sure wants to keep a secret. I'll be right there." Jonathan turned off the transmission and turned to Ellyra. "How about a tour of Command?

Chapter 5

BEING HUMAN

F ox stood in Command and Control, the hub of daily activity on *Gamma Station*. It was also the center of political headaches and disasters waiting to happen. He was overseeing the resupplying of Ellyra's ship. It needed supplies and fuel but why did the Euroo crew insist on receiving it in a ceremonial fashion? What difference did it make? *How would Juliet handle this?* he wondered. *"What's in a method? That which we call fuel given by any other method would burn as bright."*

Isabel was still seeing to the comfort of the Euroo dignitaries on board. If they were this stiff with supplies, their requirements for a proper guest room must be ridiculous. It was a good thing the Colonel didn't assign *him* that duty. The Colonel knew Isabel would be more tactful. She was so meticulous in the things she did. She remembered every detail like an actor's lines. Moreover, she was attractive.

Jonathan and Ellyra stepped into the room with Rana trailing close behind. Command and Control was a five-sided room with no door.

What did the Bugs have against doors? It was like they never considered the idea. The only doors on this space station had to be added by humans. That was also why every door looked out of place against the Chantell architecture.

The rest of the room's layout was very good. A short balcony ran around the back three walls. That's where the runners transferred internal messages, ran errands, and got the officer on duty his morning coffee. A large trench stretched around the front two walls. It was affectionately referred to as The Pit. The pit crew took care of space traffic, external communication, ship supplies, and more. The entire room worked together like the cast of a great unknown play.

"Okay, Fox, let's have it," Jonathan said.

Fox glanced at Ellyra. If the message was encoded for the Colonel, it wasn't smart for a foreign ship captain to be present. Surely, a brilliant strategist such as the Colonel would see that. He nodded in Ellyra's direction. "Sir, perhaps you'd like to take the encoded message privately?"

Jonathan blushed, looking at Ellyra. "Sorry, please excuse me a moment. I will be right back."

He crossed over to Fox and typed in his password to the computer terminal. A small screen on the control panel turned on and displayed the transmission. When it finished, he looked at Fox with a confused expression. "Put it on screen please."

Fox nodded, pressing a few buttons. One of the two large wall-mounted screens flashed and displayed a video image. It showed a bald gray-skinned alien with large black eyes and almost no nose or mouth to speak of. It was a Tumnei. One of the five elder races. They were the technological giants among the elder races. They couldn't compete with the superiority of the ancient races, such as the Draconians. But they led the scientific advances among everyone else.

"What do the Greys want?" Fox asked aloud.

Jonathan motioned for Ellyra to join them.

Ellyra walked up to Jonathan's side. "I thought the Tumnei oversaw the Earthians at *Bravo Station*."

Jonathan nodded. "They do. But at times they coordinate with us when transporting personnel from *Bravo Station*." He turned to Fox. "There should be an accompanying transcription."

"Yes sir," Fox said, pressing a few buttons on his control console. The Tumnei were a telepathic race. They spoke into people's minds, not making any audible sounds. It was very efficient since thoughts didn't need to be translated into other languages. The biggest downside, however, was that thoughts could not be recorded in a video message. Only audible sounds could. So, the Greys had to include a written message with their transmission.

The silly thing was that their mouths didn't move anyway. What was the point of seeing a video image of them staring back at you while you read a caption? It would be simpler to just send a written message. The Greys probably wanted to fit in with everyone else. They might feel excluded if they didn't also communicate with a video image.

Subtitles scrolled across the bottom of the screen. ESCORT ALIEN VESSEL 2236.5 BY 41178.2 BY 114.8 HEADING 0014 MARK 441 EXPLANATION PENDING MY ARRIVAL, DANGER IMMINENT—SUPRM. CMDR. T'KAL.

"Are they serious?" Fox asked. Could the Greys really be wanting them to gallivant across the stars in search of an endangered ship? Though, of course, it was hard to know what to believe when it came to the Tumnei.

Jonathan turned to Fox. "Oh, they're serious all right. That was the supreme commander of the Tumnei. What doesn't make sense is why they would need our help. Their ships are much faster and more powerful than ours."

Fox scratched his shaven head.

Ellyra stepped forward. "If I might be permitted to opine, Colonel Jonathan."

Even though Isabeau had mentioned that the Euroo used first names with ranks, it still sounded weird.

"Of course," Jonathan said with a nod.

"Military strength may not be the deciding factor if they had political or legal issues to evade."

"So, you're suggesting they may not have sufficient justification in this instance?"

She nodded.

Jonathan turned to Fox. "If danger is imminent, let's see just how fast we can get there."

"Aye sir," Fox said, turning to a stellar cartographer sitting at a computer station in the pit. "Chief O'Dell, I need a fix on those coordinates and the closest hypergate route."

O'Dell replied in his thick Irish accent. "Aye, sir."

Fox glanced up to the balcony and spotted one of the runners. "Vinnece!"

An 18-year-old seaman turned around. "Sir?"

When Fox had first joined the Earth Navy, he was puzzled why the enlisted rank was still called *seaman* when they were deployed in space. His drill sergeant had pointed out that changing the rank to *spaceman* just couldn't be taken seriously.

"I want a cruiser prepped for launch in five. And I prefer the *Saratoga* if she's back—this is not a drill."

"Aye, aye sir!" she said, spinning around to head back to her station. Her braided ponytail swung around and hit her in the face, briefly halting her.

Her hair had grown longer than regulations allowed for her rank. But he let it slide. She kept it neat and orderly, and it was also fun to watch her swat herself with her hair. It was an amusing encore he looked forward to.

Chief O'Dell stood. "Lt. Commander Jagger. Hypergate Washington is reportin' they be down for maintenance. They suggest detouring to hypergate Shanghai. That'll be puttin' the total travel time at 53 minutes 29 seconds, sir."

Fox sighed and ran a hand down his shaven head. "So much for our snappy response time." The Greys really needed to give more advanced warning. An hour of transit was not bad for hyperspace travel, but for a

rescue, it was horrible. In combat, a lot can happen in an hour. In fact, a lot can happen in just ten minutes.

Jonathan rolled his eyes. "It'll have to do. Inform the Chantell and request permission to leave the station."

"Colonel Jonathan," Ellyra said. "If you do not think it is too forward of me, I may be of some assistance. Seeing as you are in need to save time, I can offer you the use of my ship. Euroo vessels can enter hyperspace without the need for a hypergate. We might even be able to decrease your travel time by up to half."

Jonathan smiled. "It would mean a lot to me."

"Besides," Ellyra said with a coy smile. "I always wanted to take you out for a twirl in my ship."

He chuckled. "Out for a *spin*, you mean."

"Yes. That."

Fox rolled his eyes. Everyone likes a good romance, but did the Colonel need to fraternize with an alien captain in front of the crew? If he was going to make it a habit, at least he should put some class into his flirtation.

"Do you mind if I take some extra baggage along?" Jonathan asked Ellyra.

She raised an eyebrow. "How much?"

"Oh, say, 42 tons."

Ellyra sat in her command chair on the Center of Workmanship aboard the *Calmao*. She was pleased with herself. The situation could not have been more perfect if she had planned it. Jonathan needed help and she was in a position to help. Now she could spend some time with him, showing off her starship. She had smiled when he first boarded, watching his amazed look. He had eyed every mural and tapestry with wonder. If Earthians reacted like this aboard simple starships, they definitely didn't spend enough time decorating.

Throughout the trip, Diahlus sat to her left and Jonathan sat to her right. It was nice having Jonathan right next to her, but that isn't where she wanted him. The seating convention dictated that the seat to her right was for a visiting dignitary. She wanted him to sit beside Rana. Sitting beside her Eltashee meant he was a suitor, actively courting her. That is where he belonged.

If only he could be there now. But there were conventions that had to be followed. Things were done a certain way. Anything else just wasn't done. They had left too abruptly for Jonathan to formally announce his intentions to Rana. These things would have to wait until then.

"Sune Ellyra," a woman addressed. "The coordinates are upon us. Shall I exit hyperspace?"

"Let it be done," Ellyra ordered.

The *Calmao* raced through hyperspace, the blue tunnel of light in space. A large black hole opened at the end of the tunnel. It was the portal back into truespace. The *Calmao* crossed the event horizon. It shot out from the hyper-portal into the black starry space. The ship slowed to a stop.

"Madam," a female sensor operator announced. "Scanners are picking up two ships pursuing a third."

"On stage please," Ellyra ordered.

"As you wish."

The golden ring around the center of the floor lit up. It projected a three-dimensional hologram of the surrounding space. The two persuing crafts were tuning-fork-shaped ships of sleek orange metal.

Jonathan leaned forward in his chair. "I recognize that design. Scorpii, am I right?"

She nodded. "Confirmed. Two Scorpiian Harkon-class destroyers and one Earthian Darion-class frigate."

"What is the status of the Earthian frigate?" Ellyra asked, worried.

"Dire," she replied. "They've taken several direct hits. Their main engines are down and they are venting oxygen."

Ellyra turned to a man on her left who handled communications. "Can we hail them?"

He shook his head. "Indeed not, the Scorpii have erected a scattering field."

Ellyra shot a glance at Jonathan. "They are in no mood to talk. I suggest you launch your extra baggage immediately."

Jonathan pressed the intercom button on his chair that Ellyra had pointed to. "Eagle One and Eagle Seven, this is Mother Goose. Report in."

"Mother Goose, Eagle One. Standing by," a voice said, in a stoic military sir-yes-sir style.

"Mother Goose, Eagle Seven. Standing by," another voice echoed.

"You are go for launch, I say again, you are go for launch!"

In the cargo bay of the *Calmao*, Lieutenant Christopher Ryork sat in the cockpit of his SF-301 Trident-class starfighter. The Trident resting beside his belonged to his wingman, Lieutenant Bryce Allen. Allen was a good friend and an excellent flight lead.

Ryork's Trident starfighter held the callsign of Eagle Seven. Ryork's callsign was Ironman. When talking to Allen, they would address each other by their pilot callsigns. But to communicate with their home ship, they would use their starfighter's callsign.

Allen glanced out his canopy over to Ryork and gave him the hand signal to power on. It wasn't necessary, they had already powered on and completed the pre-flight checks. It was more of a formality since they were doing an unconventional launch.

The uptight Euroo didn't seem keen on letting them fire off their afterburners inside the cargo bay. Something about messing up their walls. Somebody needed to tell them to lighten up; char marks were an easy paint-over. When Ryork had confirmed he was ready to launch, he gave Allen a salute.

"*Calmao* cargo control, Earthian starfighters. We are ready to launch," Allen said.

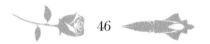

It sounded strange hearing Allen use layman's terms for their starfighters. The Euroo didn't have a brevity system, so the Colonel had instructed him to speak plainly to the Euroo. At least that wouldn't be a problem after launch.

The cargo bay door opened. It was like watching the far wall slide up, revealing the starry space beyond. The blue glow around the opening meant the atmospheric shield was holding the air inside the bay. It was a pretty impressive piece of technology. It held the atmosphere inside the cargo bay while allowing shuttles to enter and exit. But as impressive as that technology was, it didn't compare to the shield technology of the elder races. Their shields could stop more than just air pressure; they could stop an enemy's incoming fire.

The atmospheric shield of the cargo bay was going to perform a different function this time. It was called a pressure launch. It needed skilled pilots with nerves of titanium. And that was pretty much the dictionary definition of Allen and Ryork.

"Stand by for the depressurization of the cargo bay," a male Euroo voice announced. "In five, four, three, two, one."

The blue glow around the bay opening disappeared, releasing the air pressure. In a flash, the escaping air sent anything not bolted to the floor shooting out into space. Allen and Ryork's Tridents shot out like cannonballs.

"Waaaahooo!" Ryork hollered.

Quickly regaining his bearings, Ryork took hold of the stick and hit his afterburner. Allen was at his side. It was now time to dance.

Ryork checked his sensor screen. He saw five blips. The one closest to him was his wingman, Lt. Allen, the flight lead. The large blue blip was the *Calmao*, the Euroo cruiser. The yellow dot was the frigate and the two red dots were the enemy hostile ships, or bandits, as they were called.

Ryork needed to get a readout of the enemy ships. The biggest rule of engagement was to know your enemy's starcraft and to know your own. He pressed a few buttons. Details of the enemy ships streamed across his sensor screen.

47

Ryork's eyes widened. "Shogun, bandits are Scorpiian Harkons."

"Roger that, Ironman. We can't throw our weight around with the elder races. We'll have to pester them into disengaging."

Ryork smiled. Pestering the enemy was sometimes more fun than shooting them down. Since the Scorpii were an elder race, they had the technological advantage. That was usually par for the course since humans were near the bottom of the totem pole. Humans were always outclassed in technology. On the bright side, that had led to a very surprising research path compared to the rest of the known races.

"Ironman, arm EMPRAAMs, but save your heavies."

Ryork flipped a switch, arming the electromagnetic pulse missiles. Human ordnance couldn't penetrate superior armor. So, these were designed to knock out the enemy's electrical systems instead. Unfortunately, they wouldn't do much if the Scorpii had energy shields raised. "Roger, Shogun."

"Bandits are coming around for another pass on the frigate," Allen announced. "See if you can get an IFF reading on it while you follow me in."

IFF, or Identification Friend-Foe, was an electronic signal that all human ships broadcasted. It was a quick way to determine if the ship really was human and where it originated.

"Roger, Shogun." Ryork pressed a few buttons. *What on Earth!* He thought. *How can that be?* The frigate's IFF signal was from *Gamma Station.* There was no way that ship was from *Gamma Station.* Only military ships were stationed there. And the design of the frigate looked civilian.

"Shogun, that frigate has a Gamma IFF," Ryork replied.

"Roger that, Ironman. Mother Goose, this is Eagle One. Friendly echoes Gamma IFF."

"Gamma? Are you sure?" Jonathan's voice asked.

"That's affirmative, Mother Goose."

Several other voices were heard over the comm channel. It was typical to hear too many voices over a battle transmission which was frustrating. And to make matters worse, the Euroo were not aware of transmission decorum. What little Ryork had heard of them speaking was filled with too many unnecessary words. Maybe flying a mission with humans would wise them up to talking more efficiently.

"What did you learn about the ship being chased?" a male Euroo voice asked.

"It says she's one of ours," Jonathan said.

"You already told us that."

"No," Jonathan clarified. "It's saying she's from *Gamma Station*."

"How can that be?" a female Euroo voice asked.

"Someone's trying to tell me that frigate is important," Jonathan replied.

"How is that a message?" another voice asked.

"It must be an Earthian thing," the male voice concluded.

As entertaining as the background conversation was, they were coming up on those two Harkons. The Scorpii classified the Harkon as a destroyer, which did not make much sense. At least in human navies, a destroyer was a larger ship that supported the carrier group of capital ships. These looked like overgrown starfighters.

Ryork lined up his Trident starfighter with the Harkon. A targeting light flashed and a beeping sounded in his ear. "Shogun, I've got target lock."

"Roger, Ironman. Mother Goose, this is Eagle One. We have target lock, do we have permission to fire?"

"Fire at will," Jonathan's voice said. "I say again, fire at will!"

A missile dropped from under the wing of Allen's starfighter. "Eagle One, fox-2."

Ryork pulled the trigger on his stick and heard the *clank* of the missile detaching from under his wing. It rocketed away toward the Harkon. "Eagle Seven, fox-2."

Each missile hit one of the Harkons, illuminating the energy shield surrounding it. It looked like an invisible bubble of safety that lit up when they were hit. Blue electricity snaked all over the shields of the Harkons.

"Blast, these bogies are shielded!" Ryork said. "We don't have enough time to cut through them."

"Mother Goose, Eagle One," Allen said over the comm. "Bandits are endowed, again, bandits are endowed. Please advise."

"Stand by," Jonathan's voice replied.

Ryork checked the readout on his scanner. The EMPRAAM missiles didn't damage the Harkons, but they interfered with their targeting computers. The Harkons lost their lock and their orange plasma bolts missed, flying past the frigate. The Harkons would have to circle again for another pass. Ryork and Allen followed them.

Jonathan paced in front of the hologram that showed the battle. His muscles were tense and his breathing shallowed. *There has to be a way,* he thought. The frigate was losing power and oxygen; it was a drifting target. The enemy ships were energy shielded. And his two starfighters did not have enough firepower to punch through. For their electromagnetic pulse weapons to work, they had to hit the actual hull of the ship.

He turned to Ellyra. "Can the *Calmao* attack?"

She glanced over to Xer.

He shook his head. "Indeed not. We have neither precedent nor grievance to legally engage in combat with the Scorpii."

Ellyra brushed a stray lock of white hair over her ear. "When you say 'we', are you referring to the Euroo, or this ship?"

Xer returned a confused look. "Are they not one and the same in this instance?"

She shook her head. "Give me not the meaning of the law, but the letter of it."

"The law specifies the *government* may not engage. But under Article Twenty-three, a ship is considered to belong to the government to which its commander answers. So I ask again, are they not one and the same in this instance?"

Ellyra's hair color cooled into a thoughtful violet. She rose from her seat and walked up to Jonathan. She leaned in close and whispered. "Ask me for command of my ship during this battle."

Jonathan returned a startled look. He heard her words plainly. She was inviting him to request command of her ship. Was that even allowed? Maybe he misunderstood her. "What?" he finally asked.

"Command of my ship," she reiterated, staring into his eyes. "Ask me for it." Her determined eyes told him she was being serious. Why must he ask for it? Couldn't she simply give it to him? She was a shrewd one. He had learned that five years earlier. She knew something he didn't and was offering help in the only way she could. He would be a fool not to accept. His pilots were outmatched and that frigate was no longer space worthy.

His calculating mind decided this request needed to sound formal. Most things he observed about the Euroo were formal. Jonathan cleared his throat. "Sune Ellyra, seeing as the, uh, rules of engagement restrict us... may I, uh, formally command your ship for the duration of the battle?"

Diahlus jumped out of his seat, his hair color blackening. "Impertinence!"

Jonathan had no idea what an 'impertinence' was but it sounded bad. Had he misspoken? It sounded proper in his head. Jonathan paled.

Ellyra spun around giving Jonathan her back. She spoke in one long quick sentence as she stepped over to her chair. It sounded like she had rehearsed the lines to a play and spewed them out as quickly as possible. "How impertinent and improper a request, though I suppose your argument has merit. Yes, you truly have convinced me of the necessity of the situation. Under Regulation Six-five-five, I hereby grant you temporary command for the duration of the battle. Do not imagine to yourself, however, this will become a habit."

Diahlus and Jonathan exchanged dumbfounded looks.

Ellyra shot a glance over to Xer. "No, Xer. It would appear they are not one and the same in this instance."

Xer cleared his throat. "I stand corrected. We now have legal precedent."

Diahlus broke the brief silence, speaking over his shoulder. "Arm seeker missiles and open the outer hatch doors."

"As you wish," a female voice replied.

"I assume those are your orders," he said to Jonathan.

Jonathan nodded in appreciation. "Thank you, Brigadain. Can your seeker missiles penetrate their shielding?"

His hair color lightened to a formal white. "We've never had the opportunity to find out. I suspect, though, that we shall have to use every last one."

Jonathan nodded. "Target the lead Harkon and fire."

"Let it be done," Diahlus called out.

Ryork pulled his Trident fighter around a tight turn, following behind one of the Harkons. Volleys of seeker missiles erupted out of the small missile hatches on the bow of the *Calmao*. The pepper cloud of missiles raced toward the Harkons.

Jonathan's voice called out over the comm. "Eagles One and Seven, break off, break off, birds are away!"

"Roger that, Mother Goose," Allen said.

"Roger, Mother Goose, getting out of the way!" Ryork said as he veered away, engaging his turning thrusters.

The pepper cloud of missiles grew into a dense cluster as they closed in on one of the Harkons. The missiles slapped up against the invisible energy shield, illuminating it. Missile after missile, explosion after explosion harassed the Harkon's energy shield. It sputtered and collapsed.

Energy shields were impressive. Using electrical power, they absorbed explosions and enemy weapon shots. But once all their power was used up to absorb damage, they collapsed. They could be raised again once the shield capacitor was recharged but that took time. Ryork and Allen now had a window of time in which to strike a crippling blow on the Harkon.

"Ironman," Allen said. "Arm your heavies and follow me in on Bandit One. We're gonna need a one-two punch."

"Roger Shogun." Ryork armed his heavy ordnance EMPRAAM missiles. Then he pulled up beside Allen's Trident starfighter.

"Eagle One, fox-3," Allen said, firing a missile.

The targeting computer beeped in Ryork's ear. "Eagle Seven, fox-3." The missile *clanked* as it dropped from under the wing. It rocketed close behind Allen's missile, racing toward the Harkon. The first missile struck its hull. Green electricity danced across the metal surface. The second missile crashed into the hull a few seconds later. It bathed the Harkon in green electricity. The red glow of the Harkon's engines flickered and died. It helplessly drifted without electrical power.

"Hoorah!" Allen shouted with joy. "Bandit One is dead in space!"

A flash of light from Ryork's peripheral vision caught his attention. "Shogun, break right! Bandit Two incoming!"

Allen fired his turning thrusters, pulling away from his trajectory. Furious orange bolts of plasma streaked past, illuminating his canopy. Allen dove his Trident starfighter behind the lifeless Harkon, breaking line of sight. This did not deter the other Harkon. It fired its orange plasma bolts into its wingman's dead ship, destroying it. The explosion threw wreckage in all directions. Debris showered Allen's starfighter until it also exploded.

Time seemed to stop for Ryork. His flight commander, his friend, was now gone. Memories of Allen and his wife flooded his mind. They were almost as close as family. His heart felt cold and heavy. His throat was dry.

Jonathan's voice over the comm sounded faint and distant. "...I repeat, Eagle One, do you read!"

Jonathan stood in the Center of Workmanship of the *Calmao*, watching the terrible battle on the three-dimensional holograms in the center of the room. One of the Scorpii ships exploded and Lt. Allen's starfighter was very close to the explosion. This worried him.

Ryork's voice finally responded. "He's K.I.A., sir. He's gone."

A moment of dreadful silence passed. Jonathan closed his eyes and clenched his fists. His jaw tensed up. He took a deep breath and opened his eyes, forcing his jaw to relax. "I need you to pull yourself together, Lieutenant. There is still one more bandit. Can you commit?"

Ryork's static-laden voice replied. "No joy, Mother Goose. And my sensors are inop."

Jonathan sighed, glancing heavenward. What else could go wrong? Losing visual was usually not a problem with an active sensor screen. But Ryork's starfighter was also quite close to the explosion. If his sensor grid had shorted out and was inoperative, then he was blind to anything he couldn't physically see. And having lost visual, his pilot was a sitting duck.

Jonathan located the Harkon on the three-dimensional hologram. "Eagle Seven, bandit is forming up on your six o'clock. Break left and hit your afterburner. You should then get a visual."

"Tally on bandit," Ryork's voice announced.

Ellyra, Diahlus, and Xer sat, watching with bated breath. It wasn't clear how much combat experience they had. The Euroo were an elaborate and peaceful race. Jonathan couldn't count on them having as much field experience. This arena was his, and his alone. The *Calmao* had already fired all its seeker missiles, so, he couldn't help his pilot in that way. Yet there had to be something he could do.

"Bandit is scissoring me, gaining the advantage. Please advise, Mother Goose. Please advise!"

"Colonel Jonathan," Diahlus addressed. "May I advise a retreat?"

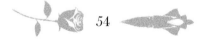

Jonathan glanced in his direction and then he continued his pacing. His calculating mind spun in circles. The obvious path had been foreclosed. He could not overpower the enemy. And their energy shield prevented his weapons from having any effect. He needed another angle. Something not obvious, something perhaps wild and crazy.

"Jonathan," Ellyra said, standing. "The Brigadain is correct. We must retreat."

"Something on that frigate is important. If we retreat the Scorpii will destroy it."

"Better that frigate than us," Xer said. "We were never a match for an elder race to begin with."

Jonathan spun around to meet Xer's gaze. "If you ever learn anything from humans, learn this expression: where there's a will, there's a way!"

"How can there possibly be a—"

Jonathan raised his hand, gesturing for silence. His eyes danced around momentarily and then he looked up with a smile across his face. "And I just found a way." He walked over to Diahlus. "I need you to power up your hyperdrive. But don't engage the drive, just let the power build."

"That could blow the primary relay conduit and rupture the drive!"

"Right, but that won't happen for about a minute or so, correct?"

"How long is a minute?"

"Your assessment is correct," Ellyra answered.

Diahlus looked to Ellyra for approval of the order.

She gave him a nod.

"Steersman, power up the hyperdrive," he ordered. "And do not, I repeat, do *not* engage the hyper-portal generator."

"As you wish, Brigadain."

A low gentle hum from the hyperdrive capacitor sounded in the room. The hum grew in intensity.

"Mother Goose, Eagle Seven!" Ryork's panicked voice came in over the comm. "Bandit One is on my tail, and I can't shake him!"

"That's it, Eagle Seven!" Jonathan shouted. "Bring the enemy into range. We are charging up the Death Ray."

"Death Ray?" Ryork's confused voice asked.

"Death Ray?" Xer mumbled under his breath.

"That's right, Lieutenant," Jonathan continued. "The Scorpii have crossed the line and we're going to send them into oblivion!"

"...oh...right," Ryork's voice said. "But I won't escape the blast radius."

"You will, uh, be remembered with honor, Lieutenant!"

Diahlus pointed to the three-dimensional hologram of the battle scene. The Harkon had veered away.

"Mother Goose, Eagle Seven. Bandit One is bugging out!"

"Quickly! Fire the Death Ray!" Jonathan shouted.

The Harkon bolted into superlight speed.

"Enemy vessel has hyper-shifted into hyperspace," a female Euroo voice announced.

"Yiiii-haha!!" Ryork hollered over the comm.

Diahlus quickly gestured to the steersman to cut power to the hyperdrive capacitor. The loud hum of the hyperdrive died down. Ellyra jumped up and hugged Jonathan. Then, second-guessing the propriety of the act, she stepped back.

"Simply brilliant, Jonathan," she said.

Xer looked confused. "What is a Death Ray?"

"A clever ruse," Diahlus explained. "It would seem that the Colonel here has deceived the Scorpiian pilot into thinking we were about to destroy his vessel with some great weapon."

Xer's cyan within blue eyes widened. "And when the enemy vessel scanned the *Calmao*, they detected a large energy buildup and assumed the threat was real! Masterful!"

Diahlus walked over to Jonathan. "Colonel Jonathan, I owe you an apology. When you came aboard, I saw you as an uncultured, arrogant, and impulsive ruffian."

"And now?"

"I *still* think you're an uncultured, arrogant, and impulsive ruffian," he admitted with a smile. "But it is clear to me that your unorthodox strategies produce spectacular results. Which makes you—on my canvas, at least—an artist." He bowed to Jonathan.

Jonathan bowed in return. "That's quite the compliment to live up to."

Diahlus smiled. "Indeed." He raised a finger. "Yet, there is one thing I do not understand. How did your pilot know you were deceiving the Scorpii and how to properly respond?"

Jonathan returned a witty smirk. "That, my friend, is part of being human."

Chapter 6

CONSPIRACY

Fox raced down the wide hallway with a hovering stretcher in tow. On the stretcher lay an unconscious man with pale skin. The Colonel had said they rescued an Earth frigate from the Scorpii, but that it was severely damaged. The oxygen had all vented out into space. The sole occupant of the frigate now lay on the stretcher, dying. The closest medical bay was Med Bay Alpha. But the Colonel had specifically requested him to be taken to Med Bay Charlie. Dr. Mallory was the chief surgeon and also the very best.

Fox wanted to stay and inspect the broken frigate, but he was also the fastest runner among the officers. *We've got to get a better way to transport passengers to the med bays,* Fox thought. The Chantell didn't build a better way because they always flew down the wide hallways. The Bugs hadn't designed this space station with a flightless bipedal species in mind.

Grrrah'Kah's men were stationed at each hallway intersection, halting pedestrian traffic from crossing. That saved time and lessened the risk of an accidental collision. *Grrrah'Kah thinks of everything*, he thought. *That bug will definitely be getting a raise.*

Fox slowed to a stop in front of Med Bay Charlie. The door slid up and Fox maneuvered the hover stretcher inside. "Here he is, Doc," he said, panting.

Dr. Mallory looked up from the bedside of Ambassador Cale. "That's the passenger Jonathan called about?"

"That's him, Doc," he answered, still trying to catch his breath. "He's not responsive but he still has a weak pulse."

Dr. Mallory rushed across the room and checked the man's pulse. "I need some room. Move the stretcher over next to the Ambassador's bed."

Fox pushed the hover stretcher beside Ambassador Cale's bed. Fox looked down at the pale man who lay on the stretcher. Both the bed and the stretcher lay side by side. Ambassador Cale on the bed and the pale man on the stretcher. The pale man looked to be in his early thirties but with a bald head and pale skin. He lay motionless. His chest didn't even noticeably rise and fall as it would if he were breathing. Suddenly, the man's hand grabbed Fox's wrist.

Fox jerked his arm away. The fear of the surprise vanished from him. And somehow, he knew what was wrong with the man. It was like a sudden flash of inspiration was transferred through the pale man's touch.

"Severe cerebral hypoxia, Doc."

Dr. Mallory rushed over and placed an oxygen mask on the pale man's face. "How severe?"

"Imminent somatic death."

Dr. Mallory cursed and feverishly connected machines up to the body of the pale man. Fox stood watching in helplessness. What was there to do? He could only watch and hope. If the man recovered, he could get some answers. But if he died, the mystery would die with him. The Greys did promise an explanation. But would they have enough of an explanation without this man?

An alarm sounded and Dr. Mallory cursed again, working twice as fast. After a few exhausting moments, Dr. Mallory stopped and breathed out long and hard. He turned off the alarm with a flick of a switch and then glanced at the time on the comm-band around his wrist.

"Nurse, time of death is o-seven-hundred-thirty-eight hours."

A computerized voice responded. "Noted and recorded."

Dr. Mallory sighed and began disconnecting the equipment. "I'm sorry."

"No worries, Doc. You did everything you could with what little time you had." Fox paused a moment. "Doc, what is cerebral hypoxia?"

Dr. Mallory looked at him. "Don't you know? You're the one who told me."

Fox shook his head. "It's strange, Doc. When that man's hand grabbed me, those words were very clear in my mind. Somehow, I knew that was the answer. Only now, I have no idea what that means."

Dr. Mallory returned a skeptical look. "Cerebral hypoxia is a lack of oxygen to the brain. When starved for long enough, the patient will lose consciousness and eventually die. As we have seen here." He shook his head. "But with how far gone this man was, there's no way he could have grabbed your arm."

Fox's eyes intensified. "He grabbed it, Doc. Just like this." Fox imitated the gesture to his own wrist.

Dr. Mallory again shook his head. "Lt. Colonel, a comatose patient has no voluntary motor control."

"Oh yeah," Fox said. "Well then, how do you explain that?" He pointed at the body. The pale man's other hand had reached over and was holding onto the wrist of Ambassador Cale.

"What the..." Dr. Mallory whispered in amazement. He leaned in closer. "It must be some kind of localized Dystonia that happened to look voluntary..."

Fox rolled his eyes. "Whatever you say, Doc."

"Look," he said defensively. "I've worked in foreign and domestic medicine for two decades. I've seen a lot of strange alien stuff. But this man is human."

60

Fox folded his arms. He knew what he had experienced. He had felt the cold grasp of the hand followed by the flash of inspiration that had now left him. But it was no use debating the issue with a medical doctor. He would have better luck debating music with a prima donna.

Fox's comm-band beeped twice. It was a transmission from the Colonel. He spoke into his comm-band. "Receive."

The black screen blinked and displayed a video image of Jonathan. "Lt. Colonel Jagger, how is the man we rescued?"

Fox looked away. It was hard to inform the Colonel that one of his best pilots was killed saving a man who died anyway. "I'm sorry, Colonel. But he didn't make it." For a few seconds, the only sounds heard were the faint noises of medical equipment in the background.

Jonathan looked down. "That's...unfortunate."

"The Doc did all he could."

Jonathan nodded and took a deep breath. "Better come on up to the conference room. Supreme Commander T'Kal has arrived. We should be able to get some answers."

"On my way, sir." He tapped the screen and it turned off.

Dr. Mallory put a hand on Fox's shoulder. "For what it's worth, I wish I could have—"

The computer screen next to Ambassador Cale started beeping softly. Dr. Mallory crossed over to the screen with a confused expression on his face.

"What is it, Doc?" Fox asked.

"Cale's brainwave activity is returning to normal...that doesn't make any sense."

"Wait, isn't that supposed to be a good thing?"

Dr. Mallory kept his eyes on the screen. "Well, yes, but how is it possible?"

Fox glanced at the time on his comm-band. "I have a meeting to get to. Let me know what you find out."

61

I sabeau paced back and forth across the dull green metal floor of the conference room. She didn't usually pace. She didn't often have enough anxiety to take up the habit. But today was different. Jonathan had mentioned that the Greys' ship had arrived. T'Kal wanted to hold their secret meeting in person this time. That meant there was a chance that they brought Cyran with them. If only they had thought far enough in advance. They might have anticipated the opportunity and brought him.

She dearly hoped they had. She hadn't seen her brother in five years. It would be so grand to see him again and feel his warm embrace. Would she recognize him? The picture she had of him was seven years old. A lot can change in seven years. Everything, that is, except the Draconians and their stupid rules. Why couldn't she at least write to him? Why was there such strict segregation between each of the space stations? And why was she one of the unlucky ones?

The door slid up. Isabeau spun around, her heart stopping. All her longing to reunite with Cyran bubbled up inside her. Her muscles tensed up in anticipation. She took a quick step toward the door and then froze. Fox stepped inside and sauntered over to a seat. Her anticipation melted away into annoyance. It was only Fox. All that suspense was for nothing, like seeing a package arrive only to find out it's not for you. She glared at him.

"What?" he asked in bewilderment.

She turned away and continued her pacing.

The door slid up again and Jonathan entered with three Tumnei behind him. The Greys stood four to five feet tall. They wore silvery skin-tight uniforms with black boots. Their large heads held two solid black glassy eyes. Their noses were so small that only a pair of nostrils could be seen. Their small mouths were the greatest mystery; they never moved.

"If you'll please have a seat," Jonathan said to them, motioning to the table.

It was always difficult to pick out which one was T'Kal and which were his bodyguards. They all looked pretty much alike and their uniforms held no distinctions. One of the Greys sat down, his head not very far above the conference table. That must be T'Kal. The other two stood at the wall behind him.

Isabeau felt a hand on her shoulder. It was probably Jonathan, instructing her to take her seat. She turned to sit down at the table but stopped. Jonathan was standing at the table already. Then whose hand was on her shoulder? She glanced back. A tall man with short black hair and a thick mustache stood at her side. His blue and white attire suggested he was from *Bravo Station*. He smiled.

She knew that smile. She had studied every curve of that smile from her old tattered photograph. "Cyrano!" She jumped into his arms, giving him a tight bear hug.

He lifted her off the ground and spun her all the way around. "Bonjour, ma petite Isabeau! Comment ça va?"

"Bien, mon cher frère! Bien, et toi?"

Cyran kissed her on both cheeks and she mirrored him. "Oui, petite sœur, moi, je vais bien!" He gave her one last tight hug.

Fox deliberately cleared his throat.

"Forgive me, my friends," Cyran said in his thick French accent. "But a five-year reunion just could not wait."

"That's okay," Jonathan said in a calm tone. "I think I know exactly how you feel." He motioned toward the table. "If you'll both please take your seats."

Isabeau and Cyran sat next to each other.

Jonathan glanced over to Fox. "Please lock the door."

"Of course, sir." Fox walked over to the door and typed a code into the keypad on the wall. The door chimed three times. Fox retook his seat.

"Thank you for agreeing to move up this meeting, T'Kal," Jonathan began. "It's difficult to keep these meetings looking random. Current events also made the perfect excuse to meet in person."

"Your gratitude is unnecessary but appreciated, Colonel Terynn." T'Kal's thoughts projected into everyone's minds.

Isabeau had heard that the Greys spoke telepathically but hadn't experienced it before. No wonder their mouths never moved. They never had to.

"But before we begin," Cyran said. "I want to thank you for rescuing Vincent."

"Vincent?" Jonathan asked.

"Yes, the passenger aboard the frigate. I had altered the frigate's transponder signal to that of *Gamma Station.* I hope you got the message?"

Jonathan looked down. "Yeah, I got the message. But I'm sorry to report that Vincent didn't survive."

Cyran paled. "Did you retrieve the body? Did you bring it here?"

Jonathan looked at him curiously. "Yes...yes we have the body in a med bay."

Why is he so concerned about a dead man's body? Isabeau wondered.

"There's a possibility he might not be dead."

"Oh no, he's dead all right," Fox replied. "I was there when the Doc called the time."

"If he is dead then this was all for *nothing,*" Cyran said grimly.

A fire lit in Jonathan's eyes. "I lost a good man in that rescue, Cyran. It had better have been for *something.*"

"What was all for nothing?" Isabeau asked. "What was so important about that man?"

"He was not an Earthian man," said T'Kal's telepathic voice. *"He was a Voonsu."*

"I beg your pardon?"

"Voonsu. They are a race of microorganisms. They inhabit deceased bodies to interact with the outside world."

Isabeau covered her mouth and nose. *Gross!*

Fox pounded his fist on the table. "I *knew* there was something weird about that guy."

All eyes turned to him.

"Something you wish to share with the rest of us, Mr. Jagger?" Jonathan asked.

Fox ran a hand down his smooth head and face. "In the med bay, I swear that guy grabbed my wrist. The Doc says that's not possible due to his condition. But he grabbed my arm and I suddenly knew what was wrong with him. Like a sudden idea popping into your head that eventually fades away."

"Yes, they form a network of consciousness. It allows them to intercept neural impulses around them."

"In other words," Cyran said. "They are telepathic."

"Well, so far you've told us what they are but not why they're so important," Jonathan said.

T'Kal tilted his head. *"Are you familiar with the story of the Skorath Prophecy?"*

Jonathan glanced up in thought. "In fairy tales mostly. From when my mother would tuck me in at night. I remember something about a foretold star that would scare the Draconians."

"Yes, that is the one. Allow me to refresh your memory: A newborn light will arise from an uninteresting corner of space, wielding a power that will frighten the star of Draconia, and claim the birthright of the ancestors."

Cyran sighed. "That, unfortunately, was where the Voonsu were supposed to come into play."

"How so?" Jonathan asked.

"The prophecy tells of the downfall of the Draconians by a new race with the power to 'frighten the star of Draconia'."

"And just what power was the Voonsu supposed to have? What could possibly frighten the Draconians?"

"Because, Jonathan, the Voonsu don't simply read people's thoughts, they can also *influence* them."

Jonathan sat forward in his chair. "Wait a second. You're telling me they can mess with somebody's mind?"

"Talk about a security risk," Fox added.

"It's perfect," T'Kal's voice said in their minds. *"It fits the prophecy's description of a power that can frighten the star of Draconia."*

"No," Cyran objected. "It would have been perfect had the Voonsu lived. Now all this talk about the prophecy is meaningless."

It didn't make much sense to Isabeau. If it was a prophecy, wouldn't that mean it was going to happen and not something that simply *could* happen? After all, wasn't inevitability what separated prophecies from useful advice?

"Well," she began. "How could the Voonsu be the fulfillment of this prophecy if they're dead? Wouldn't they have been prophesied to have died if that were the case? I thought a prophecy was peering into the future; seeing what was going to happen."

T'Kal tilted his head. *"The Commander's logic has merit. From a philosophical standpoint, if the Voonsu are to fulfill the prophecy, they cannot be all dead. If Vincent has perished, there must be more Voonsu out there somewhere."*

"You make them sound like replacement parts," Cyran said. "As if you could go and pick up new ones when needed. It was a stroke of luck finding Vincent in the first place. How are we ever to seek out more?"

Isabeau wrinkled her brow. "Can't we just visit their home planet?"

"A sensible suggestion, Commander Alexi," came T'Kal's telepathic voice. *"Unfortunately, they have no homeworld, at least, none that they are aware of."*

"Forgive my pessimism, ma petite sœur. Without a homeworld, our only recourse is to ask around if anyone has seen a race of micro-organisms about."

Fox snapped his fingers. "Wait, micro-organism? Is that like germs?"

"A crude approximation, but that technically fits."

"I'm not the only one Vincent touched," Fox said, running a hand down his shaved head.

Cyran gave him an inquisitive look. "What are you getting at?"

"Vincent touched Ambassador Cale also. And right before I left, the doc said the ambassador's brain was working again."

Cyran exclaimed something in French. "I pray this is true. Did he wake up? Were you able to talk with him?"

"Well...no. He still looks kind of dead."

"No homeworld," Jonathan thought aloud, the gears in his head turning. "From a strategic standpoint, there is only one way we can feasibly wage war on the Draconians. At least without their armada decimating our home planets. That would be to invent an enemy that has no home. There would be no stationary target to retaliate against. The Draconians would be forced onto the defensive."

"If they can actually take casualties, that is," Fox said, interrupting the thought train. "Their dreadnaughts are darn near invincible."

Jonathan shook his head. "Nothing is invincible, Mr. Jagger. Everybody has a weakness. It's just a matter of finding it. For example, the Draconians do not use defensive shield technology. I've always wondered if our EMPRAAM missiles could short out some systems."

"Even if we could," Fox replied. "We have a limited number of missiles, and they have a limitless armada of ships."

T'Kal looked at Fox. *"Please forgive the critique, Lt. Colonel. But you speak in exaggerations."*

"Forgive me, Supreme Commander. But the most prominent fleet in the sector is the 53rd fleet. That's over two hundred dreadnaughts parked within striking distance of most homeworlds. Now, that name alone tells me they have at least fifty-two other fleets. Do the math. That's more than ten thousand six hundred Draconian dreadnaughts. And that's a conservative estimate."

Isabeau breathed out in dismay. "We would be trying to fight a colony of ants, one ant at a time."

"That's why we needed the Voonsu," Cyran said, passionately waving his hands as he spoke. "They would have fulfilled the prophecy and freed us from the Draconians."

Fox turned to him. "How? You haven't mentioned them having a fleet of starships or anything. How would the Voonsu tackle an armada of dreadnaughts?"

T'Kal held a hand up. *"That is where the last line of the prophecy comes into play: claim the birthright of the ancestors. We are sure it means advanced technology from an ancient race."*

"Skorath tech?" Jonathan asked.

Fox leaned back in his seat. "You'd think if the Skorath technology was so easy to find, someone would have found it by now."

Isabeau's thoughts trailed off. It couldn't be Skorath technology. The wording of the prophecy didn't fit that assumption. If the Skorath were prophesying about their own technology, wouldn't they have said 'claim *our* birthright'? She glanced at T'Kal. He was watching the others discuss the Skorath. *I wonder if he already knows it's not the Skorath?*

T'Kal turned toward her and spoke into her mind. *"Very astute, Commander."*

Isabeau blushed. *I'm sorry, Supreme Commander,* she thought, *I'm not used to my thoughts being public.*

"No apologies necessary, Commander. But please, do take credit for your logical assertions. The birthright of the ancestors, which the prophecy speaks of, is not the technology of the Skorath."

"Right, because linguistically it doesn't make sense. And besides, they all vanished after the Great War anyway."

All eyes turned to her.

She blushed again, realizing she had made that last comment aloud.

"The Skorath are not all gone," he said into everyone's mind.

She recomposed herself. "What do you mean, not all gone?"

T'Kal nodded to one of his guards. The guard walked over to a large computer screen on the wall and inserted a crystal disk. The screen flashed and displayed a video image of an empty spot in space. The timestamp was displayed in Tumnei characters in the lower corner. Isabeau shivered as a long black ship faded into view. It hadn't moved; it had gradually appeared. The long, tubular, and uneven shape of the ship made it appear organic, like a large shadowy squid in space.

Fox braced his hands on the table and pushed himself to his feet. "Is that...?"

"Skorath."

68

The others joined Fox in standing. They gazed upon the eerie-looking vessel.

"The ship appears every ten years or so on the outskirts of a star cluster they have forbidden us to divulge."

Jonathan blinked, breaking his mesmerized gaze on the ghostly ship. "So, you have spoken with them?"

T'Kal tilted his head. *"Of course, Colonel. Each time they come; they ask us only for information on current events—nothing more. And in return, they tell us about the past."*

"Why do they want to know about what happens around here?" Isabeau asked.

Jonathan stroked his smooth chin. "It sounds to me like the Skorath don't consider the Great War to be over yet."

"Precisely our assessment. In our last encounter, we inquired as to why they had not yet counterattacked the Draconians. They replied, 'We await the return of the Antarens'."

Fox plopped back into his seat. "More bedtime stories. Out of all of them, Antares was my favorite. The classic outer space Atlantis story. A vast and powerful galactic civilization that vanished without a trace centuries ago."

"No," Jonathan said. "If I recall, it was their homeworld, Antares, that vanished without a trace. The Antarens supposedly died of some deadly plague—"

"That's not what I heard," Isabeau said. "I heard they died in a great battle..."

Cyran stood and waved his arms. "Gentlemen, gentlemen, please..." He glanced at Isabeau. "...and lady," he amended. "The main point of this conversation is this: the galactic word Antar means 'they which came before'. Or, in other words, *ancestors*. Therefore, Antares, or Antar es, means 'where the ancestors reside'."

After a long uncomfortable silence, Jonathan finally spoke. "So, the birthright of the Ancestors is the technology of the Antarens?"

"Colonel," Fox said. "If we had a technological advantage like the Antarens, we could wallop the Draconians. We'd give them a run for their money."

Antaren technology was supposedly superior to the mighty Draconians. But from a practical standpoint, it wasn't much of a guarantee they'd be able to get their hands on it.

"But as you've pointed out," Isabeau said. "This all hinges on if the prophecy is true."

"More accurately, this all hinges on if we are interpreting the prophecy correctly. And if the Voonsu are the fulfillment of it."

"And assuming the Voonsu survived," Cyran added.

"We must tread lightly here, gentlemen," Jonathan cautioned. "Whether or not we understand the prophecy—whether or not the Voonsu are the fulfillment of it—if we commit to this, there will be no going back. We will win or we will be annihilated." He pointed to the video image of the Skorath ship on the screen. "Possession of that footage alone is enough to get an extermination order called. One slip will be the end of us all. The Draconians do not give second chances."

He allowed a moment of silence for his point to sink in. Everyone who was still standing took their seats. "Supreme Commander T'Kal, let us suppose that our understanding of the prophecy is correct. Would you have a proposed course of action? Just how would this birthright be claimed?"

T'Kal nodded. *"What your bedtime stories haven't told you is that the Antarens and the Skorath were allies in the Great War."*

Fox snapped his fingers. "If they were allied with the Antarens, then they would know how to claim the Antaren technology."

"Our thoughts exactly," Cyran added.

"How much time do we have until the Skorath ship returns?" Isabeau asked.

"Approximately four months."

Fox scratched the side of his head. "Just getting the technology might not be enough. We may have to construct some more of their ships. Which means we'll need facilities to construct them."

"It can't be us," Isabeau concluded. "Humans are too closely watched. It'll have to be one of the elder races if we are to have any chance of keeping such a project under wraps."

"I'm sure we can assist in that."

Isabeau glanced over to Jonathan. He was silent, staring off into space with the gears turning in his head. "Colonel, what are your thoughts?"

He looked up. "Who we really need are the Chantell. They are the most efficient builders I have ever seen. They built this space station in under a year—it should have taken ten. And they are an elder race, like the Tumnei, so they wouldn't have nearly as much scrutiny over their actions. But we don't yet know if they'll be obedient to the Draco Senate or if they'll be willing to join our conspiracy. Four months may not be enough time to approach them delicately. We have a strong relationship with Grrrah'Kah but he doesn't have any political pull with his government. We haven't even begun forming the necessary relationships." He took a slow breath before continuing. "In light of these matters, I think we should postpone the vote until we can see if the Chantell will be on our side."

Cyran's eyes widened. "That could take years! Our window of opportunity is just four months away. I officially request we vote now."

"Cyran, be reasonable. We don't even know for sure if the Voonsu survived. If we commit to this and this whole prophecy falls apart, we would have no alibi. We'd be destroyed—along with everyone else back on Earth."

Cyran pounded the table. "Jonathan, if the Voonsu survived, then our time is now."

T'Kal motioned with his hand. *"I second the motion to vote now. The Scorpii have become increasingly aggressive in the Senate. We are in a position to assist you now. However, we don't know if the political landscape in the near future will still allow that. The Tumnei government agrees that we should act sooner rather than later."*

Jonathan turned to Cyran. "Do you speak for *Bravo Station?*"

Cyran nodded. "I have the full support of the Chancellor himself. They will back whatever decision I make."

Jonathan took a deep breath. "A motion to call a vote has been made and seconded. We will proceed with the vote. Since you already know my thoughts on the matter, I might as well go first. In light of the unknown condition of the Voonsu, the limited support the Tumnei can legally offer, and the work needed to bring the Chantell in on this, I don't think we're ready for a commitment like this. I am obliged to vote nay."

Cyran exhaled in disapproval. "We won't get another shot at this for ten more years..."

Jonathan turned to Isabeau.

She swallowed the dry lump in her throat. She was torn. She desperately wanted to be rid of the mandates of the Draconians. She wanted to be with her family again. She also agreed with Jonathan that they were not ready. A tear ran down her cheek. "I'm so sorry, Cyran. I want so much to be with you. But I have to concur with Jonathan. There are too many ifs. I vote nay."

Cyran's eyes fell to the table.

Jonathan glanced over to T'Kal.

He tilted his head. *"It is regrettable that our plan does not have your backing, Colonel. However, on behalf of the Tumnei government, I vote aye."*

Cyran stood, being the next to vote. "Aye! Every time a holiday passes, I think of my family, separated and scattered. Thousands of such families will never be able to reunite under Draconian rule." He pointed at Jonathan. "And you have never been allowed to see Earth. And I know you well enough to know you have no delusions that the Draconians will ever change their mandates. And you still have the Scorpii pitting *Able Station* against you. When will we stand together and cry out *enough?*" A tear ran down his cheek. He ignored it. "Look what has happened to Cale!" he said, pointing in the general direction of Med Bay Charlie. "Are our lives really safer doing nothing? And how about the lives of everyone back on Earth? They cannot lift a finger without questioning if it will upset the Draconians. Are their live really safer if we do nothing? How much more until you have had enough?"

Jonathan's gaze drifted to the table.

Isabeau's eyes watered. She glanced at Fox. With two votes aye and two votes nay, Fox was now the deciding vote. How would he vote? She had only known him for six months. Nothing about his posture or facial expression was hinting one way or the other. She found herself holding her breath.

Fox stood and walked halfway around the table. "I respect my commanding officer."

Cyran slowly sat down and slumped in his chair.

Fox continued. "And this very morning, my commanding officer stood right here and told me—" he slammed his fist on the table. "I have had enough."

Jonathan looked up and met his resolute gaze.

"I agree with the sentiments of my commanding officer. I too have had enough. I vote aye."

Cyran breathed out in relief.

Jonathan rose to his feet. "I don't believe I've ever heard of a man supporting me by voting against me."

Fox returned a sheepish look. "If I may quote Marcus Brutus, sir: 'There is a tide in the affairs of men. Which, taken at the flood, leads on to fortune; Omitted, all the voyage of their life is abound in shallows and in miseries. On such a full sea are we now afloat, and we must take the current when it serves, or lose our ventures'."

He placed a firm hand on Fox's shoulder and nodded. "Okay." He patted his shoulder twice and turned to the others present. "Though, this does put us in a tight situation. We have to find some way to recruit the Chantell without exposing ourselves in less than four months."

"I'm sure it's possible," Fox said.

Isabeau shook her head. "It may not be. It took the Euroo over a year."

"Wait, you're saying the Euroo already have a relationship with the Chantell?"

73

She nodded. "Yes, that's what Xer told me."

"Wait a minute," Fox said. "If the Euroo have already established trust with the Chantell, why not go through the Euroo?"

They both looked at Jonathan. His eyes widened. He took a sharp breath and waved a dismissive hand toward them. "Out of the question. My relationship with Ellyra is strictly personal."

"Colonel Terynn, are we to understand that you have a personal relationship with a member of the Euroo aristocracy?"

He pursed his lips before facing T'Kal. "The daughter of House El'Allel."

T'Kal tilted his head. *"Please forgive my impropriety, Colonel. But would it not be agreeable to use your advantage to recruit the Chantell?"*

"There are some lines you just don't cross."

T'Kal shifted his gaze. *"Some have said that about the Draconian rule. As the weaker party in the upcoming confrontation, can we afford not to use every means at our disposal?"*

"You make a convincing argument," he said, walking over to T'Kal. "But I haven't seen her in five years. And a lot can change in that time. For now, let's just say that I will consider it."

"Thank you, Colonel Terynn."

Jonathan faced everyone else. "Three votes aye, two votes nay. We go to war."

The tension in the room broke and Cyran rose, sauntering over to Fox. "Mr. Jagger, is it?"

Fox nodded. "You can call me Fox."

"A very stirring speech, Fox. I never thought I'd find anyone else so well versed in Shakespeare."

"I appreciate the praise, Ambassador."

Isabeau stood. "He quotes it *a lot.*"

Cyran smiled.

Fox chuckled. "Yes, but rarely to such a rapt audience."

Isabeau rolled her eyes.

The door chimed. Isabeau walked to the door and typed in the code to unlock the door. The door slid up, revealing Rana standing on the other side.

Isabeau's face lit up. "Rana, how are you?"

Rana returned a forced smile. Something wasn't right. She had gotten along quite well with Rana since she came aboard the station. Something else must have been on her mind. Her curt tone and fidgety fingers attested to her displeasure. But if that wasn't enough, her hair was jet black. Isabeau didn't know what all the Euroo hair colors meant but she knew a few. And black meant she was feeling angry.

"Thank you for the pleasantries, Commander Isabeau. But I am here to speak with Colonel Jonathan."

Isabeau turned to see Jonathan walking to the door alongside T'Kal. "Colonel, sir?"

He looked up. "Izzy?"

"Rana Arauri is here to see you."

He quickly tapped his com-band to check the time. "I'm sorry, it looks like I'm three minutes late—"

"Walk with me, Colonel," she snapped, turning around and strolling down the hall.

Jonathan glanced at Isabeau as if to ask what that was all about. Truthfully, she didn't know. But if Jonathan had set an appointment, maybe it had something to do with that. Isabeau shrugged.

Jonathan stepped out the door after Rana.

Chapter 7
ABLE STATION

Matt Jaimess walked through the dimly lit black hallways of *Able Station*. He didn't mind the lighting. His eyes long ago got used to it. The slithering Scorpii who built this station didn't care much for light. At least they didn't pollute the air with unbearable cold damp moisture. Those ugly squiddies didn't even try to be accommodating. You'd think *they* were the rulers of the galaxy and not the Draconians. But it was easy to see why they confused themselves; they were the favored pet of the Draconians. And that allowed them leniencies.

He stopped at a door and pressed his black-gloved hand to the plate. The doors parted and he stepped in. His black shirt and slacks with red trims were meticulously pressed and spotless. He loved the red but he could do without so much black. Before him, sat two others similarly dressed. Merin was a woman with long straight blond hair. Her hair was quite a contrast amidst the flood of black this space station had to offer. Her bright red lips didn't suit her but it was *Able Station*'s dress code.

The other man was Ross. Matt's right-hand man with dark curly hair and a baby-faced complexion. The man dearly needed to grow some facial hair.

Matt sat down. "Well?"

Merin spoke first. "We've received another message from Jerry."

"And?"

"He reports that he hit his secondary target and was apprehended."

"Clumsy fool! You'd think he enjoys getting caught."

Ross leaned forward. "He is an eccentric assassin."

"What of our mole?"

"Ir'Jad reports the plan has not yet been compromised," Merin replied. "We can begin phase two at any time."

"Tell him to just sit tight and wait for Jerry's signal."

"Matt," Ross said with a timid tone. "With their key ambassador out of the way, do we really need to advance to phase two?"

Matt returned an annoyed glance. "Lucas Cale was by far their greatest orator, but he was by no means the mastermind."

"It just...seems a waste..."

Matt's eyes lit up. Was there regret in Ross's voice? No, not regret. More like admiration. Yes, the poor fool looked up to that militaristic troublemaker. Perhaps he would have been happier if he were born a Gamm. "You admire the man, don't you," Matt accused, pointing a finger.

Ross glanced at the table, his shoulders slouching.

"Well, you'd better thank your lucky stars you were born an Abe, Ross. I didn't spend the last five years brown-nosing and butt-kissing the squiddies for nothing. When I first began, this station, and everything on it, was run by the Scorpii. Now only one Scorpiian is standing between me and full control of *Able Station*."

"Lord Vaux?" Merin asked.

"Lord Vaux."

"How will you get rid of him?"

77

Matt leaned back in his chair. "There are a few angles I can try, but none of them have a decent opportunity. For now, I will just have to stick close to him until such a time presents itself."

"But why *Gamma Station*?" Ross asked. "They are humans."

Matt took a breath and paused. "I wish it were different. We have spent too many years positioning ourselves in a place of authority. And it could all come crashing down if those prideful Gamms and decadent Euroo keep getting in the way."

"You'd think they'd want to be free from the Draconians," Merin said.

"I'm sure they do," Ross said.

"They have a funny way of showing it," Matt stated. "The Scorpii are the favored elder race of the Draconians. But instead of pleasing them, the Gamms antagonize them. Instead of rising in favor, they plummet in ire."

Ross sighed. "They may not realize what they're doing."

"That, Ross, is the crux of their problem. They don't realize that for better or worse, the Scorpii are the key to rising above slavery. The Scorpii are the dominating force in the Senate. Therefore, whoever controls the Scorpii, controls the Senate. And whoever controls the Senate dictates the future of mankind."

"What about the Draconians?" Ross asked. "They own the Senate. We're all still slaves to the Draconians."

Ross did have a point. The Draconians were the top dogs in the galactic arm and they knew it. They had long ago conquered every sentient race within reach. They had had no enemies or new prey for centuries. They were as complacent as any would be under those conditions. They didn't even seem to pay attention to the Senate hearings that they had forced all the races to participate in. There were, however, a few taboo topics the Draconians didn't like to have mentioned. And they demonstrated their displeasure with an extermination order. Their superstitious fear of an ancient race they destroyed centuries ago was ridiculous. Ridiculous even by Matt's standards.

Matt held up a finger. "Technically, yes. You are correct. But in practice, the Draconians show little interest in what goes on in the Senate. As long as we don't provoke them, they will leave us to our own devices."

"What if Colonel Terynn doesn't oppose the Scorpii?" Ross asked.

"Jonathan Terynn is a soldier. He's a clever one at that, but still just a soldier. He can only think in terms of black and white. Anyone not with him is against him. Since the Scorpii are favored by the Draconians, he will oppose them on principle alone. And we cannot afford to let him tip the balance in the Senate. The Scorpii have to remain in control for our plan to work." He leaned toward Ross. "That is why we must proceed to phase two."

"And once we control the Senate?" Merin asked.

Matt looked at her. "Then we can finally end this asinine segregation. Who are the Draconians to dictate whether I should be allowed to see my daughter?"

The tension in the air thickened. Neither Merin nor Ross spoke. They knew better than to risk a foolish comment about Eva. She had been taken from him when she was only a few years old. She was designated a Brav and sent to *Bravo Station*. No ifs, ands, or buts allowed. It still stung the chest to think about it. How could they have arbitrarily separated him from his daughter?

Was it the hand of destiny? Had fate placed him in the right place at the right time to end the Draconian nightmare? Was he to reunite not just his family, but all the families the Draconians had torn apart? The thought was not likely but it seemed to help a little. At least it eased the pain.

"How old is she now?" Ross asked.

"She would be about twenty..." *Or was it twenty-one?*

A knock sounded at the door.

Matt turned around. "What?" he asked with annoyance oozing from his voice.

The doors parted and a man in the same black with red trim clothes stepped inside. He held out a rough metal data rod; the crude data storage devices the slimy Scorpii use. Matt snatched the data rod and inserted it into a hole in the middle of the table. The table illuminated and words appeared on the table. It was an official letter from Lord Vaux.

Vaux was not the type to bother typing up letters. He preferred to talk. So, whenever a letter came from Lord Vaux, it was a serious matter. Only anger mixed with ceremonial propriety would induce him to type up a letter.

Matt read the letter with eager curiosity. Then his face contorted into sheer confusion. Then, his mood blackened. His heart raced and his blood boiled. His clenched fists shook. With a wail and a rant, Matt yanked the data rod out of the table port and threw it across the room. It clanged against the far wall and bounded across the metal floor. It was a pity there wasn't anything he could afford to break. Breaking something would have felt good.

He balled up his fists and spun to face the courier. "Tell him I'm on my way!"

The courier bowed and left.

"Matt, what is it?" Ross inquired.

"Those fools on *Gamma Station* have shot down a Scorpiian destroyer."

"How did they shoot down a Harkon?" Ross asked in dismay.

"I haven't the foggiest idea. Normally I would have said Kudos to them for the achievement. But they picked the wrong ship to shoot down. Now Lord Vaux is up in arms—well, up in tentacles—over this whole mess."

Merin sighed. "He'll take it out on all of us."

Matt pursed his lips. "The imbecile doesn't make any distinction between Abe, Brav, or Gamm. If a human has angered him, the closest human will pay the penalty. I'll think up a way to appease him again."

"Matt," Merin said. "We need to get Lord Vaux to distinguish Abes from Gamms."

"Shall I also turn water into wine while I'm at it?"

Merin looked down.

 80

"We appreciate all you do, Matt," Ross said.

Matt nodded. "Let us just hope Jerry can hit his primary target soon. We need all the leverage we can get in the Senate. If we can't pull this off, all our preparations will be for nothing."

An uncomfortable silence passed.

"You two had better get back to your posts. Lord Vaux will be doing his inspection soon."

Ross and Merin left the room.

Now that he was alone, Matt sat back in his chair and pulled out an old crumpled photo from his inside jacket pocket. The color had long since faded to amber and the edges were tattered with age and wear. He caressed the outline of his daughter's face on the photo. He had long since memorized every line and every curve. But somehow actually touching the picture felt more real to him. He took off his glove and felt the gloss of the photo. His little Eva.

If only her mother had survived the brutality of Scorpii punishment. Those hideous creatures had blood on their hands. Precious blood which was worth more than all the treasures of the known galaxy. Why had they taken out their anger on Megan? And why had he been powerless to stop it? Well, he was not powerless now. And if he played his cards right, he soon would have the power to make those pathetic squiddies pay for their crime.

Chapter 8

ANNOUNCING INTENTIONS

Jonathan jogged up beside Rana and then matched her stride. Since she cut him off in his apology attempt, there wasn't much reason to try again. If she wanted to dominate the conversation, she would have to start it. They walked in silence for a few moments.

"I won't pretend I don't know what it is you wish to speak to me about," she finally said.

Her hair was black. That wasn't a good sign. Izzy had mentioned that black was a sign of anger or contempt. The Euroo were very ornate and ceremonial in their day-to-day actions. So, it was possible that being a couple of minutes late had offended her. What didn't make sense, though, was that she wasn't cordial. Either he had crossed the line or she was upset as a matter of principle. In either event, it was best to mend relations as much as possible.

"I see my tardiness has troubled you," he began. "I—"

She abruptly stopped. "Your bad manners can be excused the first time. In the future, however, punctuality would be appreciated."

Jonathan looked at her with renewed interest. She wasn't simply starting a conversation. She was haphazardly hurling veiled insults. This was not like any experience he had had with the Euroo. They had always been overly polite and dignified. This was very different. It was as if her intent wasn't to talk but rather to agitate. *That* was it. She wasn't starting a conversation. She was probing the enemy for weaknesses, watching to see how he would react.

Well, if posturing was what she wanted, he would oblige her. The only question was in which direction to posture. Should he lean into subservience or stand toward obstinance? They both had their benefits and problems. If he were to layer on apologies and promises he might get back into her good graces but he might also appear a weak fool. If he were to stand in opposition, he would look strong but could very well fracture relations with the Euroo. Decisions, decisions...

"Thank you," he replied. "I will be sure to do so."

"Well, are you going to stand there all day or are you going to announce your intentions?"

He had practiced his line numerous times. "Rana Arauri, Eltashee to Sune Ellyra of the house of El'Allel, I come to formally announce my intentions to seek courtship of the daughter of House El'Allel."

She rattled off her own words as if they had a bad taste and she couldn't stomach them. "As Eltashee and under the customs of house El'Allel, I say to you, let it be done."

There was something more than professional annoyance behind her tone. There was a deliberate lack of civility. There was something deeper, something personal, that had crawled under her skin. It took him a moment to identify it, but it was undoubtedly there.

"You don't like me, do you?"

She pursed her lips. "My, you can be blunt, can't you? You must say whatever comes to your mind."

Jonathan frowned. "Some might call that honesty."

"And the rest might call it barbaric," she replied. "But then again, I am not sure how much can be expected of a military man."

Any hesitation he had about which direction to posture completely evaporated. If she was tossing the gauntlet, he was more than ready to receive. He lacked the talent for veiled insults and political intrigue. But he knew combat and military posturing. And if Ellyra was right and the only difference was the battlefield and the weapon, he had a fair chance to come out on top.

"I'm sure everyone agrees that honesty is a noble virtue."

She forced half a smile. "Yes, I'm sure you abound in such virtue, even if that is all that is noble about you."

Jonathan took a deep breath. She wasn't pulling any of her punches. She had it out for him for some reason. And sifting through her words to find clues was tiring. At least her last clue was easy to decipher. The key word was noble. He used that word to mean high moral character but she used that same word to highlight his lack of social class.

"We value a person's character over their social status."

"An ingenious consolation," she replied.

Jonathan took a controlled breath, slowing his heartrate. This was worse than arguing in the senate. At least in the senate you could retaliate with long-winded rebuttals. Here, it seemed, the more he spoke, the further behind he got. "You sound as though you disapprove," he finally said. "Your reasons are not arbitrary, I hope."

"One of my duties is to guide her away from fortune seekers."

His eyes widened. Could she seriously think he was after money or social status? Is that what this was all about? What kind of world did she live in? "You think I'm trying to profit from her?"

"You needn't play the fool," she said. "A military man with no connections and no influence can only improve his station by marrying the daughter of a house lord. Common is what you are."

"Common? You mean Earth military men frequently court Ellyra?"

"Not common occurrence," she said in annoyance, "common law. That which is without ceremony, honor, and dignity—entirely unbecoming of someone of her station—is said to be of common law." She looked him over, taking stock. "Common," she declared.

His stomach muscles tensed, as his annoyance rose. "Well, I'm glad the decision is not yours."

Her eyes widened, shock plastering her face. She wasn't used to a direct confrontation. And she probably wasn't expecting him to push back so hard. "Do you treat all dignitaries with such insolence as this?"

And here was her counter-attack. She didn't strike head-on as her last statement. She was attacking his flank by changing the subject. Accusing him of being rude to all his guests was a contest she could easily win. The Euroo had a much higher standard of conduct. She could pick apart every little gesture he made and turn them each into evidence of barbarism. The best tactic was not to follow her up to her high ground and instead lure the battle back to his home field. And if being direct had caught her off guard, he needed to repeat that directness.

"I wouldn't think it rude to wish Sune Ellyra to be happy in the choice she has made. I would have assumed her personal aid would be the first to support her."

She pursed her lips.

Was it his imagination, or did her hair turn even blacker? Her scrawny figure tensed up. It was a wonder how she kept herself from clenching her fists. He had to give her credit for self-control. It looked to have been bred into her. Now that shots had been fired in her direction, it was his turn to wait. Either she would return fire or mount a retreat. Her hesitation to speak again was a good sign. It meant he had struck a decisive blow. If she had to start considering her words, she was on the defensive.

"An Eltashee's greatest value is in offering advice and opinion. Such that can guide her Mistress's decisions. Surely, you understand that not all decisions are initially the correct ones."

A brilliant defense. Not only did she defend her opposition to him, but she justified it. And then, at the tail end, she managed to toss him a grenade. Clearly, she was quite practiced. There had to be some way to throw her grenade back. His accusations carried little weight. But, if he could use her own arguments against her, she would be dodging her own artillery. But the words would have to be delicately chosen. They would need to turn the discussion back to her.

Jonathan smiled. "Sune Ellyra is most fortunate to have such an abundance of advice. I feel at a disadvantage; on Earth, we have only one mother."

Rana's thin lips tensed, fighting against an impending scowl. Her practiced expression refused to betray what her hair already had. "Your time in the Senate seems to have served you well. You speak like a politician."

He clenched his hands and stiffened his jaw. A politician? Politics was the scourge of any civilization. Jonathan was a military officer, trained to command. Trained to fight. Not to weasel his way into someone's good graces for the sole purpose of buying favor. A politician? She might as well have called him a liar and a coward. A deep breath forced its way into his lungs.

A subtle smile crept into the corner of her mouth. Hardly noticeable, but present nonetheless. She read his body language and saw the extent of the damage her words had caused. Her subtle smile was not one of satisfaction only, it was a smile of victory. She had won and he had somehow lost. How could he have lost? He had chosen his words so carefully. He had been cautious enough not to fall into her trap. There seemed to be some unwritten rule that the first person to show their offense was the loser. Her well-practiced expressions were a testament to that.

Jonathan slowly breathed out, letting his hands relax. If he was going to hold his own in this kind of arena, he needed to learn to control his reactions.

"Since I am unsuccessful in dissuading you," she said, a sly pleasure lining her voice. "You will have a steep learning curve in Euroo etiquette."

She handed him a small hand-held reader device. It was already pre-loaded with a digital book. The title read, Lord Agsten's Manuel: a children's guide to etiquette.

Rana smirked. "You may thank me later. And," she added, "chapter 21 is a must."

He glanced up from the reader to find her hair color had warmed up to a happy blond. Her victory had evidently brightened her mood. She probably counted her victory as the first of many to come.

"As a first step," she continued, "You will require a formal introduction. A morning banquet has been scheduled for zero-nine-hundred. "You are to bring a gentleman to introduce you."

"Understood," Jonathan finally said, feeling like he was addressing a superior officer.

"You will need to accept the invitation before we retire for the evening."

He nodded. "Oh, I accept."

She shook her head with anticipated disapproval. "You must send word to me by way of a gentleman. For the sake of expediency, you may need to begin your reading in chapter three." She started walking past him but stopped short and turned around. "And Colonel Jonathan, do not be late."

He gripped the reader with white knuckles. "I'll send my best man."

She gave a flamboyant curtsy and departed.

Jonathan marched back to the conference room to find Isabeau waiting for him.

"May I ask how it went?"

He pressed a button and the door slid down, closing. "I crashed and burned, Izzy," he replied, frustration seeping through his words.

"That bad, huh?"

He returned an exaggerated nod. "Oh yeah. Shots were fired in both directions. And it would appear I was the only casualty." He held up the reader.

"What is that?"

"Euroo Etiquette. Her royal majesty insists I am hopelessly out of my league. And this is the proof."

She looked at him skeptically. "Why is she giving you a book on etiquette?"

He started pacing. "I had the audacity to seek permission to court Ellyra."

Her eyes lit up. "You're going to date a Euroo captain?"

He spun around. "Izzy, she isn't just some alien captain; I've known Ellyra for five years."

She walked up to him with wondrous eyes. "You're going to date her?"

The excitement on her face melted his grim mood. He didn't speak of Ellyra as often as he had in prior years. Isabeau had always been supportive. Now, her excitement stirred up his.

He smiled. "Yes, Izzy. She won't be here for long, but yes."

"Do you need any help with the customs or etiquette?"

"I'm invited to breakfast and I need to bring a *gentleman*," he replied.

"You're taking Fox with you?"

"Fox is a fine officer," he said. "But he and I don't have the same connection that you and I do. I'd feel more comfortable with you at my side."

She shook her head. "If Rana said a gentleman, she means a gentleman. Bringing a lady would give her way too much ammunition against you."

"Touché," he said, pacing again.

"Fox will make an excellent wingman. And, if memory serves, you also need to send him to formally accept an invitation. Did she mention anything about that?"

He nodded. "You must send word to me by way of a gentleman," he quoted in a high-pitched voice. Rana had all but dismissed him as a defeated opponent. Throughout his military career, he had refused to remain defeated. He had always found a solution, however unconventional, to eventually win. And it was that part of him that kept his brain searching for options. He hadn't ever given up before and he wasn't about to give up now. Losing a battle with Rana was acceptable but losing the war to her was not. He stopped in his tracks as an idea popped into his head.

"I'll send for Fox," Isabeau offered, turning to leave.

"Wait," he said, holding up a finger. "Send for Grrrah'Kah instead."

Isabeau spun around with concern in her eyes. "Grrrah'Kah?"

Jonathan nodded. "He counts as a gentleman."

"He's a Chantell! You don't just send a nine-foot-tall bug to somebody's doorstep. The poor woman could faint."

Jonathan smiled.

She gave him a disapproving glare. "You're posturing, aren't you?"

"And tell him to wear his riot armor," he amended.

Chapter 9

CONSEQUENCES

Matt jogged down the dimly lit hallways of *Able Station*. Lord Vaux always began his inspections from the north end and proceeded southward. Lord Vaux was in one of his moods and Matt needed to contain the damage as much as possible. It had taken him a few minutes to come up with something enticing enough to pacify Lord Vaux. At least that was the hope. Matt rounded the corner and halted. He almost tripped over the body of a young woman on the floor.

Her pale skin and straight blond hair were spoiled by the red of her blood. It was Merin. Matt dropped to his knees. He didn't bother checking for a pulse, there was no use. The Scorpii built the space station with no medical center. "Only the strong should survive" was the Scorpiian philosophy. If she had survived the initial attack, there would be no way to save her anyway. It was just like Megan; nothing he could do. It wasn't supposed to be this way. He had gained power and position since Megan's death. How was he still so powerless?

Matt reached over and closed her eyelids. A hiss came from his left. It was Lord Vaux. The wretched squiddy was not more than a watermelon-sized lump of flesh with a small head on top of that. Its evil grin displayed its half-rotted jagged teeth. Its two beady yellow eyes didn't have any pupils. It stood four feet tall on eight tentacle legs with another eight tentacles for arms. Lord Vaux held a bloodied dagger in one tentacle arm. At least the Scorpii referred to them as daggers. They looked like a shattered piece of sharp scrap metal strapped to a handle. A second tentacle arm was wrapped around Ross's neck.

Matt didn't bother looking at Lord Vaux. "I need him alive." He held out a rough metal data rod toward Lord Vaux. There wasn't anything on the data rod, he didn't have time to put together an actual proposal. As it was, he had been too late to save Merin.

Lord Vaux hissed a question.

"Of course, it is. What else would it be?"

Lord Vaux reached a tentacle over to take the data rod.

Matt threw it down the hallway. It clanked in the distance against the metal floor and walls. It was a bold move; Lord Vaux could kill him in an instant. It was a calculated risk, but it did have a promising reward if he could pull it off. The Scorpii respected ambition and cunning. To stay irreplaceable, Matt needed to always think up new schemes for them to take advantage of. Each new proposal proved more lucrative than the last.

If Matt correctly guessed Lord Vaux's greed, he would have the leverage he needed. But if he misjudged, he would wind up dead. He needed to take the gamble, though. He was out of time and the blood-thirsty squiddy was on a rampage. He had to get its attention and throwing the data rod had accomplished that. The downside was that Lord Vaux's wrath was now directed at him.

Lord Vaux shrieked in rage, releasing its grip on Ross's neck. It skittered over to Matt with its eight legs each taking a step in sequence. It raised its jagged dagger.

Matt turned to Lord Vaux. "Go ahead! Destroy everything you've worked for! All your gains, everything you've built, just throw it all away!"

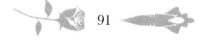

Lord Vaux hesitated to strike.

Matt stood. "I elevated you to the sole commander of *Able Station*. I gave you dominance in the Senate. And even now I have plans that will make the Scorpii the most powerful race beneath our Draconian Lords. But how can I work if you keep *killing all my men?*"

Lord Vaux lowered his jagged dagger and squawked thoughtfully. "A wise observation, my Lord."

It waved a dismissive tentacle at Matt and skittered down the hallway. Matt breathed out a sigh of relief. He was confident his performance would work, but Lord Vaux was not always predictable. This time, his gamble had paid off.

Matt helped Ross to his feet. "I should have come sooner."

Ross rubbed his neck. "You can't be everywhere." Then, he glanced down the hallway after Lord Vaux. "How do you do that?"

"Greed, Ross. It's a universal ailment with no respect for species. And you feed it with an ounce of cunning and a gallon of bravado."

Matt walked back over to Merin's body with regretful steps. "We have to end this..."

"How? How does a slave end his master's treatment of him?"

"By appealing to his master's master," he said, half in thought. "If we can get a big win for the Scorpii in the Senate, we can gain the recognition of Lord Vaux's superiors. And once that happens, I can engineer Lord Vaux's downfall."

"But what if his replacement is just as cruel?"

Matt shook his head. "There won't be any replacement; I will fill the void."

Ross hung his head. "Then I guess the only obstacle is *Gamma Station*. They won't easily give in to the Scorpii's ambitions."

"That is why we must move to phase two."

Ross looked up with a mournful expression. "But...couldn't we bring them in? What could we accomplish with two space stations working together?"

Ross was an incurable optimist. Even with all he had endured on *Able Station*, he still believed that all mankind could join hands and sing kumbaya; as if by some magic that would free humanity from the slavery they were born into. But still, there was a measure of goodness in his heart. He didn't like assassinating other humans. And the practical side of Matt's mind had to agree. Killing other humans was a waste. Perhaps it wouldn't be necessary if Ross was correct. What if he could unite the efforts of two space stations?

"All right, Ross. We'll try it your way. We are walking the fine line of treason, so I'll have to test the waters first. If they can be trusted, we'll forgo phase two."

"How will we contact them?" Ross asked. "All of *Able Station*'s transmissions are monitored. We would have to speak with them in person."

Matt raised a finger to hush Ross as a man rounded the corner. The man stopped cold and gasped at the bloody sight on the floor.

"Get another cleanup crew in here," Matt directed. "And steer clear of Lord Vaux."

The man nodded, transfixed with the horror before him. Then with sullen eyes, he retreated the way he had come. Matt took Ross by the arm and led him down in the other direction.

"You're correct. I can't just call up another would-be conspirator. I'll need to devise a reason to meet in person. Remember the Scorpii's skirmish with *Gamma Station*, where they lost a Harkon? Get me the transcript of the communication logs."

"You think there'll be something in there you can use?"

"Don't ask stupid questions, Ross. I'll be in my office."

Ross nodded and veered off down an adjoining hallway. Matt retired to his office. The cramped little room was hardly big enough to warrant a desk, but Matt couldn't function without one. The impeccably clean desk was made from imported Earth oak. Scorpiian wood was too soft and pliable to hold any weight. It was a product of their wet home environment. Beside his desk, a tall metal shelf stood against the wall. It held a few scattered knick-knacks and a data pad or two. Books were not commonplace on *Able Station*. The Scorpii didn't see any value in them; anything of value to them was stored electronically.

Matt kept his little sanctuary clean and dry. It was the one place Lord Vaux had not come, which in turn made it the one place Matt could relax. Matt picked up a data pad from off the shelf. The definitive volume on the rules and procedures of the Draco Senate. He had often perused this digital tome of loopholes and lesser-known rules. It proved invaluable in pushing the Scorpiian objectives through the Senate. He had spent years building up the Scorpii's dominance in the Senate. Now it was time to cash in on some of the hard work.

He needed to fabricate a reason to meet in person. The Gamms would never come to *Able Station*; there was too much bad blood between them. The Gamms had a convoluted sense of independence. That made them push against anything that felt restrictive. The Abes, on the other hand, sought freedom at any price. Manipulating the Scorpii and strong-arming the Senate were a few of the tools that were not beneath them. Because of this divide, there was no mutual affection to be had.

If there was to be a meeting on a space station it would have to be an Abe going to *Gamma Station*. That much was not an issue for Matt. Nothing was beneath him if it furthered the cause of freedom. The only problem was their Scorpiian overseers. They watched them like Cliverian hawks. The squiddies monitored and recorded all travel to and from the space station. What kind of excuse could he give? What pretense would be acceptable to visit a rival space station? The squiddies would be suspicious of any change in routine that was not justified.

There came a knock at his metal door. The doors had bell chimes to announce someone was at the door. Matt had instructed Ross and Merin to always knock instead. It was an easy way to distinguish if the visitor was within his trusted circle. "Come!"

The doors parted and Ross entered holding a metal data rod in his hand. "The reports you requested."

Matt took the large metal cylinder, eyeing it reverently. "Did you have any trouble getting it?"

"I almost couldn't get past Commissioner Gyne. I told him Lord Vaux wanted to know how an Earth ship destroyed a Harkon destroyer."

Matt nodded. "Technically, he did say that. Good thinking, Ross." He placed it into the data port hold in the middle of his desk. His entire desk illuminated with Scorpiian words sprawled across it. The crude scratchings that the Scorpii called letters were difficult to decipher without years of practice. They didn't look much different from the scratch marks of a small animal. Matt had made it a point to learn the Scorpiian written language. He needed every advantage he could get.

"There," Matt said, pointing to a section of the transcript. "There's our chance."

"What does it say?"

"Death Ray."

"You're joking."

Matt shook his head. "The clever Gamms bluffed the stupid squiddies into retreating. They alluded to a super-weapon called a Death Ray."

Ross snickered. "They fell for *that?*"

"What will be even more impressive is what they'll fall for next." Matt grinned in delight. "The squiddies are going to facilitate our meeting with the Gamms."

Ross regarded him with a confused expression. "How are you going to pull that off?"

"Greed, Ross. Remember, it is not a respecter of species. Inform Commissioner Gyne that we have evidence that the Gamms have a stolen Skorath weapon."

Ross paled. "Are you certain you know what you're doing?"

Matt smirked. "Pretty sure. In fact, this might even make up for Lord Vaux's murder of Merin."

"Should I inform Lord Vaux then?"

Matt shook his head. "No. Lord Vaux must learn of this secondhand. I need his natural suspicions to work for me, not against me."

Ross nodded and turned to leave. He stopped at the doorway just as the door opened. He turned back to Matt. "And you're *sure* you know what you're doing?"

"I have never been more so," Matt declared. "What will follow next will only appear to be the natural consequences of ambition."

Ross nodded and left the room. Matt sat down and slouched in his stuffed chair. Ross was right to be concerned. The Skorath were no laughing matter. The Draconians outlawed the very mention of their name. And this is what the greedy squiddies would latch on to. Any race that could be accused of using the Skorath, the Draconians had a mind to destroy.

Lord Vaux would be all too eager to wipe out one of the largest two political thorns in its side: *Gamma Station*. The trick was to get Lord Vaux to act without over thinking it. Given enough time, the half-witted squiddy would lose its nerve and back down. This opportunity would need to look juicy and time-sensitive.

Chapter 10

BREAKFAST

Ellyra sat up straight in a soft armchair with her legs crossed. Xer, her young parliamentarian officer sat on the couch at her side. Diahlus's grandfatherly figure paced across the open floor. The rooms that Jonathan had prepared were rather adequate considering the circumstances. The front door slid up. Arkamenos, her master of security, stepped inside with troubled gray hair.

"How is she?" Ellyra asked.

"She's doing rather well considering the fright she had. I'm confident she will be herself in the morning. I can return her to your quarters in a half an hour."

"Actually, I think it would be best if your wife spent the night in your quarters. I will manage without her tonight."

Arkamenos bowed. "Thank you, my lady." He turned and left.

Xer sat on the couch, staring into space. "Did the Earthian commander even know what he was doing?"

Diahlus huffed, halting his pacing, his hair color blackening. "Oh, he knew what he was doing. No man sends a monster to one's doorstep without realizing it."

"That's not what I meant. I'm wondering if he knew the ramifications of his actions."

Diahlus shrugged, his hair brightened back to formal white. "I suppose it's possible he did not. He is, after all, a military man. He was most likely trained in conquest rather than diplomacy. I suppose not much should be expected from such a man."

Ellyra leaned back in her armchair, contemplating. Jonathan's choice of *gentlemen* had been rather unsettling for poor Rana. Ellyra had never seen a Chantell before. That tall insectoid body with a twin set of cold compound eyes was already more than a match for even her wits. But this particular Chantell wore what looked like black battle armor. The result was intimidation piled upon intimidation. But Jonathan was not one to posture aimlessly. He had a purpose behind it. Figuring out what that purpose was would be the tricky part.

She turned to Xer, realizing he had been calling her name. "Yes, Xer?"

"If you will not be needing me further tonight, I will retire. I have an early morning with *Gamma Station*'s dining staff."

"You have decided to hold the morning banquet on *Gamma Station*? Could we not more easily host it aboard the *Calmao*?"

"Yes, my lady. But seeing as this event is more of a personal nature it would not be proper to host it aboard our ship. Were the Colonel an official envoy, it would be different."

Xer was right. The entire event was being hosted for her benefit. Jonathan needed to formalize his intentions to court her. If it was for official Eurosian business, then hosting it aboard her ship would be warranted. Matters of the heart, however, were best left as unofficial as possible. Sometimes there were too many cultural obligations to keep them all straight. That was why a parliamentarian officer was so useful.

"Then let it be done, Xer."

"Good night, my lady." He bowed and left.

Ellyra turned to Diahlus. "And what are your thoughts on Colonel Jonathan's recent actions?"

He sighed. "I had believed my thoughts to be the most enumerated by now," he said, continuing to pace. "Uncultured, arrogant, and impulsive ruffian," he muttered under his breath.

"Then, you agree with Xer, that his actions were thoughtless?"

He stopped and turned to Ellyra. "I dearly wish to like the man. But blunders such as this depict him nothing shy of inept."

She produced a faint smile, looking off into the distance. "Interesting...I am curious to know if that is what he intends."

He eyed her with suspicion. "What do you mean?"

She sat up straight again. "Consider yesterday's events, Diahlus. Before we encountered the Scorpii, Colonel Jonathan had brought along his Earthian ships. That tells me he is a man who plans ahead."

He dismissed her comment with a wave of his hand. "What you allude to as cunning may only be the product of his military training. Let us not forget that it was *your* brilliance that allowed him the support of our ship."

"But surely you do not suppose that his military training also included the use of a Death Ray?"

He sighed. "Granted, I must concede. He does have a mind for strategy. But I do not see evidence of it in play in this circumstance."

She rose from her chair with an air of excitement. "Don't you? When we advised him that the only logical option was to retreat, he resisted. Instead, he came up with a clever ruse to defeat the Scorpiian pilot. He found victory in an unorthodox manner. That tells me he doesn't accept defeat easily, and that he thinks outside the confines of convention."

Diahlus gave an exaggerated nod. "His choice of a gentleman was *most certainly* unconventional."

Her hair warmed up to a joyful blond, her curly locks swaying in her eager movements. "And that is the genius of it! It is as if he transformed a defeat into a victory."

He continued pacing. "Agreed. Though, Rana was hardly a suitable opponent."

"That is indeed a malady that a little instruction should remedy. As both Xer, and Colonel Jonathan himself, have equally attested, he is a military man. And as such, not well versed in politicking."

"And you feel confident that with such training he could be suitable?"

She looked down, her hair color darkening into a sullen indigo. "There is little chance of him ever becoming suitable, unfortunately."

He again halted his pacing. "Your father does not think of him as highly as you?"

She slumped back into the armchair, all excitement draining from her. "My father's regard is reserved for a probable heir."

"I see," he said, walking over to her. "That must place you in a difficult position."

"A woman should never be placed at odds with her father."

He raised an eyebrow. "Considering your station, isn't that a rather idealistic opinion?"

A small smile broke through her glum mood. "Perhaps, Diahlus. Perhaps. But it is heartbreaking nonetheless to play antagonist to the man I admire most."

"If you will forgive my impertinence, what have you against resigning to your father's wishes?"

She crossed her legs and leaned back in the armchair, staring off into space. Her hair brightened into a wishful violet. "Dreams, Diahlus. Each one a distant star that I long to touch. And when I reach for them, I find I am held down by the chain of my station and the anchor of family duty." She turned to him. "I suppose, in the end, I will have to succumb to my obligations. But in the meantime, cannot a lady have a little diversion?"

He let out a half-chuckle and pointed to the door. "That, my lady, is a bit larger than a little diversion."

She blushed and looked away, her hair burning into a burgundy. "I must admit, allowing an alien man to court me is indeed more than just diverting. It is as if I'm exploring my girlhood notions of romance." She glanced heavenward. "What I would give to let my heart guide me instead of my station."

He placed a gentle hand on her shoulder. "If I may be allowed to caution you, it would be wise to tread lightly. If you allow this to continue, certain expectations would naturally arise—especially for him. Your heart cannot be as easily mended as the hull of your ship."

She stood and paced to the other end of the room. "I am well aware of the risks. After all, a starship is most safe when it is on the ground." She glanced back at him. "But that's not what starships were built for."

He placed his hands behind his back in contemplation. "I don't suppose you would consider galivanting closer to safety?"

She smiled, her hair warming into a joyful blond. "I feel as if the launch alarm has sounded. I cannot remain standing astride the ground and the loading ramp."

He shrugged with an air of resignation. "Then, as your friend, I suggest you climb aboard and take your seat. It will be a bumpy ride, but I'll do what I can to smooth it out."

She beamed. "How have I been so fortunate to have you as my first Dommicon?"

He smiled. "Fortune had nothing to do with it, my lady. I did not come out of retirement for just any academy graduate."

Jonathan stood at the mirror by the door in his quarters. The muggy damp air from his shower still wafted in from the bathroom. The moderately bright lights didn't do much to enhance the drab green metal walls of the space station. At least it was quiet. The gentle hum of the electrical grid could barely be heard. Jonathan adjusted the collar of his formal dress-black uniform. *Get a grip, Jonathan,* he told himself. *It's only breakfast and you look good, darn good.*

His anxiety hadn't allowed him to sleep well last night. His nerves were on edge, and he needed to give a good first impression. He took a deep breath and picked up the reader device Rana had given him. Although it was titled a children's guide to etiquette, the reading was excruciating. It must have been a direct translation from the original Euroo language. The sentences were long, flowery, and filled to the brim with extra words. Words that either didn't need to be there or could have been easily said with much simpler words. If this was a children's guide, then the adult guide would be impossible to read.

What little he was able to understand made a lot of references to what "simply is not done". What it neglected to answer was *why*. Why wasn't it done? It was written as though nobody would think to question why something wasn't done.

His door chimed.

"Come in."

The door slid up and Fox entered. "You still want to go through with this? Rana might not like you."

Jonathan huffed, again readjusting his collar in the mirror. "Then I haven't lost anything."

"Okay, so what do I need to do?"

Jonathan picked up the reader again. "As far as I can tell, your sole job is to introduce me."

"Wait...don't they already know you?"

He sighed. "Yes, but I still have to be introduced and I can't introduce myself."

"Why not?

"Because it's simply not done," Jonathan recited in a mocking tone. "And for whatever reason, they don't ever explain *why* it's not done."

"Boy, they sure got you jumping through hoops."

Jonathan released a slow breath. Although it had been five years, he still remembered what he had felt for Ellyra back on her home planet. Things seemed simpler then. Could it have been the carefree vacation atmosphere? Or had it actually been very simple when he had first met her? There was no pretense of a long-term relationship. He knew he couldn't stay long and that he might never be allowed to return. So, he just let himself experience the moments.

Now he wanted something more than the fleeting moments. Now the resistance and pushback of her society were bearing down upon him. Had his first experience with Ellyra been just a fantasy then? Had the absence of adult responsibilities deceived his senses? Five years ago, there were no hoops to jump through. There was just her. But there were hoops now. A lot of them. And was it even worth it?

Jonathan sighed again and set down the reader. "Yes. Yes, they do. And the funny thing is that this is the kind of thing I would have expected for a fiancé, not a girlfriend."

"Well, at least she's worth it, right?"

"Let's just say I hope my memories pale in comparison to the genuine article, and not the other way around."

"Well, as Macbeth put it: Life's but a walking shadow, a poor player that struts and frets his hour upon the stage and then is heard no more."

"So, in other words, carpe diem?"

Fox chuckled. "Carpe diem."

They exited, walking down the hall to the elevator. Jonathan handed his reader to Fox. "Here, this is how you're supposed to introduce me."

Fox smiled. "It's been years since I had lines to memorize. I'm having fun already."

"I'm glad one of us is."

They emerged from the lift tube one deck lower. Fox memorized his line before they reached the officer's mess hall and handed the reader back. Arkamenos stood outside and greeted them.

"You've been expected. Right this way, I'll announce you."

They followed him through the noisy room, passing men and women with trays of food. Arkamenos led them to a small enclosed room at the back of the mess hall. It was called the Captain's Mess, but neither Jonathan nor his officers ever used it.

Arkamenos opened the door and stepped inside. "Colonel Jonathan and company." He then stepped aside allowing Jonathan and Fox to enter. Ellyra and her crew were already seated around the table. Rana sat beside Ellyra with black hair.

Diahlus stood. "To what do we owe the honor?"

Fox gave a flamboyant bow, gesturing with his arms as well. The natural grace with which he performed it was worth coveting. There was no doubt he had entered his element. "The honor, Brigadain Diahlus, is entirely ours. I present to you he who has been accepted as a suitor, Colonel Jonathan Terynn of *Gamma Station*."

Diahlus smiled. "If I may, I must make an honest observation. Seeing all the flair of Eurosia about your mannerisms, I wonder why *you* were never considered."

Jonathan gave Fox a confused glance. Diahlus's comment was not part of the script he had read. Fox must have given an outstanding first impression. Regardless, they were now in uncharted territory. He could only hope that Fox was good at improvising.

Fox spread his arms, feigning embarrassment. "If only every man could aspire to such a worthy endeavor. But alas, some things are simply not done."

There was something disgustingly magical about Fox's performance. Not only did it break the tension in the air but it lightened up everyone's mood. Who had his first officer transformed into? In only a few moments, Fox had everyone smiling and enjoying his company. Even Rana's black hair had brightened up into blond.

Diahlus motioned to two empty chairs. "Please, have a seat, gentlemen."

Jonathan took his seat without a word.

Fox moseyed over to his. "Thank you kindly."

Jonathan's comm-band beeped. He swatted the button to silence it.

Xer leaned in from across the table. "Lieutenant Colonel Fox, you seem so natural. Have you spent time on Eurosia?"

"Sadly, no. I have not had the pleasure. Travel for Earthians is restricted."

Xer returned a confused glance. "Then, however did your Colonel manage it? It is my understanding that he visited Eurosia some time ago."

"Yes," Jonathan said. "Five years ago—five *Earth* years ago, I exploited a loophole in some command instructions I had been given. The plan was to visit Earth. But, as fortune would have it, that plan didn't work out. I ended up on Eurosia."

"Your story sounds as though your visit to Eurosia was a misfortune," Rana said, glaring at Jonathan.

"The misfortune was not getting to see my home planet. Visiting Eurosia, however," he said, looking over at Ellyra, "was truly a gift."

She smiled in return.

"And, ah, forgive me for being the realist in the room," Arkamenos said. "But once our tenure here has concluded, will it not be difficult to...continue the relationship?"

That was the one question Jonathan was hoping to avoid. He had no idea how to keep up a long-distance relationship that was lightyears apart. He had rather hoped any questions would be limited to his career or background. Instead, it looked as if any question was fair game. Several Euroo men entered the room carrying large platters with plates of food on them. They circled the table, setting down plates in front of each person seated.

"I have no idea," he finally admitted.

Rana smirked. "A venture ill-planned is also ill-fated. Would you not agree, Colonel Jonathan?"

Ellyra leaned forward with a nervous look in her eyes. "What Colonel Jonathan probably means is that—"

"Well, that all depends," Jonathan said, "on whether or not one accepts defeat."

"And how about you?" Rana asked. "Do you accept when you are defeated?"

Jonathan stared, the corners of his mouth hinting at a concealed smile. "Do I?"

Seaman Vinnece stumbled into the room, out of breath. She must have run all the way from Command and Control. Her braided ponytail hung over one shoulder. "Please excuse the interruption. Colonel, Commander Alexi has been trying to get ahold of you on your comm. There's a live priority message for you. It's from the *Brah'Kerov.*"

The tension in the air sank, being replaced by a vague feeling of unease. The Draconian flagship was called the *Brah'Kerov*. That was also where the Draco Senate convened. Upsetting the Draconians was always a concern on everyone's mind. To do so was usually fatal.

Jonathan stood. "Thank you, Seaman. I'll be right there."

Chapter 11

THE CRIME

Matt exited the cold, damp shuttle. He strolled down the loading ramp into the massive hangar. He gazed around in wonder. He had never seen the inside of a Draconian dreadnaught before. He knew they were big, but this ship was larger than them all. It was the flagship of the Draconian armada. The walls looked like they had been hewn from black rock. Matt stepped off the ramp and onto the polished smooth floor. He glanced back up to the ceiling, towering up three stories high. A swarm of flying lizards circled above, holding glowing orbs to light the room.

Light didn't mean much to the Draconians. Most things didn't mean much to those overgrown lizards. As long as the Skorath were not mentioned, they didn't care what happened around here. And that was the advantage Matt needed both to exploit and to ruin. A Scorpiian skittered across the floor over to Matt. The squiddies didn't use clothing so it was hard to tell what their social status was. Most of the Lords carried a large dagger to punish subordinates.

This squiddy carried multiple scars on its body. And it was missing at least one of its long tentacle arms. The marks of punishment meant this was an underling. Legally, any Scorpii—regardless of station—was superior to any human. In practice, the underling squiddies were so used to subservience that even a human could order them around. But one had to be sure they were talking to an underling; giving orders to a Lord would not end well.

It squealed out an introduction.

"I'm sure you are," Matt said in a dissatisfied tone. "But I came to speak with Commissioner Rawl. It's about the position of Senate Adjunct."

It gave a little squawk and motioned with a tentacle arm for Matt to follow. The squiddy guided him across the landing bay into a smaller hallway. They passed by two ornately dressed men in black robes with gold decorations. The Senate staff were the only Abes not yet under Matt's direct control. But that would soon change. Soon they too would be liberated from the squiddies.

Piece by piece, one slow advance at a time, Matt had wiggled control away from the Scorpii. It had taken years, and he had come close to death several times. The only way he had survived was by being more cunning than they were. The only way to survive was to outwit the wretched squiddies in their own game.

Matt had been especially good at it. Good enough that, by degrees, he had gained favor with Lord Vaux. The fruits of his five years had finally paid off when he had been entrusted with the operation of *Able station*. Unfortunately, it still wasn't enough. He needed to get rid of Lord Vaux. Then, maybe the killing would stop.

Lord Vaux, however, was a shrewd squiddy. He wouldn't be so easy to get rid of as the last couple had. This required a change in strategy. A change that could only happen if *Gamma Station* would stop getting in the way.

They rounded a corner and the squiddy halted before a large door. The squiddy looked at him with apprehension. It was as though he was questioning Matt's intentions. The pathetic creature was right to be wary. Commissioner Rawl was easily offended.

"Well?" he said, placing his hands on his hips.

The squiddy squawked and then touched the door chime with a cautious tentacle. The door croaked a deep slothful moan. That horrid sound needed to be retired. How could anyone stand listening to it every time someone came to the door?

The door slid open and an irritated Scorpii stood on the other side. It hissed angrily, its beady yellow eyes glaring.

"You must forgive the intrusion, Commissioner Rawl. I am your new Senate Adjunct and I was instructed to report to you immediately."

It waved a fierce tentacle and hissed again.

"That is correct, but unfortunately, Lord Vaux killed her this morning. I am the replacement."

It turned around, grumbling little squeals beneath its breath. Matt stepped inside and the door closed behind him.

"I can understand your concerns, Commissioner. You have every right to be furious. We can only hope Lord Vaux will see the error of his ways."

Commissioner Rawl huffed a skeptical hiss.

Matt paused a moment as if he were changing topics of conversation. It needed to look natural. "Too bad we have to wait on Commissioner Gyne before we can implicate *Gamma Station.*"

Commissioner Rawl spun around squawking inquisitively.

"You mean you've not heard? They have stolen what Commissioner Gyne believes to be a Skorath weapon."

It hissed angrily, flailing a couple of tentacles around.

"Commissioner Gyne does not appear to be concerned. He thinks he can use that to punish the Gamms. And who knows, Lord Vaux will probably reward him for his efforts."

Matt flinched as Commissioner Rawl shrieked and hissed in fury.

"I understand your frustration. But there isn't anything we can do...unless.."

109

Commissioner Rawl wrapped a tentacle around Matt's neck and hissed.

"...unless someone were to implicate *Gamma Station* before Gyne does."

It released its tentacle from around Matt's neck, pacing the floor in contemplation. Matt watched anxiously. Would Rawl take the bait? It was a calculated risk on Rawl's part. To try to preempt another commissioner was ambitious and also dangerous. Failure would mean being subject to punishment. But success, on the other hand, would increase his favor with the Draconians. They always rewarded those who exposed corruption. Rawl could even be promoted to a Lord.

Commissioner Rawl continued to pace.

That was not a good sign. If Rawl thought too long, it might lose its nerve and back out. There wasn't any way he could sweeten the deal without looking suspicious. The plan had to appear to be Rawl's idea. Perhaps a sense of urgency could do the trick?

Matt turned to leave. "I'll be in the senate office awaiting the call."

Commissioner Rawl stopped and squawked a few words.

"I have to be ready to send the transmission. Any moment now, Commissioner Gyne should be calling. Either you will give the order or Gyne will. In either case, I should be ready."

It pointed one of its tentacles at Matt, squealing an ultimatum.

Matt smiled; it worked. He bowed. "As you command, Commissioner. I'll send the transmission right away informing *Gamma Station.*"

He promptly left Commissioner Rawl's office and made his way to the senate offices. In the center of the *Brah'Kerov*, stood the massive senate chamber. It towered five stories tall with four balconies. The room's vacant chamber would soon be at full capacity once the Senate was in session. The senate offices lay just outside the chamber. The largest office held the transmission terminal.

The office held the familiar walls that looked like they were hewn from rock. On a raised platform in the center of the room, sat the hyperspace transmission controls.

Matt walked up to the man at the controls. He looked up. "Ah, Director Jaimess. Where will you be sending this transmission?"

"This will need to be a live transmission to *Gamma Station*."

"Why live?"

"Let's just say I want to make an impact."

"All right, you got it." He pressed his hand over several large stone plates. The faint hum of the hyperspace transmitter grew louder. "Stand by for connection..."

The air above the platform began to swirl and sparkle. The swirling sparkles melted together into a video image of the Command and Control room aboard *Gamma Station*. The image shimmered in the movement of the air.

A black-haired woman stood in the center of the video. It was Commander Isabeau Alexi, Colonel Terynn's second officer. Despite how troublesome the Gamms were, Matt had to admit she looked attractive, for a Gamm.

"Good evening, Commander Alexi," he said with absurdly fake zeal. "Or is it good morning where you are? I can never remember." The annoying tone of voice was necessary to convince the sly squiddies. They monitored all communication to and from the *Brah'Kerov*. For an alliance with the Gamms to work, they needed to look like enemies. The nemesis charade was a simple tool to fool the simple minds of the squiddies. The only drawback was that it created distance between him and his would-be allies.

"Mr. Jaimess," Isabeau replied.

"*Senate Adjunct* Jaimess," he corrected. "I'm helping out around here, you see."

"Senate Adjunct Jaimess, I trust you have a reason for calling?"

"An astute deduction, my dear," he replied in an overly enthusiastic tone. "However, this message needs to be given to Colonel Terynn personally. Go ahead and fetch the dear Colonel, I'll wait for you."

111

J onathan rounded the corner and stepped into Command and Control. "All right Izzy, what have you—"

He stopped in his tracks, gazing up at the large wall-mounted screen. The smug face of Matt Jaimess stared back at him. The weaselly excuse for a human being must have gotten bored and wanted to fraternize with the enemy.

"Matt Jaimess."

"You still remember me, dear Colonel. I am deeply touched."

"I don't have time for this, Jaimess. So, if you'll excuse me—"

"Oh, I do believe you should make time for this. You see I'm calling on behalf of the Senate Treaty Violation Committee. It seems you Gamms have been busy; shot down a Scorpiian destroyer."

He shook his head. "There was no violation of the treaty. I acted in defense of an Earth ship."

Matt smirked. "If you had such an air-tight case, would the Senate bother summoning you?"

Something in Matt's eyes hinted there was more than what he was divulging. It was the look of a card player who had an ace up his sleeve. Was it possible that something had been overlooked? If only Ambassador Cale were here. His political mind would be very useful right now.

"All right, Jaimess. You've got my attention."

"I'm sending written instructions and coordinates at the end of this transmission. The bottom line is that if you are not here to present your defense, you will be indicted by default."

This was not the time for political headaches. A major distraction like this could undermine the entire conspiracy for liberty. Only a few months remained to get both the Euroo and the Chantell on board. That alone would be miraculous in only a few months. This new development meant he would have to accelerate his approach to Ellyra. It also threatened to detract from the precious few days he had with her.

"I'll be there," he finally said.

"Oh, I almost forgot to mention, my dear Colonel," he said in his over-acted tone. "This also applies to your Euroo conspirators. They must be present also."

Jonathan clenched his fists. His jaw stiffened. The weasel was trying to rope the Euroo into this crazy allegation. "Mr. Jaimess, is your life so meaningless that you have to invent infractions just to fill your days?"

Matt's eyes flashed and his nostrils flared—only for a second—but it was there. He had touched on a nerve. Matt recomposed his smile in a swift motion. The man seemed practiced at keeping his emotions below the surface. It could either be called politics or deceit. And knowing *Able Station,* the latter was more likely.

Matt replied in a serious tone. "Colonel Terynn, not everyone is as they seem. You would do well to bear that in mind."

Jonathan huffed. "Thanks for the tip, Jaimess. You can tell those slimy superiors of yours that we'll be there."

Matt stared a moment, his eyes hinting at the desire for further conversation. Something else was going on. But what could it be? Did he want to gloat? Or was there some other sinister ploy he had devised? He finally took a deep breath, sighing with an air of resignation. "Jaimess out." The transmission ended.

Isabeau turned to Jonathan. "What was that last part all about?"

He shook his head. "I'm not sure. But knowing Jaimess, it can't be anything good."

She lowered her voice to a whisper. "This might delay things with the Chantell."

He nodded. "I know. I'll have to talk to Ellyra today."

"She is never alone."

"That is the crux of the problem. How can I hide what I want to say within what I say?"

"I'm sure you'll find a way."

Chapter 12

BEDTIME STORIES

D r. Mallory walked into Med Bay Charlie holding his reader to his eyes, reading the morning's news. His morning routine had become automatic. Perusing his reader as he walked, he waved his hand over sensor plates, turning lights on. Then he meandered over to the coffee rehydrator. With his eyes still on the morning's headlines, he fingered the controls and started the machine.

"Jacob," a weak voice called out.

Dr. Mallory looked up. Ambassador Cale's body remained motionless on his bed.

Cale's lips moved. "Jacob."

Dr. Mallory's breathing stopped, and his heart skipped a beat. For one startling moment, nothing in the universe made sense. Then he remembered the improved brainwave activity. Was it possible for him to have recovered so quickly? With the amount of neural and vascular damage, was it even possible to come out of the coma? His reader dropped to the ground, clattering. He rushed over to Cale's side. "Lucas! Can you hear me?"

"Yes, Jacob."

A thousand questions flooded his mind. Could he open his eyes? Did he have any feeling in his arms and legs? Was he too hot or cold? What was the last thing he remembered? But amidst the tsunami of questions, Dr. Mallory settled on just one. "How are you feeling?"

"Thirsty."

He glanced up at the I.V. machine. He was still being given fluids. The electrolytes were in balance and his hydration level was stable. Why would he be feeling thirsty?

"Well, you're at a hundred percent, but I can get you some water anyway."

"No," Cale muttered, shaking his head with gentle rocking motions. "Coffee."

And suddenly the universe made sense again. One of the great many things they had in common was the way they liked their coffee; overly sweet and thoroughly saturated with cream. At least his olfactory sense was working again; he must have smelled the rehydrator's work.

"I don't think you're ready for coffee just yet."

Cale grunted in disappointment.

"Well at the very least you'd need to be able to sit up."

"Drat. Well, we'll get to that," Cale assured. "Right now, we're working on opening my eyes."

"Who's we?"

A slight smile crept across Cale's face. "Oh, that's right. You haven't met my roommates, have you?"

That was not a good sign. Hallucinations were common before the onset of several neural diseases. It was best to keep his mind grounded in reality for as long as possible. "Lucas, there is nobody else here."

"Not in the room. I meant inside my head."

Dr. Mallory shook his head. "No, we're not jumping to conclusions. Split personality disorders are extremely rare. Besides, it would have shown up in the BRT scans."

115

"Jacob," Cale said with a hint of a chuckle. "Stop trying to diagnose me and try listening."

Dr. Mallory took a slow, annoyed breath. "Okay, fine. You say you've got voices inside your head. What do they say to you?"

"They call themselves the Voonsu."

"Uh-huh...Voonsu," he said, suppressing the skepticism in his voice. "Would that be a non-profit group or some social organization?"

Cale again gently shook his head. "Jacob, we're off to a terrible start if you can't believe anything I say."

The door to the med bay opened and Fox entered. "Hey Doc, do you still have the body we brought in earlier?"

"Yes. Did the Greys tell you anything about him?"

Fox nodded. "Turns out he wasn't human after all. Some kind of microscopic race called Voonsu. And, there's a good chance they survived."

Dr. Mallory threw a confused glance in Cale's direction.

Ellyra sat in an armchair in her quarters, staring into space. Diahlus paced across the open floor. "I should have objected." She refocused her gaze on him. "There was insufficient time for debate. The Earthian frigate was on the verge of being destroyed by the Scorpii."

"Yes, of course you're right. I trusted your judgment," he said, still pacing. "Yet, a part of me feels I should have anticipated this ramification."

She shook her head. "Not even Xer, being the most well-versed in the law, saw this as a possibility. How could you or I expect your anticipation?"

Rana walked over to Ellyra's side, handing her a glass of pink liquid. She took a sip and returned it. "Thank you, Rana."

The door chimed and Rana answered it. Her hair blackened in an instant. "Are you expected?"

"No," Jonathan's voice replied. "But I was hoping to speak with Sune Ellyra."

Ellyra composed herself. "Please see him in, Rana."

She led him over to Ellyra and curtsied. "Colonel Jonathan to see you."

Ellyra motioned toward the sofa. "Won't you be seated?"

Jonathan took an uneasy breath and sat down. He kept his eyes down amidst a dark countenance.

"Can I get you something to drink? Some Porteñey perhaps?"

His eyes met hers. "No, thank you." He moved his mouth as if to speak more, but instead refrained. Something was clearly bothering him.

She waited a moment longer for him to speak, but he never did. What was on his mind? This was not the Jonathan Terynn she knew. The bold Earth man who wouldn't back down had somehow transformed into a skittish boy. Not only would this never do, but it diminished his charm considerably.

"We received your message and we, of course, are all astonishment and dismay."

Jonathan looked away. "Jaimess knows we were never in the wrong. But he has something he can use against us. That much is clear."

"Is this what worries you?"

He shook his head, re-engaging her eyes. "This is the kind of political headache I relied on Ambassador Cale for. And without him, I am charging into this half-blind."

She looked at him with curiosity. "Is that another human expression?

Jonathan took a deep breath, glancing heavenward. Then, smiling, he returned his gaze to her. "Yes, sorry about that. I guess it means I feel unprepared."

"Well, I have Xer preparing a brief in our defense. He assures me we were well within legal rights."

He shook his head again. "That's not it. He has something else up his sleeve. And that is the danger."

"You suspect he is hiding a weapon in his coat?" Diahlus asked.

Jonathan closed his eyes in exasperation. "Uh, no...when I said up his sleeve, I didn't mean..."

"Incredible," Diahlus said in conclusion, turning around in search of a drink. "We are speaking the same language and we still cannot understand you."

Jonathan glanced back to Ellyra. "Is there any chance I can speak to you in private?"

If only she could afford him the luxury. If he were simply a foreign ship captain, confidential meetings would be warranted. But now that they were officially courting, that was even less of an option. It was not proper to be alone with a suitor.

She shook her head. "Indeed not. I'm afraid that's not done. Not at this stage at any rate. Perhaps we can take a walk?"

"That might not be advisable," Rana said. "The display last time was rather unbecoming."

Diahlus walked over to Ellyra and bowed. "Allow me then to give what assistance I can by retiring to the *Calmao*. I'll send word to you when we need to depart."

"It is well, Diahlus."

He turned to Jonathan. "Colonel Jonathan, there is no need to take separate ships to answer the allegations before us. Shall I send for you as well?"

"That would be helpful. Thank you."

Diahlus bowed again and left.

Jonathan glanced over to Ellyra. "When you were growing up, were you ever read bedtime stories?"

There was a look of confidence in his eyes. Whatever he wanted to say, he must have found a way to say it discretely. But what did childhood stories imply?

"Not exactly," she said. "My father used to sing fables to me. Each verse was a story."

"My mother used to tell me tales of ancient galactic empires. And I was fascinated with the idea of a time when there were no Draconians."

"I suppose it should not be surprising considering the restrictions laid upon your race. You must have cherished those stories."

He nodded. "Yes...yes my mother's stories became a large part of who I am..."

Something in his tone implied the message he was trying to convey was rooted in his mother's stories. Could he actually be wanting to converse about his childhood? That didn't seem likely. What he wanted to say was personal enough that he wanted to speak privily. This had to be a deeper conversation, something he couldn't speak openly about.

Then her muscles tensed up and her heart raced as a sudden realization struck. Could he be evaluating her ability to be a mother? Her hair color dulled into a troubled gray for a brief moment. Her concentration pulled it back into a formal white. She focused on her facial expression, keeping it neutral. It wouldn't be seemly to put her emotions on display, as her father continually reminded her.

She forced a breath. They were both aware of the time constraints for courting. But such an intimate question, so soon, came as a surprise. How should she answer? How did he want her to answer? Was there even a right or wrong answer? Somehow, she had expected that conversation to come up after marriage.

She swallowed. "You must have had a wonderful mother indeed. And I would venture to suppose that all women, at one time or another, aspire to make such a difference in a child's life."

Jonathan's eyes shifted around in thought but they didn't give any clues as to how he evaluated her response. If only his hair would change colors. At least then she would have some clue as to how he felt. That was something else she would have to get used to.

He looked at her again. "One of my favorite stories was about a foretold star that would rise up and frighten the Draconians. Have you ever heard of a story like that?"

She shook her head. "I'm afraid not. Most of the ballads my father sang were about the Eurosian dynasties. Perhaps you will need to recite these stories to me."

He gave her a short half-smile before returning his gaze to the floor. After a moment of silence, he lifted his eyes back to her. "Have you had many dealings with the Chantell?"

This was a surprising question. It didn't seem to match the context of his previous question. Relations with the Chantell did not seem to relate to the question of children. Had he changed topics so abruptly? Or was this only another part of his strategy? His closest officers considered him a brilliant strategist. And she had personally witnessed his remarkable ability to outwit the Scorpiian pilots. This might not be so much a change of topics as it was a change of approach.

"Yes, I have had extensive meetings with them. They are exceptionally organized."

He nodded, motioning to the room around them. "They built this space station in a fraction of the time it should have taken. The unity of their hive mind allows them to coordinate at an unprecedented level."

Unity? Was he trying to imply marriage? Her breath halted in her lungs. Her heart pounded within her. She felt the slight tingle of her hair changing color. She clenched her jaw, forcing back the change in her hair. Despite her efforts, however, her hair dulled into a frightened gray.

She could still be wrong. He still might be referring to something else. But what else could it be? The private nature of the conversation, the talk of children, and now of unifying... They all pointed to one obvious conclusion. *How could I have been such a fool?* She wondered. *Diahlus warned me and I didn't listen.* Trifling with a man's heart was never so simple as a mere diversion. Diahlus warned that certain expectations would arise from continuing this courtship. It seemed she was now seeing the effects of it. She forced herself to take a breath.

"Are you then requesting a unity?"

He thought for a long moment. "Yes... I believe I am."

She stood, a deep breath invading her lungs. In three quick steps, she was beside a small table against the wall. She took the glass and downed its contents in a single swallow. It clanked when she set it down, holding one hand to her chest to slow her heart rate.

Whether she liked it or not, the time to choose had now arrived. Her foolish decision to pursue her romantic desires had trapped her against a wall. She could not accept him without disappointing her father. Nor could she refuse him without breaking his heart. The only practical choice—the only proper choice—was to refuse him. And she needed to do it right now before her romantic yearnings overpowered her judgment.

She turned around. "Colonel Jonathan..." The rest of her words refused to come. As though the faucet of her mind suddenly shut off, leaving her without anything more to say.

"Yes?" he asked, rising from the sofa.

She stared into his gorgeous eyes. Even from this distance, she saw the delicate brown with amber gems on the white canvas. The tapestry of his eyes tugged at her heart. Memories of being together with Jonathan on Eurosia flooded into her mind. His boyish wonder, his silly notions that plants should be green, and the safety she felt around him, all intruded upon her thoughts. Her memories and her heart were confederates, betraying her proper duty. Deep down she knew there was only one acceptable answer.

She took another quick breath. "Then...let it be done."

The door slid up and Diahlus entered. He bowed to Ellyra. "Sune Ellyra, the time has approached. We must depart within a quarter of an hour if we are to reach the Senate in time."

She nodded.

He turned to Jonathan. "If you'll follow me."

Chapter 13

THE SENATE HEARING

Matt strode down the torch-lit hallways of the Draconian flagship, the *Brah'Kerov*. The city-sized ship didn't have much in the way of décor. The walls looked like they were hewn out of rock. Lizards crawling on the walls breathed fire onto torches, providing the only lighting. This, however, didn't seem to bother the Scorpii who worked on board. The Draconians did as little as possible in the operation of the ship. Abes and Scorpiians did most of the labor.

Lord Vaux hissed angrily, walking beside Matt.

The squiddy behaved precisely as he should have. Just as Matt had predicted he would. He felt a smile creeping across his face and suppressed it. Control was mandatory when dealing with Lord Vaux. He wasn't just any squiddy, he was almost as sly as Matt. Lord Vaux was very ambitious. Ambitious enough to learn the ways of Earthian intrigue. Matt could almost call him a protégé. Too bad he must be eliminated.

"This is most distressing, my lord. If I had but known—"

Lord Vaux hissed again, pointing an accusatory tentacle at Matt.

"I only follow my instructions, my lord. But, if you instruct me to, I will be happy to inquire of Commissioners Gyne and Rawl whenever it might interest you."

Lord Vaux squealed contentedly, strutting with satisfaction in its stride.

Lord Vaux had not only taken the bait but had elevated him to a position to question the actions of both commissioners. Never waste a good intrigue when it can serve multiple purposes. But he did have to act quickly. This new authority over those two commissioners would only last until Lord Vaux's demise. He still needed a good excuse to get on direct speaking terms with the Draconians. Something which no human had ever done before.

Matt bowed to Lord Vaux before parting ways. Matt walked down another hallway, finally allowing his smile to caress his face. His five-year-long operation was finally coming to an end. He only needed one good foothold above the Scorpii to accomplish it. But first, he had to deal with *Gamma Station*. If the Gamms kept provoking the Scorpii, his men would keep falling to Lord Vaux's temperament. That needed to stop right away.

Although a permanent solution was already in the works, Ross had a convincing point. An alliance between two space stations, would not only double their resources but also their reach. Indeed, the prospects of the future of humanity never looked so good.

A chair-sized orb of crystals floated up in front of Matt. The Crystallines were an interesting race. How a ball of crystals could defy gravity was a pure mystery. As far as any human knew, they were a race of living crystals. Though, to say they looked like a floating crystal ball would be insufficient. They looked more like the inside of a geode. The Crystalline hovered. It pulsed colors through its crystals and hummed what sounded like musical notes.

"Good," Matt replied. "Which landing bay have they been directed to?"

It chimed another note and pulsed a few more colors.

"Thank you, I'll be right down."

The Crystalline floated away and Matt turned a corner, heading down a side passage. He didn't need to get there in any sort of hurry; it would take time to disembark. But to maintain the edge, he needed to get every advantage he could. So, if a few extra minutes to observe the Gamms could be gained, he would take it. He quickened his pace. The hallway ended in a wide staircase leading down into the enormous landing bay. It still looked about empty. Only a handful of large ships lay sprawled across the mile of polished stone-like floor.

The far end of the bay did not have a wall. Instead, the red pulsing glow of the air pressure force field separated them from the cold black of space. Through the bloody glow of the force field, a Euroo starcruiser could be seen. As it passed through the force field into the landing bay, the anti-gravity emitters engaged. They held up the massive bulk of the ship as it crossed over from the cold weightlessness of space into the gravity-rich atmosphere of the bay.

That was the great secret of the Draconians. One would not know from a casual glance that the Draconians had any advanced technology. Hiding it below the polished floor was just the first hint that the torch light and cave-looking walls were only the Draconian décor. It seemed they enjoyed the low-tech look.

The bulky Euroo ship slowly descended to the ground with its landing gear out. A ramp extended to the floor and several of their decadent crewmen disembarked. Picking out which one was Jonathan Terynn should be easy from this distance. All the Euroo had bleach-white hair, though rumor had it that they could sometimes change the color.

This short procession consisted of five white-headed Eurosians and two Earthians. The one with the brown hair was Jonathan. The other man with the shaved head must have been a recent addition in the last year. His walk was too stiff to be a diplomat. He was most likely another officer. That was good. That meant Ambassador Cale hadn't survived the assassination. That should put them in a more desperate mood. Exactly the right disposition for this to work.

Matt descended to the bottom of the stairs to patiently await their approach. Thankfully, they didn't keep him waiting long. Jonathan led the procession while talking to a Eurosian woman. *I guess he's more of a lady's man than I had given him credit for,* Matt decided.

Jonathan glanced ahead, noticing Matt, and stopped. "Senate Adjunct Jaimess."

Matt erupted into pretended enthusiasm. "You still remember, my dear Colonel Terynn. I am deeply touched."

"Oh, I doubt that very much."

"Oh tisk, tisk Colonel Terynn. Shouldn't you have learned better manners from spending time with the stiff Euroo?"

"Mr. Jaimess, I don't have time for this. As you are aware, I have some false allegations to attend to."

"Direct and to the point, as usual, my dear Colonel," Matt said with an exaggerated smile. "Perhaps I could expedite this little detour if we could speak in private."

"Mr. Jaimess, my ambassador may never wake up again thanks to an Abe assassin. I would have to be a great fool to be alone with you."

The enthusiasm drained from Matt's face. "Either that...or simply desperate for things to change."

The Eurosian woman at his side beckoned his attention with her hand on his arm. They spoke to each other in whispers for a few moments before Jonathan turned back to Matt.

"All right, Jaimess. You've got two minutes."

Whomever that woman was, she had some influence over Jonathan. That wasn't expected. Jonathan had always seemed headstrong. How she managed to tangle herself around his strong will was uncertain. What *was* certain was that Matt needed to learn more about this alien woman.

The woman took a reader from Jonathan—presumably a map of the *Brah'Kerov's* layout—and led the rest of the procession up the stairs.

Matt placed his hands behind his back and began a slow walk, Jonathan cautiously at his side.

"Jonathan," he said in a serious tone. "Let me be frank. Big changes are coming. Changes that will benefit all humanity."

"You don't say."

He stopped, turning to Jonathan with fresh annoyance in his expression. "I enjoy a good adversarial banter as much as the next man, but this is the only time we can talk unobserved."

Jonathan stared into his eyes for a few moments as if deciding something. "Okay," he finally said. "Go on."

Matt's voice lowered to a whisper. "One day, there will be no travel restrictions for humans. One day there will be no *Able Station*, *Bravo Station*, or *Gamma Station*—there will just be humans."

Jonathan matched his whisper. "You speak with the confidence of a man with a plan."

"Indeed. Such a plan would also have one defining hindrance."

"Such as?"

"Such as a daring little space station with the uncanny ability to infuriate the Scorpii."

"In my experience, that takes no great feat. One only needs to breathe to accomplish that."

Matt pursed his lips. "Be that as it may, it has forced us into taking steps to remove the obstruction."

"Such as assassinating my ambassador?"

Matt took a breath. "It doesn't have to be this way. What could the future look like if fair Brutus joined Cassius?"

Jonathan stood, staring for a few eternal moments. "Mr. Jaimess, you would be asking me to vote alongside the Scorpii—voting against my conscience—"

"Your conscience be hanged!" Matt said, struggling to keep his voice a whisper. "I'm not asking you to pollute your soul with the whims of the vile squiddies. You can keep your self-righteous bravado for all I care. All I'm asking is for you to sacrifice a few of your over-abundant morals for the benefit of your fellow man. I would think that a bargain in exchange for liberation."

"Matt, if I have to become evil in order to destroy evil, who has really won?"

Matt clenched his fists and tensed his jaw. The stupid Gamm would rather see his own race forever enslaved than do what was necessary to set them free. How foolish he had been to hope that a Gamm would ever ally with an Abe. Jonathan's righteous zealotry blinded him. He would never understand what it takes to rise above what providence had dealt to humanity. In a way, they were both fools. Only time would tell which was the bigger fool.

"Fine...fine, my dear Jonathan. You have made your position quite clear. When the walls of oppression start to suffocate your people, be sure to explain to them how your scruples are more important than their lives." Matt stormed off. He headed in the wrong direction but that didn't matter. He needed to blow off some steam. He had reached out the hand of friendship only to have it stabbed. *Stupid Ross!* Matt thought. *You're an idiot for idolizing that blind fool. And I'm also a fool for believing you.*

Jonathan walked into a small comfortable room overlooking the large Senate floor. This was the northwest waiting room. Several benches lay strewn about. A large bay window isolated it from the noise of the circular Senate chamber. Like every other room on the massive ship, torches provided most of light. Ellyra and Xer turned from looking through the bay window. Arkamenos and Rana remained seated while Diahlus paced.

Fox stood. "So, what did Jaimess want?"

"An alliance."

Fox stood dumbfounded. "You're kidding..."

"No, he quite believes he and I could be Brutus and Cassius."

Fox frowned. "Wait, they're the ones who died."

He nodded. "Jaimess probably meant Octavius and Antony."

Diahlus halted his pacing. "Pray tell, to what are you referring?"

"Ancient Earthian history," Jonathan replied. "The battle of Philippi in the Roman civil war."

"Ah," Diahlus said with disinterest, continuing his pacing.

Ellyra left the window and approached Jonathan. "What was his proposal?"

"I didn't let him get that far..."

Her eyes lit up. "Am I to understand that you refused him before hearing a proposal for an alliance?"

He stared back, his heart pounding. She had a point. He had been quick to refuse a chance to ally with the enemy. But that is how he saw them: as the enemy. He had refused on moral grounds. But did Ellyra see it that way? What did she see that he did not? It couldn't have been wrong to refuse to violate his integrity, could it? This was the gray area in politics that was so infuriating. How could black and white not always be black and white? At least in combat, battle lines were easy to see.

"Yes," he finally said. "Though when you put it like that, it does make me look hasty."

Her brow wrinkled with concern. "One never refuses without hearing the entirety of a proposal."

"He wanted me to vote in favor of whatever the Scorpii want in the Senate. I don't sell my votes, not for any price."

"Yes indeed, but even the hope of a possible acceptance can forestall calamity. Surely leaving such an opportunity available would have opened up the options for negotiation. You might have even found something besides your votes that would have been acceptable."

Negotiating hadn't occurred to him either. That was another area he would need to work on. Had living thousands of lightyears away from Earth his whole life disconnected him? What came so naturally to Matt Jaimess—and even the Euroo—was strangely foreign to him.

Jonathan took a breath. "I guess I—"

128

"Here they come," Xer announced, looking out the window at the Senate floor below.

Everyone else moved to the window. Three men walked down the center of the Senate floor below. Their ceremonial black cloaks with gold embroidery swayed in their stride. They made their way to the stairwell. They would be at the door to their waiting room in moments. The ceremonial garb indicated they were official Senate summoners. Which was a fancy title for errand boys.

Jonathan took a deep breath.

Xer turned to him. "Colonel Jonathan, are you ready?"

"Well, yes and no. I wish I knew what Jaimess was up to."

"Should it matter? We have the truth on our side."

Jonathan shook his head. "This is not about truth or even fact. Even Jaimess knows our legal ground is solid. What this is, is an attack."

"Surely you exaggerate. This is bureaucracy, not warfare."

"For all our sakes, I hope I'm wrong. Because if I *am* right, we'll be seeing a lot more shots fired before this hearing is through."

Xer stared back with a puzzled look. "I am unsure of your meaning."

"Most likely another Earthian expression," Ellyra said, walking up to Jonathan's side. "Colonel Jonathan may wish to convey that this hearing is a façade for malicious intentions."

Xer dismissed the comment with a shake of his head. "What possible allegations could they make?"

The door opened and the three summoners entered, their black robes swaying. The lead summoner held a tall smooth staff. Atop was a sculpted symbol of twin serpents swallowing a planet. That was the emblem of the Draco Senate.

"The Senate is now ready to hear remarks from the accused. Who will speak for *Gamma Station*?"

Jonathan raised his hand. "That would be me."

"And who will speak for the ship referred to as Mother Goose?"

"I will," Xer said, stepping forward.

"Follow us," the summoner directed.

"Also," Jonathan added. "I wish to invoke my right of counsel."

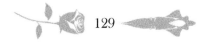

He turned back to Jonathan. "You have the right. Who will act as counsel to you?"

Jonathan pointed to Ellyra. "Sune Ellyra El'Allel will act as counsel."

Ellyra shot him a glance that seemed to ask what he was doing.

He mouthed the words, "I need you."

Ellyra took his hand. Rana walked over to Ellyra but the summoner barred her path with his staff. "Only one counsel is permitted."

Jonathan gave Rana a triumphant smile. There would be no chaperone this time, and Rana could object all she liked. That alone was worth the trip.

Xer, Jonathan, and Ellyra followed the summoners out of the room and down the hall. Torchlight shadows danced across the rough-hewn walls. They descended a winding staircase and emerged on the floor of the senate chamber. A starcruiser could fit inside the spacious room which had four balconies. Winged cat-sized lizards flew from torch to torch. They spewed blue flames onto the torches, keeping them lit.

They were led to a large stone-looking table where they each took a seat. Jonathan hadn't ever been on the ground floor. He had only ever been in the senate box assigned to *Gamma Station*. And that was on the first balcony. Jonathan readjusted his posture on the cold solid stump that was called a chair. For all their high-and-mighty technology, the Draconians sure didn't let much of it show. What did they have against padded leather seats?

He looked up to a secluded balcony overlooking the Senate floor. Three Draconians lazily lay their massive reptilian bodies. That particular balcony reserved the name, the Dais of Draconia. The less-than-interested Draconians always watched proceedings from their lofty perch. Rarely did they ever participate. And that was a good thing; capturing the Draconians' attention was always met with wrath. The most tiring game in the Senate was avoiding their notice while luring opponents into it.

In front of Jonathan, stood a taller table that sat five senators. One from each of the five elder races. Jonathan knew them by sight. P'Lare from the Tumnei, Chisss'Tah from the Chantell, Gondesh from the

Arkalan, Msmrthn from the Crystalline, and Lord Vaux from the Scorpii. The rock-like Arkalan and the floating geode-like Crystalline were uncommon sights outside of the Draco Senate. These senators made up the Treaty Violation Committee. Beside the Scorpii senator, sat a man from *Bravo Station* who acted as a translator.

Lord Vaux squealed a long sentence of squawks and other noises. Between breaths, the man translated its words. "Colonel Jonathan Terynn, on the thirty-fourth day of the second month in the current galactic year 21836, your ships attacked Scorpiian destroyers."

Msmrthn, the floating Crystalline pulsed a few colors and hummed a low-pitched sound. The man at the end of the table quickly translated its words. "That statement is out of order, the accused has yet to present their account of the incident."

Gondesh, moved his rock-like features as he spoke in a deep dry voice. "Sustained. We will now hear their account."

Xer stood, systematically recounting the events. And in typical Euroo fashion, he laced his account with plenty of extra flowery words. He kept his narrative short, arguing that an Earthian ship was under attack and that an Earthian commander defended it with deadly force. While Msmrthn pulsed a few colors in a follow-up question, Matt Jaimess strolled up to Lord Vaux and whispered to him. A sly smile crept over Lord Vaux's mouth. Matt glanced momentarily at Jonathan. What were they planning? Perhaps he *had* been too hasty in denying Matt. Was he now going to be punished for it?

Ellyra leaned toward Jonathan's ear and whispered, "Is that not the Earthian man you met in the hangar?"

He nodded. "Matt Jaimess. Supervisor of *Able Station* and the new Senate Adjunct. He's the one who wanted an alliance."

"This may be worse than I thought," she said.

"Somehow I'm not surprised."

"Jonathan, whoever that man is, regardless of his rank or station, he is the one making the decisions. You can see it in the way he moves and the way he looks. I've known several like him. They are the bureaucrats behind the bureaucrats."

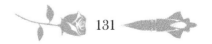

"I have a sick feeling that he is going to try to limit my ability to interfere with his plans."

"I wish I had been able to warn you sooner."

Jonathan glanced back at Xer. He had finished answering the committee's follow-up questions. Xer sat down.

Chisss'Tah clicked in his native Chantell dialect and the man at the end of the table translated. "The account appears substantiated. Article Twenty-three is specific."

Msmrthn pulsed a few colors and hummed a high note. "It would appear the treaty has been obeyed."

Lord Vaux hissed and squawked. "This confession is most troubling indeed. The Earthians of *Gamma Station* have dragged the Euroo into their aggressive business." A vile smirk crossed its lips, revealing its twisted, jagged teeth. "I'm afraid the Earthians are a bad influence on the Euroo and should be segregated."

Lord Vaux's remarks caused an instant commotion in the room. Xer protested while the committee members bickered back and forth. Jonathan stiffened in his seat. Panic shot through his veins. His heart pounded. He had just barely reunited with Ellyra. Losing that temporarily he could live with, but losing that permanently... He felt sick inside thinking of never again being able to be with Ellyra.

But that was not all, if the Scorpii could invent a way to separate him from Ellyra, the conspiracy would crumble. They only had a few short months to test the waters with the Chantell. They were counting on his relationship with Ellyra to traverse the gap with the Chantell.

Jonathan glanced at Ellyra, trying to keep his voice a whisper. "If the Scorpii find a way to keep us apart officially, is there any way to meet *unofficially?*"

She shook her head. "We have no binding union or alliance that would escape such a decree."

Jonathan stood and raised his hand.

Gondesh pounded his rocky hand on the table several times, demanding order. The commotion fizzled out and all eyes returned to

Gondesh who stared at Jonathan. "You have something to add, Earthian?"

"Affirmative. Any discussion regarding the Euroo and Earthian governments is not germane to the topic at hand. This hearing is specifically held to address the actions of one ship and one crew."

Gondesh nodded. "Sustained."

Lord Vaux squealed in delight. "Normally that would be true." It glanced up to the uninterested Draconians high above. "But we have heard reports the Earthians of *Gamma Station* have acquired a Skorath weapon."

The three Draconians animated upon hearing that name. They roared in their native language, smoke rising from their reptilian nostrils. The Draconian in the center reached out and pointed a clawed finger at Lord Vaux.

"The Skorath are forbidden! All mention, all stories, all technology is outlawed and punishable by extermination," it decreed in its slow gravelly voice. "Explain!"

Jonathan shuddered. He had no idea the Draconians could speak his language. In fact, they spoke perfect Earthian. In a way, it made sense; the Earth language was considered by most species to be a very easy language. It was still shocking since he had never before seen them participate in the Senate, let alone angrily address a senator.

Earning the attention of the Draconians was never wise. So, why did Lord Vaux do it? What did he hope to gain? He could very easily lose his life just by mentioning the Skorath. Jonathan's thought returned to Matt Jaimess. Whatever the Scorpii were attempting was cooked up by Matt, and Matt was no fool.

Lord Vaux squawked his reply. "Our records indicate these Earthians have an illegal weapon. And that they have attempted to pollute the Euroo by installing it on one of their ships."

"That's a lie!" Xer protested.

"They call it: Death Ray."

The second Draconian rumbled his deep slothful voice. "Present your evidence, Lord Vaux."

133

Lord Vaux let out a hesitant squawk. "We're still compiling the logs. But the preliminary—"

"You dare to mention They Who Shall Not Be Named and you have not brought your evidence?" the Draconian shouted, its voice echoing in the large room. It took a slow, deep breath, its internal fire illuminating its nostrils. "Take him, and hold him until the evidence is produced."

Two tall Arkalan guards, like gargoyles coming to life, walked up to Lord Vaux. They sent tremors through the floor as their heavy footsteps pounded. Their slow stride took them a moment to reach the Scorpiian. They each grabbed some tentacles and dragged it down a corridor. *Maybe this could be a good thing, after all,* Jonathan wondered. It did take one of the prominent Scorpii senators out of the picture.

The third Draconian pointed a clawed finger at Jonathan. "In the interim," it declared in its slothful, gravelly voice. "The Earthians of *Gamma Station* and the Euroo shall not associate."

Jonathan stared at the Draconian with wide eyes. The blasted Scorpii had done it; they had invented a way to separate him from Ellyra. Or rather, Matt Jaimess had. He shouldn't have dismissed Matt so easily. What Matt could not have known was how serious a blow he had delivered. Ellyra was the key to getting the conspiracy off the ground. And T'Kal was right. The political landscape was dramatically shifting under Scorpii ambition. They could not wait another ten years to try again. There would not be enough of a resistance left by then.

In a panic, he turned to Ellyra. "Is there any way we can stay together?"

She returned a startled expression. "Together?"

"Ellyra, I can't afford to lose you. There's too much at stake. Is there any way at all?"

Her hair color dulled into a frightened gray. "Well, there is a way. A common union should be binding enough."

"Then will you do it?"

A breath caught in her throat. "It isn't usually done for instances like these. It's normally used to remedy indiscretion. We would carry a blemish on our reputations."

"Remove him from the Senate floor," the Draconian ordered.

Another two stone Arkalans approached Jonathan, their feet pounding against the solid floor.

"Ellyra," Jonathan pleaded. "I can live with a little embarrassment. Please."

She stared back, her lips parted and halted in mid-breath. Her blue within blue eyes searched his. Whatever she was contemplating had to be a big deal to her. But that couldn't be helped right now. The guards were approaching and he was out of options.

"Ellyra, I need you."

She took in a sudden breath, her hair color brightening into pink. He had seen her hair turn that color before when he had promised to officially court her. Why was it pink now? Forging an alliance with the Euroo seemed far removed from sweet sentiments. Maybe pink didn't mean what he thought it meant. *I have got to figure out the hair colors,* he thought.

Ellyra glanced up at the approaching Arkalan guards and then over to Xer. "Brigadain Xer," she said in a shaky voice. "There isn't much time, I need a common union quickly."

Dismay erupted in his eyes. "My lady, your station! It is not done!"

She once again glanced back at the ever-approaching guards, then back to Xer. "That hasn't escaped me, Xer. But I must resign and order you to comply."

The shock eased off his face. "He will want my head for this."

A tear rolled down her cheek. "I'm very sorry." Without looking, she took Jonathan's hand. He didn't often get the privilege of holding her hand but he wasn't about to ask why. Nor did he dare to interrupt their conversation to ask what it all meant. There was something deeply emotional in this alliance for some reason. It didn't make sense but he hadn't ever entered into any agreements with the Euroo before. He did know they were very ceremonial and ornate in what they did. Maybe a simple agreement was too unceremonial and therefore looked down on.

Xer breathed out and picked up his reader. He punched a few of the digital buttons and pulled up what looked like a contract. He typed some things in and then held it out toward Ellyra. "Your thumbprint."

She pressed her thumb to the screen. A small light scanned her thumb. Xer then held the reader to Jonathan. "And yours."

Jonathan felt the heavy thumping of the Arkalan feet right behind him. He pressed his thumb to the screen. One of the Arkalan guards grabbed Jonathan by the arm and yanked him aside.

Xer waved his hands over his head. "Wait!" He pointed to Ellyra. "This one is to go with him; she's his wife."

Jonathan shot a startled glance at Xer. "His what?"

Chapter 14

BEGINNING AGAIN

Ellyra walked across the rusty metal floor of the Arkalan starship. She didn't dare touch anything. Every surface was covered in dirt, grime, or something unrecognizable and therefore worse. Definitely not her first choice of transportation. But it was better than being stranded on the Draconian flagship. After the decree to separate, her crew had been ordered to leave without the Earthians. The irony was that they had neglected to segregate Jonathan's first officer from her crew. She and Jonathan were now being escorted back to *Gamma Station* by the Arkalan.

A tall Arkalan, its stone-like body pounding the floor, led Ellyra through a corridor. She hoped it was taking her to see Jonathan. At first, she wasn't sure the Arkalan guards would recognize the marriage. She shuddered to think what would have happened if they had refused to accept the union. She would have been sent home as a married woman never to see her husband. It would have been worse than being a widow. At least with widowhood came the opportunity to marry again.

Marriage... it still felt so foreign to think of herself as married. A deep breath filled her lungs. She wasn't ready for this. There had been no preparation, no courtship customs had been observed, and she didn't have so much as a ceremony. Her heart sank as she recalled her girlhood dreams of marriage. Her wedding was supposed to be a grand and happy event. She had pictured that day thousands of times in her head. Her father would wear his double-breasted scarlet waistcoat. Her mother would wear her shimmering blue gown. Her best friend from finishing school would be there. Her dance instructor and tutor would stand by with warm smiles offering congratulations.

The conductor would strike up the symphony and they would play the Mezonee. She would dance the first half of the dance with her father, who would then give her hand to her groom. She could picture the candlelight of the ballroom and all the ladies in their fancy gowns. It would have been the most treasured moment in her life. And it was all gone now. There would be no ball. There would be no celebration and no ceremony. She was legally bound to Jonathan in a common law union.

Common law! Her father would be furious. How could she ever explain such a blemish on her honor? How could she ever reconcile her deed with him? This branding would doubtless carry over to the entire El'Allel name. Sadly, she might never get the chance to explain. By a Draconian decree, Earthians could no longer interact with the Euroo. And she, being an Earthian by marriage, could no longer return to Eurosia.

What have I done? she wondered. She had not only given up her homeworld, but she had given up ever seeing her mother and father again. Her heart pounded in her chest, and she felt the tingling sensation of her hair color changing. Probably to a sad brown. Was it worth it? Would the Draconians ever reevaluate the situation or was this now permanent? And what would become of her ship?

Jonathan had said he needed her. He had seemed almost desperate. It was that desperate plea of his when he said he needed her, that caught her heart. What was most important was that she could marry for love.

138

And finally, the man who had only hours earlier evaluated her to be a mother had pleaded to stay together. If his heart truly belonged to her, then she could cope with losing her homeworld and family. She could survive the new harsh reality she had thrown herself into. As long as she had his love to hold onto, she could make it.

The Arkalan stopped at the end of the hall and pressed a button, opening a thick rusty door. He motioned for her to enter. She stepped through the door to find Jonathan inside. He held his head in his hands, his elbows on the table. At least his uniform was dark in color, it would hide the stains he was certain to pick up from that table and chair. The door closed behind her.

He looked up, dismay still plastered across his face. He didn't speak at first. His eyes eluded that he had much to say but couldn't decide how to begin. He swallowed. "Wife?"

She looked down. Her tingling hair indicated the embarrassed burgundy that would match her cheeks. "I was not left with sufficient time to explain all the details." She glanced at his face. "You had asked if there was any way..."

"Yeah, it's my fault," he said, placing his head back in his hands. "I'm sorry I dragged you into this."

Fault? Her heart sank again, her hands felt cold. He must regret the marriage. Instead of the charming Earth man scooping her up in his warm embrace, he sat there in regret. Instead of a sweet reunion, tension. She had been wrong, there was no love here. He showed no concern for the sacrifices she had made for him—she might never again see her father.

She was a fool. She had unwittingly thrown away every hope and dream that mattered to her. But he still needed her, didn't he? He had indicated as much when he asked her to join him on the Senate floor. He still had much to learn by way of politics. There was much she could teach him. Hopefully, there was still a purpose for her. Without her ship and her family, what was she? Would there be anything for her in this new life of hers? He didn't want her for a wife, that much was clear by his demeanor. Then why had he courted her? Why had he formally announced his intentions?

Her breathing stopped, and a lump formed in her throat. She had told Diahlus that she knew she would have to give in to her father's wishes. She would have to marry someone who could be an heir to the Great House. She had told him she wanted to explore her girlhood notions of romance. The realization struck her. Had she never intended to give Jonathan any real chance at marriage? To her, this was all a pleasant distraction while she rebelled against her father's wishes. Had it been the same for Jonathan? Had she also been just a pleasant diversion?

She lowered her head. Diahlus had tried to warn her, and she hadn't listened. Tears welled up and ran down her face. This was all her fault. She had toyed with her heart, and like a clumsy fool, she had broken it. She turned away from Jonathan. He wasn't looking at her, but she still didn't want him to see her weeping. It would not be dignified. Her father would not approve. *Oh Father, why did I not listen to you?*

Dr. Mallory carried a steaming cup of coffee across the medical bay over to Ambassador Lucas Cale. Lucas gently rose to a seated position and accepted the mug with both hands. He looked much better. More color had come to his cheeks and he acted more like himself.

"Funny thing," Dr. Mallory said, fetching a mug for himself. "I never would have guessed you were an invalid only forty-eight hours ago if I hadn't seen it myself."

"My roommates work quickly. They do have their limitations, but they perform excellent work. I have perfect vision again—I haven't had perfect vision since I was in my twenties."

Dr. Mallory pulled up a chair next to his bed. "So, Lucas, what do your roommates get in return for fixing you up?"

"A place to live."

"A permanent place to live?"

Lucas wrinkled his brow. "Jacob, they have nowhere else to go. When their last body degraded beyond repair, they had to abandon ship, so to speak. I guess you could call them refugees."

"So will these refugees be looking for a new body anytime soon?"

Lucas took a sip of his mug. "Well, I hope not."

"You like their company all that much?"

Lucas chuckled. "It's not that simple, Jacob. My brain connections— or whatever they're called—were severely damaged by that poison. My roommates manually fulfill those functions that no longer work on their own."

"You're saying you're dependent upon them?"

"As dependent as medication or a prosthetic, I suppose."

Dr. Mallory sighed in exasperation.

How could he have let this happen to Lucas? His best friend now could not live without alien micro-organisms inside him. At least he wasn't permanently comatose, or dead. That much he could be thankful for. That much was worth celebrating. Despite his shortcoming in helping his friend, it would have to be enough that his friend was alive.

"I'm sorry this had to happen to you."

Lucas glanced up with a smile. "Now don't you go trying to pity my situation. I have far more advantages with this arrangement than I ever did on my own."

"What do you mean, advantages?"

"Well, for example, they are teaching me how to read minds."

"You can read minds?"

"Well," Lucas said, hesitating. "No, *I* can't read minds, but my roommates can. So, I guess you could say that *we* can read minds."

Dr. Mallory glanced at him in suspicion. "Lucas, what number am I thinking of?"

"I'm not very good at it yet."

"But still, what number am I thinking of?"

He stared at him a moment before smiling. "H is hardly a number, Jacob."

Isabeau entered the med bay with Cyran tailing along. It was nice to see Isabeau getting some time with her brother. Dr. Mallory didn't know the specifics, but he knew she wasn't normally allowed to see her brother. The Bravs, the Gamms, and the Abes were never allowed to mingle. It was one of the Draconians' strictest rules concerning humans. And what made even less sense was that the Draconians had divided many families from Earth. They had randomly assigned them between the three space stations. That was the story of Isabeau's family.

Most would argue there was no rhyme or reason to it. But if science and medicine had taught Dr. Mallory anything, there was a systematic reason for it. His profession had instructed him to look for the patterns within the chaos. If he had to guess, the Draconians were searching for something.

Dr. Mallory greeted each of them. "Commander. Ambassador."

"We came immediately when we heard the news," Isabeau replied.

Cyran walked up to Lucas. "Ambassador Cale, I am glad to see you are feeling better."

Lucas set down his steaming mug. "Yes, Ambassador Alexi. To answer your unspoken question, the Voonsu are very much alive inside me."

"Can I speak with them?"

"They share my eyes and ears," he replied. "Ask what you will."

Cyran swallowed. "I am very sorry, Vincent," he said with a hint of remorse in his voice. "I had no idea the Scorpii would discover you."

A white glow flashed in Lucas's eyes. Isabeau and Dr. Mallory each took a startled step back. Cyran waved a hand toward them. "It's all right, it's just something they do."

Lucas's voice sounded like a multitude of voices speaking in unison. "The Vincent was irreparably damaged. We are the Cale now."

This was not Lucas. This was something foreign. The alien microorganisms were speaking through him. A chill went up Dr.

Mallory's spine. *It would seem Lucas's roommates have chosen a name for themselves,* Dr. Mallory thought.

Cale continued. "No apologies necessary; we accepted the risk."

Cyran gave a short grateful nod. "I appreciate that. And I hope your...*new accommodations* are adequate?"

"Lucas accepted our request. In return, the Cale has restored the Lucas vessel to full functionality."

"Colonel Terynn will be delighted to have both of you."

Cale's eyelids drooped as if in fatigue. Then he blinked and took a deep breath. He smiled, and it was Lucas's smile. "That reminds me," Lucas said in his normal voice. "Where is Jonathan? I should like to speak with him."

"He is away at a special senate hearing," Isabeau explained. "I'll let you know when he returns."

"I hope he returns before the Senate convenes; we have a lot to discuss."

Chapter 15

NEW ADJUSTMENTS

Matt paced the length of the room in his office. The trip back from the *Brah'Kerov* was not pleasant. The infuriating Colonel's words kept circling his mind. Why did the man have to be such an ingrate? He had offered a way to work together toward a mutual goal. But no, the lousy Gamm had thrown it back in his face.

Ross stood apprehensive by the door. "And you're sure he understood you?"

"Yes. Ross," Matt said in almost a shout. "Colonel Self-Righteous was all too clear in his condemnation." He paused a moment, reflecting on Jonathan's words: If I have to become evil in order to destroy evil, who has really won? "His zealotry will not allow him to relent in his opposition to the Scorpii."

Ross hung his head. "I had hoped..."

"Your hope became my fool's errand," Matt snapped.

It wasn't entirely Ross's fault. The man was, after all, an incurable optimist. He wanted to work alongside the most decorated military leader Earth had produced. And it was a shame Jonathan had refused to cooperate. But that was probably where the mistake was made. Jonathan was a man of the military; he knew conflict. What more could be expected from him? All the military was good for was direct conflict. They would never understand how to fight with intrigue and subterfuge.

"I can understand your disappointment, Ross. I, too, was looking forward to the possibility."

Ross let out a deep breath. "I suppose we have no choice then?"

Matt halted, looking at Ross. "It is unfortunate."

Ross looked up with sullen eyes. "I will inform Ir'Jad to begin phase two."

Matt walked up, placing a consoling hand on his shoulder. "It is for the best. These sacrifices will not go unnoticed. Soon this ridiculous existence will change, and I will be with my daughter. And for you, Ross," he said looking over the room as if motioning to the entire space station, "this will all be but a bad dream."

Ross drew in a deep breath, and with it, courage. He nodded and left the room. Matt was left to himself. The tidy office was not much to look at, but it was home. A home he despised. It had enough comforts to exist, but it would never house the laughter of children. Nor would merry music ever echo down the corridors. *A home indeed,* he thought. *More like a prison.*

Matt sat down at his desk and pulled out his daughter's picture from the drawer. He traced the lines of her face. Soon. They would be together soon. His seven-year plan was coming to fruition. The last five had gone well; he was now second in command of *Able Station* with a means to become the sole commander of it. The next steps were the most tricky. Careful planning was crucial, and cunning allies were mandatory.

"I'm sorry, Eva," he said to the picture. "I could have shaved off a year of my planning had a Gamm actually been reasonable. I was silly to think I could trust a Gamm. But in a short while, I won't have to worry about him any longer."

Jonathan stepped through the docking port hatch onto *Gamma Station*. His first order of business would be to shower and change. The filth of the Arkalan ship had gotten on his nerves. He marched toward the other end of the bay before stopping short. His old habits hadn't entirely stolen his wits; thoughts of Ellyra entered his mind. He offered her his hand and assisted her through the docking port hatch.

Married, he thought. *How could I be married?* This was all a terrible mistake. A mistake that he had brought on—begged her, even. He needed her access to the Chantell—really needed it. Well, now he had it...along with a whole lot more. How was he going to manage this? He already had plenty of responsibilities on the space station. How was he to factor in a spouse on top of that? So many adjustments to consider and each of them demanded his attention. It was maddening.

He walked with her across the docking bay toward the exit. He still had her hand in his. Should he let go? Would that send the wrong message if he did? Speaking of which, that was yet another worry he didn't need. The awkward tension that wedged itself between them was something else to figure out. But that would have to wait, and, thankfully, it *could* wait. For better or worse, she was no longer going to be leaving in a few days. That, at least, was something to be grateful for. At least he had more time with Ellyra.

Isabeau approached with a confused look on her face. *"You* were on that Arkalan ship?"

"T'Kal was right. The political landscape is dramatically changing."

"What happened?"

"Let's just say that Jaimess is on the warpath, and I think I just made things worse."

Isabeau pursed her lips and glanced at Ellyra. "Where is your crew?"

Ellyra gave a hesitant curtsy. "They were ordered to leave without us."

"Long story," Jonathan said. "I'll give you a full brief once I wrap my head around it. In the meantime, is your brother still on the station?"

"Yes. He's scheduled to leave after the funeral."

The funeral. He had forgotten Lt. Allen's funeral was today. It had been postponed due to the senate hearing. What he really needed was for time to stop moving forward until he could catch his breath.

"That's right, the funeral."

Ellyra turned to him. "The pilot who died fighting the Scorpii?"

He nodded, "Lieutenant Allen." He turned back to Isabeau. "Izzy, I need Cyran to send a message to T'Kal. We need another meeting, and soon."

"Aye, sir." She looked once more at the docking port hatch that was now shut. "Where's Lt. Colonel Jagger?"

That's right, he had been so consumed with his own plight that he had forgotten about Fox. It was yet another new headache he needed time to sort out. And he needed to get into some clean clothes before he felt well enough to explain everything.

"All in good time, Commander," was all he could think to say.

Jonathan led Ellyra from the docking bay and down the hall. They walked in silence, passing other people but never saying a word. They stopped in front of her quarters.

He cleared his throat. "I imagine you'll want to change clothes after that trip."

She nodded. "Yes indeed, that would be refreshing."

She stood there as if waiting for something. Was she waiting for him to open the door? Or was she waiting for him to talk? They needed to talk but he couldn't, not yet. His emotions were still swimming inside his head. Only time would sort them out into manageable pieces. Time which he would have to spend alone. Only then would he be able to talk about them.

Jonathan pushed the button to open her door. It slid up and the light turned on. Ellyra stepped inside but turned back to Jonathan, her gloved hand on the door frame. "Colonel Jonathan—might I be permitted to address you by your first name?"

"I'd like that."

"Jonathan, you have returned from the peril of Draconia to your home and your command. However, it would appear that I have not been so fortunate."

He glanced down. "Yeah, I'm very sorry about that."

"It has left me pondering what is to become of me now that I am here. You had told me that you needed me. And seeing as I have neither starship nor title to command, I must ask if that still holds true."

He hadn't thought of it that way. Her diminished status might hinder forging a useful relationship with the Bugs. But that couldn't be helped. Whatever influence she had would have to do. In that way, he still needed her very much. The entire conspiracy was at risk without her.

He looked into her eyes. "I *do* need you. And I hope you can forgive me for what happened to your ship and crew. Oh goodness, and your family..." A deep breath invaded his lungs. He hadn't even considered that she was now in the same position; she could no longer visit her homeworld. But much worse, she could not see her family. She was now living the full experience of what it was to be an Earthian under Draconian rule. He looked into her eyes. "Why?"

Her eyes watered, her hair darkening into a beautiful violet. "You said you needed me."

He could only blame himself. The mistake was his, the fault was his, yet the consequences were hers. How long would she have to pay the price for his stupidity? The only way to make this right again would be to successfully revolt against the Draconians. The only way to end her strife was to double down on the commitment to liberate themselves from Draconia. He owed it to Ellyra.

"I promise you; I'll fix this."

Her hair color darkened into a brown. He really needed to learn what the colors meant. He took a breath and tapped his leg with the fingers at his side, having run out of things to say.

"I...I'll go and change too." He turned to leave.

"Jonathan?"

He turned back.

"Where shall I report once I have refreshed my attire?"

"Do you remember where Command and Control is?"

She nodded. "I believe I remember the way."

"Good. You'll find me there."

He excused himself and headed back to his quarters. He couldn't pay attention to where he was going; his mind was running in circles. Habit led him to his quarters. The funeral wasn't for a few hours so he took his time showering and dressing. It felt good to get all traces of the Arkalan muck off. As he fastened the cufflinks to his uniform sleeve, he paused. The mirror reflected the image of his hand with his academy signet ring. He had given the ring to Ellyra five years ago as a promise to reunite. Had it really been only a few days ago that she was able to return it?

His thoughts turned to Ellyra. Married. It was like a daydream; something on his distant horizon had suddenly become reality. It couldn't be all that bad, could it? After all, Rana is no longer around to prevent them from touching in public. Did this mean he could now have private conversations with her? It had to. After all, they were now husband and wife.

Wife. How foreign that word sounded. A wife had always been what other people had, never what he had. How quickly things had changed. He needed to have a frank and open conversation with Ellyra, but later, after the hubbub of the funeral was over.

Jonathan took one final glance at himself in the mirror. *Married.* He left his quarters and made his way up to Command and Control. He entered the doorless room and strolled up to Isabeau. She had been overseeing the resupply of the battlecruiser *Saratoga*. Additionally, she was finalizing the funeral arrangements for Lt. Allen. The woman was a born multitasker.

"Mind if I add something else to your plate?"

She looked up. "Sure, what can I do for you?"

"Can you take a walk with me? I'm ready to debrief."

Chapter 16

COMMON LAW

F ox sat in a fancy chair in the room the Euroo called the Center of Workmanship—whatever that meant. But at least the chair was comfortable, more comfortable than any Earth ship he had traveled on. The senate hearing hadn't quite gone as planned. At least the Euroo seemed to be taking things well. Their hair color wasn't black and Isabel had mentioned that black was bad. So, on all counts, things were going as well as they could under the circumstances.

Ellyra's crew didn't say much on their trip back to Eurosia. Diahlus didn't say more than ten words and Xer didn't say any. What was there to say? The Colonel and the Euroo captain had eloped on the spur of the moment and sailed off into the sunset. As far as elopements go, that was a pretty stellar send-off.

Fox wasn't that lucky. Since he was now stuck with the Euroo for a while, the task of answering for his commander's actions now fell to him. It wasn't the brightest thing to look forward to. But, it wasn't wholly bad either. With the elaborate language the Euroo spoke, it was like living in one of Shakespeare's plays. And if he was stranded, doomed to early retirement, there was no better place than in a Shakespeare play.

A woman in a green gown and elbow-high gloves walked over to Diahlus. "Brigadain, the coordinates are upon us."

Diahlus glanced up. "On stage, please."

"As you wish."

A gold-colored metal ring in the center of the floor lit up. It projected a holographic image of the surrounding space and their ship, the *Calmao*. It traveled through the fascinating hyperspace tunnel of blue streaking light. It was as if the starship was on stage, with the stage lights lit all around. Shakespeare was right; all the world *was* a stage. And, it seemed, so was hyperspace.

"Astrogator, you may exit hyperspace," Diahlus said.

"As you wish, Brigadain."

A bright white light appeared at the end of the hyperspace tunnel. The *Calmao* passed through it, plunging back into truespace like an actor stepping through the curtains. The ship slowed to a stop as the hyperdrive engines revved down.

A pink and orange planet lay before them. Two moons and a space station slowly circled in orbit. Fox had never seen Eurosia before; not many humans ever could. Somehow the Colonel was lucky enough to have had a chance to visit. And now, fate had determined it was Fox's turn. The *Calmao* moved closer, weaving through the planet's smaller ship traffic.

Fox gripped his armrests as they broke through the fluffy clouds and descended into the blue valley. Tall snow-capped mountain peaks poked up through the blue foliage. The amber sunlight spotlighted a large city of tall colorful glass buildings. The colors of the buildings looked coordinated as if the entire city was a painting. They whizzed through the air over the buildings, heading for the largest structure.

Three tall spires rose into the air surrounding a large, ornamented dome. It looked like a palace, decorated with pennants, draping flags, and heraldic sculptures. Immaculate lawns and gardens surrounded the palace along with hedges, fountains, and trees. An awkward feeling quietly crept into the pit of his stomach. He had crossed the threshold into a very high society.

The starship slowed and hovered directly over the large dome of the palace. Small lights began flashing on the dome as it spiraled open, revealing a landing bay inside. The ship drifted down with the grace of a leaf through the air. When it touched down, Fox was escorted out by Arkamenos. Diahlus, Xer, and Rana followed behind. Fox's boots clanked on the metal ramp as he descended. Small gusts of wind carried the familiar scent of lilacs. The rumor must be true; the Euroo had transplanted some Earth flowers.

The great domed roof overhead spiraled closed as he reached the bottom of the ramp. Servants dressed in fancy silk and linen clothes walked over to the landed starship. They began inspections and refueling. Even the most menial of servants seemed to be dressed far fancier than he was. Several feet in front of him, large ornate double doors parted. Four fancy-dressed guards with white uniforms and brass buttons entered the bay. Their scarlet capes fluttered in the slight breeze as they walked. Their shiny gold helmets sparkled and their sabers swayed at their side.

Xer turned to Fox. "Those are the House Guard. Nine-tenths of what they do is ceremonial. So, I implore you to resign yourself to whatever instructions they give you."

"I'll try my best to cooperate."

The House Guards stopped in formation in front of them. One bowed and addressed Diahlus. "Brigadain Diahlus, Lord Areo asks that you report directly to him."

"As he wishes," Diahlus replied.

The guard turned to Xer. "Brigadain Xer, Lord Areo wished the prisoner to be brought to him in irons."

Xer huffed. "Good gracious, man. Surely such measures are neither warranted nor requisite."

"Such judgments, Brigadain, belong to his grace."

Xer turned back to Fox. "I'm sorry."

153

A second guard stepped forward and pulled out two shiny brass rings. They looked like thin bracelets. He slipped them over Fox's wrists and pressed a button on his wristband. The bracelets magnetized together like handcuffs.

"Hey, hey. Pretty spiffy," Fox said in assessment.

The guard glared at him as if he had spoken a foreign language.

"It's an Earthian compliment," Xer explained.

The guards turned around in formation and ushered Fox, Xer, and Diahlus out of the landing bay. They walked down a grand hallway lined with white walls and a vaulted ceiling. Paintings of distinguished individuals and ornamental furniture lined the hall. Their boots each clattered against the polished white marble floor. The hallway ended at another set of double doors. Two of the guards pushed the doors open, allowing everyone else to step through.

They entered a smaller room with a high ceiling and lavish furniture. An aging white-haired man in a red and white five-piece suit with tails stood by the mantle with a glass in his hand. A white cape with red lining hung around his shirt collar, reaching the back of his knees. A gold medallion hung at his neck. A white-haired woman about the same age sat close by on a plush couch. Her glittering jewelry bounced light across the walls. Her red gown shimmered as she crossed her legs.

"Brigadains Diahlus and Xer," the guard announced.

The man set his glass down on the mantle and waved an impatient hand to the guards. "Leave us."

The guards each bowed and left.

Diahlus cleared his throat. "Lord Areo, may I present Lt. Colonel Fox Jagger of the Earthian outpost *Gamma Station*."

Lord Areo glared at Fox. "A pleasure," he said with an air of disdain. He turned to the woman seated beside him. "I present to you the Lady Elony of the House of El'Allel."

Fox gave a deep bow with a smile. He wasn't sure if he should say anything but it seemed fitting to say hello. "A pleasure, my lady."

"Why thank you," Lady Elony said. She turned to Areo. "Well, well, Lord Areo. It seems we have been taken as fools. There is no barbarian present."

"It would seem the reports have been somewhat exaggerated," Areo admitted. He pulled out a small device from his waistcoat pocket and pressed a button. Fox's bracelets de-magnetized, allowing him to freely move his arms.

Lord Areo stuffed the device back into his waistcoat pocket. "You will, of course, pardon the precautions. One cannot be certain of the disposition of aliens."

Fox smiled wide. "Absolutely, your grace. Were I in your shoes, I would have done the same."

"Won't you have a seat," Lord Areo offered, motioning to a chair.

Fox smiled and sat in a plush chair with ornamented wooden armrests.

Lord Areo walked up to Diahlus. "The reports, then, are accurate?"

Diahlus glanced to the floor. "A thousand apologies, my lord. The reports are true."

Lord Areo tensed his jaw and balled his hands into fists. His hair color blackened for a split second and then returned to white. He glanced over to Xer. "And is there any reason I should stay my hand from dismissing you this very instant?"

"Forgive me, my lord. When you granted me this commission, your very instructions were to uphold loyalty above all. Loyalty first to the House of El'Allel, and secondly to whomever should command me. When your daughter beseeched me this task, I did, in truth, object. Her very station alone should never be subject to such a disgrace."

"Why, then, did you comply?"

Xer took a breath, glancing down. "Although I have every right to claim I was acting under the orders of my superior, it would not be wholly accurate." He looked back into Lord Areo's sapphire within blue eyes. "When I looked into your daughter's eyes, I saw, almost as it were, an ocean of hope. Before such a scene my resolve crumbled."

Lord Areo took in a deep breath and let it out along with all his tension. "Your candor does you credit, Xer." He placed a hand on Xer's shoulder. "Can I trust that you did not grant any titles in the contract?"

"Indeed not, my lord. The Earthian had no such standing."

Lord Areo nodded. "You may go, Xer."

He bowed and left.

Lord Areo turned to Diahlus. "And what have you to say?"

"My humblest apologies, Lord Areo. I must admit the fault on my part; I did not see this conclusion approach."

Lord Areo waved a dismissive hand. "My friend, unless you can read tea leaves, interpret the stars, or read the mind of a woman, you were destined to be blindsided. To my chagrin, I have bequeathed to her my disposition and resolve."

"Lord Areo," Lady Elony said. "You are neglecting your guest."

"Quite right, Lady Elony, quite right." Lord Areo motioned for Diahlus to follow and sat in a chair across from Fox. "You will, of course, forgive my neglect. I can assure you I am beside myself."

Diahlus sat next to Lord Areo. Fox wasn't sure he wanted to be back in the conversational spotlight. For one thing, his vocabulary was rusty and the Euroo had trouble understanding human expressions. Actually, *most* aliens had trouble with human expressions. On the other hand, he hadn't been on the stage since before his military career and this was just like acting. The only possible pitfall was the culture. This wasn't ancient England back on Earth, though there were similarities. He would have to be careful what he chose to say.

"You are too generous, my lord. I do believe it is I, on behalf of my commander, who should be apologizing."

"Your civility is a credit to your race," Lord Areo said, leaning back and crossing his legs. "But in this instance, it would be best if you did not attempt to apologize on his behalf. The damage he has inflicted upon this great house is extensive."

"How extensive?"

Lord Areo motioned to the heraldic seal hanging over the mantle. The scarlet and royal blue along with the symbols matched the large flags outside the palace. "This great house has borne the name of El'Allel for over two hundred years. And without an heir from my line, the Cora'Del name will adorn this great hall instead. Having been unsuccessful in producing an heir myself, I turned my attention to my daughter's suitors. If a match could have been made with a man descending from the right line, I could have acquired an heir."

Fox sheepishly dipped his head. *Yeah*, he thought, *I can see how the Colonel may have messed that all up.* "I stand corrected, Your Grace. To think it could—" Fox blinked and took a closer look at the large heraldic seal on the wall. One of the symbols looked like a shiny black squid. Not just any squid, this one looked rigid and strangely proportioned. It reminded him of the Skorath ship.

"I beg your pardon," Lord Areo said.

Fox rose from his chair and strolled over to the mantle; his face looking perplexed. "This symbol...it's important, isn't it?"

"That, my dear Lieutenant Colonel, is Vera," Lady Elony answered. "She is the patron goddess of space travel."

"Part of the Euroo mythology," Lord Areo added.

Fox's heart thumped loudly and his breathing shallowed. A surge of excitement coursed through his body. He looked back at Lord Areo. "Your lordship, our two worlds may not be so distant after all." He pointed to the symbol again. "I'm betting the myths about Vera say she only comes about every ten years. And she probably is known for a prophecy about frightening the star of Draconia."

Lord Areo's lips parted but he made no reply. Amazement plastered his face.

Lady Elony rose to her feet. "How is it possible that an outsider could know so much?"

Chapter 17

FORGOTTEN

Ellyra spent more time than usual looking for a dress. All her dresses fastened up in the back. That wasn't a problem with a personal Eltashee to help in getting dressed. But now that she was alone, she hunted for a dress that she could easily put on by herself. One after another, she dismissed her gowns. They looked spectacular on her, and they fit so well, but each one was too difficult to put on by herself. It was a symbol of wealth and prestige to need an assistant to get dressed. But now that she was alone, she would have to try anyway. After an hour of frustration, she tossed yet another gown to the floor.

Maybe I could borrow one of Rana's dresses, she wondered. They wore a similar dress size and hers all fastened in front. Though, Rana was a bit skinnier. She crossed the divider into Rana's bedroom and looked in her closet. She selected the largest size and put it on. It wasn't a perfect fit, but it would do. She was making far more concessions for Jonathan than she had anticipated. Even day-to-day living had been forever changed. Foolish decisions made reality harsh. At least her hairstyle was already in place and didn't need to be altered.

She walked over to the door and stopped short of exiting. What lay in store for her on the other side? She no longer had a ship to command—did she still hold the rank of Sune? And what was her social status now? She was still Eurosian by blood, but now she was also Earthian by marriage. But where would that leave her with her father? She would always be his daughter, but would he look on her with any degree of favor anymore? She had ruined his last chance to produce an heir to the family name. She had betrayed his hopes for her.

She closed her eyes and leaned her head against the smooth steel door. She smelled the faint odor of motor lubrication. Such a crude and barbaric place she now had to call home. If Jonathan needed her, really needed her, she could make it in this new life of hers. As long as she had some purpose to hold onto, something to look forward to, she could do this. Jonathan had promised that he needed her. She straightened up her posture, took in a deep breath, and opened the door.

She walked down the hallway, back the way Jonathan had escorted her. At least it looked like the way she had come. *Gamma Station* did not have any decorations or furnishings. There were no tapestries, paintings, or furniture to use as landmarks to navigate by. At least there were markings on some of the walls. The wall before her read, 03 Sierra. But what did that mean?

She needed to speak with Jonathan again, but how could she? She hadn't been instructed on how to use the communication systems on the space station. There wasn't a friendly face or a familiar voice around. Amidst all the people walking around this large space station, she felt truly alone.

A young Earthian woman dressed in a military uniform walked up to Ellyra. The young woman wore her hair in a braided ponytail. "Is everything all right ma'am?" she asked. "You look like you could use some assistance."

Ellyra smiled, a feeling of relief washing over her. "Indeed, I do. I am trying—"

The young woman abruptly took a step back.

"Is something the matter?"

"Your hair changed colors, ma'am."

Ellyra smiled again. "Yes, I am Eurosian; my hair will do that from time to time."

"Well, I'm pleased to meet you, I'm Seaman Katheryn Vinnece."

Ellyra gave her the customary hug. "I can assure you; the pleasure is all mine. I am called Sune Ellyra of the House of El'Allel. I came aboard visiting Colonel Jonathan."

"Do you mean Colonel Terynn?"

Of course. She had forgotten that the Earthians addressed each other by their surnames. "Yes, indeed. That is whom I mean."

"Do you have any identification?"

"Indeed not, I am a visiting dignitary."

The statement was partly true at least. She *had* been visiting, though it *now* appeared this was to be her permanent residence. But as far as she knew, she was still a dignitary. Time would tell if that had changed.

Katheryn's eyes lit up. "Oh, you must be the visiting starship captain. The one that was with Colonel Terynn the other day in Command and Control."

She nodded. "The very same. Do you suppose you could direct me back to that room?"

"Absolutely, ma'am."

Katheryn escorted Ellyra down a different hallway and into a lift tube. They traveled up several decks before the lift tube stopped and let them off. Katheryn led her down a few more hallways and into the doorless Command and Control room. It looked just as she remembered it. The tall ceiling, the balcony, and the trench in front. Except, she didn't remember the gentleman sitting at the center console. The short blond-haired man glanced up at Ellyra.

"This area is restricted to military personnel. May I help you?"

Katheryn walked up to the man. "Begging your pardon, sir. This is the Euroo captain that is visiting Colonel Terynn.

He eyed Ellyra with suspicion before giving Katheryn a matter-of-fact response. "Well, if she is looking for the Colonel, he left with Commander Alexi twenty minutes ago."

"Any idea when he will return?"

He shook his head. "Negative. But he will be officiating at the funeral service in a quarter of an hour."

Katheryn nodded. "Thank you, Commander."

She returned to Ellyra's side. "Looks like the Colonel isn't here. But if you'd like I can take you to where the funeral service is being held?"

"He instructed me to meet him here," Ellyra protested.

"I'm sorry about that, ma'am. You can either wait for him here or you can come with me."

Ellyra sighed. This wasn't going very well. Her first meeting with her husband and already his lack of interest was apparent. Had he forgotten about her? Never in her life had she ever been forgotten. Dignity and recognition came without question to the daughter of a great lord. Now that she was the wife of an Earthian military man, she might have to get used to being forgotten.

But that couldn't be right, could it? He had counted the days they had been apart. Could a man such as that forget about her? But then, how else could she explain it? He had arranged to rendezvous in this room and yet he was not here. There was one other possible explanation. A chill went down her spine and her heart sank. Did he feel betrayed? Did he want to distance himself from her?

Could he think she had tricked him into the union? How could he possibly think that? After evaluating her ability to be a mother and then pleading for any way to remain with her. If any trickery were in play, it was not on her end. She had lost everything dear to her, including the promise of happiness with Jonathan. If only she had known beforehand how many concessions she would be required to make. If only she could rewind time and make a different choice.

161

She felt the tingling of her hair changing colors. No, this was not the time to allow her emotions to be put on display. Her father would never approve. *Oh, Father,* she thought. *What I would give to feel your embrace, even to hear you tell me you told me so.*

Ellyra tensed up in concentration, keeping her hair color a formal white. She looked at Katheryn. "It would appear I was not apprised of the changes. I would gladly accept your assistance down to the funeral service."

Katheryn smiled. "Right this way, ma'am."

She led Ellyra back down the hallway and into a lift tube. The lift tube descended one deck before halting and opening. A man in elegant clothes entered the lift tube. He was very different from the military men; he didn't wear a uniform. He wore a five-piece suit with a flourish of silk. It was much too ornate for her taste; it looked like it came from a previous generation. It was strangely familiar, however. Her heart thumped as she realized whom it reminded her of. It was the style that her father dressed in.

Katheryn straightened her posture in an instant. That much meant this gentleman held a high rank or position.

The man smiled at Katheryn. "At ease, Katheryn. There's no one around but us."

"Thank you, sir."

Then, he glanced over at Ellyra. There was something in his smile that looked familiar somehow. Ellyra gave a graceful curtsy. "Begging your pardon, sir, but I have reason to believe we have met once before."

The man smiled again. "Oh? Then allow me to discover your identity." He sized her up with a swift glance before chuckling. "Well, well, my dear. Your appearance is quite a contradiction." He motioned toward the lace in her hair. "Your rank insignia is of a Sune, which is an aristocratic commission. Yet, your dress would suggest otherwise."

Ellyra blushed, her hair tingling as it transitioned to an embarrassed burgundy. It was always difficult to stop it from changing into burgundy. But the man was right, wearing Rana's dress did suggest a lower station.

The man continued. "However, I may yet discover you, my dear. You wear the embroidered seal of House El'Allel—a house that I am very familiar with. And Lord Areo has a daughter who would have completed the Academy by now. So, I'd wager I am in the presence of the lovely Lady Ellyra."

She beamed. "Bravo, correct on every count. Though I do feel I am at a disadvantage."

"Oh, not so," he replied. "My face is familiar to you, and I have just disclosed that I know your father. And with so very few Earthians allowed to travel, that should narrow down the possibilities of my identity quite considerably."

Ellyra's eyes lit up. "Why, you must be Ambassador Lucas Cale!"

"Bravo, my dear."

"Now I remember you," she admitted. "At my last birthday party, my father introduced me to you. I remember thinking you were always cross because your hair was always black."

Lucas chuckled again. "One of the many downsides to being human. Age, at least, has decided to remedy that with plenty of gray hair coming on."

Ellyra laughed. "So, now you shall be troubled, as well."

Lucas chuckled, patting her hand.

"Forgive me," Ellyra said. "But it was my understanding that you were injured."

"Quite right, quite right. But as the Eurosian philosopher once said; Call me tempestuous, brash or folly, but never canst thou call me resigned. Tumults I defy, failures I challenge, and death I deride."

Ellyra politely clapped. "Bravo, Ambassador. You have read Kalmeedes."

He smiled brightly. "I have never read a more stubbornly optimistic man. It carried me through some of my most difficult negotiations on Eurosia."

"Are you retired now?" she asked.

He shook his head. "Indeed not, my dear. I serve as the political counsel to Colonel Jonathan Terynn in the Senate. I guess you could say I'm his 90 in such matters."

His 90. How could Jonathan need her if he already had a 90? Maybe Jonathan only needed her until Lucas was well again. Had her usefulness just come to an end? Her heart sank and her lungs refused to take a breath. Had she now lost everything? She could not return to her homeworld and she was no longer needed here. Her family and friends were lightyears away, and Jonathan had forgotten about her. Fresh moisture gathered in her eyes and her hair tingled.

The feeling of simply being in the way tugged at her heart. She stiffened her jaw and forced the tears back. She had to concentrate on keeping her hair color from muddying. There wasn't enough resolve left inside her to keep both her tears and hair at bay. One of them would break loose and betray her feelings. Her grieving could not remain locked up. Her hair dulled into a heartbroken brown.

Lucas's smile faded. "Is something the matter, my dear?"

She could not explain, not right now. If she allowed her emotions any leeway, they would break through her barricade and stream down her face. Such a public display could never be dignified. Her father would not approve. For now, she needed to only tell enough of the truth to dismiss his question.

She offered a weak smile. "I perceive that as of late I could benefit from Kalmeedes."

"Going down, sir?" Katheryn asked.

Lucas glanced over at her with a sheepish grin. "My apologies, Katheryn. Yes, I'm heading to the funeral service."

She nodded and pressed a button for the lift tube to proceed.

Lucas turned back to Ellyra. "Tell me, my dear, what brings you to *Gamma Station?*"

She glanced down. How much could she tell him? Her heavy heart yearned to confide in him. His dress, his mannerisms, and even his laugh reminded her of her father. She could always confide in her father. Could she confide in Ambassador Cale? Jonathan hadn't openly talked about their marriage yet. Perhaps he didn't want it public. And that was understandable. A common-law marriage was always looked down on, at least on Eurosia. It couldn't be the same here, could it?

Here, things were supposed to be different. The Earthians had always appeared so carefree and open. They had always worn so very few of the chains of propriety. Why had things changed now? Had their carefree nature been only an illusion? Had all the baggage of society really been lying under the surface all along? It was perhaps best that she say nothing of the marriage. At least until she could confirm with Jonathan how he wished to handle it.

She met his gaze and gave a polite smile. "I am visiting Colonel Jonathan."

"Splendid. Will you be with us long?"

She took a breath. "I can assure you I do not have any plans to leave as of yet."

The lift tube came to a stop and the doors parted. Everyone exited.

"Excellent news," Lucas said. "Then you must visit me and tell me all about the current events on Eurosia. I have dearly missed it since being reassigned."

She smiled, walking alongside Lucas down the hallway. "I would be delighted to arrange it." She glanced up and froze in place.

Jonathan and Isabeau approached from the other end of the hallway, still conversing. The anguished throbbing of Ellyra's heart tugged at her. Unwanted. Alone. Unnecessary. Forgotten. She fought against the crushing weight on her heart, straining to take each breath. *Whatever my station now is,* she thought, *I shall carry the dignity of House El'Allel.*

Chapter 18

THE FUNERAL

J onathan strolled down one of the many hallways of *Gamma Station* with Isabeau at his side. It was a relief to finally unload all his worries onto a listening ear. The irony was that usually, it was Isabeau who needed to talk and Jonathan who did the listening. It was a fitting turn of events. He had told her all about the senate hearing and his brash request of Ellyra. And somehow, he felt lighter. Sharing his burden had lightened it.

"So...needless to say, until I can figure out a way to get Fox back, I'll need you to cover his duties."

"I had a feeling that was coming."

A slight chuckle escaped, further lightening his mood.

"Well, on the bright side," Isabeau said. "You won't have to worry about all those courtship customs and restrictions."

Jonathan chuckled in exasperation. "True. I won't be going to battle with Rana anymore."

Isabeau gauged his facial expression. "Looks like that's a downside."

Blood rushed to his cheeks. "Okay, okay. I'll admit, I enjoyed the challenge."

"Reveled in, would be more accurate."

He smiled. "Izzy, you've got all the confession out of me that you're ever going to get."

She smiled in return. "How is your wife handling all this?"

Jonathan's stomach tightened and he drew in a large breath. Wife. It still sounded so foreign. "Well, I think she's taking it rather well. I'll ask her once we have a chance to talk."

Isabeau stopped in her tracks, staring at him in disbelief. "You haven't spoken with her?"

Jonathan halted and gave her a confused look. "Well...on the way back from the *Brah'Kerov* I told her I'd find a way to fix all this."

She shot him a disapproving glance. "That's not *talking.*"

They continued walking.

"I know, I know," he admitted. "Things have been happening so fast...I feel like I'm swimming in problems and it's all I can do just to keep my head above water."

Isabeau bit down on her lower lip. He knew that sign. She was hesitant to tell him something. It was her way of resisting the urge to tell him he was wrong. But right now, he couldn't afford to be wrong. There was too little time to get their plan in motion.

He sighed. "Okay, Izzy. What is it?"

"Don't wait to talk with her."

"I've got plenty of time for that. She doesn't have to leave now."

She shook her head. "Take it from a woman, Jonathan. She will need to talk. Don't put it off."

He hung his head in resignation. He didn't know as much about women as he needed to. And besides that, Izzy had almost always been right about people. Her love of languages extended into the arena of unspoken words. Following her advice had often saved him from catastrophe.

"Okay, I'll speak with her after the funeral service."

"Speaking of which, I spoke with Cyran."

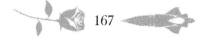

167

Jonathan looked at her with interest. "Did he arrange another meeting?"

She nodded. "T'Kal agreed to delay his departure. I've scheduled it for after the funeral."

"I guess I'll have to talk with Ellyra after that."

"Maybe you can bring her?"

He stopped walking and faced her, lowering his voice. "The matters we discuss in those private meetings could land an extermination order on us and the Greys. Bringing a brand-new face without prior discussion would be a breach of trust. T'Kal is risking the lives of all his people every time we meet. This will have to be done properly."

She glanced down. "You're right."

Something caught Jonathan's attention from the corner of his eye. Lucas approached with Seaman Vinnece and Ellyra in tow. His heart fluttered a moment at the sight of Ellyra. She had changed into a blue gown that shimmered in the light as she walked. Her muddy-brown locks of hair swayed with each step.

He whispered to Isabeau. "Izzy, what does brown mean?"

"Pardon, sir?"

"Euroo hair colors. What does brown mean?"

"Sadness or remorse," she explained as the three walked up to them.

"Jonathan, I heard you had returned," Lucas said, stealing his attention.

He took a breath before replying. "Ambassador Cale. Yes, just barely." He glanced over to Seaman Vinnece. "Thank you, Seaman. I'll take it from here."

She nodded and walked on past.

Turning his attention back to Lucas, he motioned toward Isabeau. "Commander Alexi informed me you are back from the dead, so to speak. Having you back at my side is a huge relief."

Lucas smirked. "Still so formal. Why don't you ever call me Lucas?"

Jonathan smirked. "You're a great man, Ambassador. I've never really considered myself to be your equal."

Lucas gave a dismissive huff. "So says the hero of Mesa Sol."

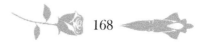

Awkward tension loomed in the air around Jonathan. He glanced down, feeling the blood rushing to his cheeks. He knew better than to go to battle with the ambassador. Lucas knew what buttons to push. Yet that was where the challenge—and the fun—lay.

Lucas continued. "At any rate, you'll have to start calling me Lucas anyway. I, along with my...*roommates*, as I call them, have put together a little arrangement. When you wish to speak with me, address us as Lucas. When you wish to speak with the Voonsu, address us as Cale."

"A bit nostalgic, Ambassador? It sounds like a splendid way to get me to call you Ambassador Lucas."

Lucas chuckled. "I will admit, it brings back memories of Eurosia."

Jonathan glanced at Ellyra. "Forgive me, you've probably already met, but this is Ambassador Lucas."

Ellyra politely smiled. "Yes indeed. He is an old friend of House El'Allel, though my memory of him was faded."

"Colonel," Isabeau addressed. "The time."

Jonathan glanced at the time displayed on his comm-band. It was getting late; the funeral service would soon begin. They needed to get to the probe launch bay quickly. Punctuality was a mark of the military. "Thank you, Commander." He motioned for everyone to proceed down the hall. "This way."

They reached the probe launch bay in good time. The wide expanse of the bay gave ample room for the many rows of chairs along with the silver casket. The blue and white flag of Earth draped over the casket. *Gamma Station* had its own flag, but who really cared about *Gamma Station?* It was Earth that everyone was really attached to. Using the Earth flag was, in a small measure at least, a way to reunite with the home planet.

A small mobile podium had been rolled into the bay. A transparent wall stood to the left. Officially, it served as visual confirmation of the sensor probe's trajectory. Unofficially, it was a place to escape from the day by gazing out across the cosmos. It was Jonathan's favorite habit. Today, it would serve a different purpose. Looking out through the transparent wall, seven starships were lined up in a single row. They were the battlecruisers Earth had assigned to *Gamma Station*.

Since the Chantell were to study human military tactics, *Gamma Station* needed warships. They were also to defend themselves. It was both a blessing and a curse; the freedom of your own ships but without the protection of an elder race. The small reddish-brown planet that *Gamma Station* orbited could be seen beyond.

Jonathan glanced back at Isabeau. "Please direct Sune Ellyra."

She nodded and motioned for Ellyra to follow her. "Spouses are seated right over here."

"Spouse?" Lucas asked, eyeing Jonathan and then Ellyra.

Jonathan took a breath and gave an awkward smile. "Long story."

"I enjoy long stories," Lucas insisted.

"I'm sure you do." Without waiting for a reply, Jonathan strolled through the crowd of personnel. He reached the front of the rows of chairs and spotted Grrrah'Kah, sitting without a chair. Chantell didn't need chairs. They simply squatted down on their abdomen and were still taller than most people.

He walked over to Grrrah'Kah, who was studying words typed into his reader. He had asked Grrrah'Kah to say a few words about Lt. Allen. "Master Sergeant," he said.

Grrrah'Kah looked up. "Terynn Colonel."

"Are you ready for this?"

He twitched his antennae. "Why you ask Grrrah'Kah to speak? Grrrah'Kah no talk Earthian well."

"You speak just fine, Master Sergeant. I asked you to speak because the two of you were close. Besides, it would mean a lot to his wife to know what kind of impact Lt. Allen had on your life."

Grrrah'Kah jerked his head, mimicking a nod. "I vision what you mean."

Jonathan smiled and patted him on the shoulder before leaving. He walked past the soldiers in dress uniform who were to perform the flag ceremony and stood at the pulpit. He glanced at the comm-band on his wrist. One minute to go. He stood, waiting.

At the back of the room, Cyran stood against the wall with T'Kal at his side. He hadn't expected any of the Greys to attend. They didn't care much for ceremony. They were perhaps the opposite of the Euroo. Yet somehow, he felt gratitude swelling inside that T'Kal would attend.

Jonathan checked the time once more. Nineteen hundred hours on the dot. He cleared his throat. "Company, attention."

The low moaning chatter of voices subsided. All eyes looked at him. "We have gathered to honor the sacrifice of Lt. Bryce Allen, who was killed in action. And since I am not a man for eloquent words, I had asked Lt. Colonel Fox Jagger to say a few words. Unfortunately, logistics have prevented that." He held up an unfolded paper. "So, I pilfered this from his quarters. I have no clue whom it is quoting, but the words are fitting." He cleared his throat again. "The muted trump hath sounded the sullen notes of the soldier's last tattoo. The stars of the heavens, their bowing light doth bid adieu. Glory and honor adorn the fallen in silent dignity. Whose sacrifice hath hallowed the celestial battleground with their last measure of nobility."

Jonathan reverently folded the paper back up and put it in his uniform jacket pocket. "I have asked Master Sergeant Grrrah'Kah to say a few words." He took a few steps back from the podium.

Grrrah'Kah stood and walked up to the podium, his four legs pounding against the floor as he walked. Taking one final glance at his reader, he looked at the audience. "Allen Lieutenant friend was," he twitched, putting extra effort into enunciation. "Before Allen Lieutenant came, Grrrah'Kah no hive here have. Allen Lieutenant made Grrrah'Kah friend." He took another glance at his reader. "Allen pilot was. Allen life gave. Allen others did save...Allen Lieutenant always a life save. Allen always someone help. His heart like Chantell was; loyal to forever."

Grrrah'Kah walked back toward his seat but stopped momentarily in front of the casket. It was empty, of course. Not much is recoverable after a spaceship explodes. But it didn't matter. The air was thick with emotion, and few eyes remained dry. Grrrah'Kah reverently bowed his head and fanned out his four mighty wings. Then he returned to the front row of seats and sat without a chair.

Jonathan retook his position at the podium. He glanced to his left and nodded. A soldier in an elegant dress uniform held up a shiny brass bugle and played the slow melody of Taps. After the melody, the dress-uniformed soldiers picked up the flag from the casket. They ceremoniously folded it into the triangular shape of the tricorn. They moved with sharp determined motions. When the flag was folded, one of the soldiers held it like a delicate pillow and turned on his heel. With one slow determined step after another, he approached Lt. Allen's widow.

With one hand, she held a tissue to her eyes. With her other hand, she held the hand of her three-year-old son. The soldier offered the flag to her. "On behalf of the President of Earth, the United Earth Navy, and a grateful world, please accept this flag as a symbol of our appreciation for your loved one's honorable and faithful service."

She accepted it, holding it to her bosom. "Thank you," she whispered hoarsely.

The soldier then took one deliberate step backward before turning on his heel. He walked back with one precise step after another. Jonathan turned to the transparent wall and the seven Earth battlecruisers outside.

"Atten-hut!" a soldier bellowed.

The whole room stood at attention.

"Company, face right!"

Everyone faced the transparent wall.

"Company, salute!"

Jonathan leaned into the microphone. "We hereby commend the body of Lt. Bryce Allen to the starry heavens. From the stars were we born, to the stars shall we return." He nodded toward the dress-uniformed soldiers. They loaded the casket into the probe launch tube and sealed the hatch. Another soldier at a neighboring console pressed a red button. Allen's casket was propelled out of the launch tube, streaking across the starry sky. A ray of brilliant light glowed from the edge of the planet as the sun slowly peaked around from behind.

Jonathan tapped a button on his comm-band. "Gamma Fleet, salute!"

The seven battlecruisers each fired a cannon. They belched out thundering yellow bolts that exploded a way off. The explosions resembled fireworks in space. The seven ships fired a second time, and then a third time, making in total, twenty-one shots.

Jonathan finished his salute and addressed the audience once more. "Company, dismissed."

As the audience slowly dispersed, Ellyra strolled over to Jonathan's side. "It was a lovely service."

He managed a weak smile. "Thanks. Thankfully, I don't have to do it often."

"I especially enjoyed that poem at the beginning."

"If you'd like to read it again," he said, pulling out the paper and offering it to her.

She reached out but the paper suddenly tore. Startled, Ellyra took a step back. Jonathan stared at the paper; a small hole was torn through it. A pungent bitter-sour odor assaulted his nose.

"Jonathan," she said in alarm, pointing to him.

He ran his hand up his uniform shirt and to his throat. He plucked out a small dart. He stared at it in confusion. What was going on? The room began to spin and his vision blurred. Ellyra screamed his name as everything went black.

Chapter 19

THE ANCIENT MAGIC

F ox sat at a fancy table of reddish-brown wood in the house library. The library was a large room with tall bookshelves lining every wall. Rolling ladders gave access to the high shelves. A single high stained glass window allowed the natural sunlight in. Lady Elony turned a few pages in a large leather-bound book. The thick worn pages turned easily under her hand.

"Here it is," she said, turning the book to face Fox. "The Song of Vera."

Fox stared blankly at the alien text on the page. With the Euroo speaking his own Earthian language, he had forgotten he couldn't read or speak theirs.

Lady Elony noticed his hesitation. "Shall I translate it for you?"

He flashed a sheepish smile. "That would be most appreciated, your ladyship."

"A ship shall sail from beyond the amber realm, where the dragon thinks not to look, its maiden voyage with children at its helm. When in subtle strength shall they bare their teeth, the star of Draconia's courage shall be forsook, for upon them the ancient magic to bequeath."

Fox smiled. There was too much in common to be a coincidence. It was a different telling of the Skorath Prophecy. How many variations of the prophecy could there be? And were they purposely different or the product of exaggeration through the centuries? Scholars couldn't be expected to know it was a prophecy and not some cute verse to interpret and rephrase.

The most important similarity was the final line; upon them the ancient magic to bequeath. If ancient magic didn't sound like alien tech, then what did? The birthright of the Ancestors had to be ancient technology. Fox's heart raced. Excitement plastered his face. Before him lay a crucial piece to the prophecy puzzle. But who could he announce his finding to? Who was there that he could converse with? The Colonel was many lightyears away, prohibited from any contact.

"You appear to be a man very pleased with himself," Lady Elony observed. "Such a joyous yet contemplative smile is rare upon anyone who hasn't found something."

"Indeed," he said, nodding. "It seems silly, but I feel like I should report to my superior...only he is now in another galactic sector."

She returned a warm smile. "I don't think it silly; ceremony and ritual are always important."

He leaned back in his chair. "Do you think it would be too forward of me to ask Diahlus if I could give my report to him?"

Her smile bloomed. "You could not have chosen better. Diahlus is a longtime friend of the House. His wisdom reflects his age well." She turned to a servant standing against the far wall. "Vash, please send for Brigadain Diahlus."

"It is well, your grace."

It didn't take very long to get Diahlus to the library. When he entered, his broad smile accented his blond-colored hair. He had the same grandfatherly disposition that he did on *Gamma Station*. Lady

Elony had already taken her leave to attend to another matter. Diahlus sauntered over to where Fox sat.

"It is the first time I have been summoned on behalf of an Earthian."

Fox smirked. "I hoped you wouldn't mind."

"Not in the least, Lieutenant Colonel Fox. Now, how might I be of assistance?"

"I think I have found something interesting. But, to bring it into context, do you mind if I ask you a few questions first?"

"Go right ahead."

"How much do you know about the Skorath?"

Diahlus frowned. "Only that the Draconians want us to call them They Who Shall Not Be Named, and that they once were an ancient race."

"What would you say if I told you they visited this planet?"

"Eurosia?"

Fox nodded.

"In all honesty, I would sooner call you a wit than believe it."

Fox smiled in amusement. "Fair enough."

Diahlus continued. "Because if such a visitation had taken place, there would be evidence of it."

"You mean like, artifacts and documented accounts?"

"In part, yes, but it would run deeper than that. There would be a significant cultural impact as well. One does not encounter a vastly superior race and not have their beliefs fundamentally changed."

Fox fought to suppress a smile. "Such as mythology, for example?"

Diahlus nodded. "Precisely; such as mythology, religion, and art."

"What I found may have hit on two of those points."

Diahlus shook his head. "I'm afraid I do not follow your train of thought."

"Right, right," Fox said in concession. "Human expressions." He ran his hand down his bald head and across his face. "How about I put it to you in another way? Let's suppose the Skorath did visit a couple of thousand years before you became a spacefaring race. Being technologically advanced, let's suppose they dramatically impacted your culture—as you said."

Diahlus took a seat across from Fox. "All right, for the sake of argument, let us make such an outlandish supposition."

Fox grinned. "Now your ancestors wouldn't have described them as technologically advanced, right?"

Diahlus shook his head. "Indeed not. We would not have understood their technology. It would have been something magical, unexplainable. The Skorath would have been seen as magicians, or gods even."

"In which case, one of the gods of your mythology would have been attributed to the Skorath, am I right?"

He nodded. "Yes, that stands to reason. Though, there are several mythologies and dozens of gods between them."

"There'd have to be some way to figure out which one."

Diahlus shook his head. "Not necessarily. Indeed, there would be clues in the iconography. The early painters would have included some kind of symbol that represented them. The trouble is not knowing anything about the Skorath. Without knowing what they looked like, the shape of their starships, or anything else, we don't know what to look for."

Fox paused in contemplation. His eyes widened as a new realization struck him. It all started to make sense. "Diahlus, that's what the Draconians have been trying to do all along."

Diahlus leaned in closer with a confused expression. "I'm afraid you shall need to explain."

"The Draconians have outlawed everything about the Skorath. Even speaking their name is illegal. Diahlus, it's as if they are trying to erase the Skorath from history."

"But what possible reason could they have for doing that? What benefit does it serve?"

Fox leaned closer across the table. "To stop anyone from identifying the Skorath."

"Again, what possible benefit could it serve?"

177

Diahlus had a very good question. How could he answer it? There were no answers, only more questions. It had to serve some purpose, otherwise, the Draconians wouldn't have bothered. "Diahlus, I don't know why. But I'm sure they have a reason. Why would they bother trying to hide something if they weren't afraid of it?"

"So, you believe the Draconians fear the Skorath?"

Fox shook his head. "No, they won the Great War. What they're probably scared of has something to do with us learning more about the Skorath. They stand to lose something, and I just wish I knew what that something was."

Diahlus leaned back in his chair with a relaxed posture. "Alas, we may never know. The Draconians have all but succeeded in erasing any knowledge of the Skorath."

Fox smiled. "Unless someone saw something they weren't supposed to."

Diahlus sat up straight. "What have you seen?"

"Let's just say, I now know the shape of a Skorath starship."

"What does it look like?"

Fox turned the book around and pushed it across the table, showing the open pages to Diahlus. Fox reached over and pointed to the black squid-looking symbol.

Diahlus looked up. "You cannot be serious."

"Oh, trust me; that shape is unmistakable."

Diahlus's eyes returned to the page momentarily, then he glanced back at Fox. "Why are you telling me all this?"

"Because you have a starship, and I have a riddle to solve."

Chapter 20

JERRY

D r. Mallory eagerly stepped over to a machine that stopped spinning. He knew he was running late but the first sample was about ready for testing. The funeral service had already begun and he needed to haul jets to get up there. But the sample was almost ready. The tantalizing reality of a possible remedy for Teterophalezine could not be ignored. Yes, attending the funeral was important but so was this. When it all came down to it, people died all the time. This was a possibility to eliminate the deaths caused by the vicious 'phalezine.

He glanced at his comm-band. How could it be so late? The funeral could be half over by now. He moaned with irritation as he took out one of the small vials of clear liquid. He put a few drops into a nearby petri dish. He eagerly set aside the vial and plastic dropper in favor of putting the petri dish under a microscope. He pressed a few buttons on the microscope and his monitor screen flashed on, showing the closeup.

Dr. Mallory nodded in approval. "Looking good, looking good," he whispered to himself.

The initial cell reaction was a good sign. That meant it had potential. Why couldn't he have figured this out sooner? Admittedly, the promising results were owed to Bug tech and a sample from Vincent's brain tissue. If this serum panned out as a real cure, he would have to share the credit with the Chantell and the Voonsu—even though he did all the work. It was a minor detail he could get over. After all, it could save a lot of lives.

He checked the time on his comm-band again. *Blast!* he thought. *I've missed the entire funeral service.* A guilty sense of relief spread over him. He would definitely get an earful for not attending the funeral. But at least he could continue analyzing the sample. After all, this was important work. The research to save a life should be just as important as the service to honor the passing of a life.

Dr. Mallory filled a syringe with the sample vial as he heard footsteps enter the med bay. He grew tense with annoyance. Why of all times did he have to get a walk-in patient right now? He just needed another twenty minutes. He began his patient evaluation without taking his eyes off the screen. "What seems to be the problem?"

A pleasant voice replied. "I seem to be coming down with an unnatural fixation for a bitter-sour-smelling plant extract, Doc."

Dr. Mallory froze. His heart raced with panic. There was something else in that voice, something creepy. And then there was his description, a bitter-sour-smelling plant extract. There was no doubt; he was standing in the same room as the assassin.

Dr. Mallory slowly looked over his shoulder. The assassin took a few steps closer with a makeshift dart gun in his hand. It wasn't the most elegant of weapons. In fact, it looked homemade. Such a primitive weapon would be easy to slip past security scanners.

"How?" was all Dr. Mallory could think to say.

"How?" the assassin repeated him in dismay. "I've come here to put an end to your pathetic life and the only question you can ask is how? Not who are you or what do you want? You Gamms always were weird."

The assassin wasn't very well informed; Dr. Mallory was a Brav. But that detail didn't seem important enough to waste one's last words correcting it. "All right, who are you, then?"

The assassin smiled in triumph. "Jerrol Hosskin at your service. But you can call me Jerry."

Dr. Mallory huffed. "At the Scorpii's service, more like."

Jerry's eyes lit up with enthusiasm. "Oh no, my dear doctor. Make no mistake about it, I truly am in the service of humanity."

"By murdering members of it?"

Jerry smirked. "Tisk, tisk, doctor. Even a surgeon such as yourself should know that to save the patient one must cut out the cancer."

"It takes a treacherous mind to think of his fellow brothers and sisters as cancerous," Dr. Mallory declared.

Jerry's nostrils flared. "Treachery! You Gamms have quite the audacity to speak of treachery when you fight against every effort to liberate humanity. You who cannot see past the ends of your noses. You who refuse to sacrifice a little pride in the name of preservation, dare to speak of treachery? You brought this fate upon yourselves." He took a step closer. "What I do is at the very heart of patriotism."

The man was insane. He actually thought murdering humans was somehow saving them. Politics was more confusing than statistics. At least with statistics you could go back and look at the raw data and see where you went wrong. With politics, it was a lot of argument around various points of view. This man, however, took it to the extreme.

Dr. Mallory shook his head in disapproval. "A rather psychotic opinion—"

Jerry snapped the trigger and a small dart leaped from its confines, striking Dr. Mallory in the chest. Instinctively, he plucked it out and looked at it. The potent bitter-sour odor crept to his nose. The room began to spin, and his knees buckled. He collapsed, knocking medical equipment to the floor. The syringe rolled out of his hand, across the floor, and under the neighboring exam table.

"Do forgive my abruptness, doctor. You see, I don't have time for any lengthy discussion; I am in quite a hurry, actually." He reloaded his

181

dart gun while standing over Dr. Mallory. "It's nothing personal. But, you see, you've already cured one of my targets from my 'phalezine, and I cannot let you continue."

It sounded like Jerry was giving him credit for saving Lucas. Even though it wasn't entirely accurate, it was still nice to get some recognition out of the whole headache. Especially if it would be his last.

Jerry swiped everything off the lab table. All the serum samples crashed to the floor, splattering the clear liquid. Jerry then moved over to the computer and inserted a crystal disk. The computer flashed gibberish across the screen.

Dr. Mallory's heart raced yet his pulse weakened. All his 'phalezine research was being destroyed. His vision blurred and he strained his eyes to focus. He reached over to his comm-band and pressed a button. It was the wrong button. He meant to press the adjacent one. He tried again. His muscles acted confused. It was as if conflicting messages were being sent to them. His vision faded entirely.

Ellyra cradled Jonathan's head in her arms. His breathing faded as she lay kneeling on the floor beside him. The cacophony of shouting voices and screams faded into dull background noise. She could hear her heartbeat banging in her chest. The nauseating bitter-sour odor assaulted her nose. She had heard of teterophalezine, or 'phalezine as it was sometimes referred to. But this was the first time she had ever smelled it. Her husband had been shot with a poison that had no known cure. She stared down at the man she had cared for, the man she wanted to be with. Only now, she felt empty. Where was her remorse? Instead of sorrow, she felt a hole. A piece of her heart seemed forever lost.

She felt a hand on her shoulder, the touch pulling her back to reality. An Earthian soldier dressed for combat addressed her, his weapon held at his side. "Ma'am, I need you to step aside; we need to take him to a med bay!"

The soldier shouted over the noise of panicking and officers giving orders. She glanced back down at Jonathan and nodded. The soldier took Jonathan by an arm and a leg and hoisted him over his back. He hustled through the dense sea of people toward the exit. As she followed him with her eyes, she spotted a short Tumnei against the back wall.

She hadn't met many Tumnei. The Earthians would sometimes call them Greys. What was a Tumnei doing on the space station? They were assigned to oversee the Earthians at *Bravo Station*. Her eyes widened in realization. Her heart surged with the warmth of hope. They were the answer. They were one of the five elder races with superior technology. And the Tumnei excelled in the study of biology. If there was any chance of Jonathan surviving, the Tumnei were it.

She pulled up the hem of her gown, allowing her to scramble to her feet without stepping on it. Years of practice made the maneuver automatic. She no longer needed to consciously think about her dress. Once on her feet, she pushed her way through the throng of service personnel toward the Tumnei. Fresh tears tickled her cheeks.

Her approach was all wrong. She had not formally been introduced, and her tear-saturated appearance was not fit to be seen. It just wasn't done. *Jonathan will die if I don't,* she thought. And that thought pushed her onward. Standing before the Tumnei, she curtsied. "Begging your pardon, sir, might I beg a boon of your kindness?"

He looked at her, her image reflected in his large round solid-black eyes. *"For the sake of expediency,"* he said into her mind, *"may I have your thoughts?"*

Such an invasion of privacy was also not done, but there was no time for propriety. She nodded. Then, she felt him inside her head, as if her mind were a filing cabinet, and his fingers thumbing through the files. There was something else. His mental touch carried with it a small connection to his own mind. She now knew his name was T'Kal.

"As you wish," his voice replied in her mind.

As you wish... it was the formal Euroo acknowledgment. This Tumnei was well versed in Euroo culture. Whatever his station was, he was a man of prominence. This made her request all the more improper. But how could it be helped? The man she loved was dying.

T'Kal waved a hand over his wrist and a holographic keypad appeared in the air. He typed a few holographic buttons, and then, in a flash of brilliant white light, he was gone. Ellyra glanced toward the door. Jonathan was also gone along with the man who was carrying him. She breathed out a sigh of relief. For the first time since arriving back on *Gamma Station*, her shoulders felt a little lighter. Jonathan had a good chance of living. Even if he didn't want her and would forget about her, she would sleep at night knowing he was alive.

Isabeau flinched at the blinding white flash of light. She'd seen flashes like that before. It was the Tumnei's teleporter beam. How it worked and still obeyed the laws of physics was anybody's guess. She glanced toward the bay door. Jonathan and the chief that she had instructed to carry him to Med Bay Charlie were gone. Had T'Kal taken them? She glanced toward Cyran at the back wall.

He shrugged with a look of confusion plastered on his face.

Ellyra stood nearby. The poor woman must be scared and confused; being suddenly married and now quite possibly a widow. Standing so close to where T'Kal was, she might have some answers. Isabeau finished giving instructions to the sergeant that stood before her. He handed her an E.M. Pistol.

Isabeau pulled back the charge lever. The power cell activated with a high-pitched hum. Then she ran her finger across the safety switch, making sure the safety was on. She now had a manhunt to perform on the station. And this time, it would be without the guidance of Jonathan's cleverness or Fox's tenacity. She was on her own. She marched over to Ellyra and Cyran.

Ellyra noticed her approach and curtsied. "Commander Isabeau."

"Sune Ellyra, did you talk with T'Kal?"

She nodded. "I asked him, with their vast knowledge of biology, if he could help Jonathan."

She had a point. The Tumnei excelled in biology as well as several other technologies. Ellyra was one step ahead of her. Even amidst all the terror and chaos, Ellyra managed to keep her wits about her. Which made sense since she was a starship captain. A lot of training and experience were required to captain a ship. It could be the dresses she wore instead of military uniforms that made it so easy to forget she was so capable. Jonathan had chosen well.

"Excellent thinking, thank you. I trust you will be staying with the Colonel?"

A look of hesitation shone in Ellyra's eyes. What was she afraid of? Shouldn't she want nothing more than to stay with Jonathan? Something was not right. Had Jonathan been putting her off for too long? Had the day's events been too much for her?

Ellyra glanced down. "I would not wish to be a burden."

How could she think she was a burden? It was her right, as his wife, to be at his side. Jonathan must have messed things up big time. But like all truly important matters, it would have to wait. A killer was on the loose and she was in command.

"Ellyra, Jonathan is like a brother to me. I would feel much better knowing you were at his side."

Her eyes lifted to meet Isabeau's. Her hair color brightened into a light blue. That was a new color—just when Isabeau thought she had them all figured out.

"I would be delighted to impart comfort to you by staying with Jonathan."

Ellyra's tender eyes threatened to spill more tears as a smile crossed her lips. The poor woman needed a hug. And thankfully, hugs were a part of proper Euroo culture. She hugged Ellyra, also exchanging a sense of comradery in that gesture. "Thank you."

Isabeau turned to Cyran, who was looking quite uncomfortable. "Will you escort Ellyra to T'Kal's ship?"

He nodded. "Mais, bien sûr. Absolument!"

Isabeau smiled. It was such a comfort to have her brother there, speaking to her in the language she cherished. It was a shame he had to leave tomorrow. At least he left her with warm memories to help her through the next lonely years without him.

Cyran motioned for Ellyra to precede him toward the door.

Ellyra took a few steps and then turned back to Isabeau. "Commander Isabeau, do not hunt for this assassin in any normal fashion."

Isabeau returned a confused look.

"Assassinations are planned around the target's habits and patterns," she explained. "So don't follow your normal patterns."

If only Jonathan were here to lead this hunt. He always knew what to say. He would often quote some famous general. There was one he would repeat from time to time; If you know yourself but not the enemy, for every victory gained you will also suffer a defeat. Jonathan would often quote it when he didn't understand who he was up against. Ellyra seemed to understand quite a bit. The feuding great houses on Eurosia had given her valuable insight.

"Thank you," Isabeau said. "I'll take all the advice I can get."

Ellyra curtsied and then followed Cyran out of the bay.

Isabeau rejoined a group of marines suiting up to join the manhunt. All the marines that were on guard duty had already been dispatched to search the deck. Now every available marine and SEAL was preparing to comb the decks of the station one by one. One of the marines had a decorative emblem on his helmet. It was a representation of the original Cobra Squad insignia. It appeared that Jonathan's war stories had now become a fashion statement.

"Manitez, Carter," she said, addressing the two nearest marines. These were two of the rail gunners that Fox trained for aboard-ship shooting. Rail gun shooting was usually disastrous. Those rapid-fire cannons could punch holes through the bulkheads and depressurize the deck. Fox's idea was to use trained snipers on the rail guns for accurate short, controlled bursts. There was no telling what possible application Fox had in mind. But if Ellyra recommended unconventional methods, then rail gunners would surely fit the bill.

Isabeau's comm-band beeped. It was Grrrah'Kah. Good. She needed all the experienced crewmen she could get. "Grrrah'Kah, I need you to take two squads. We have another assassin on the station."

"New is not," he replied in his poorly constructed Earthian language. "Same."

She shook the confusion from her head. "I'm going to need you to rephrase that."

"Commander Alexi, prisoner gone is. Assassin new is not, but same is."

"What?" she said in dismay. How could that happen? He was locked up in the brig. Should she be glad there wasn't another assassin using a rare poison or horrified that he found a way to escape? A prisoner escape was another headache she'd have to unravel once this chase was over.

A young lieutenant tapped Isabeau on the shoulder, "Deccio just reported in. Med Bay Charlie has been hit. The place is a mess, and a doctor has been killed. I'm taking Tango Squad down to look around."

A sick feeling sank into the pit of her stomach. It wasn't just political targets that he was killing. If she couldn't stop him fast, more people would die. Isabeau nodded to the lieutenant then turned her attention back to her call with Grrrah'Kah. "Just find him," she finally said, "and I want him shot on sight." She pressed the button that ended the call and turned toward Manitez and Carter, the two rail gunners. "Let's move."

Chapter 21

IR'JAD

Jerry slid down the metal ladder, his feet thumping against the green metal floor. What a shame that *Gamma Station* security never checks the maintenance access tunnels. Otherwise, he might get a real challenge. He didn't blame them. Like most military outfits, they relied too heavily on automated security systems. If only they knew how easy it was to outsmart an automated system.

Jerry strolled to the other end of the dim access corridor. His conspicuous black cloak brushed up against the narrow walls. Without breaking his stride, he pulled out his palm-sized communication transmitter. It beeped once. "Ir'Jad, inform Mr. Jaimess that the primary target is down, and that pesky doctor's home remedy has been dealt with."

An artificial voice answered back. "Are you ready for extraction?"

"Not yet. I'm going to finish what I started with their ambassador."

"Those are not our orders," Ir'Jad's monotone voice said in protest.

That egg-headed technician had no sense of professional pride. How could he? His whole race was as devoid of passion as it was devoid of purpose. In the end, though, it didn't matter what he thought. Ir'Jad was a good asset. Without him, it would have taken months just to figure out how to penetrate *Gamma Station*. Staging the assassinations would have taken even longer. He would have to endure his puerile objections.

"Good boy, Ir'Jad. So glad you can read. Now be ready to extract me on my next signal." Jerry closed the device in his palm, severing the transmission.

Having reached the end of the narrow corridor, he put his ear to the door. A crude but effective means of determining whether the coast was clear. He opened the door and slipped into the hallway. The red glow of the overhead lights meant the station was still on high alert. That was good; that meant he still had a challenge. The fun wasn't in the killing, that was only the job. The real thrill was in escaping the armed pursuit.

Having the station on alert was also beneficial. It cleared the halls of all the annoying pedestrians. An escape was hard enough without foot traffic to slow things down. It also gave him more leeway in not being spotted. Though it wouldn't matter in a few moments anyway. Once the secondary target had been eliminated—again—Ir'Jad would extract him back to safety. Then the long trip back to *Able Station* would begin.

He rounded the corner and put his ear to the second door. Nothing. He was supposed to be here. He always returned to his quarters at this hour. Was he just being quiet? There was only one way to find out. Jerry pulled out a long metal card with a black stripe down the center and slipped it between the door and its jam. Sparks popped and a trickle of smoke danced up to the ceiling. The door slid up and Jerry hopped inside.

Lucas sat in a leather armchair perusing his reader. He looked up with a startled expression, seeing Jerry walk in with his dart gun poised to strike.

Jerry smiled. "Well, well. Second time's the charm, eh, Ambassador?" He pulled the trigger before Lucas could respond.

The dart sprang from the gun. Lucas raised his reader like a shield. The dart bounced off the back of the reader with a high-pitched *clang*. Of course, the silly Gamm would deflect the dart with a narrow reader device from twenty feet away. The odds of timing that correctly were staggering. Whatever Matt said about this Gamm, he had more lives than a cat. But luck cannot be counted on forever. Aiming for another part of the target's body should suffice.

Jerry pulled out another dart to reload his gun as Lucas leaped out of the chair toward him. Jerry smiled. This target had some fight in him. He was forced to abort the reload in favor of moving out of Lucas's reach. Lucas swung a second fist and knocked the dart gun out of Jerry's hand.

Jerry dropped the dart and landed a punch into Lucas's face, sending him staggering backward. The trouble with dignitaries was too much arguing and too little physical exercise. In a battle of fists, quicker is always better. Jerry kicked Lucas's leg. He groaned, dropping to one knee.

Jerry pulled out a dagger from under his cloak and walked up to Lucas. "I must say, you're so much more fun up close."

Lucas fell to a seated position on the floor, panting. Then his back straightened up and his eyes flashed white. Jerry paused. What in the galaxy had he just seen? Had the target's eyes really pulsed with a white glow? What had that silly doctor done to the man? Jerry had seen some crazy cybernetics in his time but nothing to compare to glowing eyes. All the same, it was safer to dispatch this one from a distance. Jerry spun around and retrieved his dart gun.

"Jerry," a strange voice called.

The target knew his name. Weirder still, the voice sounded like a hundred voices all speaking at once. A chill shot up Jerry's spine. The intelligence reports had to have been wrong. This man was definitely not human. Whatever he was, he was creepy.

"What are you?"

"We are the Cale, of Voonsu."

Jerry shrugged. "Never heard of you. And I can't say that I really care." He pointed his dart gun at Cale, but then something was wrong. The gun didn't fire. He tried again. It still didn't fire. He glanced at his hand. His trigger finger wasn't responding. Could he flex his finger? Nope, it did not move at all. It was like his finger wasn't listening to him anymore. He switched the dart gun to his other hand. Now his other finger wasn't responding.

His eyes widened with panic and his heart pounded. What was going on? What was wrong with him? He was losing control somehow. Then the whole hand twitched quite on its own. Both the hand and arm moved in concert, turning the gun to point at himself. His breathing became erratic and his heart raced.

"Stop!" he commanded his arm. It still moved the dart gun toward his own head. What was going on? "Wait!" he shouted, trying to stop it with his free hand. Still, the gun inched closer to his temple. It was like his arm was possessed. It was no longer under his control. The end of the dart gun pressed against his head.

"Goodbye, Jerry," Cale said in his eerie voice.

"NO!" Jerry shrieked in terror as his finger pulled the trigger.

Click! His heart launched into his throat, but the dart gun had not fired a dart. A sense of relief surged through him. It had not been reloaded. He was safe from his precious 'phalezine. The dart gun clattered to the ground. His hand and arm were now listening to him again. He panted, trying to calm his erratic heartbeat.

Cale rose to his feet. His eyes flashed brightly once again. His voice still spoke with an eerie echo. "You will tell us what we want to know, or you will reload your gun."

Isabeau marched down the hall with Chief Colton, one of the SEALs, at her side. His Li-Tech thrummed as it scanned for life signs. The two rail gunners brought up the rear. They marched

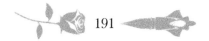

with large Rail Guns on swivel arms mounted to their chest plates. Having the Rail Gun mounted to the soldier's chest plate made the large weapon easier to carry. The mounted swivel arm allowed the gun to be maneuvered around as needed.

Three soldiers armed with E.M. rifles led the way. Section by section they swept Romeo deck along with six other teams. Chief Colton pointed to two red dots on the Li-Tech scanner.

Isabeau tapped her comm-band. Her voice projected through the loudspeakers in the halls. "Attention all personnel on Romeo deck, section 34. Hold fast and tap your comm-band." The red dots each blinked and turned blue. "Eliminate those from the search."

Chief Colton nodded and pressed a few buttons on the Li-Tech.

Isabeau's comm-band beeped. It was an incoming call from the security station. She tapped her comm-band and it showed a video image of Sergeant Herrmann.

"Commander, Ambassador Cale called in reporting that the assassin has been apprehended. I've sent a squad to his quarters."

Her anger curled into a ball in the pit of her stomach. She wanted the assassin shot on sight. Now, according to regulations, if an enemy surrendered, she had to give him quarter. That was yet another unfortunate headache she would have to deal with. Keeping a prisoner that could escape—and kill—again was not something she looked forward to. Why couldn't they have just shot him on sight?

"Thank you, Sergeant."

"There's more," he said.

More? What more could there be? She tilted her head in confusion. "I'm listening."

"The ambassador also reports the assassin has an accomplice on Sierra deck, section 12."

"How does he know that?"

Sergeant Herrmann shrugged. "I'm heading down there to find out for myself."

She nodded. "Acknowledged," she said, tapping the comm-band again to end the call. She tapped a few more buttons. "Grrrah'Kah, converge on Sierra 12."

She turned to Chief Colton. "You can save the Li-Tech for Sierra 12. Let's move."

The men all grunted a *hooyah* in unison and broke into a light run. The pounding of their feet on the green metal floor echoed down the hallway. Isabeau glanced behind, half expecting to see the rail gunners lagging behind. Instead, they kept pace with the rest of the unit. The fitness evaluation for operating the Rail Gun must have been substantial.

A stray strand of Isabeau's straight black hair flew into her face. She remedied it with an annoyed toss of her head. Her heart pounded as loud as the stomping of their boots. She was heading straight into a deadly situation. It wasn't her preference. She specialized in administration. But with Fox gone and Jonathan shot, she was the commanding officer. And the commanding officer cannot afford to show weakness.

She swallowed hard, forcing her fears down as far as they would go. If she could stretch her concentration enough, her military training would take over. All the drills and exercises that had been burned into her reflexes would take over. At least, that's what the boys often talked about. She had yet to experience it. What if she never would? Maybe it only happened to the infantry who saw action. What if a decade of administration had ruined her chances?

Chief Colton shoved Isabeau against the wall. She tumbled to the ground, her E.M. pistol slipping from her fingers and clattering to the ground. What had gotten into him? Striking an officer was a serious offense. The loud barking shots of the E.M. rifles echoed in the hall. Isabeau opened her eyes and saw a large smoking hole in Chief Colton's helmet.

She shivered. Colton hadn't assaulted her, he shoved her out of the way of an incoming shot. A shot that was intended for her. Someone had actually tried to kill her. A huge wave of gratitude for his actions washed over her, followed by sadness. He had given his life to save hers.

Her hands trembled but she didn't shed any tears. There was too much adrenalin for tears. Tears would come later. For now, there was a killer to end. She snatched per E.M. pistol from the ground and quickly checked the sight alignment. It was a little off but she could compensate.

She looked ahead to where the marines were shooting. A small section of the outer wall shimmered like a mirage as supersonic aluminum rounds pounded against it. Whatever it was, it was a field of energy that camouflaged the shooter behind it.

"Stealth field, sir," Carter said, pointing to it.

"Stealth *shield*," Isabeau corrected. If it was only a stealth field, their ammunition would pass through instead of deflecting off. This was *not* good news. Energy shield technology had only been achieved by some of the elder races. Alien technology was not something she had expected.

A hot red bolt of energy flew down the hall toward them. The soldiers dropped to the ground letting it fly past them. The enemy shooter was protected behind that shield and could gun everyone down with impunity. The E.M. rifles were not strong enough to punch through the shield.

"Carter, when I give you the signal, I want you and Manitez to fire your Rail Guns."

Carter shook his head. "Negative, Ma'am. That's an external bulkhead. We could unintentionally rip a hole into space and depressurize the entire deck."

Ellyra had been right about this assassination setup. It had been planned around how the crew normally operates. "That's exactly why the shooter chose that spot," she explained. "The only weapon we have that's powerful enough to crack that shield is the Rail Gun. And he knows we won't normally risk shooting at an exterior wall. So that's exactly what we're going to do."

"But ma'am—"

"That's an order, soldier!"

He swallowed. "Yes, ma'am." He turned to Manitez. "Short, controlled bursts."

194

Manitez nodded. "Hooyah."

Isabeau held her breath in anticipation. Either this was the right call and victory was near, or it would be the last order she'd ever give. If she was wrong and they ended up depressurizing the deck, everyone there would be killed in moments. Every regulation in the book said she should not take the risk. But that is exactly why it had to work.

Carter and Manitez stood up and each pulled back their safety lever. The Rail Guns hummed to life. The sounds of servos and micro hydraulics filled the tense air as Carter and Manitez swiveled the Rail Guns, aiming for the stealth shield.

"Fire in the hole," she said.

Isabeau plugged her ears, shielding them from the loud *crack-bang* sounds of the Rail Guns. Trails of singed air traced the paths of each shot. The stealth shield shook wildly under the massive pounding. Carter suddenly held up one fist, signaling a cease-fire.

The shield collapsed in a small explosion of sparks and black smoke. Isabeau took in a deep breath of relief. Not only had Carter and Manitez shot accurately, but they also had gauged when the shield would collapse. Accuracy would not have mattered if they had kept on shooting after the shield had collapsed. These men were true professionals who honed their craft well. She was definitely going to see to it they received a commendation.

The thick smoke faded, revealing the dead body of the enemy shooter. It was a bald gray-skinned alien with large black eyes, lying in a pool of light-blue blood.

"It's a Tumnei," Manitez said in disbelief.

Chapter 22

SEARCHING FOR A CURE

E llyra stood in a low-ceiling circular room aboard a Tumnei starship. The walls and ceiling were bright white. They even seemed to glow white. The floor was harder to tell what color it was; a thick fog covered it. What was the purpose of the fog? She didn't know much about Tumnei culture, but it looked a little odd.

She stood next to Jonathan's medical bed; a white table suspended in the air with a stasis field covering it. Like a force field, a stasis field also kept matter and energy out like a protective bubble. The difference was that a stasis field rendered the occupant in suspended animation. Within the stasis field, Jonathan would not age and the poison could not progress—he would live. Unfortunately, it also meant he was perpetually "asleep".

She ran her fingers across the surface of the stasis field, feeling the tingling static-electric sensation. Was this now as close as she would ever get to touching him? Would she never again feel his warm hand on her face? How had she lost it all so soon? Only a week ago, she was the daughter of the largest of the Great Houses on Eurosia. She was also a new starship captain, ready to take on the galaxy. Now she was a disenfranchised widow standing over what amounted to a fancy casket.

A Tumnei walked over to Ellyra and spoke in her mind. *"Your species finds comfort in rest. May I offer you something to sit on?"*

Her image reflected in his large black eyes. Tumnei physiology gave them all expressionless faces. Yet, she could see genuine concern within his dark glass-like eyes. She offered a weak curtsy. "That would be of great comfort, thank you."

He turned to leave.

She held up a finger. "Forgive me, but I haven't had the pleasure of an introduction."

He turned back around. *"My name is called R'Com."*

"A pleasure to meet you, R'Com."

R'Com tilted his head in confusion. *"If my introduction causes you pleasure, then I am glad to have provided it."*

She had forgotten that the Tumnei were a race of very literal thinkers. She would have to be more judicious in her choice of pleasantries. The short man stalked out of the room, the fog swirling around his feet as he walked. Perhaps *he* could tell her what the fog was for.

She glanced up seeing the Tumnei walk back in. Only, it wasn't the same Tumnei, was it? They all looked so similar. And their uniforms didn't seem to have any distinctive markings. And this Tumnei's eyes didn't hold the same concern that R'Com's did. She wanted to ask his name, but she wasn't sure she had been introduced to him yet. The proper thing to do was to wait for him to address her. But her legs were stiff from standing and her nerves stretched thin. The temptation to break propriety was overwhelming. She took a breath in preparation to speak but held her tongue instead.

Finishing school had trained her manners so thoroughly that her muscles responded automatically. It appeared she would do the proper

197

thing and wait until spoken to. *This is so silly*, she decided. *I'm worried about manners with a race who are the epitome of practicality.*

The Tumnei bowed. *"No regret is necessary."*

Why did he bow? The Tumnei don't use ceremony. And then there was something with how he spoke. Although they were only words in her mind, they still held an element of individuality. The only way to describe it would be to say she recognized the "voice".

A feeling of warmth spread over her, and a smile found its way across her face. "T'Kal," she said as she curtsied. "I am flattered that you honor me with a formal greeting."

"Experience has taught me that impracticality has its benefits."

Ellyra walk over and gave him a formal hug. It was awkward. With the Tumnei standing about four feet tall, it was like hugging a child. Despite the height difference, there was still comfort in that hug. T'Kal wasn't just a friendly face, he made her feel like they were kindred spirits.

"Thank you for helping Jonathan."

T'Kal glanced over to Jonathan within the stasis field. *"Your gratitude is accepted, though it is not necessary. This Earthian is special to us."*

Half a smile crept into her expression. "My father often says that Earthians are a new and exciting race." She glanced down, her smile evaporating. She had been too enthralled with Jonathan, even against her better judgment. Her carelessness had led to her current predicament.

T'Kal looked at her. *"You have a strong emotional attachment to him."*

And just like that, her tears came flowing freely. Something about T'Kal's words gave her body permission to grieve. It was as if being called out was all that was necessary. Her hair soured into a hysterical orange. Aside from its horrid color, it was freeing to finally allow her deepest emotions to be on display.

"Yes," she admitted between sobs. "I love him."

198

She had finally said it aloud. She loved him. She loved him and she was losing him.

"Love is a mystery to us. From a practical standpoint, it serves no purpose. It doesn't even have its own dedicated emotional response."

She looked at him, her tears subsided by the confusing declaration. "Dedicated emotional response?"

T'Kal nodded. *"For example, when you are angry, your adrenal gland stimulates and your muscles tense. When you are frightened, your heart rate increases and your sense of alertness and attention is stimulated. When you are sad, fluid is released from the tear ducts. Love does not appear to have its own emotional response. It instead draws upon responses of all the other emotions."*

Ellyra pushed a stray lock of her curly hair over one ear. "On Eurosia it is said that love is the clay that is molded into whatever shape is needed."

He tilted his head in contemplation.

"But as to its purpose," she continued. "I am quite fond of an Earth saying that Jonathan told me. Love conquers all."

"I fail to see how an emotion can affect a temporal outcome."

Ellyra sniffled. "I like to think it has merit."

R'Com walked into the room. He and T'Kal exchanged a look. Since Ellyra couldn't hear their conversation, she evidently was not privy to the discussion. R'Com nodded and left the room again. Wasn't he supposed to bring a chair?

T'Kal faced Ellyra. *"Perhaps your saying might prove to have some merit after all."*

"I do not understand your meaning."

T'Kal waved his hand in the air and a holographic keypad appeared. He pressed a few holographic keys. A low humming sounded throughout the ship. Then, in a bright flash of light, one of *Gamma Station's* soldiers appeared. He held out a cracked syringe to T'Kal.

"Supreme Commander T'Kal, this was found in Med Bay Charlie. Whoever ransacked the place took great pains to destroy Dr. Mallory's 'phalezine research. Commander Alexi believes he was working on an antidote. Hopefully, this can help you with the Colonel."

Ellyra's eyes lit up. Her heart thumped in her chest. Was she dreaming? "Are you telling us, sir, that there is a cure?"

He glanced over to Ellyra. "We think so, ma'am."

T'Kal took the syringe and glanced back to Ellyra. *"As I said, perhaps your saying might prove to have merit after all."*

Chapter 23

IN SEARCH OF VERA

T he wind blew through Fox's hair as he stepped through the ornate metal door into the landing bay. The domed roof spiraled open, revealing the pink sky overhead. It was the second time he had been in the landing bay. At least this time he wasn't wearing handcuffs. Instead, he wore a dark blue calf-length cape with a scarlet lining. Lord Areo had it tailored for him, remarking that it was indecent to travel without a proper cape.

One of the fancy-dressed House guards tapped him on the arm, signaling him to move forward. Fox broke his gaze from the majestic sky and walked toward the starship's loading ramp. The sweet scent of lilacs swirled in the breeze. *It is really a shame to leave this place so soon,* he decided, ascending the metal ramp. Diahlus stood at the top with Xer at his side, their scarlet-lined capes swaying in the morning breeze.

"I trust you slept well?" Diahlus asked.

Fox smiled with anticipation oozing from his excited eyes. "Not a wink."

"Well, I do not know what a *wink* is, but by the looks of you, I can safely conclude you are in good spirits this morning." He glanced down at the reader device in Fox's hand. "What have you brought?"

Fox held it up. "I took some notes before leaving. If I'm correct, it should lead us straight there."

"And if you are not correct?"

Fox grinned and shrugged. "At least it'll be a grand adventure."

Xer lowered his voice. "How did you ever get Lord Areo to agree to this?"

"I didn't," Fox admitted. "I convinced Lady Elony. *She* convinced Lord Areo."

"Well, you've certainly obtained the lay of the political landscape," Xer said, motioning for Fox to enter the hatch.

Fox crossed the threshold into the *Calmao*. He strolled across the velvet carpet soaking in the memory. The Euroo were a cultured and elegant people. It was like stepping through the curtain and appearing on stage. A stage with actors in costume that never broke character. How had he become so fortunate?

Diahlus tapped him on the shoulder. "When you've finished stargazing, perhaps you'd be so good as to join us in the Center of Workmanship?"

Fox's cheeks flushed. "Gentlemen, please forgive me. You have no idea what it means to me to be amongst you. There is so much to admire, I don't even know where to begin."

Xer huffed an impatient sigh. "Might I suggest the Center of Workmanship?"

Fox gave a gracious nod, making sure to add all the flair of his former acting career. They led him to the large command room with chairs and computer consoles arranged in a circle. He took his seat beside Diahlus. While the crew prepared the ship for departure, Fox perused his reader. He scrolled through the notes he had typed in. Every book Lady Elony had brought out on the subject of Vera had clues hidden somewhere in the text. It had to. Most mythologies began around tangible events. So, this myth had to have begun with the visit of a Skorath ship to Eurosia.

Diahlus had asked what concern Eurosia would be to an ancient race such as the Skorath. What reason indeed? Fox had spent hours racking his brain for any reason at all. If there was a reason—which he was sure there was—it was tied to something they didn't yet understand. If they knew more about the Skorath and their motives, then the reason would become clear. The challenge, then, was to learn more about a race that had disappeared and was forbidden to learn about.

If only he could talk to T'Kal; he would probably know more. But placing a personal call to the supreme commander of the Tumnei turned out to be a lot harder for an unknown Earth officer such as himself. He had also tried to send a message to Cyran, but again, that proved difficult. Cyran was the *Bravo Station* ambassador, and his secretary said the soonest appointment he could get would be next month.

With the muffled thunder of its thrusters, the *Calmao* lifted off the ground. Gracefully, it floated up and through the open spiral dome roof and into the pink sky. The dome roof spiraled closed as the *Calmao* flew past the fluffy clouds and the red light of dawn.

A woman in a simple green gown walked up to Diahlus's side and handed him a reader. "The stellar cartography report you requested."

He took it and flashed his grandfatherly smile. "Thank you, Miss Layna." He held it up, showing it to Fox. "Every known star map in the regions you've spoken of. If the fabled Vera is anywhere to be found in your notes, surely, we shall discover where."

"Great! Where shall we start?"

"Oh, not so, my dear Lt. Colonel Fox. *You* shall decide where we go. Should this spontaneous endeavor of yours prove fruitless, it shall be of your own making."

In other words, if they failed it needed to be *his* fault, not theirs. He couldn't complain; he was getting starship travel out of the whole deal. Perhaps Shakespeare wasn't correct after all? What if all the world wasn't a stage but actually a bureaucracy?

203

He smiled. "Fair enough." He glanced at his reader once more. "How about we start with Ez-radom?"

Diahlus cringed at his pronunciation.

Xer cleared his throat. "Perhaps Fox means Ezsh'rolthom?"

Diahlus nodded. "Indeed." He turned to his left. "Steersman, lay in a course for Ezsh'rolthom. Power up the hyperdrive."

"As you wish."

Fox stared at his reader. How in the galaxy did they get that pronunciation from those letters? Lady Elony translated it for him, so, the letters should be correct. It was nearly like trying to learn French. Isabel had once written down some phrases for him but only half of the letters were pronounced. The Euroo language was proving to be every bit as elusive.

He looked over to Xer. "Yeah...that."

The hum of the hyperdrive rumbled throughout the ship. The woman in the simple green gown walked up to Diahlus again.

"Course laid in, Brigadain. We are now in position to open the hyperspace portal."

"On stage please," he replied.

The gold ring in the center of the floor lit up. A three-dimensional diagram of the surrounding space floated in the air. The *Calmao* drifted away from the planet Eurosia, past the orbiting space station.

Diahlus turned to his right. "Astrogator, open the hyper-portal."

"As you wish."

A twinkle of light flashed in front of the *Calmao*. The hyperspace portal opened, like a large drain in space with sparkling particles being sucked into the blue tunnel of light.

"Let it be done," he ordered.

The *Calmao* moved into the hyper-portal and vanished.

Chapter 24

TO SAVE HUMANITY

Matt once again strolled down the dimly lit hallways of Able Station. Too much black and too much darkness. Since when did he mind the dim light? Had his visit to the *Brah'Kerov* spoiled him with all those overhead orbs and torches? Had he been given a glimpse of real light and now craved it? It didn't matter in the end; he was not yet in a position to change anything. How much longer did he have to wait until he could drastically fix things? He was still under the thumb of the vile squiddies. He still had more work to do. Liberating one's entire race from slavery was no small feat. Matt knew this, yet the long years of waiting and positioning were wearing on even *his* patience.

He stopped at a door and pressed his black-gloved hand to the plate. The door slid open and he stepped inside. Ross was seated at the table, as usual. Beside him sat someone new to these meetings. She wore her dark curly hair over one shoulder. And the uniform-standard red lipstick complemented her well. Matt noticed his hands were clenched into fists. He relaxed them. *Calm yourself, Matt,* he told himself. *It will do you no good to lose control.*

He knew the woman; her name was Cossette. She was the daughter of Undersecretary Hammond. She was pleasing to look at, no question. And that was precisely the root of two problems. She seemed to light up whenever he was around and had, on occasion, sought opportunities to talk with him. That was a difficult feat considering she was from a lower circle of influence. Her tenacity was what first attracted him. And for a brief moment of weakness, he considered getting to know her. Then the memories of his dead wife flashed before his eyes.

How could he betray Megan by considering being with another woman? It was an emptiness in his heart that he would have to endure. And with his wife murdered and his daughter taken from him in her infancy, he would have to endure it alone.

Lord Vaux was the other problem Cossette presented. The blood-thirsty squiddy killed humans when it wanted to unleash some anger. He had already lost Megan and Merin to its brutality. He would not allow Cossette to be added to the list.

"Mr. Jaimess," Cossette said, standing. "I am so pleased to be on your staff. I won't let you down."

No, he thought. *I'm sure you wouldn't if fate would have afforded you half a chance.* He pulled out a metal data rod from his jacket pocket. There wasn't anything of interest on it, but it would serve his purpose. "Thank you, Cossette. I need you to take this down to data forensics and get a full analysis."

She walked around the table and accepted the cup-sized metal cylinder with eagerness. "Right away, Mr. Jaimess."

After she exited Matt rested his hands on the conference table, glaring at Ross. "What in the galaxy were you thinking, hiring a woman?"

Ross flinched with a look of shock on his face. "Matt, she's the most qualified—"

"In another time and place that would have been acceptable!" he shouted. "Have you forgotten what Lord Vaux did to Merin?"

"I'm sorry, Matt...I..."

"It's not your fault..." Matt grumbled turning away. The incurable optimist was doing his job and being as efficient as ever. But, efficient as Ross was, his dim wit could get another woman added to the morgue. She would have to go before Lord Vaux returned. The squiddy would not be in a great mood after the humiliation of the Treaty Violation Hearing.

"Tell her there's been some mistake," Matt said.

"You're going to get rid of her?"

Matt spun around in contempt. "I will *not* have her blood on my hands!"

The door opened and Cossette dashed inside, holding a data rod in her hand. All data rods were made of rough dull metal, but over the years Matt learned how to tell them apart. The one Cossette now held was not the same one he had given her.

She held it out to Matt. "Mr. Jaimess, this message just arrived from *Gamma Station.*"

He snatched the data rod from her hand, noticing the sweet scent of her hair. Why did she have to do that to her hair? He needed distance, not fondness. It didn't matter anyway; he was going to dismiss her. He couldn't let Lord Vaux get its tentacles on her. He inserted the data rod into a hole in the center of the conference table. The table illuminated and words appeared on it.

"A message from Ir'Jad?" Ross asked.

"Two messages," Matt said, still reading it. "The first is from Ir'Jad..." He looked up from the text on the table and smiled with satisfaction. "Jerry eliminated his primary target."

Ross let out a sigh of regret.

Silly man, Matt decided. Ross had no sense of victory. It was true, another human being had to die, but it was for the good of all mankind. With Jonathan Terynn in the way, Matt could not give the Scorpii a victory big enough. If the prize wasn't good enough, Matt would not be able to gain any more influence over them. He had worked too long and sacrificed too much to let it all go to waste. Megan did *not* die for nothing. He was so close to freeing his people from the Scorpii.

Ross's eyes fell to the table. A sense of regret tugged at the pit of Matt's stomach. Ross hated anytime they had to kill another human. The Scorpii are the enemy, he would say, not ourselves. Perhaps Ross deserved pity. It wasn't his fault he was born an Abe. If only he could have been born a Brav, and been spared this life of suffering under the tentacles of the Scorpii.

He looked at Ross. "It had to be done."

"I know..." Ross muttered. "Thank you for trying to reason with them."

Matt leaned back in his chair, breathing out long and hard. "In that, I grieve with you. If only things could have been different. Perhaps in another lifetime, we could have been allies."

"Does this mean Jerry and Ir'Jad will be coming home?" Cossette asked.

Matt sat up straight and continued reading the words on the table. "Odd...the second message is an automated notification..." Matt studied the words in confusion twice over until a realization struck him. His heart sank, and his heart pounded in remorse. He lowered his head and clenched his fists.

"What is it?" she asked.

He slowly sat back in his chair. "It's an automatic message from Ir'Jad's shuttle. It had been programmed to automatically return to *Able Station* if anything happened to Ir'Jad."

Cossette stared back in disbelief.

Ross looked up. "He's dead?"

Matt nodded.

"But how? He had a shield."

"I don't know, Ross," Matt said, annoyance oozing from his tone. "Somebody screwed up, that much is certain. Without Ir'Jad, it will be difficult to find out what's happening on *Gamma Station*. I'll have to shake some political branches and see what falls."

"That reminds me," Ross said. "The *Brah'Kerov* sent over the itinerary for the Senate Convention. As the Senate Adjunct, you are commanded to notify the senators of the member races of the time and place."

Commanded. That was a word Matt hadn't heard in quite some time. He heard it frequently when he first came aboard *Able Station*, but it had become less common as he grew in power. That word was a sickening reminder that humans were still slaves.

Matt stood. "Ross, get my shuttle ready. I'll need to make the announcements from the *Brah'Kerov*."

"Your shuttle has already been prepped," Cossette proudly declared. "I saw to it when the message arrived for you."

Matt stared in confusion. "How did you know I'd need to leave?"

She gave half a smile. "It wasn't hard to guess. You are the new Senate Adjunct and a message arrived from the Draconian flagship. And it arrived right around the time when the next convention should take place."

Matt felt a smile creeping across his face. He forced a neutral expression. He hesitated to endanger a woman by keeping her on his staff. But despite that, she was clever and efficient. Ross was loyal but he didn't have the shrewd mind she seemed to. "Very good. Be sure to get me that forensics report."

"Of course," she said, leaving the room.

Matt stared at the door she left. "Ross, whatever you're paying her, double it."

"You're keeping her? What about Lord Vaux?"

Matt held up a hand. "I know what I said. She just might be worth the danger." He looked at Ross. "Just keep her out of sight whenever Lord Vaux is aboard."

Chapter 25

AN AWAKENING

Jonathan took a deep breath. His sore chest muscles protested. He raised his eyelids and blinding white light flooded in. He shut his eyes, groaning from the stinging brightness. It was better in the dark; it was less painful. He could rest in darkness. But darkness was the absence of knowing. Was knowing worth the pain? He took another deep breath. *Lilacs,* he thought. No, not really lilacs; it was more like lilacs with a faint cinnamon smell.

Where had he smelled that fragrance before? Was it on Eurosia? Yes, Ellyra had shown him her favorite garden spot. She had stood near a blossoming shrub with glowing white berries. She had giggled with a bright smile when she had seen him sniff the Vrozsha shrub. Cinnamon and lilacs. Vrozsha. It reminded him of her. Did this mean Ellyra was nearby? His breathing deepened and his heart thumped. Excitement tingled like electricity. He had to know.

Another deep breath. He opened his eyes, once again confronting the stinging bright light. He blinked and squinted, trying to fight against his desire to shut his eyes. Somehow, it was important to know if she was with him. Gradually, his eyes adjusted and the world around him came into focus. The blinding light still flooded his senses but the intensity of the pain began to lessen. What was this place?

The brilliant white ceiling hung precariously low and faded seamlessly into the walls. There were no light fixtures. So, where did the light come from? It seemed to come from all around. Moving his eyeballs around to see caused a dull ache in his head.

The faint sound of breathing came from his left. He turned his head to the side. Ellyra lay beside him, breathing softly as she slept. Where was this place? Had he died? Was this Heaven? No, the headache wouldn't quite fit into that scenario.

Ellyra shifted and a lock of her light blue hair fell across her face. He hadn't seen light blue as a Euroo hair color before. She looked so peaceful sleeping beside him. Did light blue mean she was feeling peaceful? She must have stayed awake worrying over him until she completely exhausted herself. At least she had enough sense to climb onto the bed rather than curling up on the floor.

Jonathan lifted a stiff arm toward Ellyra. With great care, he brushed aside her lock of hair, trying not to wake her. That was better; he could see her whole face now. He studied the lines of her eyelids, the shape of her nose, and the contours of her lips. He had seen her before, but not like this. She looked relaxed and delicate somehow. There was something precious and endearing about watching her as she slept. In that moment, there were no outside worries. There were no Draconians, no Scorpii, no assassins, no politics or procedure; there was only him and her.

If he touched her face again, would she awake? He wanted to touch her again. It would be embarrassing if she did awake to his touch. Getting caught red-handed would only intensify the awkwardness he felt. But, did it have to? Shouldn't he be permitted to touch her face? They were, after all, married, right? Then why was it so nerve-racking to touch her?

Jonathan shook the thought from his head. It still didn't seem real. How could he be married? He signed a contract, true, but that didn't make it feel real. Is that why he had a hard time touching her? He cringed. No, it was definitely guilt. Technically they were married, but there had been no ceremony and no vows. Nothing was endearing about a document and a couple of thumbprints. Without making some commitment from the heart, it didn't seem real. And without that, it would be wrong to touch her. It would be taking advantage of the situation. And taking advantage of a woman was a line he would never cross.

Jonathan placed his hand on his forehead, the pressure easing the throbbing. It was his fault Ellyra was in this mess. He needed to figure out a way to fix it. But how? He couldn't rewind time. There had to be another way, something he hadn't thought of yet.

A small gray man walked into the room. It was a Tumnei. He must be on T'Kal's starship. That would account for the strange bright ambiance and lack of décor—not to mention the low ceiling. The small gray man walked over to Jonathan and spoke into his mind. *"I have been instructed not to interfere with the female's sleep. I also need to run another examination of you."*

Jonathan nodded.

"You needn't restrict your replies to bodily gestures. I can hear what you think."

Jonathan smirked. How could he have forgotten that? *I'm thankful for that,* he thought. *What happened?*

"You were poisoned via projectile injection."

Jonathan's memories raced through his mind. He remembered the funeral service. He remembered talking with Ellyra. Then he remembered the small dart that pricked his neck and the bitter-sour smell.

Teterophalezine? he asked in thought.

"That is correct. With the serum provided by Gamma Station, the poison was neutralized before it caused any irreparable damage."

Serum? From *Gamma Station?* Doc Mallory must have figured out an antidote. Jonathan breathed a sigh of relief. He now owed his life to Dr. Mallory. He would need to thank him when he got back to the space station.

"I will now perform the examination." He waved his hand in the air and a holographic keypad appeared. He touched a few holographic keys and a wide blue beam of light began sweeping down the length of the bed. When the blue scanning beam had finished, it disappeared.

"Scan complete. You may now return to your study of the female."

Now, wait a minute, he thought. *What are you implying?*

The Tumnei tilted his head. *"The increased level of blood in your cheeks signifies you are experiencing embarrassment. There is no reason for this emotion. It is quite natural for the male of the species to inspect its females when searching for a suitable mate."*

This conversation was proving less helpful than the 'phalezine. It needed to end now. So, he didn't bother arguing with the small gray man. One did not argue with a Tumnei without knowing their facts and figures. And right now, Jonathan wasn't in any position to refute biology or sociology. The quickest ending to the conversation was to drop the subject and hope it didn't resurface later.

Thank you, he thought.

"Your gratitude is accepted, though it is not necessary," the Tumnei said before leaving.

Jonathan turned his attention back to Ellyra, still slumbering next to him. That lock of hair had fallen across her face again. If he tucked it behind her ear, it might stay. He brushed the lock of her light blue hair out of her face and behind her ear. The smooth, warm skin of her ear felt good to touch. Without thinking, he lightly caressed her ear with his finger.

Ellyra took in a deep breath and opened her eyes. Jonathan yanked his hand back to his side. Why did he have to touch her? His foolishness woke her up.

"Jonathan," she said, half startled. She lifted her head and placed her hand on his cheek. "Thank the stars, you are all right."

Her hair darkened into a rose-red color. That was also a color he hadn't seen before. How many hair colors were there? The complexity of colors was building. He brushed aside her hair with the back of his fingers. It wasn't in her face; it just seemed the thing to do.

Several tears broke free and rolled down her cheeks. "I have been so worried for you each day."

"Each day?" he asked in confusion. "How long have I been out?"

"Three days."

It would be too much to hope she was joking. How could he have missed 72 hours of his life in the blink of an eye? Moreover, how could she have stayed by his side for that long? No wonder she was exhausted. Had she eaten anything? The Greys would have seen to that, right? What had Ellyra endured to stay at his side? Why did she endure it?

A breath caught in his lungs as a realization struck him hard. She cared about him. She worried herself about his well-being, she stayed with him, and now she was shedding tears of joy over him. He was a fool; not once had he thought about what *she* was going through.

"Ellyra, I have been so blind," he finally said. "I have been so focused on what I am to do next that I entirely neglected you."

She smiled amidst new sobs erupting. Fresh tears caressed her cheeks. She may have been resisting an urge to nod. How could he have been so neglectful? He wrapped his arm around her. It was an odd hug, lying beside her, but that didn't matter. He needed to make up for spoiled time. The woman he cared for needed his attention.

He wiped away her tears, inadvertently brushing her lips with his fingers. Her hair brightened up into pink. She closed her eyes and leaned toward him. He pulled her close and gave her a long kiss. His heart raced and a surge of guilt pounded at the back of his mind. What was he doing? That kiss didn't count as taking advantage, did it? That was never on his mind. To say that he was married seemed too convenient an excuse to cross the line. He abruptly pulled away.

Ellyra opened her eyes, taking in a deep breath.

Jonathan quietly panted, catching his breath. He stared into her blue within blue eyes. He hadn't planned to kiss Ellyra, it just happened.

"I...I'm sorry, I..." What was there to say? Sorry for kissing you, seemed more like an insult than an apology. He needed some time alone to clear his head. But it couldn't be very long; he had neglected her once and didn't want to do it again. So, he said the only thing that came to mind.

"I should take a shower."

Chapter 26

BRAIDING ROSES

Ellyra sat on an oak chair facing a table with a large vanity mirror. One of the few comforts from home she could travel with. And if *Gamma Station* was her new home, this was one of the few things proper about it. Katheryn stood behind her, brushing her joyful blond hair.

"And you are certain this will not interfere with your daily obligations?" Ellyra asked.

Katheryn shook her head. "Not a bit, ma'am. I'm not on duty for another 30 minutes."

"I really do appreciate your kind offer to assist."

"No problem at all, ma'am. A friend in need is a friend indeed, I always say. Besides, I have two younger sisters on the station and I enjoy helping them with their hair. And you have very fun hair."

Ellyra giggled. "Yes, I suppose it is quite a novelty at the moment. Exciting perhaps."

"Yeah, there's been a lot of excitement around here. I sure am glad the Colonel is doing all right."

Ellyra's thoughts returned to the Tumnei starship. She could almost feel the tingling sensation on her hand from the stasis field. She had been so close to losing Jonathan to an eternal slumber. She smiled, reliving the memory of waking up to his touch on her ear. Then there was his tender kiss...

"Woah!" Katheryn said, halting her brushing.

Ellyra looked up at the mirror. Her hair color had changed to a romantic pink.

"Okay, now I am really curious what you were thinkin' about."

How much should she say? Indeed, Katheryn was a new friend, but she barely knew her. It wasn't like talking to Rana. It was not proper to disclose personal details with someone so new. It was best to be vague and discreet for now. "Forgive me, Katheryn. It would seem my hair has made it evident that my mind was more agreeably engaged."

"Thinkin' about the Colonel?"

Her hair tingled; it was changing color again. And there was no question that it was becoming an embarrassed burgundy. And that was always the hardest color to suppress. Still, Ellyra fought for control. She focused all her attention on keeping her hair color the same. She tensed up all her muscles, willing it to stop changing. But to her chagrin, it changed anyway.

"Wow," Katheryn said. "I guess that's a big 10-4."

Ellyra blushed. *Why do I even bother trying?* she wondered. The truth could be read right off her hair. Her father would not approve. Then again, he was many lightyears away. Did it really matter if he would approve?

"My dear Katheryn, please forgive me if I decline to give you all the details," she said with a smile. "But if you will tell me how much you already know, I might be inclined to satisfy your curiosity in some small measure."

Katheryn continued brushing Ellyra's hair. "Well, rumor has it that you and the Colonel are in a relationship. Some even speculate

217

marriage, but I don't believe everything I hear. If the Colonel was getting married, I'm sure we would have heard about it."

"Then let it suffice for me to say that he and I are indeed in a relationship." *Albeit a rough and confusing one.*

Katheryn smiled. "That's so nice, I'm happy for you. And if you don't mind me saying, I do think it's about time the Colonel found someone special."

"It sounds like you know a bit about his personal life," Ellyra said.

Katheryn blushed. "Now you got *me* telegraphing my emotions,"

Ellyra smiled again. "So sorry."

"No, no," Katheryn said dismissively. "A turnabout is fair play. As a general rule we aren't supposed to pry, but Colonel Terynn is kind of a legend. And not just here, they talk about him back on Earth too. Ambassador Cale talks about him a lot."

"Lucas?" she asked.

Katheryn nodded. "Yeah, he knows the Colonel very well."

Talks about him a lot, she thought. If there was free information on Jonathan, then she was overlooking an obvious asset. But it was not proper for a lady to call upon a gentleman who was not family. But it wasn't exactly uncalled for. Lucas had extended an open invitation to her and she would simply be accepting. Surely that was acceptable. Surely no one would object so long as there was a suitable chaperone. It was a tantalizing opportunity that couldn't be passed up.

After Katheryn finished brushing Ellyra's hair, she taught her how to braid it. It wasn't very dignified to have to ask how to style her own hair, but her new life required concessions. Dresses that button up in front and styling her own hair were just the beginning. Finding a chaperone— let alone a suitable one—would be difficult. The people she knew on *Gamma Station* were limited. But she never had gotten anywhere in life by quitting when it was difficult. Somehow, she'd get an appropriate chaperone.

After Katheryn left, Ellyra paced across the length of her room for a while. Then she walked over to the wall-mounted communication screen. She pressed the button to call the operator.

"I'd like to speak with security please," she said. "I have a security concern to report."

Lucas stood in his room, perusing the news report on his handheld reader. The news was always fresh and yet always the same. The Draco Senate was proposing new regulations on space travel. Their justification was saving the galaxy from the decay of interstellar space. And the term they coined was cosmic meltdown. The Scorpii claimed they had scientific evidence to support their assertions this time.

He shook his head. "The musicians may have changed, but the tune is still the same."

The Scorpii had become desperate. Without a clear and present threat, they could not seize any more control over the member races. But if they could create an excuse great enough to warrant regulating space travel, they would be poised to cripple economies. No one would oppose them in the Senate ever again. He and Jonathan would have to keep an eye on the Scorpii. The next Senate convention should be called into session soon.

His door chimed.

He glanced at his comm-band with a confused expression. He didn't have any appointments scheduled for this hour. Who could it be? He crossed over to the door and pressed the button. The door slid up, revealing four security guards and one woman: Ellyra.

"Ambassador Cale?" one of the guards asked.

"Please, I insist you call me Ambassador Lucas now."

"Very well. Please forgive the intrusion, Ambassador. SecOps was notified by an anonymous tip. This woman is an alien starship captain that has been wandering the station unsupervised. So, for any meetings with high-profile staff, such as yourself, we've been ordered to escort her."

Why that clever young lady, he thought. *I'll bet she couldn't find a chaperone and decided to create one.* The irony was that a military entourage was closer to what the daughter of House El'Allel would be used to. It was also more fitting. On Eurosia, she would have had several men at arms to escort her places. Now, she had managed to convince the station security to escort her around *Gamma Station.* She was no longer the simple little girl he had met on Eurosia all those years ago. The woman now before him was clever and resourceful. *Jonathan, my old friend, you have chosen well.*

Lucas stood back from the door. "Yes, please come in."

Two of the guards remained outside his door while the other two escorted Ellyra inside. It was important in Euroo culture for a lady to have a chaperone when calling on a gentleman outside the family. Otherwise, he would have dismissed the guards, telling them it was unnecessary.

Lucas motioned for Ellyra to take a seat. "Welcome, my dear. And judging by your arrival, I'd say you have certainly put Kalmeedes into practice."

She smiled, her hair brightening into an excited blond. "As it has been said, 'Failures are but a finite resource; the more errors I employ, the fewer there stand between me and my goal'."

He now needed to add *scholar* to her list of virtues. It was proving quite entertaining having someone to quote Kalmeedes with. "Bravo, my dear, bravo. Now, may I get you something to drink? Cascheñey perhaps?"

She smiled again. "You have Euroo drinks?"

"Now, seriously, my dear, how could one ever expect to spend any real time on Eurosia and *not* come away forever spoiled from enjoying anything less?"

"I concede to your point with my whole heart. And yes, I would love some Cascheñey."

Lucas walked over to a table at the side of the room. He retrieved a fancy crystal bottle of pink liquid along with two glasses. He handed her one and poured. "I trust a woman of your station can identify the year."

She smelled it and then took a small sip, rolling it around in her mouth. She glanced back at him with a broad smile. "Fifty-third," she declared.

He nodded with a smirk. "Fifty-third." He sat down in an armchair across from her. He took a breath to speak and then noticed the security guards standing against the wall. The only downside to this kind of chaperone was that he needed to be discrete. That meant speaking just cryptic enough for the extra ears to be unable to understand.

"You must forgive my sensitive ears. During the funeral service, Isabeau seated you next to the officer's spouses. My first inclination was to question if the seating arrangement was accurate."

Her hair darkened into a gloomy indigo. "Yes, the seating was accurate. The abrupt union was in response to the Senate's injunction against *Gamma Station* and the Euroo."

Lucas sat forward. Very little in the Euroo culture was abrupt. One of the few exceptions was a common-law marriage, which could be enacted by a simple contract. Because it was devoid of any ceremony, it was looked down upon. Could Ellyra be serious? Her station as the daughter of a great house made such a marriage a complete scandal. Her reputation would be branded.

"He asked this of you?"

She looked down. "More accurately, he asked if there was any way to still be together after the new sanction."

Lucas took a sip of his pink drink. "It's not an easy thing to dismiss one's reputation."

She looked up, a tear rolling down each cheek. "He said he needed me." Her eyes returned to her lap. "But I am finding that need may no longer exist."

Lucas set down his glass. Did Jonathan have any idea what kind of sacrifice she made for him? *Dear lands!* he thought. *She has given up everything for him.*

She sniffled, more tears silently making their journey down her face.

He pulled out a handkerchief and offered it to her. "A very rough beginning, indeed." He looked heavenward, searching for something to say—something comforting and useful. His mind sifted through memories and anecdotes from his past. With so many memories, stories, and words of wisdom, it should have taken a while to find the right thing to say. But with Lucas, the right thing usually came quickly.

"I am reminded of the groundskeeper at the Naval Academy back on Earth, one of the few times I was permitted to visit. His name was Winston. He was such a man that everyone could tell him their troubles and he would have useful advice. On a particular day—I remember it being a Friday—I overheard him talking to a pair of academy students. One of them had asked how she could continue believing in love and romance when she kept experiencing pain and sorrow."

Ellyra looked up again with renewed interest in her eyes. "What did he tell the young lady?"

"Love, he said, was like braiding roses. At first, their thorns prick at every attempt to weave the two together. The process is long and painful, but once braided, the pair of roses are inseparable. Their thorns turn outward to ward against any threat that would come between them."

Ellyra's hair brightened into a wishful violet as another tear ran down her cheek. She dabbed at it with the handkerchief.

"The key to such a success," he added, "is not giving up after a few thorn pricks."

A smile crossed her lips. "Thank you."

Chapter 27

THE SUMMONING

Jonathan sat at the only chair in the middle of Command and Control, next to a large control panel. The evening shift was busier than usual. Mostly because Jonathan wasn't as organized as Isabeau. But she needed a day off. Three days of filling his command without any support had drained her. The room had reached a lull in the hubbub of activity and Jonathan wanted to catch up on current affairs in the Senate. A lot could be missed in 72 hours of unconsciousness.

He perused the newspaper on his handheld reader. "Cosmic meltdown," he grumbled under his breath. What would the Scorpii think of next? Aside from the ludicrous name, their proposed solution was exactly the same as last time. It didn't take a genius to read between the lines. They wanted more power and authority.

"Colonel Terynn," Petty Officer McKinsey addressed. "Supreme Commander T'Kal's ship is requesting clearance to leave the station."

Jonathan stood. "Put it on screen, Petty Officer."

One of the two large wall-mounted screens flashed. It displayed a video image of an extremely white room with a thick fog rolling across the floor. Several Tumnei crewmen sat with holographic computer screens floating in the air. In the center of the room, T'Kal sat in a white swiveling chair. He tilted his head as if to speak and a caption ran along the bottom of the video image. IT IS GETTING CLOSE TO THE TIME FOR THE DRACO SENATE TO CONVENE. I MUST RETURN AMBASSADOR CYRAN TO *BRAVO STATION*. I, THEREFORE, REQUEST PERMISSION TO DEPART.

"Permission to depart, granted. And give my best to Cyran. Tell him we'll take good care of his sister."

T'Kal nodded as a new caption scrolled across the bottom of the screen. I WILL, OF COURSE, RELAY YOUR REGARDS. T'KAL OUT. The video image ended, returning the screen to displaying statistics and graphs.

Jonathan sat back down, lifting his reader to pick up where he had left off.

"Colonel Terynn," Petty Officer McKinsey said. "We have an incoming message on the Alpha Channel. It's from the Draconian flagship, *Brah'Kerov*."

Jonathan rolled his eyes, tossing his reader onto the console. It was about time for the Draco Senate to convene. It was too bad it had to happen so soon after his recovery. He would have liked more time to prepare. "On screen, Petty Officer."

The large screen flickered again. It displayed a live video image of Matt Jaimess in his typical black and red *Able Station* uniform. Behind him hung the twin serpent crest of the Draco Senate. He instantly burst forth into his absurdly fake zeal. "Good morning, Commander. Or is it good evening where you are? I can never—" He paused, all the enthusiasm draining from his face as he stared at Jonathan.

Jonathan placed his hands behind his back. "Why, Mr. Jaimess, you look as if you have seen a ghost."

Matt blinked.

Jonathan strolled a few steps toward Matt's image on the wall-mounted screen. "Commander Alexi has the day off; I'm filling in."

Matt slowly breathed out. "Colonel Terynn..."

"Disappointed to see me alive, Mr. Jaimess?"

As if snapped out of a trance, Matt erupted back into his phony enthusiasm. "Merely surprised, my dear Colonel. I had expected to see Commander Alexi as I have for several days now. But I must say, you look to be in remarkably good health."

"Good health and a strong constitution. It takes a lot more to get me down."

"I am so pleased to hear it."

"Perhaps you should get to the point, Mr. Jaimess."

"Direct and efficient as always, my dear Colonel. The reason for this communiqué is to inform you of the time and location of the next Draco Senate convention. It is scheduled to be held in two days' time. Details are included at the end of this transmission."

"Noted," Jonathan said, turning to walk back to his console.

"Colonel," Matt said with an air of caution.

Jonathan turned back around.

"If you need to sit this one out to recuperate," he said in a serious tone, "We will gladly see you again at the next convention. Such a precaution may even be...advisable."

There was something in Matt's tone of voice that made his suggestion seem more like a threat. Of course, Matt wouldn't want him participating in this session of the Senate. The Scorpii were making another power grab and didn't want the opposition. There was no way he was going to let the Scorpii get any more power than they already had.

Jonathan smiled. "Thank you for expressing your concern for me. After the past few days, I had begun to wonder if there was any love coming from *Able Station.* I'll be sure to relay my humble gratitude to you in person. See you in forty-eight hours. Terynn out." He pressed a button on the console, ending the transmission.

225

He walked back around his control panel back and flopped back into his chair. He would need to inform Ambassador Lucas about the call to convene. Not many things had gone his way in the last few weeks, but at least he now had Lucas back. He would need his keen political mind in this next war of words.

He turned to the stellar cartographer down in the pit. "O'Dell, plot a course to the destination coordinates from that last transmission. I want an estimated travel time."

"Aye, aye sir."

Jonathan glanced up to the balcony and spotted Katheryn. "Vinnece!"

She stopped and glanced down at him. "Sir?"

"Please inform Ambassador Lucas to report to Command and Control."

"Aye, aye sir."

Just then, Lucas walked into the room. Jonathan glanced back up to Vinnece. "Belay my last, Seaman."

Lucas walked up to him and spoke in a soft voice. "Jonathan, might I have a word with you concerning Ellyra?"

Jonathan knew there was much that needed to be said in regard to Ellyra. Most of which was his fault. But now wasn't the time. Stopping the Scorpii's latest power grab was more pressing. As was orchestrating the fastest possible transportation route.

"I'm glad you're here, Ambassador. We just received the call to convention."

"Uh, fine. Now I really must speak to you about Ellyra."

Jonathan felt the restless jitters in his hands and his anxiety grew. "Ambassador, I appreciate your concern. But right now, we have much bigger fires to put out. Matt Jaimess is on the warpath, we have been banned from interacting with the Euroo, and now, the Scorpii are making another move to seize more authority." *Not to mention,* he thought, *I still need to approach the Chantell about the conspiracy. Otherwise, we may not ever get this prophecy off the ground.*

"Imagine, if you will," Lucas said, "finding yourself stripped of your rank, alienated from society, and never again able to see your family. Not only your duty but your very purpose called into question."

What kind of nonsense was Lucas up to? While he enjoyed the occasional mental exercise, now was not the time for a philosophical discussion. He waved his hand dismissively, walking over toward the pit. "Can we save soul-crushing tragedy scenarios for when we get back?"

Lucas called out behind him. "Because that is exactly what has happened to your wife!" His words echoed off the walls.

The room grew still and quiet. Jonathan turned around, hearing the small grinding sound of a fleck of dirt under his boot. He walked back over to Lucas, his steps echoing. Every eye in the room was looking at him. He didn't appreciate his tattered love life being thrown on display. But to Lucas's credit, he did try to speak privily. He had only himself to blame.

Chief O'Dell stood up. "Colonel," he said with an Irish accent. "I have a course plotted to Gamma Lepordis VII. Total travel time—"

Jonathan held up his hand to O'Dell, signaling for silence. He kept his stare on Lucas. "All right, Ambassador, you've got my attention."

Lucas motioned toward the exit. "Do you mind if we...?"

Jonathan waved his arm for Lucas to lead the way. He followed Lucas out of Command and Control and round the first corner.

"Please forgive the outburst, Jonathan. I would not have done it if I wasn't afraid for you."

"Afraid for me?"

Lucas nodded. "You have been so focused on the front lines that you have not even noticed the enemy breaching your flanks."

Jonathan tried not to smile. Lucas knew him well enough to use combat metaphors. And although Lucas didn't have an extensive military vocabulary, he did know how to get his point across. In other words, Lucas was saying something very important was being overlooked. "All right, Ambassador, you've disarmed me. Go ahead and be frank."

"Have you any idea what Ellyra has sacrificed for you?"

Jonathan glanced down. His heart sunk into the pit of his stomach. Guilt swept over him like a winter breeze. "I know that she cannot return to the Euroo homeworld and that I have neglected her. She cares enough about me to have stayed at my bedside for 72 hours." He looked into Lucas's eyes. "I know I've been a fool, but I'm trying to make up for it."

"You comprehend only the tip of the iceberg, I'm afraid. Do you know what else she has given up for you?"

"Well, she's stuck with me. Some kind of marriage contract."

"It's called a common-law marriage. To put things into perspective, in Euroo culture a common-law marriage is usually reserved for those in scandalous affairs. Such a social branding leaves reputations in utter ruin. I have seen House Lords disown children rather than take on such a blemish to their family name."

Jonathan felt weak in the knees. What had he done to Ellyra? How could he ever face her again knowing that he ruined her reputation and probably her entire life? A sudden sense of dread mixed with light-headedness washed over him. He steadied himself against the wall. "Why did she do it?"

"Two reasons; she loves you and you told her you needed her."

Images of T'Kal, Cyran, Fox, and Isabeau sitting around the conference table flooded his mind. He remembered them asking him to approach Ellyra in order to get close to the Chantell. If only he had refused, this whole mess could have been avoided. Why did he have to give in? Why couldn't he have thought of another way?

Jonathan closed his eyes and breathed out a deep breath. "Ambassador Lucas, how do I fix this?"

"Right now, that dear woman needs a sense of purpose. I recommend you make good on your promise to need her."

Jonathan straightened up and smoothed out his uniform jacket with a sharp tug at the hem. "Sun Tzu said that even the finest sword plunged into salt water will eventually rust. It's time I take care of what I have."

Jonathan walked back into Command and Control with Lucas in tow. He glanced up at the runners on the balcony. "Vinnece, contact SecOps and have them prepare a comm-band for Sune Ellyra."

Katheryn's eyes widened with excitement. "Right away, Colonel!" She spun around and got socked in the face by her braided ponytail.

Jonathan suppressed a smirk before turning to Chief O'Dell. "Chief, what is the estimated travel time to the *Brah'Kerov*'s current position?"

"Travel time is estimated at forty-six hours and some change, sir," he replied in his thick Irish accent.

Jonathan turned to Lucas. "Get your things together; we all have to leave in under two hours."

"We all?" he asked with a confused expression.

Jonathan nodded. "Ellyra is coming too."

Chapter 28

RUNNING IN CIRCLES

Fox sat, slumped in his seat aboard the *Calmao*. He stared at the three-dimensional holographic display of the star system. There didn't look like there was anything to find. But that was how it was with the last twelve star systems they checked. All empty. All silent.

"Any response yet?" Diahlus asked, pacing the floor in front of the holographic display.

"Indeed not," came a reply from behind.

"How long have we been broadcasting the signal?"

"Three-quarters of an hour."

Diahlus blew out a breath of disappointment. "You may discontinue the signal." He then sat down next to Fox. "It would appear we can cross this one off the list as well."

Fox hung his head.

Diahlus placed his hand on Fox's shoulder. "It is regrettable that we have exhausted all the locations of which you have taken notes."

Fox ran a hand down his shaven head and across his face. "Yeah, tell me about it—that's just a human expression, by the way. I was so sure..."

Diahlus shrugged. "Perhaps we might extend our search to the western frontier."

"No. It has to be somewhere along the northern edge of Euroo space."

"Fox, I do not wish to criticize your convictions, but why, may I ask, are you so thoroughly convinced the Skorath are here?"

Fox stood in irritation and paced through the holographic display of the star system. He clenched his fists. How much could he say? There was no way to ask Jonathan for permission to bring Diahlus into their confidence. The conspiracy for freedom could be jeopardized by one misjudgment of character. It wasn't worth endangering the plan to rebel against the Draconians. Jonathan still had Ellyra. And hopefully, he was working on bringing the Bugs into the conspiracy.

In the meantime, Fox was left out of the loop. He was no longer able to rejoin *Gamma Station* and had no plausible excuse to contact the Greys himself. There had to be some way to help decipher the Skorath Prophecy. He had to find a way to help out. And right now, all he had to go on was the uncanny references to the Skorath in Euroo mythology. There was even a version of the prophecy in their mythology. It was so old and probably a dozen times retold before it was written, but it was indeed the prophecy.

And if the added clues in Euroo mythology could help him find the Skorath, then he had to try. But how much of the conspiracy could he disclose to Diahlus? If he told him too much, there was a risk the Draconians could find out. And if they found out about a conspiracy, they would exterminate the Greys. Yet, if he said too little, Diahlus would feel he wasn't trusted and that would make him less willing to help. Fox needed to walk a razor edge of just how much to say.

Fox walked over to Diahlus and lowered his voice to a whisper. "What I *can* tell you, is that the Skorath have been spotted somewhere in these northern sectors. And with the references to Euroo mythology, that narrows the search down to these thirteen star systems. So, you see, they have to be here."

Diahlus shook his head. "Except that we visited each one and transmitted a hail for close to an hour at every location. There isn't anyone out there willing to talk."

Fox looked up in surprise. His heart thumped as a surge of hope washed over him. *Of course! Why didn't I think of that?* he thought. "Diahlus, you're brilliant!"

Confusion settled on his face. "I am? How so?"

"Willing to talk!" he said as if announcing a lottery winner. "It's not necessarily that there isn't anyone out there, but that they aren't willing to respond. And why would they? They've been in hiding for centuries."

"That is one way to interpret our results. However, we have no evidence that anyone is even listening."

"Don't you see? It's Chekhov's gun!"

"I'm afraid you will have to explain."

Fox ran his hand down his shaven head again. "Okay, Chekhov's gun is a narrative principle in storytelling. In the words of Sergius Shchukin, if you say in the first act that there is a rifle hanging on the wall, in the second or third act it absolutely must go off. If it's not going to be fired, it shouldn't be hanging there."

"And how does this storytelling principle relate to the Skorath?"

"Diahlus, the Skorath would not have inserted themselves into Euroo myth unless they wanted to be found."

"If they wanted to be found, would they not have responded to our relentless hails?"

Fox took a deep breath. "Anyone who is hiding and yet needs to be contacted will set up a procedure. Like a password or something to ensure they aren't being contacted by the enemy."

Diahlus stared a moment in thought. "If what you say is true—and I am not yet convinced that you are—then the Skorath are waiting to be contacted on *their* terms?"

"Exactly. We just need to decipher how they want to be contacted."

Diahlus took his seat. "Well, I certainly do not envy your task ahead. Do be sure to let me know when you have had another stunning revelation to this mystery."

Fox frowned. "Thanks for the vote of confidence." He couldn't blame Diahlus for not wanting to help pore through several volumes of mythology. Most of the helpful material was very dry to read. It nearly put Fox to sleep. At least Diahlus had appointed him a translator.

A gentleman turned around in his seat. "Brigadain Diahlus, we have an incoming message on the priority channel."

Diahlus turned to face him. "On stage please."

"As you wish."

The hologram of the star system flickered and changed to a hologram of Lord Areo. He gave a slight bow of the head. "Diahlus, I need the *Calmao* to intercept a starliner. House Creo is sending an envoy to the Scorpii."

Diahlus's hair blackened. "After all we have done for them, they intend to defy the Great Houses?"

"It isn't a matter of defiance this time; it could be outright treason. I have heard reports that Creo intends to form an alliance with the Scorpii. In exchange for military aid to usurp control of Eurosia, they promise to side with the Scorpii in the senate."

Diahlus's hair paled into gray. "They would incite a civil war?"

"I do not believe Lord Inson has given his actions enough thought to properly predict the outcome. Their ship is heading for Scorpii space by way of Anon's Nebula. Intercept their ship while I see what evidence I can find here."

Diahlus bowed. "As you wish, my lord."

The hologram faded and disappeared. Diahlus dropped into his chair. "The greedy imbecile is going to start a war," he grumbled. After a moment of staring off into space, he turned to Fox. "I'm afraid this will prematurely end your research."

Unfortunately, that was all this endeavor was to Diahlus; a research project. That was the other downside to leaving him in the dark about the conspiracy for freedom. With no emotional commitment, this was

all just some hobby. Authorized or not, Fox needed to tell him. If he didn't, they would return to Eurosia and possibly get entangled in a civil war. There was no guarantee he would ever get another chance to find the Skorath.

"Brigadain Diahlus," Fox said. "I have not been fully honest with you, and knowing what I know may affect your decisions."

Diahlus looked him over a moment. "Then it is perhaps best that you do not tell me. As of now, my thoughts and convictions are aligned with a single duty to my house. I cannot allow war to come to Eurosia."

He had to admire Diahlus in at least one area. He was a man of duty and principle. But right now, he needed to be a man of vision. If Fox was close to solving the Skorath Prophecy, he was within arm's reach of the promised "birthright of the ancestors". And if the birthright was indeed the technology of an ancient empire, then this research project was more important than ten civil wars. It had the potential of leveling the playing field with the Draconians. But how could he convince Diahlus to hear him out?

Fox thought for a silent moment. There were many things he could say. He could ask, what if there was a way to prevent war *and* find the Skorath? Such a question sounded more like a feeble plea than anything else. He could try some cryptic line such as, what I know could spell the downfall of the Scorpii. That would buy him at least a follow-up question, but it would not guarantee Diahlus would hear him out. Diahlus was not a political thinker, nor a philosopher. As articulate as the man was, he was the closest thing the Euroo had to a practical man. And the only thing a practical man appreciated was the bottom line.

"Diahlus, I'm involved in a conspiracy to start a revolt against the Draconians in the next few months. If we fail, billions of people will be executed by the Draconians. But if we succeed every homeworld will be liberated from the Draconians as well as the Scorpii."

Diahlus stared at Fox as though he had grown two extra heads.

"Sorry to drop that on you," Fox said. "But what we're out here searching for could save Eurosia as well as the rest of the slave races.

234

And we are *so* close, Diahlus. Couldn't you please give me a little more time?"

Diahlus's hair color lightened up to violet as he pondered.

Fox sat in uncomfortable silence, waiting for a reply.

Diahlus eventually cleared his throat. "If we head to Anon's Nebula the long way, around Creeson's Pulsar, it would delay our stay in this region another day. And it would put our trajectory in the path of several of your target solar systems."

Fox breathed a sigh of relief. He had got through to Diahlus. One day was not much leeway, but it was something he could work with. "Thank you, Diahlus. You won't regret this."

Diahlus turned toward him. "We only have time enough to stop at one of those locations."

Fox's mouth dropped open. "Wait...you're telling me I have to choose? I have one day to figure out how to contact the Skorath, and I only get *one chance* to pick the correct solar system?"

"I'm afraid that is all the time I can spare. I will have your meals brought to your room and provide a second interpreter."

Fox rose to his feet. "No pressure..." he said under his breath. "I'm only gambling on the fate of the known galaxy." He turned to leave.

"Fox," Diahlus called after him.

Fox spun around. "Yes?"

"May Vera guide you."

Chapter 29

THE GREATER GOOD

Matt walked down the torch-lit hallways of the *Brah'Kerov*. The rough-hewn walls cast small shadows in the torchlight. In his hand, he held a data rod. Unlike the majority of the data rods Matt had carried, this one was valuable. The data that it held had the potential to cause the extermination of an entire race. It had been recovered from Ir'Jad's ship. How Ir'Jad had come across it didn't matter. All that mattered now was that it gave Matt enough power to tip the balance in the Senate. If he was reckless in his use of that power, everything he had worked for could come crashing down. But if he used it wisely, he could finally open the door to liberating his people from the vile squiddies.

He stopped at a fork in the hallway and stared down the other passageway. There was one other minor detail that needed attention. He needed to rescue Lord Vaux from the Draconians. They had led him away from the senate floor after he accused *Gamma Station* of using a Skorath weapon. The Draconians declared they would hold him until evidence was produced. Matt lifted the data rod to his eyes. Here was the evidence that would set Lord Vaux free.

He glanced back at the foreboding passageway that led to the holding cells. It would be so easy just to forget about Lord Vaux. If the evidence never came, the squiddy would rot. A smile crossed Matt's lips. Justice could not look any sweeter. He lowered his hand and let out a sullen sigh. But that would not put him any closer to freeing his people. Lord Vaux would be replaced by the next ambitious Commissioner. And Matt would have to begin again getting into the good graces of the next lord.

Could it be that bad? Could the next lord be less barbaric? So many unknowns and so little time. No, he couldn't continue living like this; bowing before the squiddies and hoping every day they wouldn't massacre his crew. At least with Lord Vaux, he already had an established relationship. He had already greased that wheel enough to manipulate it. He could push Lord Vaux into the next phase of his plan. But if he were to free Lord Vaux, it would take out its anger on the *Able Station* crew again. More death. More loss.

Matt clenched the data rod with white knuckles. With Colonel Terynn alive, there was no choice but to advance to the next phase. If he didn't, Colonel Self-righteous would blockade every avenue to advance in the Senate. *It's for the greater good,* Matt told himself. *I must free my people.* With a deep breath, he marched down the hallway toward the holding cells. He just had to hope Ross would keep Cossette out of sight. They would have to endure Lord Vaux's outrage one last time. If they could hold out long enough, Matt would put an end to the barbarous squiddy while elevating himself to an all-new high. High enough to wrestle away control of *Able Station* from the Scorpii.

A bead of perspiration ran down his forehead. He ignored the tickling sensation as long as he could before wiping it away with his free hand. This was not going to be an easy sell. To look convincing, it needed to appear as if he would fail. He had perfected this performance with the Scorpii, but he had little interaction with the Arkalan. Hopefully, the same principles would apply.

When he reached the end of the hall, a whiff of the Arkalan grime assaulted his nose. Those creatures sure put off a lot of odor for being supposedly made of rock. Matt stepped into a large room lined with stone-carved cages with metal bars. It was too dark inside the cells to see Lord Vaux. All the better for the performance. It would be more convincing if the squiddy heard his voice before seeing him. That was a trick he had learned from the last lord of *Able Station.*

"You there!" Matt called out to one of the two tall stone-looking Arkalan guards. "Release the Scorpiian in the ninth cell." He pointed at Lord Vaux.

The overgrown rock-like man took three thunderous steps closer. "By whose command?"

"Oh don't be a nincompoop; just open the door."

The Arkalan guard grinned and glanced over to his companion. "An Earthian giving orders. I thought I had seen it all."

The second Arkalan thundered a few steps closer. "The only time an Earthian gives orders is right before it dies for insolence."

The Arkalan were twice the height of a door and bulky. They towered over Matt with evil grins. A physical altercation would prove instantly fatal. This is where the delicate dance of words became crucial. It still needed to look realistic, so playing the part of the fool was necessary.

Matt backed up a few steps. "Now just a minute, there's no reason for things to turn nasty."

One of the Arkalans picked up a long metal rod. It was twice the length of a man and too large around for a man to hold. "Tell us again, little Earthian, what your order is."

Matt clenched the data rod. *Not yet, I still need to sell it a bit more. It has to look like I'm defeated.* He backed up a few more steps. "If I said something wrong, I do apologize."

The Arkalan raised the metal rod, preparing to bring it down hard on top of Matt.

Matt held his hand forward. "Wait! That's what he told me to say!"

The Arkalan halted his swing, showing a confused expression. "Who told you what to say?"

Here it is, Matt thought. *Time to throw the hammer down on these morons.* "Why, it was his Excellency, Creus-Thanus."

Both Arkalan guards took a step back. Anytime the name of a Draconian was mentioned, it warranted great care. And even these brainless brutes knew enough to be cautious. Offending a Draconian was no laughing matter. It didn't matter that it was a complete fabrication. Creus-Thanus would never stoop to speaking to an Earthian directly. That was a fact that these overgrown gargoyles hadn't figured out yet. All that mattered was that it took a lot more effort to disprove the claim than to comply.

The Arkalan lowered his metal rod and grumbled to his companion in their native language. The other one nodded and replied. Even though Matt couldn't understand their words, he knew they were debating whether to obey or seek verification. Most simply obeyed but every now and then there would be someone willing to verify Matt's claims. He was prepared for that scenario. He rubbed his finger across the rough metal edge of the data rod, hoping not to have to use it for this.

The Arkalan guards moved over to Lord Vaux's cell and opened it. Lord Vaux skittered out like a spider fleeing from danger. It probably had had enough of the holding cell and didn't want to give them a chance to change their minds. It stopped in front of Matt.

Matt motioned Lord Vaux toward the exit.

Lord Vaux hissed and swatted Matt across the face with a tentacle. Matt dropped to his knees. He had forgotten to bow to Lord Vaux. The idiotic squiddy still fancied itself as being in charge. *It's for the greater good,* he reminded himself. He had to endure its brutality a little longer. *Your time will come, Lord Vaux. And when it does, I will be the one pulling the trigger.*

Matt wiped the blood from the corner of his mouth and stood. "Forgive me, my lord."

It squealed contentedly, strutting out and down the hallway. Matt squeezed the data rod. He was free to begin the final phase of his plan. The sour irony was that he had to give Lord Vaux a huge victory in the process. He took a deep, regretful breath. *It's all for the greater good. Freedom is almost within reach.*

J onathan wandered through the moving sea of people. The foreboding hallways of the *Brah'Kerov* looked cheerful with the crowd of senators and delegates moving all about. He held onto Ellyra's hand, guiding her through the vast throng. Close behind her walked Lucas. Jonathan had walked these halls dozens of times over and yet each time he came, it stirred up the same feelings.

Every alien he passed belonged to a world that the Draconians had conquered. And while he had memorized the five elder races, he had long ago lost count of the younger races. Some he knew, others he wasn't sure he had ever seen before. Were the Draconians still conquering? Were they still expanding their empire or did their dominion reach so far that he would never meet every race? So many slave races. So many reasons to wish for things to be different.

At least there was hope. If T'Kal was right about the prophecy, then *Gamma Station* would be the catalyst for shifting the balance of power in the galaxy. He had a chance to make a difference. It was a chance to improve the lives of everyone on the homeworld of every alien in this crowd.

Lucas tapped Jonathan on the shoulder. "I saw Senator Clarence. I'm going to say hello."

Jonathan tapped his comm-band to see the time.

Lucas smirked. "Don't worry, Jonathan. I'll be seated before the call to order."

He nodded as Lucas veered off a different path through the crowd.

Ellyra squeezed his hand and asked a question. It wasn't loud enough to hear over the cacophony of conversations. Jonathan leaned in closer.

She pointed. "That man over there. In the black and red uniform. Is he the one we saw at the Treaty Violation Hearing?"

Jonathan's eyes followed the direction she indicated. Matt walked beside a Scorpiian at the far end of the hallway. Images of his last in-person encounter with Matt flooded his mind. He had asked for an alliance between *Able Station* and *Gamma Station*. And like an idiot, he had shut down the possibility on account of his morals.

But, then again, was it really so foolish to shut him down? He was, after all, asking him to vote against his conscience and side with the Scorpii. Politics should not be like warfare. A senator's duty was to scrutinize the legislation and make an informed decision. It was not to not pick teams and draw battle lines between each other. And that is what was so broken about politics.

Thousands of people so ready to believe themselves at war with one another. And legislation being nothing more than the ammunition they volley. But what if Ellyra was right? What if there was a way to make an acceptable alliance with the Abes? What could they achieve together? With the resources of two space stations, and the information-rich tie they have to the Scorpii... His mind spun with possible scenarios. They would be better able to plan their revolt against the Draconians. Matt could even influence the Scorpii in their favor.

"Matt Jaimess," he replied. "The one who wanted an alliance and I refused before hearing him out." He glanced into Ellyra's blue within blue eyes. "I need to talk with him. If I can resurrect interest in an alliance, perhaps we can..." He stopped short, realizing he still hadn't told her about the conspiracy for freedom. She would not know what he was talking about.

"Perhaps we can do what?"

There wasn't time for an explanation. There was little time left before the call to order. "I'll explain later." He towed her along, weaving through the senators and delegates. Jonathan grumbled under his breath. The sea of people was so dense that it was taking a long time to navigate through them. Little by little, they made their way down the hall. Matt was not yet close enough to talk to or even to notice Jonathan. Matt finished conversing with the Scorpiian and bowed.

Not good. Matt had finished his conversation but they were still pushing through the thick cloud of people. The Scorpii skittered away with its tentacle legs. Matt stared after it for a short while and then headed back the way he had come.

Jonathan's heart raced. His opportunity was slipping away. He started shoving people aside as he rushed to get through. He had to get to Matt before the convention began. A roar sounded behind Jonathan. He glanced back. One of the alien senators he had shoved aside angrily pushed back. That sent Jonathan tumbling to the ground. Seeing the commotion, the crowd moved aside, giving them some clear space.

He had never seen that species before. But it looked angry. Jonathan scrambled back to his feet, his hands and feet in a combat stance. He didn't come to the convention to brawl with the local delegates. But his military training had been baked into his reflexes.

The angry senator drew a small knife from his belt. Unarmed combat was one thing, unarmed versus armed combat was another thing entirely. Jonathan shifted his feet and hands into another combat stance. This one was to defend against an edged weapon. As long as his opponent wasn't better trained, Jonathan would win. If the angry senator was better, on the other hand, Jonathan could die.

Ellyra jumped between them, speaking in a strange language, and motioning to Jonathan. The senator calmed his breathing, put away his dagger, and replied to her.

Ellyra then turned to Jonathan. "Caldezians do not like to be touched. For them, it is a matter of honor. I promised him it would not happen again."

Jonathan lowered his hands and straightened up. "It was my fault, I—" he turned and shot a glance down the end of the hallway. *Blast!* Matt was gone. Jonathan clenched his fists, his blood pumping, and his heart sinking. He had lost his opportunity. He closed his eyes, lowering his head. The painful realization tugged at his heart. He could have stopped the assassinations and started a collaboration. He would have to try again another time. Could the political landscape still allow for another chance?

Chapter 30

THE SENATE CONVENTION

The crowd of people began dispersing almost all at once. Jonathan tapped his comm-band. It was almost time for the call to order. The proceedings would begin in moments. They had just enough time to get to their assigned delegation box. Jonathan again took Ellyra's hand and led her through a door and up a flight of stone-looking steps. The disappointment of the morning still tugged at his heart, like an anchor dangling into his stomach. He shook his head to clear his mind.

They reached the next landing and Jonathan guided her through the first doorway. It opened up into a narrow walkway in an immense open room. Small flying lizards soared overhead carrying large glowing orbs to light the room. Other small lizards crawled along the walls, spewing blue flames onto torches. The Senate Chamber held rows upon rows of balconies. Each one portioned off sections of seats into balcony boxes.

Each delegation was assigned a permanent balcony box. *Gamma Station* had been assigned box 131. The open air smelled of warm breath and perspiration. The noise of thousands of overlapping conversations rumbled throughout the enormous room.

"Is that the one?" Ellyra asked.

He glanced up. She had pointed to the sign for box 131. "Yep, this is it."

"Why are all the signs written in Earthian?"

He shrugged. "The Draconians consider it to be an easy language. Most of the proceedings are conducted in Earthian. I've never questioned it; it certainly makes *my* job easier."

She stared at the sign a moment longer before following him. He opened the door to box 131 and motioned for her to enter. She smiled and curtsied before entering. Jonathan closed the door behind him. The box had four chairs with ample space to walk around. Jonathan found this particularly helpful when he wanted to pace. At the front, a railing separated them from the large void in the center of the Senate Chamber. Jonathan joined Ellyra at the railing.

All the people in all the balconies resembled the glittering sand on the shore. Every one of them was a distinct person from a conquered world. Yet from within the box, the strange landscape of people looked unified somehow. *If only they really were unified,* Jonathan thought. *I can't imagine even the Draconian armada would have enough ships to fight us all at the same time.*

"Oh, look," Ellyra said, pointing to another box at the other end of the room, one balcony higher. "It's Ambassador Trrrz'Kizits."

She pointed to the Chantell delegation.

"The one standing in front of Senator Vzzz'Tah?"

She shook her head. "The one just to the left of the Senator."

Jonathan only knew the Chantell senator by reputation and didn't know anyone in his delegation. If Ellyra personally knew a Chantell ambassador, then half their work to approach the Chantell was already done.

"How do you know him?"

245

A warm smile caressed her face. "They had a border dispute with the Vareshi tradesmen. My father offered to assist in the negotiations."

"Perhaps you could introduce me?"

She nodded. "It would be my pleasure."

"How do you know him? Is he a friend of your family?"

She blushed, her hair turning burgundy. "Not exactly, no. My father took me along—he figured it would be an educational experience. I was young then. I hadn't yet learned when not to speak."

He furrowed his brow. "You spoke out of turn?"

She took a breath and hesitated a moment on her words. "To say that I spoke out of turn would be far too forgiving a statement. In fact, to say that I spoke would also be generous. You see, I conveyed precisely what was on my mind regarding the matter. And I said it rather forcefully."

Jonathan's eyes widened. He knew she was capable and accomplished, but he had no idea she could be a spitfire as well. He grinned. "You shouted during the negotiations?"

Ellyra blushed again, turning partly away. "It was the first time I ever saw my father unable to keep his hair from turning burgundy."

There was something almost magical in her retelling. The regal side of her seemed to melt away, leaving a wistful, dreaming, child-like version behind. His heart swelled with longing. What would things be like if he could simply let go of his mountain of responsibilities? What would life be like if he could run away with Ellyra and live out each other's childhood dreams? He took her gloved hand in his.

At his touch, she looked back into his eyes. "I guess one could say that I impressed the Chantell ambassador. So much so, that he often inquires after me."

He stared into her blue within blue eyes. Had they always been so lovely? He brushed a stray lock of her hair over one ear. Instantly, her hair brightened up to a romantic pink. She took a breath, closing her eyes. Images of their first evening on Eurosia flooded his mind. Back then, he had been able to allow the pressures and responsibilities of his life to fade into the background. While he had been with her, time didn't seem to exist; he had been free to simply be with her.

The only trouble he had had in the galaxy was that he had to return home and could not stay. That was when he gave her his military academy signet ring. Something for her to return; an excuse to reunite. He would have given anything to stay with her. The difference now, was that he no longer had to leave her. She was his. His to cherish. Even if the galaxy fell apart, he could still be with Ellyra.

He leaned in closer.

Lucas cleared his throat. "So sorry to interrupt, Jonathan, but as you may not have noticed, we've been called to order. They are announcing the agenda as we speak."

Jonathan shot a glance at Lucas. How long had he been sitting there? Ellyra looked at Lucas as well, her curly locks brushing against Jonathan's shoulder as she moved. Her hair had returned to its embarrassed burgundy color.

The spell that drew him deep into her eyes had been broken. A sense of awkwardness seeped into the air around them. *Not like this,* he determined. *I will not be so easily defeated.*

He graciously smiled at Lucas. "If you'll excuse us for just a moment, Ambassador."

"Why, certainly, I–" Lucas stopped short.

Jonathan pulled Ellyra close and planted a long, gentle kiss.

Ellyra opened her eyes, taking in a deep breath. Her heart fluttered like the beating of a bird's wings. Jonathan's kiss was a welcomed surprise. What did it mean? Was he saying he wanted her? Or was it all just a show for Ambassador Lucas? It was all confusing. She had just come to terms with being unwanted, alone, and forgotten. Now Jonathan had been taking her hand, taking her with him, and pouring on the attention. What did it all mean? It wasn't at all like the Jonathan she married. It seemed more like the Jonathan she had met on Eurosia.

Her father once said that when a man receives a close encounter with his mortality, he often awakens to his better senses. Could this be what happened to Jonathan? Could his near-fatal encounter with Teterophalezine really have awakened him? Did this mean that things were different now? Could it be that he wanted her now?

She took in another deep breath. Did she even dare to hope that he could love her? It was the second time since returning from his brush with death that he had kissed her. Both were powerful, with feeling and tenderness. Could she trust that he had somehow changed? Could he want her now?

The echoed voice of an Earth man slowly crept into her awareness. The ambient sounds all around her came into focus. It was like waking up from a daydream. The man's blue and white robes were stereotypical of *Bravo Station* Earthians. The Tumnei oversaw the Earthians there and emphasize the study of academics and science. As a result, the vast majority of linguists were Bravs.

A Scorpiian squealed and squawked, standing on a dais at ground level.

The Brav, who stood a little way off, translated it. "Silence on the floor! May I remind you that we are in session now? Continued outbursts will be punished."

A Crystalline, a chair-sized floating ball of crystals resembling the insides of a geode, flashed a few colors and resonated a gentle hum of musical notes.

The Brav again translated. "Commissioner Rawl, although your desires for order are amiable, you do not have the authority to threaten the delegations. Nor do you have the floor to speak. Return to your box at once."

Commission Rawl hissed in anger, then skittered away from the dais.

Ellyra turned to Jonathan. "Are the Scorpii always so disagreeable?"

He gave her an exaggerated nod. "The only Scorpiian that isn't overly ambitious is one that isn't feeling well."

She smiled at his wit.

"I have something for you," he said, pulling from his pocket what looked like a metal bracelet. "Let me see your arm."

She held out her right arm and Jonathan fastened it around her wrist. She caressed its edges with her gloved fingers. The silver metal shined in the torchlight. She ran her fingers across the smooth black glass plate in the center. "I do thank you for your kind gift. May I inquire what it is?"

"It's a comm-band. It's an easy way for you to contact me. Outside of *Gamma Station,* it only has a range of a few hundred meters but it should be sufficient."

She smiled, caressing her comm-band. This was the Jonathan from long ago; the Jonathan who wanted her. He had just given her the greatest gift; she would no longer be alone. He had given her the means to call him and the permission to do so. Her hair tingled, transitioning to a loving red as a tear sparkled in her eye.

"This is, perhaps, the greatest gift you have ever given me."

He smiled, staring back with his gorgeous brown and amber eyes. Gently, he took her hands in his. "Ellyra," he said, lowering his voice. "I almost lost the chance to tell you that I love you. I will not squander my second chance. I want you by my side."

Two tears broke loose and rolled down her cheek. At that moment, it was easy to believe that he loved her. No longer would she be alone. Never again would she be unwanted or forgotten. It was finally true; he wanted her. More tears caressed her cheeks. Her heart felt light, as if it would carry her across the stars.

Memories of her girlhood dreams of romance flooded into her mind. All those years of longing for romance instead of family duty swelled inside. In each of those years, she would have given anything to marry for love. And now, it seemed, that despite her marriage contract's origin, she would live out her marriage in love.

She wrapped her arms around his neck and kissed him. How was she so lucky? The shackles of family duty had fallen away. She was free. Free to love the man that *she* chose. All the other cares in the galaxy faded into insignificance. Her ship, her social standing, her reputation, and even her exile no longer mattered. All she wanted was him. And he was hers.

"Forgive me, Jonathan," Lucas said. "But the Scorpii are making their play."

Jonathan abruptly pulled away. He wiped his lips, removing the remnants of her lipstick. "Sorry Ambassador, that couldn't have been the most comfortable display to sit through."

Lucas smirked. "Think nothing of it, Jonathan. The better part of my career has been in getting two parties to come to terms."

Ellyra blushed. What had come over her? Such a display was quite unseemly.

The Crystalline chairman floated in the void between the balconies. It pulsed green and blue while chiming several harmonic notes. The Brav wasted no time translating the discussion.

"The Chair recognizes Commissioner Gyne, the delegate from Scorpii."

Commissioner Gyne waved a few nonchalant tentacles and squawked.

"The scientific data is now conclusive. We are destroying the fabric of space with every ship we send across the cosmos. If we do not act now to save it, our posterity will suffer. We must take action for the greater good of everyone to prevent Cosmic Meltdown. We have drafted a bill that will safeguard the fabric of space from our carelessness."

"The blasted Abes have been tutoring them again," Jonathan said offhandedly. "Their speeches are getting more convincing."

"Yes, but they're atrocious at hiding their intentions. I'll pick them apart from their own legislation."

Jonathan raised his hand. "Not yet. If we slam them right away, the other races won't join in; they'll just watch the two of us duke it out. But if we wait and give the others a chance to voice their disagreement, it will sound like we are agreeing with everyone else."

Ellyra squinted, looking across to the other balcony at the Scorpii delegation. An Earthian sat among them. By the looks of the black and red uniform, it was an Abe. As the senators of the various other races voiced their disagreement with the Scorpii proposal, that Abe sat in his chair as if the world didn't matter. Something was very wrong. On Eurosia, the Great Houses often conspired against each other in parliament. And the men to be feared were the clever ones who seemed unconcerned.

"Jonathan," she said. "Something is amiss. Is that not Matt Jaimess sitting in the Scorpii box?"

"What, pray tell, is *he* doing there?" Lucas asked in wonder.

"Well, he's the new Senate Adjunct. I guess he gets around now?" Jonathan said.

Lucas shook his head. "No, the Senate Adjunct does not have any duties while the Senate is in session. Whatever he is doing is entirely of his own volition."

"Well, at least he doesn't look very interested in the proceedings."

Ellyra put a hand on Jonathan's shoulder. "That is not the look of a bystander. The quiet man who appears unconcerned is he who has a plan."

Jonathan sighed. "Unfortunately, there's no way to know what he's up to until we play our hand. Which also means we're at a disadvantage."

The floating Crystalline pulsed a yellow and blue along with musical notes.

"The Chair recognizes the senator from Chantell Prime."

A flying lizard flapped its wings, carrying a microphone pole over to the Chantell senator. The flying lizard lowered the microphone for the senator to speak.

"Space old is," he said, twitching in his poorly-constructed Earthian language. "Much travel had. Not evidence ever seen is."

A light on the railing by the Scorpii box lit up.

The Crystalline pulsed green and blue while chiming again.

"The Chair recognizes the delegate from Scorpii."

Another flying lizard flew the second microphone pole over to the Scorpiian who hissed and squealed.

"Are you a science denier?"

The light on the railing by the Earth box lit up.

The Crystalline turned to see, then chimed and again pulsed yellow and blue.

"The Chair recognizes the Senator from Earth."

Senator Clarence cleared his throat. "Nobody is denying the possibility of Cosmic Meltdown. We just think the measures in this bill are too drastic."

Jonathan shook his head in disappointment. "Clarence, you coward," he grumbled. "Of course, we deny the existence of an imaginary crisis."

"Have we waited long enough?" Lucas asked.

He nodded. "Carpe diem."

Lucas pounded a large metal button on the railing. Their box light lit up.

The Crystalline pulsed purple and green, and chimed some notes.

The Brav man who was acting as translator took a quick sip of water. "The Chair recognizes the delegate from *Gamma Station*."

One of the flying lizards flew a microphone pole over to Lucas. He cleared his throat. "My friends, what we have here is a conflict of interest. The notable Scorpii have alerted us to what they call a crisis of utmost importance. And the remedy they propose is to give them control over our hyperspace travel. Make no mistake, this is not a remedy to a problem but a grab for power."

The Scorpiian senator hissed irately and the Brav began translating his rebuttal. Ellyra squinted back across to the Scorpii box. Matt sat back, spinning a data rod in his hand. What was he up to? It didn't have anything to do with the debate; otherwise, he would be anxiously listening to every word. Instead, he sat there through the entire debate, fidgeting with a data rod.

When the Crystalline announced the voting would begin, Matt stopped spinning the data rod and sat up straight. Whatever he was planning to do, it was going to happen very soon. She again put her hand on Jonathan's arm.

"Whatever Mr. Jaimess plans to do, he evidently plans to do it now."

Jonathan glanced over to Lucas. "What can he possibly do during the vote?"

Lucas shook his head. "There are no motions that can come before the assembly once the voting has begun. He can request a point of information, but that is all."

Jonathan stared off into space, mentally counting. "With Earth, *Bravo Station*, the Euroo, the Bugs, and the Greys, we should win with a vote to spare. If he intends to influence the vote, his only opportunity would have been during the debate."

The Scorpiian senator pressed his button with a tentacle arm. The box light lit.

"The Chair recognizes the senator from Scorpii."

A flying lizard flew one of the microphone poles back over. The Scorpiian squawked and casually flailed its tentacles around in mild conversation.

"We must pause the vote to satisfy the request of the Draconians; providing conspiratorial evidence involving They Who Shall Not Be Named."

The Crystalline chimed musical notes while pulsing red and orange.

"That motion is out of order. The voting—"

A loud booming voice of a Draconian echoed through the senate chamber. "Proceed."

Matt walked over to the Scorpiian senator and whispered to it, handing it the data rod. The Scorpiian squealed, holding up the cup-sized data rod in one of its tentacles.

The Brav translator cleared his throat. "Here is video proof."

"Bring it," said the Draconian in its slothful booming voice.

The flying lizard which held the microphone pole for the Scorpiian snatched up the data rod. It flew it over to the Draconians on the secluded balcony overhead, called the Dais of Draconia. The Draconian lying in the center stretched out its massive reptilian arm.

The flying lizard dropped it into its hand. The Draconian glanced over to its two companions and roared in their native language.

The empty air in the center of the senate chamber swirled into a column of sparkling mist. The Crystalline floated out of the way as the sparkling cyclone displayed a wavy video image, like a shimmering projector screen. The misty screen showed a starry background with a Tumnei timestamp in the bottom corner. After a moment, the squid-like image of a Skorath ship faded into view.

Jonathan's jaw dropped. "How did they get that?"

Chapter 31

THE
TRANSGRESSION

Jonathan stood dumbfounded while the three Draconians roared in indignation. That was the video image T'Kal had shown during the last meeting. How did Matt Jaimess get his hands on it? More importantly, what would the Draconians do? Everything about the Skorath—even mentioning their name—was outlawed. The Draconians still roared in their native tongue. Side conversations erupted across all the balconies.

Lucas leaned into Jonathan's ear. "It sounds like you know what that is."

Lucas had still been recovering from the assassination attempt when T'Kal had shown the footage and explained the prophecy. Why hadn't he taken the time to get Lucas up to speed? The past few weeks had flown by faster than light speed. Jonathan had asked Isabeau to arrange a second meeting, but then he got shot and lost three days. So much to tell and so little time to tell it.

He glanced over at Ellyra who held a startled and confused look in her eyes. He held out his hand to her and drew her close so he could speak to her and Lucas at the same time. The cacophony of voices speaking over voices and the howling roars of the Draconians provided the best opportunity to share sensitive information without being overheard.

"I only have time to say this once," Jonathan began. "So please listen well. Ambassador, while you were unconscious in Med Bay Charlie, the council met in person. We were shown that video footage of a Skorath ship."

Ellyra placed a hand to her mouth to suppress a gasp, her hair color fading into a troubled gray.

Jonathan continued. "We believe the Skorath prophecy that foretells of the downfall of Draconia could be true. And that your roommates, the Voonsu, could be the fulfillment of it. And if that is accurate, we could be the catalyst in liberating the known galaxy."

"Video footage of that kind could get the Tumnei exterminated," Lucas said in worry.

"And somehow the blasted Abes got ahold of it..."

"The Tumnei spy?" Ellyra asked.

"The what?" Jonathan asked.

"The assassin on *Gamma Station* had an accomplice. It was a Tumnei with a stealth shield and a portable teleporter. T'Kal said his name was Ir'Jad; a technician who disappeared from Bravo Station some months back."

Jonathan stared back, bewildered.

Lucas chuckled. "That was while *you* were unconscious."

"All right, fair enough," Jonathan said. "I guess we all have gotten a little behind in sharing intel."

"I do not understand," Ellyra said. "Why would a Tumnei—even an enemy spy—risk the extermination of his entire race?"

"Well, all that matters now is how the Tumnei are going to handle this."

"What if they don't?" Lucas asked in a sober tone.

What if they don't, indeed? The Greys were the glue that held the entire conspiracy together. They were the link between the Voonsu and the Skorath. Without them, how could they get in contact with the Skorath? The Skorath were the most crucial piece to this whole puzzle. They should know how to access the technology of the Ancients. And that advanced technology was the only thing that can stand against the dreaded Draconian armada.

"They have to," Jonathan finally replied. "Because if they get wiped out, our only hope for freedom will die with them."

One of the Draconians bellowed in its deep gravelly voice. "They Who Shall Not Be Named is forbidden! All knowledge, all technology, and all mention are strictly illegal. The penalty for violation is extermination."

The Tumnei senator waved his arms about in explanation as the Brav translated the telepathic conversation.

"We did not know this image was of They Who Shall Not Be Named. How could we have? To us, this vessel is an anomaly. If we had known, we surely would have reported it."

"Ignorance!" The second Draconian shouted. "Let this image educate you and be your only warning. There will be no second chances."

Jonathan released his breath in relief. The Greys had played their cards well. Playing innocent was a smart move. The one loophole inherent in a law that forbids all information on a subject, is that no one knows when they've stumbled upon it.

The Draconian on the far end pointed its large scaly finger at the Tumnei balcony box. "Your ignorance proves you are not fit to supervise younger races. You will no longer oversee the development of the Earth species at *Bravo Station*." It then pointed its massive finger at the Scorpii box. "As a reward for your diligence in exposing this corruption, you will now oversee the Earth species at *Bravo Station*."

257

The swirling mist in the center of the Senate Chamber dissolved and vanished. Silence loomed in the air for a long while. When the floating Crystalline ventured that the Draconians were finished, it moved back between the balconies. It flashed white and pink and chiming notes.

"The, uh...voting will continue."

The Scorpiian senator squawked and motioned with its tentacles.

"Since *Bravo Station* is now under new management, we feel they are not yet sufficiently organized to vote."

The *Bravo Station* senator slammed his button, illuminating his box light.

"The Chair recognizes the senator from *Bravo—*"

"This senate will *not* recognize the prodigy of a transgressor!" a Draconian interrupted with disdain. "They shall not vote."

The Brav translator swallowed nervously and hesitated. "The uh, Chair does *not* recognize the senator from *Bravo Station*. We will continue the vote...without *Bravo Station*." The lizards flew the two microphone poles to each balcony box for the delegation to give a Yea or Nay vote.

Jonathan cursed and began pacing. "They just took out our vote lead by eliminating the votes! I should have seen this coming..."

"They circumvented the rules; there's no way you could have foreseen this," Lucas said.

Jonathan gave an exaggerated nod, pointing in the direction of the Scorpii balcony box. "I knew full well what kind of a man Matt Jaimess is. Ellyra even warned me about it, but I did nothing!"

He continued pacing. "Victorious warriors, Sun Tzu said, win first and then go to war, while defeated warriors go to war first and then seek to win."

A slight breeze blew from the flapping wings of the lizard. It had flown the microphone pole over to their balcony box. Jonathan marched over to the microphone. "Nay!"

The lizard then looked at Lucas.

"Nay," he said.

The lizard flew on to the next box.

Jonathan resumed pacing. "The irony is that Matt Jaimess has no idea just how badly he has crippled us."

"Crippled?" Ellyra asked.

"Yes," Lucas explained. *"Bravo Station* is the link between us and the Tumnei. They cannot legally have any interaction with us. Not unless they are escorting their Brav Earthians to us."

"And without the Bravs," Jonathan said, "we are cut off from the Tumnei all the same."

He paced faster across the floor space. His heart raced as his calculating mind spun in circles. It must have taken a lot of time and effort to plan such an elaborate coup d'état as seizing *Bravo Station.* Why had they done it? What was in it for them? The Scorpii could hate as well as any man, but they never did anything for spite. If there weren't a reward, they wouldn't have done it. But what could it be?

Then, the realization hit him. *Of course,* he thought. *It's now so obvious.* He spun around and marched over to Lucas. *"Bravo Station* was just a means to an end. What they're really after is the Euroo."

"What?" Ellyra asked in alarm.

"Think about it," Jonathan explained. *"Gamma Station* and the Euroo are the two biggest thorns in their side. Eliminate them, and they will have no real opposition in the Senate. The Scorpii really need this bill to pass. What would happen if the Scorpii get to regulate everyone's energy output for space travel?"

Lucas's eyes widened. "They could argue that the Euroo—who are very elaborate in everything they do—are not being eco-friendly. They could decide they should be 'supervised' the way Earthians are. The language in this bill is flexible enough they could make up any penalty they wanted. They would control Eurosia."

Ellyra's hair color soured into orange. It was definitely not a good color for her. "We can't let that happen!" she said with hysteria seeping through her tone of voice. "We have to do something!"

Jonathan closed his eyes, letting his mind circle around scenarios. They couldn't win with votes; they no longer had enough. There must be an abstract way, something not normally thought of. They were not

defeated yet. As Sun Tzu said, "Attack is the secret of defense; defense is merely the planning of an attack". Somewhere there was an avenue for attack. But where was it?

Jonathan paused his pacing and glanced up with a smile running across his face. He marched over to the railing and hit the button. The balcony box light lit up.

"You can't make a motion in the middle of a vote," Lucas said.

Jonathan grinned. "I can still ask a question."

Chapter 32

THE QUESTION

M att leaned back in his chair, letting a contented smile cross his lips. It was finally finished. The Scorpii would gain an immeasurable increase in power. And in that chaos, he would seize control of *Able Station*. All the Abes would be under *his* control, not the wretched squiddies. All that now remained to be planned, was how to best dispatch Lord Vaux. Matt had kept a log of all the best accident ideas he had come up with over the past five years. Any of them would do.

The next order of business after Lord Vaux's demise would be to institute a hospital on *Able Station*. No more needless death due to the stupid squiddy philosophy of only the strong survive. Men were not meant to live like animals. His five years of patient planning and careful construction would now start to pay off.

A flying lizard carried a microphone pole over to the railing. Commissioner Gyne and Lord Vaux each squawked in the affirmative. The dry-mouthed Brav recited their votes like the imbecile that he was.

He sounded like he really thought his translation work was important. If that Brav only knew what real work was, what truly important work looked like, then he wouldn't sound like such a joke.

Important work took sacrifice—real blood, sweat, and tears. It looked like losing Megan, and his daughter, Eva. Real work took courage to make the tough decisions. But all those decisions were worth it now. *Able Station* was going to be free and the vile Lord Vaux would soon get what was coming to it.

The balcony box light for *Gamma Station* lit up. Matt straightened up in his chair. What was Colonel Self-Righteous up to? The time for debate was over. He knew that as well as anyone. And if not, that fossil of an ambassador of his most certainly did. What could he hope to accomplish? Didn't he know he was beaten?

It was a silly question. Everyone knew that the Hero of Mesa Sol never knew when he was defeated. That was the one aspect of Jonathan that he had forgotten. But tenacity alone couldn't save him, could it? No, for him to carve out some resemblance of a victory out of this vote was too remote. Miracles were something only found in fairy tales. Matt had checked and double-checked his list, and not a single thing had been omitted. Every step in his plan had been accomplished one right after the other. Nothing was overlooked. But then why was he nervous?

The Crystalline turned to Jonathan. It pulsed orange and yellow while chiming several notes.

"The time for debate is passed. We are voting now."

There! You see, he thought. *Even the stupid geode-for-brains shut down his pathetic counter-attack.* Matt relaxed again. Colonel Self-Righteous had failed again.

Jonathan shouted something. It was too faint for Matt to hear. The Crystalline moved in closer to hear him. Jonathan shouted again.

The Crystalline pulsed purple and blue.

"We have a point of information."

Point of information? That was his plan? Asking a procedural question? What a desperate attempt. Too bad there was nothing he could do to affect the vote now.

A flying lizard flew a microphone pole down to Jonathan. "Point of information, Mr. Chairman. Are we now voting on the penalties this bill would inflict on the Draconians?"

What did he say? Penalty on the Draconians? Matt's heart pounded. Beads of nervous sweat formed on his brow. *Why that arrogant, mischief-making pomp!* That wasn't a procedural question and he knew it. The problem was that the hovering crystal moron couldn't tell the difference.

"After all," Jonathan continued. "The Draconians spend more drive fuel than all our worlds combined. And we are looking to you, honored Scorpii, to save us from Cosmic Meltdown. Are we also voting on the penalties this will impose on the Draconians?"

Another flying lizard flew a microphone pole over to the Scorpii box. Lord Vaux shot a vicious glance at Matt before turning its attention to the microphone. It hesitated and then peeked a nervous glance up at the Dais of Draconia. The Draconians' eyes glared and their nostrils smoked.

Unbelievable...Colonel Terynn was using the very same tactic. He incited the anger of the Draconians to circumvent the rules. A slight sense of delight bubbled up deep within him. Colonel Terynn was a worthy adversary after all.

Lord Vaux turned around to Matt and hissed irately. What was there to do? All of his planning was for the sabotage of their votes. Never once did he consider that two would be playing at this game. There wasn't time to think up a response, let alone a believable one.

Matt stared blankly back at Lord Vaux. He couldn't think of a single thing Lord Vaux could say that would undo what Colonel Terynn had started. There had to be a way—there was always a way, but he needed time to figure it out. Time that Lord Vaux did not have.

Lord Vaux glanced once more up at the intense scrutiny of the Draconians' silent stare. Then it turned back to the microphone. It squawked regretfully.

"We rescind the bill."

The Crystalline pulsed red and green, and chimed again.

263

"The bill is withdrawn. The vote is now voided. On to the next agenda item."

Lord Vaux skittered over to Matt with fierce anger behind its beady yellow eyes. It whipped several of its tentacles down on Matt, beating him. Matt fell to the floor of the balcony box, shielding his head with his arms. He groaned under the brutal thrashing.

Matt had escaped Scorpii punishment for thirty years. His cunning and planning had always given him a way to avoid it. He had always outsmarted the pathetic squiddies before. But now, his luck had run out. Lord Vaux had chosen him to be the next victim of his wrath. At least death would come swiftly. That much he could be thankful for.

Lord Vaux wrapped two tentacles around Matt's neck and lifted him to his feet. Matt glanced at the sheathed dagger at Lord Vaux's side. That was usually how it would end the punishment. Should he bother closing his eyes for the final strike? Would it really matter in the end if he saw it coming? He hadn't ever shown any weakness to the squiddies before, why should he start now?

Lord Vaux drew the dagger. The long, rusted metal blade looked more like scrap metal strapped to a handle than an actual dagger. This was it then; he was to die here and now. Matt's chest tightened in agony. The throbbing and aching from the squiddy's thrashing were intense, but it paled in comparison to the sting in his heart.

What would become of his people now? Five long, arduous years of planning, scheming, and preparing was now destroyed. As soon as the wretched squiddy ended his life, *Able Station* would be right back where it started. It would be under Scorpiian taskmasters again. He had fought so long to be rid of them. Now it was all for nothing.

What were all the deaths for? What did Megan die for? It wasn't fair. It wasn't supposed to end this way. He was supposed to seize complete control of *Able Station* and liberate his crew from the bloodthirsty rampages of Lord Vaux. And Lord Vaux was supposed to pay for killing Megan. Now there would be no one to avenge her. Matt would also never get to see his daughter. Eva would never know her father.

A feeling of nausea swept over him. It was as if his heart had been torn from his chest and tossed away. *At least the end will come quickly,* he thought. It wasn't much comfort, but it was all that was left.

Commissioner Gyne squawked, skittering over to Lord Vaux. It lowered Lord Vaux's dagger. Was the pathetic squiddy actually trying to save him? There wasn't a merciful organ in their entire grotesque bodies. If Commissioner Gyne wanted him alive, it was because he was still useful. Being useful did not guarantee his life, it just extended it a while longer.

Lord Vaux let go and Matt collapsed to the floor. What was the point in sparing him now? He had effectively been stripped of all credibility and clout. There was no going back. Instead of being the conqueror, Matt was now the conquered. His reputation of being the irreplaceable asset had crumbled with the defeat of the vote. In one fell swoop, Jonathan Terynn had kicked the legs out from under him, toppling his five-year project, his plans for revenge, and all hope for a brighter future.

The truly merciful thing would be to end his suffering. Instead, Commissioner Gyne had prolonged it. Matt wiped away some blood from his mouth. Depending on the injuries, it would take a couple of weeks to die, if his sorrow didn't pull him into the grave sooner. He wouldn't even get a quick death. It was just as well; there wasn't anything left to lose.

Chapter 33

THE GUIDE

F ox paced around the elegant room. The soft ebony carpet dampened the pattering of his footsteps. Diahlus had said the room was rather crude in appearance but would be adequate. The sparkling chandelier overhead and the ornate wooden table were anything but crude. The blue plants sat in painted vases and the air held a hint of citrus. If this was crude, then the best rooms on *Gamma Station* must have been downright barbaric.

Fox walked past the small corner table where a plate of dinner rested untouched. The meals were regular but his appetite was fleeting. He only had nine hours left before he had to choose which location they would try for the last time. He had only one chance to guess the correct system. And that was only the first part of the problem. He still had no idea how to contact the Skorath if he should be lucky enough to pick the correct star system.

His pacing brought him back around to the table where a finely-dressed gentleman held a reader, translating into Earthian.

"...thus he plunged his sword into the depths of the ocean, proclaiming the end of the war—"

"Yes, yes, yes," Fox interrupted, rolling his eyes. "Then Euseclimeese formed the first council and all that fun and important stuff. Look, either we've been at this for too long or there just isn't any more to find in Euseclimeese."

"Another volume, your Lieutenant Colonelship?"

Fox chuckled. That was an address he hadn't heard before. He should have been flattered but it sounded too ridiculous to take seriously. "Myles, you can just call me Fox."

"As you wish, Fox. Shall we try another volume?"

Fox shook his head. "No, we might get better results if we take a break. Rest, it would seem, might be the only course I haven't sought an answer through."

Myles stood. "It is well, Fox." He excused himself with a bow and exited the room.

Fox plopped into a plush armchair. If Vera was indeed a Skorath, and if she wanted to be found, there should be some clues to finding her. *If I wanted someone to find me,* he wondered, *what clues would I give?* A map would always be handy. But something so obvious could be seen by the Draconians. No, that would never do. The clues would have to be more subtle. Something that would be meaningless to the Draconians yet helpful to the right people. If only it could be as simple as a map.

Fox returned to the tray of food. It was cold now. He picked up a piece of what looked like meat and tasted it. For several hours cold, it was quite exquisite. Piping hot, it would have been irresistible. His appetite still evaded him, however. If he was too stressed to concentrate, why should he be able to eat? It was the never-ending battle between human limits and the greater good. And while the latter begged for an encore, there was nothing left to give. *The greater good be hanged,* he thought. The scene had ended, and the curtain closed. This time, unfortunately, the show could not go on.

The door chimed. Had Myles forgotten something? Fox crossed over to the door and touched the round crystal on the wall. The door slid open, revealing a lovely lady in a simple green gown. She wasn't dressed like the officers, so she was in a lower social class. She curtsied, a few stray strands of her pulled-up white hair brushing her rosy cheek. Fox's breath halted.

"Miss Layna, reporting as instructed. I am at your service to translate literature."

"Oh yes," Fox said. "You must be the relief translator Diahlus mentioned."

She nodded with a professional smile. "That I am."

He *was* about to get some sleep. His fingers danced with jitters at his side. It was quite a shame such a lovely creature should come all this way only to have to turn back. Especially if the reason was solely for a nap. *Turning her away would be inconsiderate,* he reasoned. *And besides, how can I think of myself when there's a galaxy to liberate?* It would be selfish not to appreciate the time she was contributing. How could he think of sleep when such a beautiful assistant was here to help? What was a little nap compared to the greater good? After all, the show *must* go on.

"Why, yes, of course," he said motioning for her to enter.

She stepped inside, followed by a gentleman in a simple black suit. She turned to the gentleman. "Vandin, this may take some time. You may wish to take a seat."

"It is well, miss," he replied, sitting in an armchair away from the table. Chaperones appeared to be a thing in the Euroo culture—even aboard starships.

Layna noticed the reader device on the table and approached. She inspected the title of the volume loaded onto it. "Classical literature then?"

"Yes, I've been pouring through Gorazhio and Euseclimeese."

She smiled with an air of excitement about her. "Oh, you are ready to begin Kalmeedes then?"

He shook his head. "No, I'm just reading these two."

268

"Oh, but you really must. If you have never read Kalmeedes, you are missing such a great philosopher."

She had a point, all right. A very big point. As far as he could tell, Kalmeedes was regarded as one of the greatest. And he dearly wanted to dive into some of his writings. But Kalmeedes lived in the wrong time period; he came after all the stories of Vera.

"I would love to dive into Kalmeedes. But unfortunately, my research is confined to the preceding century."

The excitement drained from her eyes. "What a shame," she finally said. "There is none greater than Kalmeedes."

Her smile was contagious. "Well, if we have any extra time," he said, "I'd love for you to introduce me."

Her hair color warmed to an excited blond. "It would be my pleasure." She sat down and began navigating through the digital book on the reader. She glanced up. "You seem to have the illustrations turned off."

Fox nodded. "Yes, the pictures were distracting me from listening to the words."

"Have you never studied the iconography of the period?"

Fox blinked. "Okay, I have no idea what you asked."

She suppressed a cheery giggle. "The artwork of the period often depicts a lot of what the written text leaves out. There are many details that were common knowledge at the time and were never explicitly written. But they are always portrayed in the artwork."

"So...the puzzle pieces I am missing might be in the pictures?"

She stared back with a confused expression. "Puzzle pieces? By what do you mean?"

Fox ran a hand down his bald head. "That's right, I need to ease up on my human expressions." He took a breath to begin again. "So, what you're telling me is that the clues I seek may be in the pictures?"

She nodded. "There is, of course, no guarantee. But it will definitely broaden your understanding of the culture." She tapped a few buttons, enabling the graphics.

"Okay," Fox said, sitting across from her. "Where shall we begin?"

"Well, that would depend on your focus of research. Perhaps you wish to begin with the life of Gorazhio?"

"I'm actually more interested in the stories of Vera."

She raised her eyebrows. "Oh, the central mythology? Yes, I believe that would be an excellent starting point."

"What do you mean by *central* mythology?"

"Only that most of the succeeding legends and myths were heavily influenced by the stories of Vera." She navigated a few pages and turned the reader around to show Fox. "This, for example, is the most common depiction of Vera." The picture resembled an old painting of a woman in silken robes and jewelry. The yellow glow of an aura was painted around her.

"And this," Layna said, pointing to a green jeweled necklace around the woman's neck. "This is what Kalmeedes referred to as the guide."

"Wait, Kalmeedes talked about Vera? Didn't he live a century later?"

"Yes," she explained. "But he made references to Vera numerous times in his famous debates with the Kad'Noran. In fact, his reference to the necklace was an off-hand mention during one of the debates."

"I see..."

"And here," she said, navigating quite a few pages later, "is the last portrait of Kalmeedes." She showed the reader to him.

Fox's eyes lit up. "Hey, I think I've seen this painting before. It's hanging in one of the hallways near the ship's command room, right?"

She nodded. "On the wall just outside the Center of Workmanship. Do you notice any similarities with the depiction of Vera?"

Fox pointed to a green jeweled necklace on the portrait. "That's the same necklace." He glanced back at her. "Why would Kalmeedes have been painted with the same necklace?"

"He was a well-known proponent of Vera, so to depict that in the iconography, he was painted with Vera's necklace."

Fox pointed to some ornate writing within the portrait. "What do these words say?"

"They don't say anything."

He glanced at her with a puzzled expression. "How can words not say anything?"

"They don't mean anything," she explained. "They are not words in any language. At best they could be invented names."

"How do you pronounce them?"

She pointed to the words. "This one says, Kalisahr. And that one says, Vendier."

Fox repeated them under his breath. "I wonder what they mean..."

Layna huffed an exasperated sigh and smiled. "Lieutenant Colonel Fox, these words do not mean a thing." She pointed to the necklace in the portrait. "However, this necklace—The Guide—*does* mean something."

He stared at the necklace a moment. "Why did he call it, The Guide?"

She shrugged. "Perhaps you'd like me to read you some passages from his debate with the Kad'Noran?"

She scrolled through a few more pages on the reader until she found what she was looking for. "Then said Kalmeedes unto them of the Kad'Noran, How well ye stand there making to look as if saviors to Eurosia. Ye speak as if our welfare were thine only concern. In truth, ye teach the hypocrites their craft; being both author and finisher of that work. As well might man stretch forth his feeble arm heavenward to grasp The Guide of Vera, or to trace its path, than to blind the eyes of this people to your doings."

She looked up at Fox. "Shall I continue reading?"

He held up a halting finger. Something within that passage stood out. It mentioned two things: reaching heavenward and tracing a path. Fox stared up at the ceiling and reached his arm out.

"Might I inquire what you are attempting?" she asked.

"I'm stretching forth my feeble arm heavenward," he replied.

"Well," she said with hesitation, "if that helps immerse you—"

"Heavenward!" His heart thumped as excitement washed over him like the thrill of a casting call.

She eyed him curiously. "You look as if you have made a discovery."

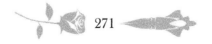

271

He glanced at her. "It's the stars, Miss Layna. Reaching heavenward is reaching toward the stars."

Her eyes narrowed in suspicion. "I fail to understand the grandeur of your discovery."

Fox stood, too animated to remain seated. "It *is* a map after all!"

"What is it that is a map after all?"

He couldn't blame her for not catching on and sharing in his enthusiasm. He hadn't even had time enough to explain what he was looking for. His mind raced, too thrilled to settle on any one set of words. How to explain was the question. "Miss Layna, I don't have time to explain. But I believe the necklace really is a guide; a guide to finding Vera."

She took a breath to interject but Fox rattled on. "I'll bet the green jewel on the necklace represents a green star in this sector."

"Lieutenant Colonel Fox, while I do appreciate your gusto for the fanciful, I should point out that there are no green stars."

"What?" he asked. "Not even one in this sector?"

She shook her head. "I am afraid you do not understand. There are not any green stars in the entire galaxy."

"How can you be so certain that there aren't any in the whole galaxy?"

"Because there cannot be; it is simply not possible. Star colors are determined vastly by their temperature. The hotter the star, the bluer the star. And the cooler the star, the redder the star. Green simply isn't possible for a star. It's not in the thermal color spectrum."

Fox's heart sank. The necklace was almost too perfect a solution to the puzzle. Having it debunked drained all the joy out of the discovery. Fox sat and slumped in his chair.

Layna cocked her head to the side with a sympathetic smile. "I am dreadfully sorry to have destroyed your triumph. The number of green objects in the celestial sky really is limited."

Fox regarded her with a curious look. "What *is* green in space?"

"Just nebulae I'm afraid."

Fox slowly rose to his feet, his heart pounding. "Love is blind and lovers cannot see the pretty follies that themselves commit..." he mumbled. "I have been obsessed with star systems when I should have been searching for a nebula."

Chapter 34

THE SARATOGA

Jonathan lay on the thin-cushioned bunk aboard the battlecruiser *Saratoga*. The trip back to *Gamma Station* seemed to take forever. He was tired but sleep would not come. Losing *Bravo Station* to the Scorpii had severed their connection to the Greys. And without T'Kal, they had no contact with the Skorath. What good would it do to bring in the Bugs now? The entire conspiracy was now crippled. The remnants of the Voonsu lived inside Ambassador Cale—well, Ambassador Lucas now. That much was good; they still had the Voonsu. But without the support of the Tumnei government, how could they build ships to put the Birthright of the Ancestors to good use? And how could they even gain that technology without access to the Skorath?

The Greys were an indispensable link in the chain. And *Bravo Station* was their only excuse to legally interact with them. That chain had now been broken. The Greys wouldn't risk it now. With how close *Bravo Station* was to the Tumnei homeworld, the Scorpii would turn it into an observation post to closely watch the Greys. Under such scrutiny, they wouldn't risk any involvement in the conspiracy.

As far as the conspiracy for freedom was concerned, the Tumnei were gone, the Skorath were gone, and their chances of success were also gone. He could always take a lesson from the Abe's playbook and try to infiltrate *Bravo Station.* Perhaps then they would be close enough to send a discreet message to the Greys. But that could take months or years to set up. With a little over three months remaining before the Skorath ship was due to return, that wasn't feasible.

There must be a way, he thought. *I just need to find it.* He sat up in his bunk, careful not to disturb the bunk below him. The wide metal room was furnished with two sets of twin bunks. He had taken the top bunk of one set, allowing Ellyra the bottom bunk. Across the room, Ambassador Lucas occupied the other twin bunk. Hopefully, Ellyra was able to get some sleep. Amongst all the chaos, somebody ought to get some rest.

Ambassador Lucas still sat in silence, conversing with his Voonsu roommates. With any luck, the Voonsu might have some ideas on how to move forward with this whole prophecy deal. It was a hollow wish, however. He didn't put much trust in luck. As Sun Tzu said, "The general who wins the battle makes many calculations in his temple before the battle is fought. The general who loses makes but few calculations beforehand".

Luck was nothing more than an illusion, an excuse to explain away preparations. If he could not think of a way to salvage the conspiracy, he would have to get used to life under the Scorpii's whims. Jonathan descended the bunk ladder. Ellyra slept soundly. He reached over and brushed a lock of her peaceful light-blue hair away from her face. There was a strange comfort in watching Ellyra sleep. The beautiful lines and curves of her face were without worry or anxiety. She looked to be at peace.

Perhaps sleep only came to those who were at peace. Jonathan's heart hung with a dreadful weight. He did not deserve her. He loved her and yet was using her to get closer to the Bugs. And quite by accident, he had fallen in love with her again—if such a thing was possible. Five years ago, on Eurosia, he had loved her. Yet now, as he watched her, that love seemed so shallow in comparison. What he felt now was something deeper. Something he couldn't put his finger on. Somehow, he needed her near him. All his idle thoughts turned to her. He sat on the edge of her bunk and gave her a gentle kiss. Ellyra took in a deep breath and opened her eyes.

"Oh, I'm sorry," he said. "I didn't mean to wake you."

Her hair color warmed up to a joyful blond and a smile crossed her lips. "Oh, my dear Jonathan," she said with the slightest hint of a yawn. "May I forever wake up to such an agreeable sight?"

He stroked the side of her cheek with the back of his fingers. "Yes, but only on condition that I get to fall asleep looking at you."

She smiled again. "I am confident that such an arrangement can be made." She reached up and ran her fingers through his hair. "Can this really be happening?" she asked. "Can you really belong to me?"

He smiled with warmth in his cheeks. "I know what you mean. I have to keep asking myself if this is all for real. If such a beautiful lady could see something worthwhile in this old soldier."

Her hand traced the contours of his cheek. "When I look at you, I see not a soldier, except the kind that dons a suit of metal, glittering under the sun. Who comes riding aloft a swift horse with lance and shield."

"I wish I had your gift for words. Next to them, my compliments seem so bland."

The overhead loudspeaker clicked on. "All hands, this is the captain. We're on approach to Hypergate Moscow. If you have any personal messages to transmit, get them submitted in under five."

Jonathan looked up in thought. "Moscow. Dean Bowmont commands that hypergate." He returned his gaze to Ellyra. "I haven't spoken to him in a while. May I introduce you?"

She glanced down at her attire. "Oh, I do not think I am suitable to be seen."

He chuckled. "If it makes you feel any better, I'll just tell him we were away at an important meeting halfway across the quadrant and haven't had the chance to freshen up yet."

She smiled again. "It would seem you have the talent for words after all."

She took his hand and he helped her up. He guided her through the narrow steel hallways until they came to the bridge. Jonathan stepped through the door with Ellyra in tow. Several men and women sat along computer consoles facing a large screen on the wall. The screen displayed a video image of a small space outpost attached to a giant metal ring. Most hypergates looked like an upside-down diamond ring, and Hypergate Moscow was no exception.

"Permission to enter the bridge?" he called out.

Captain Cynthia Prescott swiveled around in her chair in the middle of the room. Her chin-length red hair bobbed as she moved. A smirk curled up in the corner of her mouth, contrasting her British nose and no-nonsense scowl.

"Granted," she said, crossing her legs and smoothing out her perfectly pressed uniform jacket. "Well, well, fancy seeing you, Jonathan. We've been traveling for over twenty-eight hours. What took you so long to pay a visit?"

Jonathan walked up beside her chair. "Sorry, Cindy. I've had a lot on my mind. Have you already contacted Moscow?"

"I would imagine having all the duties of a commander and all the responsibilities of a politician would have that effect. And yes, Hypergate Moscow says we are twelfth in line for hyper-jump." She motioned toward Ellyra with her chin. "Who's the posh darling?"

He put his arm around Ellyra. "Cindy, this is Sune Ellyra, my wife. Ellyra, this is Captain Cynthia Prescott, skipper of the *Saratoga*."

Ellyra curtsied. "A pleasure."

Cynthia's eyes widened. "Blimey, a wife? I never figured Jonathan to be much of a knotsmith."

"Well," Jonathan explained, "It was rather short notice."

Cynthia turned back to Ellyra. "Well, well, dearie, you must tell me all about yourself. Sune is a Euroo captain rank, is it not?"

Ellyra smiled. "Why, yes, it is."

She shot a glance at Jonathan. "Married someone of equal rank, did you? Well, you can't pull rank now." She turned her attention back to Ellyra. "D'you have your own ship?"

"Yes, the *Calmao*. A Sunderis-class starcruiser; though, my commission is not necessarily clear at present."

Cynthia nodded. "Bureaucrats and their rubbish. In my experience, most are lacking between the ears."

"Cindy," Jonathan said. "I was wondering if—"

"If you don't mind, Jonathan, we birds are busy chattering." She turned back to Ellyra. "So, how did you meet?"

Jonathan tensed his jaw and resisted the urge to roll his eyes. This was not the conversation piece he had pictured when he introduced them. *Relax, Jonathan,* he told himself. *I've been through rougher storms than this.*

Ellyra's hair color faded into a romantic pink. "Five of your years ago, Jonathan had a chance visit to Eurosia, though his intentions were to secure transport to Earth."

Cynthia chuckled. "That's our Colonel for you. He gets ambushed on Mesa Sol and comes back a hero. Then he fails to stow away to Earth and comes back with an honest bride. Luck should have been his middle name."

It was nice to see Ellyra making friends, but did it have to happen at his expense? Couldn't they do it without him in the spotlight? Those old war stories always got blown out of proportion. He hadn't done anything particularly ingenious or revolutionary. He just did what any commander would have done. And somehow, he was treated as a hero. Why were his actions so fascinating that the military academy taught them?

"You'll have to tell me because I've been quite curious," Cynthia said. "Jonathan has always been an efficient man but deep down I'd wager he has a romantic side. So tell me, how did he propose?"

Jonathan's cheeks flushed and his heart pounded. That was not the most romantic part of the story. Far from it. This conversation needed to end quickly. "Cindy, I'd like to talk with Dean Bowmont. Could you please arrange a call?"

She held up a finger. "Just a moment, lovie; we're getting to the good part."

Ellyra shot a hesitant glance at Jonathan. "Well, he uh...he..."

Cynthia shifted her gaze between them. "Jonathan *did* propose, did he not?"

He looked away, taking a deep breath. "It's... complicated," he finally said.

"What rubbish is this?" she demanded. "You can win a medal of honor but you can't blooming propose?"

"It wasn't planned, Cindy."

She rolled her eyes. "Well, that's about as romantic as an ox passing a kidney stone." She turned back to Ellyra. "What in the galaxy induced you to accept him then?"

She gave a hesitant shrug. "He said he needed me."

Cynthia scowled at Jonathan. "Dodgy," she concluded.

He couldn't really deny it, his intentions at the time were to use Ellyra to recruit the Bugs for the conspiracy. Whether he liked it or not, her condemnation had some measure of accuracy. He took a deep breath, standing stiff as if at attention. Somehow, he felt like he was getting a stern dressing down from a superior officer. "Thank you for pointing out my deficiency, Cindy. I'll be sure to remedy that."

She smirked. "See to it that it is proper." She swiveled her chair to face forward. "Gordon, open a transmission to Captain Bowmont."

Gordon, the communications officer, pressed a few buttons on his console. "Aye ma'am, opening a transmission to Hypergate Moscow."

A moment later, the large screen at the front of the room switched to a video image of a heavy-set man with dark skin and a cheery demeanor. "Ha ha ha, Jonathan! What's been happening, my man? You don't set foot in these parts often."

Jonathan breathed out in relief. The awkward tension in the air faded. "It's good to see you, Dean. The Draco Senate convened all the way in Gamma Lepordis. And Hypergate Chicago just went down for maintenance. So, we're on a detour. And as far as what has been happening, I would like to introduce you to my wife, Ellyra."

She curtsied. "A pleasure to meet you, Captain Dean."

"Congratulations! Man, this is stellar news." He looked back at Jonathan. "Tell you what, I'm gonna give the two of you a wedding gift. It's not much, but after traveling all the way from Gamma Lepordis it might just be what the doctor ordered. I'm gonna bump you up to the front of the line and get you home quicker."

Jonathan smiled. "Thanks, Dean, I appreciate it."

"It's the least I could do for the newlyweds." He turned to Ellyra. "Oh, remember to be patient with Jonathan. He's brilliant with strategy but his track record with relationships isn't nearly as polished."

She politely nodded. "I shall endeavor to provide sufficient allowances."

"I wish the two of you the best of luck. Bowmont out." The screen changed back to a view of the hypergate.

"Skipper, we've received clearance from Moscow to proceed into jump position," Gordon announced.

"Ahead one-third," she called out. "Bring us to positive three-one-five on the z-axis."

"Thrusters ahead one-third, indicate pitch and turns for twelve s-knots," the conning officer directed. "Set elevation to positive three-one-five."

"Thrusters ahead one-third, indicate pitch and turns for twelve s-knots, aye sir," a voice responded.

"Set elevation to positive three-one-five, aye sir," another voice replied.

The image of the massive metal ring of the hypergate grew nearer on the screen. Small red lights flashed all around the perimeter. Electricity snaked all across the surface of the hypergate ring. A pale blue flash of light erupted, opening a tunnel into hyperspace. The *Saratoga* rumbled and shook. Jonathan held onto Ellyra to steady their balance.

"Why is the ship shaking?" Ellyra asked.

"Hypergates emit a lot more gravimetric turbulence than Eurosian ships."

The helmsman turned to the conning officer beside Cynthia. "Elevation is now positive three-one-five, sir."

The conning officer was ultimately responsible for the navigation of the ship. All engine orders had to pass through him. "Very well," he replied.

"Full thrusters on my mark," Cynthia ordered.

"All thrusters ahead full, on Skipper's mark."

"All thrusters ahead full, on Skipper's mark, aye sir."

Cindy pressed a button on the arm of her swiveling chair. The loudspeaker clicked on. "All hands, this is the captain. If you're not holding onto something, you'd better do so now." She swiveled her chair around to Jonathan and Ellyra. "You two had better take a seat."

Jonathan led Ellyra to a chair in the back and sat down beside her. Faster-than-light travel was more of an experience aboard Earth ships. It wasn't the smooth pleasant ride he enjoyed on the *Calmao*.

"Status?" Cynthia asked.

"Moscow is relaying communication transmissions through the hypergate portal," Gordon said.

"All this technology," she said under her breath, "and we're still waiting on the blinking mail."

"Transmit complete," Gordon announced. "We are clear to enter hyperspace."

"Thrusters on my mark," she reiterated. "Three, two, one, mark!"

The *Saratoga* rocketed forward, passing through the portal, and disappeared into hyperspace.

Chapter 35

A NEW DIRECTION

Matt clutched his aching side as his transport shuttle touched down in the landing bay of *Able Station*. It was good to be home, even if that home was infested with squiddies. The pain in his ribs outweighed the throbbing in his head, back, and arms. There weren't any broken bones, but the stinging pain in his ribs was arguably worse. The pilot and co-pilot walked in from the cockpit and helped Matt to his feet. Legally, they were not supposed to assist anyone who had been punished. The idiotic creed of the Scorpii that only the strong should survive carried penalties if anyone assisted.

"You shouldn't be seen helping me," he said, wincing in pain.

"Don't be silly, Matt.," the pilot said. "After all you've done for us, this is the least we can do."

He put Matt's arm around his neck and helped him down the shuttle's loading ramp. When they reached the bottom of the ramp, Ross was not there. Ross always met him in the landing bay. He turned to the pilot. "Did you inform the station of our arrival?"

He nodded. "As you instructed."

Where in the galaxy was Ross? Perhaps that woman he hired had been too much of a handful for him. When would he ever learn? He should have stuck to the stereotype. The idea was to blend in and not attract any attention from the squiddies.

"Help me to my office," he said.

The pilot nodded and assisted in the long trek to his office. The long maze of hallways on the space station felt, for the first time, extremely tedious. He walked one slow step over another, trying to relax the aching rib muscles. When they got to his office, the door had already been slid open. Who was in his office? When he stepped over the threshold, he paused. His office was in shambles with fragments of his desk and shelves all about. In the middle of the floor, lay the body of Ross with lifeless eyes.

"What happened here?" the pilot asked in horror.

Matt's knees buckled and he dropped to the floor, groaning under the throbbing of his ribs. The pilot steadied him and helped him sit against a wall. Matt's heart sank lower than ever before. What was the point of surviving now? Everything he had built, everyone he had assembled and trained, had all been taken away. When he had left the *Brah'Kerov*, his five-year plan had been completely destroyed. But now, after the Scorpiian retribution, his entire life's work was erased.

"Lord Vaux has taken out his anger on the crew again," Matt finally answered. "And I was so close to permanently ending this brutality." Matt clenched his teeth and shut his eyes, waiting for his tears to flow. But they never came. It was not entirely unexpected. Failure in one area usually led to failure in another. He could not save his people, so why should he be able to grieve?

"Find out how many have died," Matt said.

"Of course," the pilot said, turning and leaving.

He sat in silence breathing in and out, staring off into space. What was left now? Could he rebuild his life's work from the ground up? At another time, that might have been a fair question, but with a broken body it could never be done. There would be no return from a complete loss. He hung his head. He might as well have died on the *Brah'Kerov*.

He took a slow, deep breath. Was he going crazy or was there a sweet smell in the room? He took another slow deep breath. There was definitely a sweet scent. Where was it coming from? Matt groaned as he shuffled against the wall, inching forward into the room. The scent grew more fragrant the further inside he reached. There was something very familiar about that smell. Matt's eyes lit up. It was the smell of Cossette's perfume.

"Cossette?"

A muffled voice replied, "Mr. Jaimess!"

It came from the back wall. Matt struggled to his feet, stopping short and nearly shrieking in pain. He rested for several moments. His ribs complained far too much. Unless he could use his leg muscles only, he would never be able to stand. Concentration, now, was the key. He relaxed his stomach and arm muscles while pushing all his energy into his legs. Slowly, he slid his back up the wall and locked his knees. His thighs burned from the exertion.

Her muffled voice called again. "Mr. Jaimess!"

"Where are you?" he said, his blood pumping.

"Mr. Jaimess," she again called, this time pounding against what sounded like a thin metal sheet. That was a sound he knew well. At the back wall, a non-descript coat closet had been installed. Matt never used it because he kept forgetting it existed. It blended in with the back wall so well. But it wasn't very wide, Cossette would have to be quite skinny to be able to squeeze inside.

Matt slowly walked, using the wall for support, to the back wall. After a brief rest, he reached out and unlatched the coat closet door. Cossette had indeed managed to squeeze inside. But with so little room to move inside, there was no way for her to close the door herself. Ross must have helped her inside.

Tears ran down her horrified face. "It was looking for me," she said.

"Lord Vaux?"

She tried to nod. "After it saw me, Ross hid me and wouldn't tell it where I was."

Matt's heart pounded in his chest. He had misjudged Ross. The feeble man had not been so feeble in the end. *Oh Ross,* Matt thought, *it would seem that this day has made a failure of me and a hero of you.*

More tears ran down her face. "It beat him," she said. "I could hear it all."

Matt beckoned for her to come out. "I should have joined him."

She sniffled and squeezed her way out of the thin closet.

"How long ago did this happen?"

She shook her head. "Hours?"

Matt closed his eyes, waiting for another wave of throbbing pain to subside. "I'll see about smuggling you back down to the lower decks. The squiddies rarely go down there."

She shook her head, a new determination in her eyes. "I don't want to run. I want that squiddy dead."

Matt took a deep breath, careful not to flex his side muscles. "I was almost in a position to dispatch Lord Vaux. But that all came to an end tonight. I have lost everything I built."

"What do you mean?"

Matt rolled his eyes, suddenly aware that that action also hurt. "Colonel Terynn pulled the same tactic on me and got the entire vote thrown out. Hence why Lord Vaux was so furious."

"But, how? There's no way he could have out-planned you."

"Oh, his excellence is not in how intricate his planning is. The genius of Jonathan Terynn is in his ability to read the current situation like a map and to compensate. The man thinks outside the box and does so on his feet."

But surely you haven't lost everything," she insisted, "You still have a brilliant mind."

"My dear Cossette," he said in a condescending tone, "knowing how to succeed and actually being able to do it are two very different things. I have lost all my assets, and with them, all desire to start over."

"Not all your assets," she said. "Jerry is still alive on *Gamma Station.*"

Matt shook his head. "He is incarcerated and I have nothing of value that the Gamms would trade for him. That is, *if* the Gamms would even be willing to trade. Colonel Self-Righteous and his morals will be the end of us all."

"Mr. Jaimess, listen to me. There's still a chance you can negotiate with them, but you'll have to appeal to his nobler motives."

Matt stared into her eyes. What was she planning? And how long had she been planning it? "I'm listening," he finally said.

"Go to them as you are now. Show them the damage they have caused." She pointed to Ross's body on the floor. "Let them see what they have caused to fellow humans. Then beg for Jerry's release."

Her plan did have merit. It was ambitious and fresh. And getting Jerry back would go a long way to rebuilding his network. She just might be right; maybe he hadn't lost everything after all. But there was still one critical obstacle.

"What about the squiddies? They monitor all transmissions."

"All *hyperwave* transmissions," she corrected. "They won't be able to track any messages sent through the hypergate network."

"Of course," he said, his eyes widening. Why hadn't he thought of it before? They didn't have to use the Scorpii transmitters. The hypergates were all Earthian installations. If they took a shuttle to a nearby hypergate, they could send a message all the way to *Gamma Station* without the squiddies ever knowing. The unfortunate challenge was that each hypergate sent messages on its own schedule. That was not a problem for recorded messages. Those only needed to be forwarded on to their final destination. With a live transmission, however, a whole line of hypergates needed to be held open at the same time. The only catch was getting the cooperation of every hypergate in the path to *Gamma Station*. It would not be an easy task.

"All right, Cossette. You've convinced me."

"I'll get right on it," she said, spinning around to leave.

"And Cossette," he said, calling after her.

She turned around. "Yes, Mr. Jaimess?"

"From now on, call me Matt."

 286

Chapter 36

21753

Isabeau sat at the command console in the Command and Control room of *Gamma Station*. It was another busy day of headaches. The auxiliary power grid went down, the mag-clamps on docking port six were on the fritz again, and the Chantell had just announced another inspection. Isabeau dropped her reader onto the console and put her head in her hands. Some days, it just wasn't worth getting out of bed in the morning.

Katheryn walked up beside Isabeau.

Isabeau looked up. "What is it, Seaman Vinnece?"

Katheryn handed her a mug of coffee. "Begging your pardon, ma'am, but you look like you could use another."

Isabeau returned an exasperated smile. "Thank you, seaman." She took a sip.

"Permission to ask a question?"

Isabeau nodded. "What's on your mind?"

"We've been wondering. Is there any news about whether Lieutenant Colonel Fox Jagger will be returning to the station?"

She looked down at her mug. "I don't know, seaman. But I sure hope so. That will be all."

Petty Officer McKinsey stood up at his station in the pit. "Commander, the *Saratoga* is on approach."

Isabeau glanced down at her console. "Have them dock at port five."

"Aye, aye ma'am."

Isabeau had just taken another sip from her mug when McKinsey stood again. "Commander, we have an incoming live transmission from Able Station."

"Live?" she said in dismay. Holding up hyperspace travel by keeping a hypergate occupied was inconvenient to the waiting ships. Enough so that hypergate commanders rarely did it. But, with a big enough emergency—or enough money, you could persuade the hypergate commanders to endure the backlash of angry ship captains. But to get a communication line all the way from Scorpii space meant occupying a dozen or so hypergates at once.

"That's got to be enormously expensive without the Scorpii transmitters," she said. "Patch it through to the main screen."

The wall screen blinked and showed a video image of Matt Jaimess. His usual overly cheery façade was absent. His smile was strained, and his voice weak. "Good morning, Commander Alexi. Or is it Good Afternoon where you are? I can never tell." He coughed and stiffened as if in pain.

What had happened to him? He looked like a shuttle crash survivor. Was this his latest choice of antics or had something dreadful actually happen to him? How should she respond? Maybe it was best to play it safe. "Mr. Jaimess, it looks like you had to drop a pretty penny for this transmission."

He strained another smile. "I wish something as simple as poor logistics could be blamed for this pricy long-distance call. But, seeing as the clock is ticking, I must get to the point of my call."

"I'm listening."

288

"I have come to ask for the impossible. I've come to ask for Jerry's release."

"Absolutely not!" a voice answered from behind.

Isabeau spun around.

Jonathan had entered Command and Control with Ellyra. "He is charged with the murder of two men and the attempted murder of two others—myself included." Jonathan marched up to Isabeau's side with fists clenched but stopped short. "What happened to you?"

Matt wheezed a short breath. "Scorpii punishment. You see, my dear Colonel, we both had a lot riding on the outcome of that vote." He coughed again and wiped some blood from the corner of his mouth. "I suspect neither of us truly understands the extent of the damage we have caused each other. But I must congratulate you on your victory; this Moriarty bows to his Holmes."

Matt wheezed another short breath. "I should have been killed, but the vile squiddies still find me useful for now. But my men were not so lucky. Everything I have worked for is now gone."

"Are you telling me this to provoke my sympathy?" Jonathan asked.

"I tell you this to beg for a chance to rebuild."

"Rebuild? So that you can send more assassins—murder more of my crew?"

Matt coughed again, clutching his ribs. "Believe it or not, my dear Colonel, but you and I are a lot alike in many ways. My only goal has been to free my people from the brutality of the Scorpii. And I assume, in your own diluted way, you seek something similar. The problem was that you kept getting in the way."

"So sorry to inconvenience you, Mr. Jaimess. Some of us live by principles."

He took another labored breath. "I didn't come to argue, Jonathan. I came to beg. I have lost everything, and I need Jerry to rebuild. And I will be honest with you, I have nothing to offer in exchange. Except, perhaps, to say that I will no longer trouble you; that avenue has been foreclosed."

There was something sincere in Matt's voice, but when had he ever been sincere? Though, when had he ever been severely injured? Was this for real or was it a new manipulation tactic? "How do we know this isn't a trick?" Isabeau asked.

"That's a fair question," Matt admitted. "I don't know that I can say anything that would satisfy you. I am no longer in a position to free my people. But, with Jerry's help, I can put an end to the squiddy that butchered my team."

"And if I say no?" Jonathan asked.

"If you say no, you will have the guarantee that I cannot harm your men. And you will have the guarantee that more Abes—more humans—will die at the hands of the squiddies."

Jonathan turned and looked into Ellyra's eyes, considering.

"Jonathan," Matt said, cringing with pain. "I've sent my shuttle to *Gamma Station*. It should be there by now if it has not been delayed. If you choose to help me, put Jerry on board. I must lie down now. Let me just say that it is a great pity that you were not born an Abe...oh, the things we could have accomplished together. Jaimess out."

The screen blinked again, showing statistical information. Isabeau turned to Jonathan. "Is he for real?"

Jonathan took a deep breath. "Real or not, we have just been given a new lease on life."

"What do you mean?"

"You probably haven't heard yet; the Scorpii now control *Bravo Station*."

"What? How?"

"Do you remember the footage of the Skorath ship that T'Kal showed us?"

Isabeau nodded.

"Somehow the Scorpii got their tentacles on it. And Matt used it to get the attention of the Draconians. Anyway, long story short, the Tumnei were censured and the Scorpii now control *Bravo Station*."

Her nostrils flared and her muscles tensed. "That gozark deserves what he got! That was our only connection to—"

Jonathan put his hands on her shoulders. "Izzy, what matters now is that the Scorpii control *Bravo Station* and that Matt is in deep with the Scorpii. If we help Matt with his problem, perhaps he will help us access *Bravo Station*. And if we can do that, we can regain our chances to make this prophecy thing work."

She pursed her lips. "Colonel, he tried to kill you."

Jonathan nodded. "I will agree it is a risk. But right now, we need miracles. T'Kal was right, the political landscape is changing. This may be our only chance. We have roughly ninety days to get the Bugs on board and reestablish communication with T'Kal and Cyran."

How could she argue with his reasons? They would be letting a killer go free, and at the same time, breathing new life into their chances for freedom. It was a very complicated moral decision that, thankfully, wasn't her call to make. Her gaze fell to the floor. "I understand, sir."

Chief O'Dell stood up from his station in the pit. "Commander, we have an unscheduled shuttle requesting permission to dock."

She glanced over to her console. "Chief, have them dock at port two."

"Aye, aye ma'am."

She looked into Jonathan's eyes. "Request authorization to release the prisoner."

"Request granted."

She glanced up to the balcony. "Vinnece, have SecOps send a security team to escort the prisoner to docking port two for departure. And send him with some medical supplies."

"Aye, aye ma'am."

Ellyra put her hand on Jonathan's shoulder, prompting him to turn around. "It pleases me to tell you how impressed I am with the manner in which you handled that situation. You not only set the groundwork for an alliance, but you also managed to get something in return. It must have been a terrible decision."

"It seemed like the right thing to do...and the wrong thing to do as well. I guess time will tell if I did the right thing or not."

Petty Officer McKinsey again stood. "Commander, we have an incoming transmission on the Alpha channel. It's from the Draconian flagship *Brah'Kerov.*"

Isabeau exchanged a glance with Jonathan. "It can't be Matt Jaimess, he just called from *Able Station.*"

"Let's see who it is," Jonathan said.

"On screen, Petty Officer," she ordered.

The large screen on the wall flickered. It displayed a distorted video image of a man in his sixties with a forward-set jaw and a crescent moon of gray hair. His loose blue and white clothing bore the hallmark of *Bravo Station.* The man stood next to an assistant who frantically punched keys on a console. The man's lips moved but no sound followed.

"Please pardon my intrusion, Jonathan," Ellyra said. "But is not that the senator for *Bravo Station* whom we saw at the Senate Convention?"

Jonathan nodded. "Kipp Tyler." He looked back at McKinsey. "What's wrong with the signal?"

"Sorry, sir. The signal is being disrupted from the source."

Kipp's assistant spoke, motioning with his hands as if giving an explanation. Kipp sighed and hung his head a moment. Then he looked back into the camera and held up two fingers. Then he switched it to one finger. Then, he fanned out all five fingers and added two more. Then he dropped his other hand, leaving the five fingers showing. Then he switched it to just three fingers.

"Two, one, seven, five, three," Jonathan said, turning to Isabeau. "Remember those numbers: two, one, seven, five, three."

She nodded, repeating them under her breath while she searched for a reader to type them onto.

"Are we recording this," Jonathan asked over his shoulder.

"Negative, sir," a voice from the balcony replied.

"Start recording."

"Aye, sir, recording started."

Kipp again held up his fingers, showing the same pattern of numbers. Then Kipp and his assistant both looked to the side with startled expressions on their faces. His assistant ran while he held up his arms as if to brace himself from being hit. A bright yellow and orange light flooded the video image. It completely washed out the entire scene with blinding light. The video image abruptly sputtered and ended in static.

Ellyra gasped, her hands instinctively at her cheeks.

Isabeau's reader fell to the floor. The clatter echoed in the still room.

Chapter 37

THE ORDER

"**B**ack it up!" Jonathan shouted amidst the cacophony of voices, gesturing with his finger to rewind. "Back it up!" Shouted orders and clamoring voices filled the room with noise.

"Don't tell me you can't find anything," Isabeau said to a frustrated crewman. "It's the only clue we've got. I want you turning the database inside out and upside down until we figure this out!"

"Right there!" Jonathan said. He pointed to the screen displaying the recorded half of Kipp's transmission. "Okay, playback from here." The bright yellow and orange light filled the screen and the recording ended with static. "Okay, replay that sequence frame by frame."

The recording played in slow motion, the bright light consuming the entire screen. The noise in the room quieted as most of the eyes in the room were on the screen.

"Freeze frame!" Jonathan shouted. "Now reduce the exposure."

The image refreshed, darkening the blurred yellow and orange light.

"Can we clean it up?"

"Aye, sir," said a voice from the balcony.

The screen refreshed the image several more times. Each time the yellow and orange blur became clearer until it was at last in focus. It looked like a great flame of fire stretching across the screen.

Isabeau walked up to Jonathan. "What in the galaxy happened? It must be an explosion of some kind."

The image sent a chill down Jonathan's back. It was as frightening as it was disturbing. An explosion could be possible, but there hadn't ever been a report of an explosion on a Draconian ship. It couldn't be ruled out, but there was another, more plausible explanation. Jonathan's heart pounded and the air seemed to thicken. The only trouble with the other explanation was that if it was true, then the stakes were now at an all-time high.

Jonathan shook his head. "An explosion on the Draconian flagship? Possible, but not likely."

"Then how would you explain it, sir?"

"What is more likely, is that what we are looking at is the fiery breath of a Draconian."

Ellyra gasped. "But the Draconians never get their hands dirty. They always have others enforcing their rules. What could possibly be so provoking as to induce them to get personally involved?"

"Whatever it is," Isabeau said, "Kipp Tyler was trying to warn us about it."

"Two, one, seven, five, three," Jonathan repeated.

Isabeau spun around. "We really need those numbers figured out, seaman!"

The young seaman gave an exasperated sigh. "Ma'am, it could be anything. Keltracite is number 21753 on the galactic periodic table of elements, the rhyme meter pattern in a Veldosian haiku poem is two then one then seven then five then three, the 217th decimal of pi is—"

Isabeau shook her head. "No, no, no, we're looking for something on a galactic scale. These numbers are somehow connected to the Draconians."

295

Ellyra put her gloved hand on Jonathan's shoulder. "Jonathan, those numbers are also a galactic year."

"That would put it at about eighty years ago."

She nodded. "Eighty-three to be precise."

"Anything relevant in that year?"

Her eyes glistened with moisture as she solemnly nodded.

Jonathan put his hands on her shoulders, peering deep into her blue within blue eyes. "If you know something, please tell me."

A tear rolled down her cheek. "That was the last year of the Xandraxi."

"Xandraxi? I don't know if I've ever met them."

She shook her head. "You never will. They are no more. They openly defied the Draconians that year. So, the Draconains declared an extermination order against them. Every member race of the Senate was ordered to attack and destroy the Xandraxi or face extermination themselves."

Another tear escaped and traced its path down her cheek. "My grandfather was Sune of a ship that the Euroo sent in obedience to that order." She sniffled. "The Xandraxi never had a chance."

Jonathan's eyes widened and his breathing halted. What had he done? Had the Draconians declared an extermination order against humans? What in the galaxy had he done? *I'm such an idiot!* he thought. *I knew the Draconians were on edge because of the whole Skorath ordeal, why did I push it?*

Jonathan heard the drumbeats of his heart in the silent, still room. He took a deep breath. "I need to speak with Earth command."

Isabeau turned to the pit crew. "O'Dell, McKinsey, McNamar, plot a live communication line with Earth. Contact each hypergate commander and inform them this is a *priority* emergency!"

They each acknowledged and pounded the keys at their consoles. Jonathan slouched under the mental barrage of consequences. His lungs refused to breathe and his heart sank into the pit of his stomach. How could *Gamma Station* put the prophecy to good use when there would soon be no more *Gamma Station?*

Jonathan forced a deep breath. Would it even matter anymore without any human beings left to liberate? Could there be some mistake? Maybe this wasn't the intended meaning of 21753? Was there another explanation? Surely there had to be.

"What's the holdup?" Isabeau asked.

"It's Hypergate London, ma'am. The commander says the best she can do is twenty minutes."

Isabeau hopped down into the pit and took McNamar's headset. She put it on and sat down at his computer station. She stared at a video image of the hypergate commander. "Hello, Miranda."

"Isabeau!" Miranda said with cheery excitement. "What's up—" Her smile melted at the sight of Isabeau's complexion. "Babe, you look like you've seen a ghost. What's wrong?"

Isabeau swallowed. "Miranda, we could be in some very serious trouble. We need a live transmission with Earth Central Command."

"Dang, girl. I'm gonna put your transmission through right away." Miranda snapped her fingers to a crewman on her left and gave him some instructions.

"I appreciate that, Miranda. I know you have one of the busiest hypergates."

She nodded. "You bet. Stand by for activation."

The screen on the wall flickered and displayed the globe icon of Earth Central Command. After a few moments, the screen changed to show a dark-skinned older man in uniform holding a cigar in his hand. The nameplate on his desk read, Fleet Admiral Jared Mays.

Admiral Mays looked up. "I take it you got the bad news?"

"Bits and pieces, sir," Jonathan admitted. "Have the Draconians issued an extermination order against us?"

Admiral Mays leaned back in his chair. "Yes and no." He sucked on his cigar and breathed out a puff of smoke. "As of 18:30 hours Earth time, the Draco Senate met in special session, which you obviously weren't invited to. The Draconians did declare an extermination order, but the order was not issued against all humanity—thank heavens. Ambassador Clarence, the Tumnei senator, and the Scorpiian delegate for that matter, all pleaded with the Draconians that the three space stations should each be treated as a separate protectorate. The Draconians agreed. That limits the scope of the extermination order to just the three thousand plus men and women aboard *Gamma Station*. It won't extend to the other two space stations—let alone the 16.5 billion people here on Earth."

Jonathan pursed his lips.

Admiral Mays sat up straight in his chair. "I know what you're thinking, how could I be so callous toward your men? Well, you pissed off the Draconians real good. And while I applaud you for it, you got to understand that saving as many lives as possible is my *top* priority."

"I'm sorry," Jonathan finally said, almost in a whisper.

Admiral Mays took a deep breath, stammering for the right words. "The order is already in effect. Everybody is ordered to attack and destroy you. Anyone aiding *Gamma Station* will be considered in violation of the order and also subject to extermination. Earth can't help you, Jonathan."

Jonathan swallowed with a dry throat. "I know."

Admiral Mays put the cigar back in his mouth only to promptly pull it back out. "I have ordered Hypergates Arizona and Warsaw to undergo 'routine' maintenance. That'll slow down the traffic from the younger races in your direction for a couple of days. That's as long as we dare try the patience of the Draconians." He threw his cigar at the ashtray on his desk but it missed and landed on the floor. He wiped one hand down his face. "Get every last ship you can and evacuate the station. The Greys will be trying to delay their arrival too. But I fear the Scorpii will be heading your way as fast as they can."

Jonathan nodded once. The air grew heavy. Jonathan's heart tripled in weight. He stared hopelessly at Admiral Mays for an eternal moment.

Admiral Mays swallowed. "I love ya like a son, Jonathan..." He abruptly looked away, his jaw quivering. He blinked a few times, taking in a deep breath. Then he recomposed himself, returning his gaze to Jonathan with a fierce resolve in his watery eyes. "Don't you go down without a fight!"

Jonathan solemnly nodded.

"Mays out."

The transmission ended and the wall screen returned to displaying statistical data. A faint beeping sound cut through the pin-drop silence that loomed in the air. Isabeau returned the headset to McNamar and walked up the pit ramp.

Jonathan sullenly looked around the room at the crew. *I killed them,* he thought. *I killed them all.* Every set of eyes was on him, waiting on bated breath for some encouragement, for some comfort. What comfort could he provide? What hope was there? They could not outrun a fleet of ships; the hypergate network would not be allowed to assist. And without the speed of hyperspace, the slowest ships in the galaxy would overtake them in a few hours. They also could not hide; most of the elder races had advanced sensor systems. Fighting seemed the only option left. But they wouldn't last long against several fleets of warships, especially the Scorpii.

"Orders, sir?" Isabeau asked.

What orders were there to give? Any option he chose was doomed. After a long moment, he swallowed and spoke softly. "Carry on, Commander." He turned and walked toward the doorway.

Isabeau marched after him. "Sir?"

He knew what she wanted; some guidance and direction. But there was none to give. He continued walking.

"Sir?" she again asked, louder this time.

Irritation began to build inside Jonathan. How could she demand anything more of him? He had nothing left to offer. If only she would stop insisting.

"Colonel?"

Jonathan spun around with a scowl. "That will be all, Commander."

She stopped in her tracks, a look of shock mixed with betrayal in her eyes. "Aye, sir," she finally said.

He exited Command and Control and walked down the hallway. After rounding the first corner, he heard Ellyra's voice behind him.

"Jonathan!"

The irritation continued to climb. Couldn't they see he needed some time alone to think? Why did they have to pester him? He spun around to face her. "Yes?"

"Please don't leave them, Jonathan. They need you."

He dismissed her comments with a wave of his hand. "They don't need me."

"Forgive me for contradicting, but they do need you."

He looked at her with intensity in his eyes. "I'm the one who *killed* them!"

"And the one who is going to *save* them," she said staring into his eyes.

Jonathan stammered for words, motioning aimlessly with his arms. She didn't understand. How could she? All was lost and nothing could be salvaged. At least Matt Jaimess had something to rebuild. Jonathan was not so lucky. Rebuilding the space station and resurrecting a crew of over three thousand was a little beyond his capabilities.

"How?" he finally asked. "How am I supposed to save them? We cannot run, we cannot hide, and we cannot fight. What am I supposed to do? I can't even take advantage of my deal with Matt Jaimess. The prophecy is as dead as we are."

"Hang the prophecy then. This is a fight for survival now."

He closed his eyes, shaking his head. "A hopeless fight for survival."

Ellyra attempted a weak smile. "Then are you not the most qualified man to win a hopeless fight?"

He regarded her curiously.

She nodded. "Yes, in the weeks I have been here, I have heard about your war stories. Ambassador Lucas talks fondly of them and refers to you as the Ace of Cobra Squad, the Hammer of the Ursar, and the Hero of Mesa Sol. I'm told that your homeworld's naval academy teaches what you did there. And your first Dommicon, Fox, even emulates them."

The air grew thick and his heart pounded. His irritation faded and his muscles relaxed. It was so long ago, but could she still be right? Was there still any brilliance left in him? And would there be enough to overcome odds as great as these?

Ellyra took a breath. "And it was my pleasure to witness how you defeated two Scorpiian Harkons—the second one you defeated with mere words."

Jonathan swallowed.

Ellyra smiled. "And the one impossible story that is closest to my heart, is the one about the Earth colonel that was doomed to never return to me. And yet, despite the opposition of my family's house and the decree of the Draconians, he now belongs to me."

That last story wasn't completely accurate. It was partly an accident. He opened his mouth to protest but she continued.

"So, you see, my dear Jonathan, the impossible becomes possible with you. Even if the answers have yet to present themselves, you somehow find a way. Do you not owe it to your crew to carry on until you find the way? Your own military leader just instructed you to 'not go down without a fight'. And that, it would seem, is precisely what you are the best at doing."

Jonathan took in a slow breath, letting all the tension out. She was right. His entire military career had been trademarked by accomplishing what should have been impossible. If there was a way to survive, he could find it.

He swallowed. "Thank you, Ellyra. What would I do without you?"

She displayed a confused look on her face.

Jonathan quickly raised his hands. "That's just an expression that means I'm awfully lucky to have you."

She smiled.

Jonathan took her hand. "Let's get back to Command and Control."

Chapter 38

THE NEBULA

Fox walked with Layna down the corridor to the Center of Workmanship. He paused just outside the door and glanced at the portrait of Kalmeedes. Such a large painting made it easier to see all the little details that were obscure on the small portable screen of the reader. Kalmeedes wore the green jeweled necklace and also held his hand up.

Fox mimicked the gesture with his arm. "Well, Kalmeedes, are you reaching heavenward too?"

Layna snickered, covering her mouth. "Please forgive my impropriety, Lieutenant Colonel Fox, but you are talking to a painting."

Fox smiled playfully. "Well, that would explain why he never disagrees with me."

She failed to suppress her giggles. "We best not keep Brigadain Diahlus waiting now that we have arrived at the Emerald Heart nebula."

Fox walked up to the double door, which parted when he came near enough. He stepped inside with Layna tailing behind. Fox halted, seeing

Diahlus conversing with the holographic images of four other men. The first was the unmistakable image of Lord Areo, but the other three Fox hadn't ever seen before. Fox leaned over to Layna. "Who else besides Lord Areo is Diahlus talking with?"

"House El'Allel commands four ships. Those are the Sunes of the other three ships. Sune Vaynar of the *Kaliptica*, Sune Domir of the *Pentora*, and Sune Rae of the *Aloriel*."

"Looks like an important meeting," he said.

Diahlus along with the three Sunes bowed to Lord Areo. Then the holograms faded out as the transmission ended. Diahlus walked over to Xer and handed him a reader device.

"Is this a copy of the order?" Xer asked.

Diahlus shook his head. "Indeed not. It is a transcript of the Draco Senate session. Something happened to cause all this. Lord Areo wants you to review it and submit a legal opinion."

"As you wish, Diahlus."

Fox walked over to Diahlus. "What's the news?"

Diahlus ran a hand through his wavy frightened gray hair. "I've just received word that the Draconians have issued an extermination order against *Gamma Station*."

"What?" Fox said in alarm.

"I'm afraid so," Diahlus said. "And Parliament has ordered each house lord to send every battle-capable ship to *Gamma Station* in obedience to the order."

"You're going to attack?" Fox blurted out.

"Calm yourself, Lieutenant Colonel Fox. Legally, we must attack. But Lord Areo has ordered *his* ships to flank speed. We are to get to *Gamma Station* before the Scorpii do and evacuate Ellyra at all costs."

"And what of the ship House Creo is sending to ally with the Scorpii?" Layna asked.

"That matter has been put on hold," Diahlus explained. "Despite Lord Areo's assertions, Parliament has ordered every ship to *Gamma Station*. It's Parliament's concern now."

Fox stood there, stunned. An extermination order against *Gamma Station*. "They're not going to stand a chance."

Diahlus turned back to Fox. "Which is why all we can do is rescue Lord Areo's daughter."

"Colonel Terynn, Isabel, Grrrah'Kah, the rest of the crew...they'll be slaughtered!"

Diahlus huffed a breath. "Perhaps, I can convince Lord Areo that Ellyra would not leave without Jonathan. But that is absolutely all I can do."

Fox's pulse raced. His blood ran cold. How could this happen? Something had to be done. But what could be done? Fox's eyes lit up. "The Skorath! The Skorath can help. They're an ancient race with technology that rivals the Draconians. They can save *Gamma Station!*"

Diahlus waved a dismissing hand. "Fairy tales."

Fox marched right up to Diahlus. "I have *seen* a Skorath ship, Diahlus. They are real."

"Even if they are," Diahlus said, "as you have pointed out, you have no idea where they are."

"Here!" Fox asserted. "They are right here!"

"The Emerald Heart nebula?"

"Yes, it's the only nebula in this sector that is large enough to be seen from Eurosia. And it's green."

"Then you had best contact them before we get underway."

Fox rolled his eyes, glancing heavenward. "I haven't figured that part out yet. I need a couple of hours to—"

"You have five minutes," Diahlus said.

Was he crazy? How was he supposed to discover and decipher and test how to contact the Skorath in five minutes? The problem was that Diahlus didn't believe it was possible. *Was this whole excursion just to humor me?* he wondered. *Am I really the only one who believes there's anyone out there to contact?* Diahlus was asking for the impossible.

"What? Five minutes? How am I supposed to pull this off in five minutes? Diahlus, I need more than that."

"Four minutes and thirty-eight seconds," Diahlus said, glancing at the ornate hanging clock.

Fox threw his hands up in desperation. "Okay, okay!" Diahlus was not going to give him any more time. This was all he had to work with, and it would somehow have to be enough. "Skip the communication probe. Just open up a broadcast transmission to whoever might be listening and I'll just talk."

"As you wish, Fox," Diahlus said, turning to a crewman on his left to relay the instruction.

Fox sighed. Where should he start? Perhaps a simple hello? Or maybe reciting the Skorath prophecy might do some good. There was no way to know what the Skorath were wanting without any time to research. Why did the stupid Draconians have to spring this?

Fox took a deep breath. *Relax,* he told himself. *The stage is lit and the curtains have opened. Ready or not, it is showtime.*

Diahlus looked back at Fox. "Transmission open. You have four minutes to speak."

"Greetings," Fox said, holding his arms out. "We come in peace...mostly."

Diahlus rolled his eyes and sat down.

Fox glanced back at Layna. "What are those two names in the painting again?"

"Kalisahr and Vendier."

Fox continued. "Kalisahr and Vendier, we really need your guy's help right now...take me to your leader."

Arkamenos and Xer exchanged confused glances.

"I know you're out there and that you're listening," Fox said. "You even told us that a newborn light will arise from an uninteresting corner of space, wielding a power that will frighten the star of Draconia, and claim the birthright of the ancestors. Well, we're here...sort of. Actually, the Voonsu are back on *Gamma Station* but that's a small detail we can work out later. I know you guys are not due to show yourselves for another few months but we need your help. The race of prophecy is about to be destroyed. We know you've been looking forward to the

305

fulfillment of your prophecy longer than we have. Well, if you don't act now, it'll all be for nothing!"

Diahlus glanced again at the clock.

Fox sighed, clenching his fists. "Why won't you answer?" He took a few sullen breaths. "Please answer..."

Diahlus walked over to Fox and put a hand on his shoulder. "I'm sorry, Fox. Most of the important things in life have to be taken on faith, not proof. If Vera truly exists, she may have to be sought after in prayer rather than starships. But it was a valiant effort."

Fox's chest muscles tensed. The air was difficult to breathe. His heart hung low. The show was over. The curtain had closed. But there would be no curtain call for a failure. Despite his best efforts, he had let his crewmates down. If only he could curl up in a bunk and drift off to sleep. Maybe some of the pain in his chest would ease up in soft slumber.

He looked into Diahlus's aquamarine within blue eyes. "Diahlus, when we get to *Gamma Station,* will you leave me there? I don't want my crew to die alone."

Diahlus swallowed and nodded. Then he returned to his chair. "Steersman, power up the hyperdrive and set course for *Gamma Station.*"

"As you wish, Brigadain."

Diahlus turned to Xer. "And, if you would please hurry on that report of the Draco Senate session."

Xer picked up the reader. "Right away."

Fox hung his head and walked to the door. Layna reached out to lay a comforting hand on his shoulder but he rushed out the door. When the double door closed behind him, he kicked the wall beneath the hanging portrait of Kalmeedes.

He took a deep, sullen breath and looked into the eyes of the painting. "You were supposed to be the greatest, Kalmeedes. Perhaps you were just as much a fool as I am." The stubborn eyes of the painting mocked the weight of Fox's heart. The outstretched hand seemed almost to wave goodbye.

Fox huffed. "Even you are eager to say goodbye to me. Well, let me tell you something, you blue-eyed, overgrown—"

Fox blinked. "You're not saying goodbye, are you?" His skin tingled with goosebumps and his heart pounded. Fox widened his eyes and took in a huge breath. "You're saying hello, aren't you?" His eyes darted down to the two words inscribed in the painting. Those were the two words that Layna had said were not words in any language and at best were made-up names.

Fox shook his head. "They're not words in any *known* language!"

Fox dashed back into the Center of Workmanship and shouted, "Stop! It's a greeting!"

Diahlus whirled around, startled. Then his hair blackened and he scowled. "Fox, I am going to have to ask you to remove yourself—"

"I have the answer!"

"I can spare no more time. Now please, desist immediately."

"Open the transmission one more time, please?"

Diahlus tensed up and pointed to a tall man at the front of the room. "Please assist the Lieutenant Colonel in vacating the Center of Workmanship."

"I know what to say, Diahlus," Fox said, pleading. "Open the transmission and let me say one short sentence. Do this for me and I swear I will escort myself to my quarters and stay there."

"Agreed!" Diahlus snapped. He turned back around. "Steersman, halt the hyperdrive. Commsman, reopen the broadcast transmission for one minute only."

"As you wish, Brigadain."

Diahlus glared at Fox. "One minute beginning now."

"Thank you, Diahlus," Fox said. He took a deep breath and cleared his throat. "Kalisahr Vendier, Skorath!"

Fox breathed in quiet pants, listening. The entire room fell silent, staring at Fox. He scratched an itch on his bald head and continued listening. Why didn't they answer? Wasn't that the solution to the puzzle?

"Time," called a man at the other end of the room. "Shutting down transmission."

Fox's heart sank. What did he do wrong? That should have been it. Did he read too much into the painting and let his imagination get carried away? He felt Diahlus's stare. It was time to keep his end of the bargain. Fox closed his eyes in regret and hung his head. "If you would please excuse me from the room, Diahlus, I have an obligation to keep."

Diahlus's hair changed to a regretful indigo. "For what it's worth, Fox, I truly hoped you would succeed."

Layna rested a hand on his shoulder. Tears rolled down her cheek. "I shall go with you," she said.

Fox and Layna turned to exit the room. The loudspeakers in the ship rumbled with a deep ancient voice. "Kalisahr Vendier, Euroo."

Chapter 39

THE CALM BEFORE THE STORM

Ellyra sat on a couch in her quarters, her head on Jonathan's shoulder. She hadn't ever been alone with a gentleman in her quarters before. Somehow, it felt wrong, as though it were the ultimate breach of propriety. Such things just weren't done. *But I'm married now,* she told herself. *Surely such things are done in marriage.* How many times would she have to have this conversation with herself? How many times would she have to give herself permission to be alone with her husband?

Jonathan typed a note on his reader, thoroughly entranced in his preparations. Ellyra blinked a few times. With all the excitement, there hadn't been much time for sleep. Now it seemed that sleep was intruding upon their time together. She took a deep breath, trying to stay awake.

"You sound sleepy," Jonathan said, not looking up from his reader. "I warned you this might be boring."

She took in another deep breath. "Yes, that you did. But at least I find it calming."

"It's not much of a date," he said. "I would have rather spent this time getting to know you better. Instead, I'm getting to know this space station better."

"Well, I am certainly not about to give the two of you any time alone. I believe I may be frightfully jealous."

Jonathan chuckled. "I'm sorry this is taking so long. But as a great general on Earth once said, 'The general who wins the battle makes many calculations in his temple before the battle is fought. The general who loses makes but few calculations beforehand'."

"What was this general's name?"

"Sun Tzu," he replied, typing in another note.

She readjusted the position of her head on his shoulder. "Is that the man you quoted while at the Senate Convention when you said victorious soldiers win before the battle?"

He smiled. "The very one."

Ellyra lifted her head and glanced at his reader. "It would appear you have a plan."

"Not exactly," he explained. "I have *half* a plan."

"Half a plan?"

He nodded. "It's a good idea, but how to get the Scorpii to fall for it is another problem altogether."

"Oh," she said, twirling her finger around in his hair.

Jonathan abruptly stopped typing.

"Oh, do forgive me, Jonathan," she said, retreating her hand back to her side.

He smiled and turned to her. "Have I been neglecting you?"

"Oh, Jonathan," she said in protest. "We have so much at stake right now. Please do not halt your preparations on account of—"

Jonathan hushed her with his finger to her lips. "I have been neglecting you, haven't I?"

She nodded with his finger still at her lips.

He dropped the reader onto the coffee table, leaned in, and began kissing her. Her hair tingled. It was probably turning pink or burgundy, but did it really matter which at this moment? She put both arms around his neck.

An alarm blared a single note five times. Her heart launched into her throat and she jumped to her feet. Her pulse raced and she gasped for breath. "I knew this was improper!" she said, placing her hand on her chest.

"What?" Jonathan asked in dismay.

She held out a halting hand toward him. "Please forgive me, Jonathan. We should never have done this. I *knew* better."

"Ellyra," he said sternly. "That's the alarm for battle stations. It has nothing to do with us."

She took a few controlled breaths, hoping to slow her heart rate.

The loudspeaker blared "General Quarters, General Quarters. All hands man your battle stations. This is not a drill. This is not a drill. Inbound hostile starcraft." The alarm repeated.

Her breathing slowed and her hair tingled again. It was definitely becoming an embarrassed burgundy. Of course, the alarm would be for an emergency. Who ever heard of a propriety alarm? She lowered her hands and recomposed herself. "I...um..."

Jonathan nodded. "We'll have to work on this."

She nodded, blushing.

He held out his hand to her. "We need to get to Command and Control quickly."

"We?" she asked.

He nodded. "I want you by my side."

She smiled and took his hand.

They jogged down the halls of the station and even climbed a flight of stairs. Ellyra breathed heavily, trying to keep up. Most of her exercise consisted of leisurely walks in the gardens outside Palace El'Allel. Running up a staircase was a new and challenging experience. They finally jogged into Command and Control. Isabeau frantically shouted orders and the runners dashed across the balcony. The pit crew talked over one another, relaying instructions and reporting back.

"What's our status, Izzy?"

"We have incoming from Terks," she said, her French accent bleeding into her pronunciation. She picked up one of several readers from the command console. "Seventy-eight Icks-class marauders and eight Perks-class transports."

"The Bugs are attacking us?" Jonathan said with wide eyes.

"How could the Chantell possibly travel here so quickly?" Ellyra asked.

"They're from Terks—well, Trkzpizks or *however* you pronounce it. They're from the planet below that *Gamma Station* orbits. I just would have hoped they'd have given us more time."

"We've been friends for so long, I would have expected that too," Isabeau said, not looking up from her console.

"Perhaps they also fear the ramifications of disobeying the extermination order," Ellyra said.

"Perhaps," Jonathan said, nodding. "Izzy, how long before we can evacuate?"

"We're nowhere close, Colonel. Only three cruisers have been loaded, and we don't yet have all the supplies rounded up."

"Worst case scenario, if we have to evacuate now, how long could we last?"

She sighed with an air of frustration. "A couple of weeks, sir."

Jonathan glanced heavenward, closing his eyes and taking a deep breath. "No pressure," he muttered under his breath. He turned back to Isabeau. "Open a transmission. I'll see if I can talk to them. But if this goes nowhere, I want you signaling the evac and getting out of here."

"Aye, sir," she said. She turned to the pit crew. "McKinsey, open a transmission to the lead ship."

"They're a hive society, ma'am. They don't have a lead ship."

She pursed her lips, forcing herself to relax her fists. "The one in the center of their formation, Petty Officer."

"Aye, ma'am."

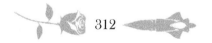 312

A moment later the large screen on the wall blinked and displayed the video image of a small, humid cockpit illuminated by orange light. Small vents spewed hot moisture into the air. The large locust bodies of the Chantell sat around consoles of switches and dials.

Jonathan cleared his throat. "I take it, you've been notified of the extermination order against us?"

One of the Chantell jerked its head up and down, mimicking a head nod. "Us informed is."

Jonathan began pacing. "Listen, George—you don't mind me calling you George, do you? We had hoped that since we've been friends for so long, that you would give us some more time."

George's head moved in short jerking motions. "Much time, you not have. Come now, we do."

"George, we don't want to fight you."

George twitched his antennae. "Fight, you must."

Jonathan glanced heavenward. "Why must it be this way? Look, I know you're scared about the stipulations of the order. But you've *got* to give us more time."

"Time, there is none. Surrender."

"Listen—" Jonathan blinked. Why were they demanding a surrender? The extermination order didn't allow for the guilty party to surrender. Everyone was mandated to attack and destroy. Did the Bugs misunderstand the order? "But we can't surrender to you," he explained. "That won't fulfill your obligation to kill us."

George jerked his head from side to side as if to shake his head. "Understand not. *Chantell* surrender."

"You're going to help us?" Isabeau asked with wide eyes.

George cocked his head to the side. "Help, violation is. Commandeer, you must."

"You *have* been studying us," Isabeau said with a bright smile.

"May Heaven bless you, George," Jonathan said. "We accept your surrender. Petty Officer McKinsey will contact you separately on coordination." He turned to Isabeau. "Get those bug transports docked and start loading them up with equipment."

313

"Aye, Colonel."

Jonathan turned to Ellyra and smiled. His eyes of brown with amber gems glistened. Something about him looked straighter, sturdier. Was it a sign of renewed confidence? Had her precious Jonathan found his proverbial footing? There was also something missing from his eyes; the gloom had left.

She walked up to him. "I believe I am starting to understand your picturesque eyes."

"Oh?" he asked, raising his eyebrows.

"I see in them that our situation has changed from dire to hopeful."

"Ellyra, we're not alone," he said, his voice catching in his throat. "We have friends."

Her eyes watered. "A man, such as you, does not command loyalty. But rather, as the flower to the bee, he attracts it."

He pulled her into a warm hug. "Ellyra, I think we are going to be okay."

She wrapped her arms around him, basking in his warmth. Things were better than okay. All her girlhood dreams of romance and affection were coming true. She was in the arms of a man with mettle, who cared for her more than his social standing. How could fortune have smiled upon her so abundantly? She was in the arms of the man she loved, and he loved her. Her hair tingled as the color changed to a loving red.

Chapter 40

FRIENDS

A faint beeping sound caught Jonathan's attention. He slowly opened his eyes and lifted his head from the back of the couch. He must have fallen asleep. His reader had fallen to the floor. How long had he been asleep? Ellyra's head lay on his shoulder, her peaceful light-blue locks of hair tickling his neck. The rhythm of her slumbering breath was the only other sound in the room. He lifted his arm to see his comm-band. His early morning alarm had been sounding for several minutes. They both must have been very tired to have slept through his alarm. *Well,* he thought, *at least Izzy will be happy I got some rest.*

The only problem was that it sucked time; time that he could be spending in council with his commanders. He gently scooted off the couch and slowly laid Ellyra down. It would be such a shame to wake her; she looked so peaceful. He glanced down at the comm-band around her wrist and smiled. It was time for a little fun. He typed a simple note on his comm-band and tapped the button to send the message. A second later, her comm-band beeped twice. It would make a great tutorial for her on how to retrieve messages.

Now, to find out how much time he had squandered while napping. He picked up his reader from the floor and carried it into the other room. Five precious hours had been lost. With the Scorpii fleet on their way, every minute counted. With his most conservative estimate, the Scorpii would arrive within a day. That would extend another six hours if the Scorpii were bringing their slower heavy attack ships. Being an elder race, the Scorpii had a large enough technological advantage that they didn't need an entire fleet to destroy *Gamma Station*. A dozen Harkon-class destroyers would be enough. But the Scorpii seldom did anything halfway. This time, it would be to Jonathan's advantage.

Jonathan looked up from his reader as the room began to shudder and shake. He reached for the dresser to steady himself.

"Jonathan!" Ellyra's panicked voice called from the other room.

Jonathan bolted through the doorway and into Ellyra's arms. "So sorry, my love."

"What's going on?"

He shook his head. "I don't know." He pressed a few buttons on his comm-band. "Colonel to Command and Control, status report."

"Large gravimetric field dangerously close to the station, sir!" a panicked voice responded.

"Sound General Quarters."

"Aye, sir."

The alarm blared. "General Quarters, General Quarters. All hands man your battle stations. Space storm warning."

Jonathan and Ellyra again raced back to Command and Control. Despite being thrown into a combat lifestyle, Ellyra was handling it quite well. It was a far cry from the simple and peaceful lifestyle he had observed when visiting Eurosia. It was far more physically demanding and yet Ellyra didn't complain. Aside from being a great political mentor, she was fast proving to be a competent crew member.

They jogged into Command and Control. The large screen on the wall displayed a video image of a distortion in space. Bright blue light and green particles spewed out like a large angelic fountain in space. Jonathan glanced over to the man at the command console. "What have we got, Commander?"

"It's emitting large graviton wakes like a storm, but the energy output is off the scale."

"Is there any danger to the station?"

He shook his head. "Negligible, sir. That is, assuming it stays right where it is."

Isabeau dashed into command and control, her hair still wet from her shower. "Status?"

Jonathan pointed to the screen. "Some kind of storm—"

Out of the cosmic mists flowing out from the distortion, a massive ship emerged. The disc-shaped ship pushed through the distortion, slowly turning on its axis. When it completely crossed through, the distortion collapsed and disappeared. The shaking and trembling of *Gamma Station* subsided.

"It's a saucer," Isabeau said.

Jonathan shook his head. "The Greys hate it when we call their ships saucers."

She shrugged. "Well, they probably don't appreciate being called Greys either."

"Touché." He turned to the pit crew. "O'Dell, can we identify it?"

"Aye, sir, working on it."

"She's enormous," Jonathan said. "Almost as big as *Gamma Station*."

"McNamar, have they charged their weapons yet?" Isabeau asked.

"Negative, ma'am."

"I wonder what they're waiting for," Jonathan said. "She could destroy the station all by herself."

Chief O'Dell stood. "Colonel, the registry index lists her as the *Azeltar*. Tumnei Fleet-Killer class warship."

"That explains the strange distortion," Isabeau said. "The Grey's new flagship is supposed to be testing a quantumspace drive."

Jonathan turned to her. "How do you know that?"

 317

She pursed her lips. "Well, let's just say I don't spend my off-duty time reading up on dead military generals."

He smiled. "Fair enough."

Petty Officer McKinsey stood. "Colonel, incoming transmission from the *Azeltar.*"

"On screen, Petty Officer."

The wall screen flickered and displayed a video image of the bridge of the *Azeltar.* Brilliant white walls lined the bridge. A thick fog rolled across the floor under bright white lights. The Tumnei crew all sat in hovering chairs. Holographic computer terminals floated in the air. Their uniforms were darker gray with faceless shiny black helmets. These were battle uniforms.

Jonathan cleared his throat. "I sure hope you're here to help us."

The Tumnei in the center chair pressed a button on his arm. The black glass of his helmet turned clear, revealing the face of the Tumnei commander.

"T'Kal!" Jonathan shouted with joy. Then his smile suddenly fell. "The Scorpii will be here in a matter of hours. If they see you, your race will be in violation of the order. Your homeworld won't be safe."

T'Kal gestured with his hand and subtitles streamed across the bottom of the screen. FOR AN INTELLECTUAL SPECIES, YOU SOMETIMES FAIL TO COMPREHEND THE OBVIOUS. OUR STUDY OF YOUR SPECIES HAS AFFORDED US AN OPPORTUNITY TO ASSIST YOU WITHOUT VIOLATING THE ORDER.

"Without violating the order?"

T'Kal tilted his head as more subtitles scrolled across the screen. THE HIGH COUNCIL OF THE TUMNEI GOVERNMENT HAS REPORTED ONE OF THEIR SHIPS AS STOLEN. THE DRACO SENATE HAS LOGGED THIS SHIP'S REGISTRY IDENTITY AND CLASSIFIED IT AS AN UNALIGNED ROGUE VESSEL.

"You're still taking a big risk, T'Kal," Jonathan said. "You know we're fighting an impossible battle."

More subtitles scrolled. THE REWARDS FOR FULFILLING THE PROPHECY ARE TOO GREAT TO LET SLIP AWAY. BESIDES, THE HIGH

COUNCIL DECIDED IT WAS MORE PRACTICAL TO PUT OUR TRUST IN THE HERO OF MESA SOL THAN TO BE SUBJECTED TO THE WHIMS OF THE SCORPII.

"They got that right," Isabeau said under her breath.

Jonathan smiled again. "You're a sight for sore eyes, T'Kal. We'll gladly take all the help you can give."

T'Kal abruptly looked to his left for a moment and then returned his gaze to Jonathan. More subtitles scrolled. SCANNERS DETECT INBOUND VESSELS IN HYPERSPACE.

Jonathan exchanged a worried glance with Isabeau. "Could I have been wrong in estimating the Scorpii's arrival?"

She shook her head. "No, I checked your math. Nobody from Scorpii space should be able to get here for another twelve hours minimum."

He looked back T'Kal. "We'll have to continue this conversation later. Terynn out." The screen blinked, ending the video feed. Jonathan turned to the pit crew. "McKinsey, contact the Chantell. Tell George to stand by in case we need him to scramble his marauders."

"Aye, sir."

"Sir," another voice shouted, "hyperspace portal opening at our 3 o'clock!"

"On screen."

A patch of starry space in front of *Gamma Station* rippled like water when a stone is dropped in. A blue tunnel of light opened in the center and three egg-shaped ships flew out. The three frosted-glass-looking ships flashed colorful lights as they slowed to a stop in front of the station.

"Colonel," Chief O'Dell called out, "three Euroo vessels just came out of hyperspace."

Jonathan spun around to Ellyra. "Can you tell if they are from your house?"

She stepped closer. "Yes, they are from House El'Allel. It is the *Kaliptica*, the *Pentora*, and the *Aloriel.* I wonder where the *Calmao* is?"

"Sir," McNamar said, "Incoming transmissions from the Euroo ships."

Jonathan took a breath. "Conference them together on screen."

"Aye, sir."

The wall screen blinked again and displayed three video images at once. Three men with formal white hair stared at Jonathan. Each one dressed in an elegant suit with a cape.

Jonathan gave a short bow. "Greetings and welcome to *Gamma Station*. I trust your trip was uneventful?"

"Please spare us your pleasantries, Colonel Jonathan," one of them said. "We are here at the behest of Lord Areo, lord of House El'Allel and member of Central Parliament. I regret to inform you that due to the impending calamity from the Extermination order, you are hereby ordered by his lordship to surrender his daughter—post haste—for return to Eurosia."

Jonathan smirked and turned, motioning to Ellyra. "She can speak for herself."

"Sune Vaynar," Ellyra said. "It is a pleasure to see you again. Words alone cannot convey my gratitude to my father for seeing to my welfare. And though I am terribly embarrassed to have to send you back empty-handed, I am ever grateful for your swift arrival."

"Sune Ellyra," Vaynar said. "I am pleased to see you are in health. Though, I do, of course, ask that you resign yourself to your father's wishes and return with us to Eurosia. It is for the good of your welfare that we are sent to you."

She gave a professional smile. "Perhaps you might just convince me to act in accordance with the good of my welfare. By all means, it would please me greatly if you three would join me aboard *Gamma Station* as my guests. Then, we will be able to properly discuss my return to Eurosia."

Chapter 41
UNDESERVING

M att sat on a plastic crate on the dark metal floor of *Able Station's* landing bay. The dim lighting and dark colors threw shadows around the room. The gravity net eased the constant pain. The bay's artificial gravity was always kept a little on the lighter side. It assisted with loading and unloading cargo. For Matt, however, it lessened the throbbing. But even without it, his pain was light compared to the weight of his conscience. Why would destiny afford him a new chance, only to make a hypocrite out of him?

He spun a data rod around in his hand. Fate was a cruel mistress who never tolerated weakness. Matt took a long look at the data rod. He wasn't mad at *it;* he was mad at who sent it. You *made a liar out of me,* he thought. *I made a deal, and you broke it.* He pulled his arm back to throw the blasted thing across the bay, but then he paused. He couldn't throw it; there was something about it that commanded a strange reverence. It was no longer simply a data rod; it was now the gravestone of his would-be ally.

A dark red light flashed in the dim light. A klaxon groaned a short alert. Men and women in black coveralls stormed into the bay to receive the incoming shuttle. The loud clanking and moaning of the mooring cranes rumbled beneath the floor.

"Shuttle entering the outer bay," an overhead loudspeaker announced. "Stand by for pressurization."

The room filled with the sound of the faint hissing of air being released. The center of the bay floor separated like large doors. A platform raised the shuttle from below the floor. The service crew descended on the ship, connecting a fuel line and resupplying. The side door of the shuttle slid open and Jerry stepped out wearing his ridiculous black hooded cloak. He slung a satchel over one shoulder with an insufferable cheery smile as he approached.

"I thought for sure I was going to rot in that cell. And yet somehow you pulled off an extraction anyway."

"You can wipe that stupid grin off your face," Matt said with a scowl. "We have a lot of work ahead of us."

"I was told you had been injured but I didn't want to believe it. Matt is impervious, I told myself."

"Your flattery is appreciated, but my spirits are a little beyond the reach of flattery at the moment."

Jerry smiled, noticing the data rod in Matt's hand. "What news do you bring? And please don't spare a single juicy detail; I have been out of circulation for quite a while."

Matt held it up. "It's the squiddies' formal announcement. The Draconians have just declared an extermination order on *Gamma Station*."

Jerry paled. "How in the galaxy did you pull that off?"

Matt tensed and his nostrils flared. "I had no part in it, you imbecile!" He gasped under a sharp stinging pain in his ribs.

"Forgive me, Matt. You don't look pleased. Where two years of planning has failed, a stroke of galactic luck has succeeded. With *Gamma Station* out of the way, the Euroo are no longer sufficient to stop our advances in the Senate."

Matt wheezed a breath. "Even if we were in a position to take advantage of that—which we no longer are—the victory is hollow, devoid of any satisfaction."

Jerry shrugged. "I can understand that. I too would have preferred my 'phalezine to take care of that blasted Colonel. But I suppose a couple fleets of warships pulverizing their space station can equally get the job done."

The pathetic man could not see beyond his ego. Matt rolled his eyes, again reminded of how much that hurt. "My friend, if you were any denser, the planets would revolve around *you*. I have spent my whole life outwitting the brainless squiddies and the pathetic Bravs. But it wasn't until the other day that I realized just how formidable an opponent Colonel Jonathan Terynn really is."

Jerry chuckled. "Is that why you're ornery? Your admiration for the Gamm Colonel has grown just in time for his atoms to get scattered across the sector?"

Matt closed his eyes and clenched his teeth, waiting for the throbbing to subside. "Jerry, whenever I have told someone that I would kill them, I have killed them. Whenever I have told someone that I would save them, I have saved them. And whenever I have told someone that they were a moron, it was because they were. I have always kept my word." He held up the data rod again. "Until today, when the impetuous Draconians made a liar out of my promise." He glanced at the data rod again as he twirled it in his hand.

But did it matter? Was he only allowing sentiment to cloud his better judgment? People died every day; that was the way of things. Why then should he care if the good Colonel should perish? Yet somehow, deep down, it mattered. Why did it matter?

"It doesn't matter..." Matt said, hoping the declaration would sound convincing. "Colonel Terynn will be dead and that is all there is to it."

Jerry chuckled again. "That's the Matt we all know and love." He gave Matt a jovial pat on the shoulder.

Matt flinched. "Not so hard!"

"Which reminds me," he said setting down the satchel. "I come bearing contraband." He opened it and began pulling out tiny bottles, bags of gauze, disposable syringes, isopropyl alcohol, and a couple of plastic tubes filled with medication tablets.

Matt picked up one of the bottles and studied the label and the handwritten instructions on it. "Where did you get this?"

"I stole it right from under their noses," he said with a grin. "I figured you'd need a little help after I heard of your injuries."

Matt lowered his eyebrows. "My friend, you're a terrible liar."

Jerry straightened up, his smile vanishing. "I am insulted by your insinuation. Is it that hard to believe that I would help you in any way I could? How will you ever know if you don't give me a chance?"

Matt sighed. "Perhaps you're right. I haven't given you a chance." He looked Jerry in the eyes. "Do me a favor, fetch me exactly three cc's of water. No more, no less."

Jerry smiled with a nod and turned to leave but abruptly turned back to Matt. "How much is a cc?"

Matt held up the tiny bottle to show Jerry the label. "Well, if you were the one to write these instructions, you would know."

"Well, you see—"

"Don't even try," Matt said with disdain. "Stick to assassinations and spying; *that* is what you are good at. And leave the intrigue to me."

Jerry's jovial smile returned. "My most humble apologies, Matt. I should have known never to match wits with you. But how am I ever to expand my horizons if I never venture out?"

"Careful where you venture, Jerry; most hallways around here lead to ruin."

"Of course," he said in resignation.

"A woman named Cossette is in my office. Report to her once you have settled. We have much work to do."

Jerry nodded and left. The resupply crew began filing out of the bay, having finished their work on the shuttle. Matt examined the tiny bottle's label once more. The good Colonel sent these supplies with Jerry. That much was obvious. But what was the motivation behind it? What could he possibly hope to gain? Matt already owed him a favor for releasing Jerry. Why the extra measure? Matt set down the bottle and rolled up his sleeve.

It couldn't be a bargaining chip; it was too specific. The hastily written instructions were specific to him. These were not random supplies. Each one had dosage and care instructions. A doctor wrote them. How did they even diagnose his injuries? Was his appearance over the transmission enough for a doctor to tell what was wrong? Did such competence exist?

Matt took the cap off a syringe and plunged the needle through the lid of the tiny bottle. He filled the syringe to 2 cc's, checking the bottle's label for accuracy. According to Ir'Jad's report, Jerry killed one of their precious few doctors. And yet one of their doctors sent medicine anyway. Matt glanced heavenward, taking a deep breath. This was a gift he did not deserve.

He injected the medicine into his arm, slowly breathing out. The pain started to dull. He breathed out again, this time in relief. It was a welcome feeling to have the throbbing and aching quieted down. The good Colonel had given him a new lease on life. Matt was going to live. The cruel irony was that his greatest opponent would be his savior.

He picked up the data rod once more and examined it again. Life was never fair. The one most deserving of a second chance was sentenced to extermination, while he—the least deserving—would live. What he last told Colonel Terynn had been wrong. It wasn't a pity that Jonathan wasn't born an Abe; it was the other way around. Matt clenched his eyes shut. What would life have been like if he were around such people? A heavy sensation moved up his chest and into his throat. His chest muscles tightened. Was the medication not working? No, this was not pain. But it was some involuntary reaction.

The skin beneath his eyes tickled. He wiped his eyes and examined his fingers. They were wet. A *tear?* Were these tears? Tears were only for the weak and afraid. Why, then, did he have tears? He glanced back at the data rod and another tear escaped. The heaviness in his heart now made sense. Maybe it would have been worth dying with the Gamms if it meant he could have lived among them.

He stared at the data rod, squeezing it. "What we could have accomplished, you and I..."

Chapter 42

THE SKORATH

Fox stood motionless on the bridge of the *Calmao*, careful not to move. He glanced all around. Had he just imagined it, or had the Skorath actually responded? He turned to Diahlus whose hair color had changed to a frightened gray. In fact, all the Euroo's hair was now gray. At least that meant he hadn't imagined it.

The golden ring in the center of the floor lit up and displayed a holographic representation of the *Calmao* and the surrounding green nebula. A massive black ship, easily ten times the size of the *Calmao*, faded into view. The green backdrop of the nebula made it easier to see the dark squid-like appearance of the Skorath ship. The room fell still and silent.

Diahlus whispered across the room. "Is it really them?"

Fox nodded. "There are more things in heaven and earth, Horatio, than are dreamt of in your philosophy."

Diahlus returned a confused look. He probably hadn't read Hamlet.

"What do we do now?" Fox whispered.

"Do you not know?"

Fox rolled his eyes. "You had me scrambling just to get this far," he explained in a hushed tone. "You didn't exactly give me enough time to think this through."

"Forgive my impertinence gentlemen," Layna whispered. "But is it not impolite to whisper while in company?"

"Quite right," Diahlus said, clearing his throat. "Lieutenant Colonel Fox, if you wouldn't mind speaking to our, uh, guest?"

He shrugged. "What should I say?"

Diahlus's eyes widened. "Do you not know?"

He sighed. "Diahlus, either there is an echo in here, or we have discussed this before."

"Just say *something*," Layna said, urging.

What was there to say? With all the emphasis on finding the Skorath, he hadn't put any thought into what he should say once he found them. But how hard could it be? Ancient, powerful, mysterious aliens couldn't be all that hard to talk to. Maybe it would be as easy as starting any ordinary conversation.

Fox cleared his throat. "An excellent weather we are having, is it not?"

Xer and Arkamenos exchanged confused glances.

"What are you doing?" Layna whispered in a horrified tone.

"Making conversation," he said.

"What does the weather have to do with anything?"

"Brigadain Diahlus," Arkamenos said, "should we not re-open the transmission?"

Diahlus nodded. "Commsman, open a transmission to the Skorath ship."

"As you wish."

Diahlus turned back to Fox and waved an arm as if to say: be my guest.

Fox scratched an itch on his bald head and stroked his goatee. "A newborn light has arisen from an uninteresting corner of space. And it wields a power that can frighten the star of Draconia. But they cannot claim the birthright of the Ancestors if they get their atoms scattered across the sector."

The loudspeaker rumbled to life with the deep ancient voice. "Rock after rock has been overturned with nothing beneath."

Fox smiled. The only thing more exciting than meeting an all-powerful ancient race was meeting one that spoke in metaphors. He rubbed his hands together in anticipation.

"Does that mean something?" Xer asked, setting down his reader device.

Fox nodded. "They said they've been looking everywhere for the race of prophecy and haven't found them." He cleared his throat again. "We have found the Voonsu. They are on *Gamma Station*, but they will be destroyed unless you help them."

The loudspeaker again rumbled. "The bee stings but once. Shall the flood precede the rain or the snow precede the cold?"

Fox ran a hand over his bald head and down his face. This was going to be a lot harder than he had imagined. Somehow, he had expected the Skorath to be itching for a fight. Shouldn't anyone who had been waiting a long time to retaliate be eager for their chance? Shouldn't they at least have wanted to see the race of prophecy? What was wrong with them? Had several thousand years of inactivity made them complacent? With that long of a time to prepare, how could they possibly not be ready?

"But the prophecy? The Voonsu are going to be wiped out before they can fulfill it. Isn't this what you've been waiting for?" he asked in exasperation.

The ancient voice rumbled. "We await the return of the Antarens."

Fox threw up his hands in defeat and began to pace. This conversation was going nowhere fast. How could he convince them that the prophesied race had been found? Moreover, how could he convince them that they were about to be destroyed? For an ancient, wise race, they seemed rather dense.

"Well then...how do we find these Antarens?" he asked in desperation.

329

"Speak of what is," rumbled the voice over the loudspeaker.

Fox thought a moment. T'Kal had mentioned that the Skorath always asked about current events in exchange for knowledge of the past. Were they proposing the same deal? What good would that do currently? Isabel and the Colonel needed help right now. Though, on the other hand, he wasn't getting anywhere by arguing with them. There didn't seem to be any other solution than to play their game.

Fox turned to Diahlus. "Current events. What do we have on current events?"

Diahlus looked around and picked up a reader close to his chair. "I have today's status report on the ship, but I doubt it would be of any interest to them."

Fox grimaced. "Yeah, we probably don't want to put them to sleep."

"The Draconian's extermination order?" Xer offered.

Fox snapped his fingers and pointed at Xer. "Yes! That's what we want. Can you transmit it to them?"

"As you wish," Xer replied, pressing a few buttons.

Fox glanced back to the holographic picture of the Skorath ship. "We're sending you another rock to turn over."

Fox nervously tapped his fingers against his leg for a few minutes until he grew bored of that and considered whistling. He glanced at Xer. "You did send it, right?"

"Indeed."

"Well, they sure are taking their sweet time reading it."

The loudspeaker rumbled again. "Another rock has been overturned. And the ground is barren."

"Oh, come on!" Fox complained. "How can you say there's nothing there? It proves they're about to be annihilated."

"Be still, young Kalmeedes," the voice said, rumbling through the loudspeaker. "The destiny of every leaf is to fall from its tree."

Fox stood, breathing heavily. What did this mean? Were they not going to help after all? How could that be? What about the prophecy? What about gaining ancient technology and revolting against the Draconians? Was it all a myth? T'Kal did mention *if* they were interpreting the prophecy correctly. Did this mean they had the interpretation all wrong? Did it also mean he had failed to get help for Isabel and the Colonel?

Fox's heart sank. He had put everything into this prophecy. "O Gertrude, Gertrude," he quoted under his breath, "when sorrows come, they come not single spies, but in battalions." The air grew heavy and melancholy. Fox motioned with his hands, willing some words to come out, but nothing came.

Chapter 43

THE COUNCIL OF
WAR

Ellyra walked down the wide hallways of *Gamma Station* with Jonathan and the three Euroo captains in tow. Letting the Euroo captains believe they had a chance to persuade her to return to Eurosia was not the politest thing to do. If these men were from a rival house, it would be a different story; it would be politics as usual. But these men were from her own house and acting under direct orders from her father. The slightest degree of deception would be frowned upon. However, it couldn't be helped.

Ellyra stopped in front of the door to the assembly hall. Like all human additions to the Chantell-built station, the door looked out of place. She touched a button on the wall and the door slid up. She motioned for them to enter. The overhead lights turned on as the men stepped into the room. They walked among several rows of chairs. The three Euroo captains, Vaynar, Rae, and Domir stood side by side until Ellyra motioned for them to take a seat.

Domir shifted in his chair. "It is not the most ideal setting for a discussion."

He was correct; the matter at hand called for a private chamber or small office for discussion. Meeting in such a large room with so many chairs was not proper unless you were addressing a large body of people. But this room was precisely where they needed to meet. She knew each of them well enough to know the kind of persuasion this would take. So, a demonstration was in order. And if she timed it right, it would arrive right on cue.

Jonathan took two chairs out of another row and turned them around to face their guests. Ellyra sat down beside Jonathan, holding his hand. "You will please pardon the accommodations," she said. "Finding an adequate room aboard an alien-built space station can be quite the challenge. I do hope you will overlook the impropriety."

"Quite right," Rae said, settling into his chair. "Certain allowances shall of course be extended due to your circumstances."

"You are most kind," she said with a polite head nod.

"Now Ellyra," Vaynar began, "about your father's wishes. What hesitations can you lay before us to alleviate?"

She squeezed Jonathan's hand. "Well, my first hesitation would be in leaving my dear husband to an untimely death. I do not think I should much like being a widow before I have really become accustomed to being a wife."

Domir sighed. "Your father doesn't much care for your husband. To use his words precisely, that Earthian menace brought ruin upon his own head and is worthy of the consequences."

Rae glanced at Jonathan. "We, of course, mean no slight upon your Colonelship. We are merely relaying the message."

Jonathan smirked. "Don't worry, I'm not offended. Taking flak comes with the territory."

"Oh, I trust my father would not object to such a simple condition. Especially if such a condition would expedite his daughter's compliance."

"Only the daughter of El'Allel can transform a mandate into a negotiation," Vaynar said, grumbling under his breath.

Ellyra smiled at Vaynar. "I am flattered that you should think so highly of my competence."

"Fine," Rae declared. "We shall bring Colonel Jonathan as well. We would ask, however, that you take it upon yourself to quell your father's ire."

"Darling, don't forget the evacuation," Jonathan said.

Ellyra gave a sympathetic smile. "Oh, that is right. My husband is evacuating the entire space station and they look up to him to fulfill that commitment, you see. It would be best that he first be allowed to complete that endeavor before we extradite to Eurosia."

"Are you mad?" Domir asked in dismay. "We came racing down here ahead of the Scorpii to rescue you from an untimely death at the hands of the aforementioned. And here you speak as if you have a previous engagement. What could possibly be more pressing than your life?"

Jonathan tensed up. He wanted to speak. It was almost a shame he had agreed to let her handle it. Ellyra paused a moment. A quick response was always followed up by a quick rebuttal. But a slow response, on the other hand, was always met with consideration. The pause was the necessary ingredient that would open up these men to understanding.

Ellyra brushed a stray, curly lock of her formal white hair over one ear. She looked into Domir's green within blue eyes. "Sune Domir, you have a lovely wife and two beautiful children." She glanced at Rae. "And your mother will be celebrating her fourteenth year." She turned to Vaynar. "And your son has recently entered the Stellar Academy. You must be so proud of him."

She looked at each of them with pleading eyes. "I ask you, gentlemen, is there anything more important than your own life?"

Domir looked down. Rae gave a big sigh, closing his eyes. Vaynar leaned back in his chair. "Gentlemen, I do believe we have been had. The daughter of El'Allel is not negotiating, she is recruiting."

"Please, do not think ill of me, Vaynar. There is a chance to save these people."

"A *hopeless* chance," Vaynar said. "The whole of the Scorpii's forward strike group is on their way. Do you allow yourself to be deluded into notions of outrunning or outgunning an elder race?"

Ellyra had chosen her seat so that she could discretely check the clock behind the men. Vaynar had spoken his inevitable concern just a little early. She needed to stall for just a moment longer. "I appreciate your candor. And I am glad you have called attention to the most obvious of challenges that threaten us. You speak of hopelessness and the approaching enemy fleet. May I ask of you, if there were anything that could convince you that our impending struggle is not hopeless?"

Vaynar huffed. "You would need a fleet of ships at least as well armed as the Scorpii." He turned to Jonathan. "And unless I am mistaken, Earthians have nowhere near the technological advances of the elder races."

Jonathan feigned consideration for a moment. "You'd be *half* right."

"Half right?"

Jonathan nodded with a smirk as crew members began entering the assembly hall and taking their seats. He raised a hand, beckoning a large Chantell to join him. The Chantell stomped over with his four heavy feet.

Jonathan stood. "George, thank you for coming and I appreciate the good work your wing of marauders is doing."

"Pleased, I is," George said while twitching his antennae.

Jonathan turned to Vaynar. "George, I'd like to introduce you to Sunes Vaynar, Domir, and Rae."

George lowered his head and fanned out his four gigantic wings, knocking over several chairs in the process. Vaynar, Domir, and Rae each bowed in return, their hair colors each dimming into a frightened gray. More people flooded into the large room. Then the blinding white light of the Tumnei teleporter flashed. T'Kal and several other Tumnei appeared at the front of the room.

"If you will excuse me, gentlemen," Jonathan said. "I need to speak with Supreme Commander T'Kal for a moment."

Vaynar turned back to Ellyra. "How did you secure so many allies despite the stipulations of the extermination order?"

"They come not for me," she said, glancing at Jonathan as he made his way over to T'Kal. "They come because of him. Not to save him, but to be saved *by* him. He represents all their dreams of freedom from Draconian rule."

"Such a thing is not possible," Vaynar replied in astonishment. "Such a small fleet—led by one of the youngest of the starfaring races—cannot possibly defy the Draconians."

Ellyra gave a warm smile. "Did not Vera, herself, declare, A ship shall sail from beyond the amber realm, where the dragon thinks not to look, its maiden voyage with children at its helm. When in subtle strength shall they bare their teeth, the star of Draconia's courage shall be forsook, for upon them the ancient magic to bequeath."

Vaynar stood, staring with wide eyes.

"So, you see, gentlemen, to them, the hour of Vera's prophecy is at hand. The next chapter of our own history is being written at this very moment. I invite you to stay not for vain ambitions or naïve imaginations, but as a fulfillment of prophecy and obligation." She again motioned to the ever-increasing body of people filing into the room. "To these people, there is more at stake than their own lives."

Rae swallowed. "Lady Ellyra, the daughter of El'Allel has the full support of the Sune and crew of the *Aloriel*."

"And of the *Pentora*," Domir added.

Ellyra acknowledge with a graceful nod and then turned to Vaynar.

He took a deep breath and sighed. "The daughter of my lord shall also have the support of the Sune and crew of the *Kaliptica*."

She curtsied. "My friends, I cannot thank you enough."

Isabeau's voice called from across the room. "Please take your seats, we're going to start."

Ellyra motioned for the Euroo men to take a seat and then walked over to the side of the room to watch. Jonathan had anticipated that all the seats would fill up. So, it was only proper to give seating priority to the military leaders.

Jonathan stood and addressed the room. "Thank you for assembling quickly. It's good to know that basic training has done well in drilling punctuality into every one of us."

The room rumbled with muffled chuckles. "Now the reason this is a council of war and not a logistical meeting is that we don't intend to simply evacuate. The enemy will hunt us down and finish what they started. So, we have to make it look like they destroyed us. That won't be an easy task but we have a plan."

Jonathan tapped a button on his comm-band. The large wall screen lit up, displaying a tactical map with statistics. "I'm going to provide each division commander with a copy of this briefing because I'm going to go over it rather quickly. The ship captains need time to coordinate and the SEAL teams need time to practice. We only have a matter of hours remaining. Are there any questions before we begin?"

Jonathan pointed to a raised hand. "Name and rating?"

"Operations Specialist 2nd Class Danzy, sir. The Scorpii don't use teleron bursts for their transmissions the way we do. How do we prevent them from calling for reinforcements or otherwise informing their commanders of the situation?"

Jonathan smirked. "A very detailed question, Petty Officer. It sounds like you've given it some thought."

"Yes, sir, I have."

"I'll be going over combat communications in just a bit. But the short answer is that we're calling in a favor that should take care of the problem."

"Thank you, sir."

Ellyra smiled. Seeing Jonathan act with a purpose, being a man on a mission, warmed her heart. This was the confident man she admired. He stood tall like her father and addressed his people with a similar dignity and passion. Like her father, Jonathan was born to lead.

She heard a familiar voice in her head. *"Forgive the intrusion, Sune Ellyra, but your species' culture does not approve of allowing a female of your position to stand for want of a seat."*

She glanced over to T'Kal who was looking right at her. She blushed. *It is very kind of you to notice,* she thought. *I did not wish to be an imposition on someone of greater need of Jonathan's discussion.*

"It would be regrettable for you to consider yourself unimportant to fulfilling the Skorath prophecy. Although our circumstances have changed, you were recognized as an important link in bringing the Chantell into the liberation effort."

Wait, she thought, *an important link?*

"Correct. Despite Colonel Terynn's initial hesitance, we saw in you an important avenue to approach the Chantell. So, it is hoped that you would realize your value and importance."

What did this mean? Had Jonathan come to her only to use her connections with the Chantell? But that couldn't be right, could it? He loved her, didn't he? He had said that he did. Her heart sank and her pulse raced. The air grew heavy and thick. Had she been wrong about Jonathan all this time? Had his only endeavor in pursuing her been to recruit the Chantell as an ally?

At the senate convention, he had asked if she could introduce him to the Chantell ambassador. And he also had spoken an awful lot about political ties with the Tumnei and *Bravo Station*. He was indeed a calculating man, a man of strategy. Was she, then, only a pawn in some strategy? But...he said he loved her. He had gifted her the comm-band, had caressed her ear while she slept, and had kissed so tenderly. It just couldn't be true.

Her mind raced back to the memory of the first senate hearing. He had asked if there was any way they could stay together. Surely, that meant he intended to be with her, not just to use her. Then, her mind caught hold of the very next thing he had said: Ellyra, I can't afford to lose you. There's too much at stake...

A breath caught in her throat as if her lungs refused to work. Her heart felt like an anchor. Her vision clouded as tears formed. He had said there was too much at stake. He hadn't been talking about their relationship. Jonathan, a man of strategy, had been talking about the greater good, the bigger plan. He had no intention to marry her. It was all a mistake. His words to her on the trip back now made sense. He had said it was his fault and apologized for dragging her into it. The marriage was a mistake, an error, an unintended side-effect of his plans.

Her chest felt tight, as if wearing a corset improperly. She forced in a large breath, trying to hold back her tears. How could he have said he loved her if it was all a mistake? If he did not love her, he should not have kissed her. Not only was it improper but it was deceptive. How could anything he said be trusted? How could he have used her as a common tool? She could only blame herself; Diahlus had warned her not to venture too far from safety. She had blinded herself with her idiotic notions of romance. Her father had told her that such notions should be left behind. But, she hadn't listened.

Her hair tingled. She squeezed her eyes shut, concentrating. She could not let her hair change to a hysterical orange, not now, not during Jonathan's meeting. It would be a confusing signal to Vaynar and the others. She needed to leave. She couldn't let anyone see her hair turn that color. Nor could she let anyone see the tsunami of tears threatening to storm. She turned and marched out the nearest door as the floodgates of her heart spilled open.

Chapter 44

THE FAVOR

Matt sat at his desk in his office. It had been cleaned up since Lord Vaux's murderous rampage. Ross's blood had been cleaned up, yet somehow, it still felt unclean. Matt took a deep breath. *Don't worry, Ross,* he thought. *The time is coming really soon, and your blood will be avenged.* Matt closed his eyes and shivered at the memory of Ross lying on the floor. This had to end. Thanks to Cossette, he now had Jerry back. But having Jerry back was not enough to end the killing. That would require a substantial amount of power and influence—which he no longer had.

It was another uphill climb to get back to where he had been, but in the meantime, he could at least serve some justice. Now that he had to start over again anyway, it did not matter which squiddy he had to brown nose up to. The one redeeming perk was that Megan's killer would die sooner than expected.

Matt glanced at the door, hearing two knocks. That was Cossette's knock. "Come in."

She entered, walking up to him with enthusiasm in her eyes. "I found her."

Matt's eyes lit up. "Are you *sure?*"

She pulled out a small printed photo from her breast pocket and laid it on the desk. Matt slid it closer for a better view. Then, he opened his desk drawer and pulled out his old and tattered photo of Eva, and laid it next to the new photo. The similarities were there. Could it really be her?

"She still has your eyes," Cossette said, smiling.

Matt pulled off his black gloves and felt the edges of the new photo. "She has her mother's hair." He glanced at both pictures side by side again. The years had been good to her. "Did you find out her profession yet?"

Cossette shook her head. "Sorry, Matt. The squiddies still won't give us access to *Bravo Station's* records. Jerry had to bribe three undersecretaries and a commissioner just to get his hands on this photo."

That was typical of the spineless monstrosities. They craved power and control. They would never see *Bravo Station* as an extension of *Able Station.* To them, it was one more thing to control, one more thing to fight and squabble over. He would need to climb to the top of the influential ladder once more in order to have a chance at *Bravo Station.* His daughter would unfortunately have to wait a bit longer. But at least he had her current photo.

"It must be so frustrating for you, Matt," Cossette said, placing her hand on his.

Matt stiffened. Why was that woman reaching out to him? And why was she wearing that lovely perfume again? What could she want that he could provide? He had been stripped of all influence with the vile squiddies, his body was bruised and broken, and he was *not* a conversationalist. Why was it so important for her to get close?

Cossette noticed his tension and retreated her hand, a look of worry in her eyes. The last thing he wanted was to hurt her feelings. *What has gotten into me?* he wondered. *Since when do I care about such things?*

341

Yet the look in her eyes was not quite panic and also not quite nervousness. It was somewhere in between. Such a lovely person should not have to cry or feel guilt over wanting a simple human connection. Around here it was probably the only medicine the squiddies couldn't take away.

Matt attempted a weak smile. "The pain medication must be wearing off. It's probably close to the time for my next dose."

She breathed a sigh of relief with a sparkle in her eyes. It was good to see her relax. It felt better to know she was comfortable.

"I'll get it for you," she said, walking over to the metal cabinet. She retrieved a single tablet and brought it back. She had a conspiratorial look in her eyes. What was she planning? After her embarrassment a moment ago, she couldn't be bold enough to try again. And yet, somehow, it was exciting to see if she really would. Any woman daring and ambitious enough to try a second time deserved to touch him.

"I'll be gentle this time," she said, carefully picking up his hand and turning it over. She placed the tablet in his hand, covering his palm with her fingers. She lingered an unnecessary moment before letting go. Her touch was not as invasive as it should have been. Why did he welcome her touch? *A side effect of the medication,* he decided.

The door chimed. "Come in," Matt said, irritated at the interruption.

The door slid open and a man walked in carrying a data rod. "Sorry for the intrusion, but I thought you would want to see this right away."

"What is it?" Matt asked, taking the data rod.

"It looks like a message from *Gamma Station* directed to Earth Central Command."

"How did it wind up way out here?"

He shook his head. "Not a clue, Mr. Jaimess."

"Very good," Matt said in conclusion. "You may go."

The man left and Matt plugged the data rod into a port on his desk. The surface of his desk displayed a video recording of Jonathan Terynn. Matt took a sudden breath at seeing him. The good Colonel was not yet dead. The stupid squiddies must be taking their time getting down there. Matt twisted the data rod a quarter turn and the video played.

342

"CentCom, this is Colonel Jonathan Terynn. This transmission should reach you *in time*. We are not *able* to *station* our men according to our *need* for *battle*. Our *communication* has been *disrupted*. The game is afoot. Terynn out."

"That makes no sense," Cossette said. "If their communication is disrupted, how are they even sending the transmission?"

Goosebumps coursed over Matt's skin and his heart thumped. The greatest news had just sounded in his ears. A broad smile stretched across his face, the excitement building. "That's because it's a message, my dear Cossette." He pointed to the shelf. "Bring me that computer."

"I don't understand," she said, setting the small Scorpiian computer on his desk.

Matt quickly turned several small dials. "I need to patch into the Scorpiian transmitter on the station."

"What is going on, Matt?"

"The game is afoot, Cossette."

She wrinkled her nose in confusion. "The last line in the recording?"

He nodded, continuing to turn the many dials of the computer. "During my last conversation with the good Colonel, I compared him and me to Sherlock Holmes and Professor Moriarty."

"Are you saying his message was intended for you?"

He nodded again. "Colonel Terynn is giving me a chance to repay my debt."

"But what does it even mean?" she asked.

He abruptly stopped and turned to her. "Did you not listen to the inflection in his voice?"

She returned a blank stare.

He grinned. "In time. *Able Station*, need battle communication disrupted."

She looked up with her mouth open, the gears turning in her pretty head. "But, how?" she asked. "How can disrupting communication do any good against a fleet of Scorpiian warships?"

Matt smirked. "I told you that the genius of Jonathan Terynn was in his ability to read the current situation and think outside the box. He

has a plan. And oh, it will keep me up at night wondering just what it could be." He turned back to the computer. "We just need to find a way to intercept the transmission lines from *Gamma Station's* location."

She pursed her lips. "I think I know what you need," she said, pulling the computer over to her. She swiftly turned the dials with acute flicks of her fingers and thumbs. "Do you want the transmissions blocked or routed through?"

Matt smiled. Where had Ross found such a remarkable woman? "I want them blocked. And if you can manage it, erase any log of the transmission ever being sent."

She nodded. "You got it."

He looked again at the data rod plugged into his desk. "Oh, the things we shall accomplish together," he muttered under his breath.

Chapter 45

THE BATTLE

Jonathan paced across the bridge of the *Saratoga*. The last eighteen hours had been exhilarating. All the preparations and training had been done hastily but at least they were completed. And all in time to meet the Scorpii. Now, it was a nerve-wracking waiting game. It was past time for any speedy fleet to arrive, which meant the Scorpii were bringing their heavy cruisers. They could arrive at any moment.

Jonathan turned back to Cynthia, sitting in her prominent chair on the bridge. Her perfect posture and crossed legs portrayed no hint of jitters or nervousness. *How does she do it?* he wondered. "Any word from Ellyra yet?"

"Not since the last time you asked," she answered in her nonchalant British tone.

Jonathan rolled his eyes and continued pacing. "Sorry, I'm just a little worried, that's all. I haven't seen her since the council of war." He glanced at his comm-band. Should he try calling her yet again?

"No need to wear a hole in the floor, Jonathan. I had Gordon make sure she was aboard."

He spun on his heel and marched toward the door. "I'm going to go look for her."

Cynthia swiveled her chair toward him. "Splendid timing. When the Scorpii arrive, we'll be sure to ask them to kindly wait until you get back."

He passed the bridge doors and headed down the narrow corridors of the *Saratoga*. It was a strange feeling walking down hallways that were the exact opposite of those on *Gamma Station*. It was a little disconcerting to have to turn sideways just to pass another crewman. For such a large ship, couldn't the corridors have been built wider? Jonathan climbed down a short ladder to the deck below.

"Colonel on deck!" a crewman called out.

Several men and women dropped what they were doing and stood at attention. Jonathan quickly surveyed them. "I'm looking for Sune Ellyra."

They stole glances at each other.

Jonathan sighed. "I'm looking for a woman in a fancy dress, white hair—well, usually it's white—and very blue eyes. Has anyone seen her?"

They shook their heads. "Negative, sir."

"Colonel," one of them said, "most of the guest quarters are located on deck eight."

Jonathan nodded. "Thank you, Seaman."

He looked around at everyone. "Carry on."

They relaxed and returned to what they were doing. Jonathan returned to the ladder and climbed down to the next deck. He checked the wall plate; it was labeled Deck 8. Scouring the decks for Ellyra was an unnecessary waste of time. He gave her a comm-band so he wouldn't have to go climbing all over the ship to find her. Why wouldn't she answer? Did something happen to her?

He rounded the corner, nearly bumping into a young chief carrying a large piece of equipment. Jonathan quickly told him to carry on and kept on walking. Several crew quarter cabins came into view on his left.

He pressed his thumb to a plate near the wall. The door chimed but nobody answered.

Jonathan huffed and moved on to the next door, pressing his thumb to the plate. The door chimed. Katheryn answered. Her eyes widened and she stood at attention.

"Colonel, sir."

"At ease, Seaman. I'm looking for Sune Ellyra's quarters."

She stepped back. "This is it," she said, motioning for him to come in.

Jonathan stepped inside with a puzzled look on his face. He hadn't expected to find anyone else in Ellyra's quarters. At least she had a friend to help her. He looked around the small room. "Where is she?"

"In her bunk, sir." Katheryn gestured toward the door at the back of the little room.

Jonathan approached and was about to knock on the door when it opened. Ellyra stood with black hair and fierceness in her blue within blue eyes. Why was her hair black? That's the color Rana's hair was when she didn't like him. What was she upset about?

"Ellyra—"

"Tell me truly, Jonathan," she said, interrupting him. "The day you came to me, prior to leaving for the senate hearing, did you come to inquire after my hand in marriage or to access my connection to the Chantell government?"

Jonathan paled. His heart raced and his breathing halted. It wasn't that simple. It was true that he was trying to recruit her into the conspiracy so they could approach the Bugs. But that did not invalidate his feelings for her. This was a conversation he had hoped never to have. How could he explain in a way she would understand? He didn't even fully understand it himself.

"Ellyra, that had nothing to do with—"

"It is a simple question," she said, stepping forward with watery eyes and a trembling jaw. "I implore you as an honorable man to speak the truth of the matter. Had you come to use me?"

Jonathan's heart tugged at him. She was calling him out as a matter of integrity to be truthful. How could he refuse her? But, then again, how could he tell her? He never wanted to hurt her, and telling her the truth would definitely hurt her. How could he possibly protect her from harm when the one thing she wanted was what would hurt her? It would be better not to tell her.

Jonathan's heart pounded in his chest. Omitting the truth would be just as bad as lying. And she counted him an honorable man. A lie would not be honorable. Whether it would hurt or not, she deserved a straight answer. He would have to give it, knowing full well there would be backlash and pain on both sides.

He swallowed and hesitated a moment. "Yes," he finally said.

Ellyra took in a sharp breath, as though someone had slapped her in the face. Tears broke loose and her hair color soured to a hysterical orange. She stammered a moment, struggling for something to say. Jonathan took a step forward but she held out a halting hand toward him.

She sniffled as tears ran down her face. "You had no right to tell me you loved me."

"But it's true," he insisted.

"How?" she blurted out. "How can I trust anything you say to be true? You have deceived me, intended to use me, and...and you kissed me." She sniffled. "How am I to trust what you say is true?"

Jonathan's breath halted. Each of her words struck him like a bullet to the chest. His hands trembled at his side. What was there to say? What could he possibly say that she would believe? He said the only thing that he could think to say, and it came out almost in a whisper. "I don't know."

The loudspeaker blared the five-note alarm. "General Quarters, General Quarters. All hands man your battle stations. Up forward on the starboard side, down aft on the port side. Inbound hostile starcraft!"

Adrenaline coursed through Jonathan's veins and his heart leaped into action. Jonathan instinctively bolted for the door to get to the bridge but stopped short. He glanced back. "Ellyra, I..."

She glared at him with a mixture of fury and hurt in her eyes. "Go," she said.

Jonathan swallowed. His time was up and he had lost his first skirmish. There was nothing he could do for Ellyra at the moment. He had to hope there would be a next time. As long as he had breath, there would be no rest until he found reconciliation with her.

"Aye, ma'am," he said. Then, he turned and left, heading for the bridge.

He weaved his way through the sea of people getting to their battle stations. He found his way to the stairs and followed the flow of foot traffic. Cynthia's voice echoed from the loudspeaker. "Colonel Terynn to the bridge. Again, Colonel Terynn to the bridge."

"...as fast as I can go, Cindy," he mumbled, climbing the stairs behind another crewman.

Jonathan dashed onto the bridge and Cynthia swiveled her chair around. "Our company has arrived," she said.

"How many?"

"More than forty ships in total. Eight Korell class battleships and about three dozen Harkon class destroyers—their whole ruddy forward strike group."

"We're still going to be fine," he said in a soothing tone.

"*Eight* Korells?" she said in dismay. "We ran our drills expecting half that!"

Jonathan smiled, slowly shaking his head. "Shouldn't matter, we just need to get them a little closer."

"I certainly hope you're right; we're not in any condition to go cleaning up after a damp squib."

"Where are they?"

"On the other side of the planet Terks, attacking *Gamma Station*—just as they should." She turned to a man seated at a control station to her left. "Gordon, pull up the tactical map on the view screen."

"Aye, aye ma'am." He punched a few buttons and the screen flickered. It displayed a computer-generated image of the planet Terks. A blue circle represented *Gamma Station* next to a large blue triangle

that represented the *Azeltar*. Many small red triangles and eight large triangles were closing in on *Gamma Station*.

"Have they detected the fleet?" Jonathan asked.

"Negative, sir," Gordon replied. "They seem to be all concentrating on attacking the station."

Jonathan smiled. "It's gonna work."

Cynthia pointed to the screen. "Assuming eight Korells do not drain the Greys' energy shield too quickly."

Jonathan nodded. "Get me a group transmission with strike group commanders."

"Gordon," Cynthia said.

"Aye, ma'am."

A moment later, the screen switched to a three-way video feed of T'Kal on the bridge of the *Azeltar*, Sune Vaynar in the Center of Workmanship of the *Kaliptica*, and George in the cockpit of a Chantell marauder.

"Can we also get a visual?" Jonathan asked.

"Gordon," Cynthia said, "patch in the video feed from the surveillance satellite."

"Aye, ma'am."

A moment later, the view screen also displayed a video image of the battle. The swarm of tuning-fork-shaped Harkon destroyers vomited up volleys of orange energy bolts. They slammed into the clear energy shield which the *Azeltar* extended around *Gamma Station*. The eight double-crescent-shaped Korells followed close behind. They fired small orange beams of energy.

"T'Kal, how are you holding up?"

Subtitles scrolled across the bottom of the screen. WE ARE HOLDING OUR OWN, AS YOU WOULD SAY. OUR SHIELD IS SLOWLY DRAINING, BUT THE KORELLS HAVE NOT YET CHARGED THEIR PRIMARY WEAPONS. HOWEVER, YOUR RUSE APPEARS TO BE WORKING, THE SCORPII SEEM TO BELIEVE WE ARE STILL ON *GAMMA STATION* AND HAVE COMMITTED EVERY SHIP TO ATTACKING IT.

"There's been a slight change of plans," Jonathan explained. "We have twice as many Korells as we planned on. We need to get them as close as possible, so I need you to pull out slowly. Make them think you're damaged. A wounded prey is irresistible."

More subtitles scrolled. COLONEL TERYNN, AT A REDUCED VELOCITY, THERE WOULD BE NO GUARANTEE WE WOULD REACH A SAFE ENOUGH DISTANCE.

"Give me the best you can, T'Kal, I'll accept whatever you can give me. But it needs to look convincing." He turned to Vaynar. "Sune Vaynar, just as a reminder, we cannot start evacuating the transports and frigates until after we open Pandora's box. Otherwise, the Scorpii will detect your hyperspace portals and come after you. Where we are going, there are no hypergates. You will need to coordinate with every ship in the convoy to follow you into hyperspace before your hyperspace portals close."

"As you wish, Colonel Jonathan."

Jonathan turned to the Chantell. "George, your primary mission is to protect the evacuation fleet, but I'll need you to hold back. Don't engage immediately. In case things don't go according to plan, I want you to be my contingency plan. If anything goes wrong, race in and swarm."

George twitched his antennae. "I vision, Colonel."

Jonathan smirked. The proper phrase was, I see. But there wasn't time for any lessons now. Jonathan turned to Cynthia. "Captain Prescott, you must hold the line until the *Azeltar* reaches us. And remember, she'll be coming in sensor blind."

"No worries, Colonel. We've timed the whole process. We'll be ready for her."

"Good, because whatever happens, you must protect the *Azeltar* until she can power up her quantumspace drive. Your strike group will evacuate with her to the rendezvous."

She smirked. "Last one there buys the beers."

He smiled in return. "Are your SEAL teams prepped?"

351

"Aye, aye Colonel. They are nuts about getting on in a kerfuffle with the Scorpii. It will be a shame if we don't end up needing them."

"I know," Jonathan said. "But if everything goes as planned, they won't have to."

Large thick beams of orange energy shot out from the eight massive Korells. Their beams raked the Azeltar's energy shield. Subtitles scrolled across the bottom of the screen. COLONEL TERYNN, THE KORELLS ARE DISCHARGING THEIR PRIMARY WEAPONS. OUR ENERGY SHIELD IS RAPIDLY DRAINING.

"Listen up!" Jonathan said with determination in his eyes. "We are *not* in battle with the Scorpii, they are in battle with *us!* And that's a mistake their offspring's offspring will never forget. Elder race or not, the Scorpii have chosen to tangle with the wrong opponent. For military might does not lie in the metal of ships, but in the mettle of the men and women who operate them. Goliath will *rue* the day he picked a fight with David!"

The bridge crew of the *Saratoga* erupted in applause. Cynthia straightened her uniform jacket with a tug on the hem. "Bravo, Jonathan. With any luck, you may yet make an optimist out of me after all."

He grinned. "I make my own luck."

"Gordon," Cynthia said. "I need a ship-to-ship with the other cruiser captains."

"Aye, ma'am."

She turned to her left. "Pierson, monitor the shield strength of the Grey's ship. Call out when it reaches thirty-five percent."

"Aye, aye Skipper."

A moment later, the screen flickered and displayed the bridges of the other six battlecruisers. Among the six other captains, Captain Brumanhoff's thick mustache pulled up in the corner of his mouth as he smiled.

Cynthia gave them all her customary no-nonsense glare. "Gentleman, our orders are to hold the line until the Greys' ship arrives. She'll be sensor blind, so we are to guard her booty until she can activate her blinkin' super-light drive. If you encounter any problems, work it out; you are all fine tacticians and we're not being paid to lollygag."

Each of the battlecruiser captains nodded.

"Brumanhoff," she said, "you captain the only Pathfinder-class strike cruiser Earth assigned us. As the fastest ship, you probably fancy yourself the quarterback of Gamma Fleet."

"Of course, Captain," he replied in his thick Slovak accent.

"That stealth field generator the Greys gave you had better be online."

He flashed a smile. "Online and ready to go, Captain."

"And your SEAL teams are ready to deploy if we need them?"

He nodded. "We're ready for 'zem."

"Splendid. Your callsign is Pandora. When I give you the signal, you will open her box."

"Understood."

"Skipper! The *Azeltar's* shield is down to thirty-five percent!"

"Speaking of which," Cynthia said as if discussing the weather. "Pierson, get me a visual from the surveillance satellite."

The *Azeltar's* large circular shape slowly backed away from *Gamma Station*, turning on its axis. The Harkons and Korells followed the *Azeltar*, moving ever closer to the station. Their fury of orange energy bolts and beams still pounded on its shield.

"Everyone except Pandora shut down and power cycle after three minutes," Cynthia ordered. "Pandora, open your box. I say again, open your box."

"Aye, Captain. Sending remote signal to *Gamma Station* now. Welcome to oblivion, comrades!"

The fusion generators aboard *Gamma Station* surged to life. They grew brighter and brighter red until the entire station exploded. The brilliant flash of light completely whitewashed the screen for a long second. A shockwave bubble erupted from the center of the station, tearing it apart. The bubble expanded, engulfing most of the Scorpiian ships, shattering them upon contact.

"Pulse wave approaching!" Gordon shouted.

Cynthia turned to Gordon. "Shut down now!"

"Shutting down," Gordon said, feverishly punching keys on his console. Computer screens and overhead lights turned off until the only light seen was the red glow of the chemical emergency lights.

"Pierson, start the clock!" she ordered.

He tapped his comm-band. "Aye, Skipper. Three minutes starting now."

Jonathan nervously glanced at the time on his comm-band. Three minutes was a long wait when so much hung in the balance. Those Korells didn't look like they were very close to the station before it self-destructed. The plan should still work fine. *We'll still be okay,* he thought, *as long as we took out at least four Korells in the blast.* He checked the time again. This plan also required the *Azeltar* to still be able to open a quantumspace portal. If their super-light drive went down, the plan would be irrecoverable.

"One minute remaining," Pierson called out.

"Count us down at five," Cynthia replied.

Jonathan checked his comm-band once more and then began to pace. His thoughts turned to the evacuation convoy. Vaynar should be coordinating the evacuation of the transport ships and equipment frigates. Timing them to follow a Euroo ship into the hyperspace portal before it closed was a matter of precision. That's why he had stationed Isabeau on the *Kaliptica* with Vaynar. If anyone could coordinate such a large convoy in such a short window of time, and under pressure, she could. If things had been different, she could have made an excellent hypergate commander.

Pierson called out the time. "...five, four, three, two, one, mark!"

"All systems, power on!" Cynthia ordered.

The room erupted in voices replying and coordinating. Computer consoles turned on and the overhead lights flickered to life. Jonathan halted his pacing, waiting for the main screen to turn back on. He needed to know what was going on out there. The absence of knowing was certain failure.

"Get my bloomin' view screen up now!" Cynthia shouted.

 354

"Working on it," Gordon replied.

After an uncomfortable moment, the large screen lit up and displayed the video image from the surveillance satellite. The scene looked strangely desolate without the familiar sight of *Gamma Station*. Small dots of wreckage floated outward from the center of the blast. Only seven Scorpiian ships remained, badly beaten and listing.

The bridge crew erupted in cheers and applause. The helmsman whistled loudly and shouted, "Take *that*, yo momma's boys!"

Cynthia sat back with a smile and crossed her legs again. "I'll bet the Scorpii never figured on us braying a wallop like the big blokes."

Jonathan sighed in relief. Then he tensed up, his heart thumping. The seven remaining ships were all Korells. His breathing grew shallow and quick. They were not close enough to the blast. Either the SEAL teams would need to pull double duty or something else had to be thought up. Escaping would not be a problem, but if even one enemy ship remained, there would be evidence that the Gamms survived. And the only way to prevent a chase was to make it look like they were already dead.

"Skipper," Pierson said. "One of the Korells is broadcasting a transmission."

"Probably calling for reinforcements," Cynthia said. "Are they receiving a reply?"

"Checking..."

Jonathan clenched his fists in nervousness. It was now the moment of truth; did Matt keep his end of the bargain? If the battle communications had not been blocked, the Scorpii government would be alerted that the Gamms were not destroyed. Jonathan swallowed. His fleet of ships would be hunted.

"Negative, Skipper. Not a single transmission is coming from Scorpii space."

Jonathan breathed out with a sigh of relief. *Thank you, Matt,* he thought.

"Skipper, Echo Squadron is breaking formation. It looks like they're going to assist the *Azeltar*."

"What is the status of the *Azeltar*?" Cynthia asked.

"Their energy shield has collapsed, and a lot of their primary systems are down."

"What is the status of their super-light drive?"

"It appears to be active, ma'am."

Cynthia uncrossed her legs and crossed them with the other leg. "Get me a ship-to-ship with the squadron commander."

"Initiating transmission, aye Skipper." The overhead speakers clicked on.

"Dannigen, what in the blazes are you doing? Get back into formation."

Dannigen's static-laden voice responded. "The Greys' ship isn't going to make it back to the line before those Korells recover. They're sitting ducks!"

Jonathan took an instinctive step forward but halted. He forced his hands to relax. It was best to let Cynthia handle it. She was in command of the strike group, and it was the mark of a poor general to micromanage. Going down the ranks was just as important as going up.

Her stern eyes narrowed. "Get your infernal self, and your squadron, back in formation."

"But they're not going to make it!"

"Before I blast you myself!" Cynthia shouted.

Only the crackle of static sounded through the overhead speakers for a moment. "Aye, Captain. And with all due respect, you may have just sentenced us all to death."

"Your confidence in my leadership is positively tear-jerking." She turned to Gordon. "Signal the fleet, we're moving the line—and to keep their starfighter squadrons in formation." She turned her attention back to the audio transmission. "Dannigen, you're a brilliant pilot and a natural leader. But when it comes to tactics, you're an imbecile. Follow formation and be ready to engage those Korells." Without waiting for a response, she turned to Gordon and gave him the kill gesture. He terminated the transmission.

Jonathan smiled. "Skipper? That doesn't sound like a very *proper* title."

She smirked, glancing at Jonathan from the side. "That might be precisely why I like it."

"Skipper!" Pierson called out. "Hyperspace portal forming off the starboard bow."

"Now what?" she asked in a huff.

"Admiral Mays put the hypergates in our path on maintenance. So, none of the younger races except the Euroo can get here," Jonathan said. "It won't be the Tumnei or the Chantell. The Scorpii are already here and can't call for reinforcements. That leaves the Arkalan, the Crystalline, or the Euroo."

"Put it on screen," Cynthia ordered.

The screen flickered and displayed a video image of a patch of space rippling like calm water after a stone is dropped. A light blue light shone from the center of the ripple.

"I sure hope it's the Euroo," Jonathan said. "We already have one great house on board with us. I wouldn't mind getting some more."

Several crewmen gasped watching the screen as a large black ship emerged from the hyperspace portal. The light from the distant sun illuminated a rough black surface that resembled hewn rock.

"None of the above," Cynthia said in a sarcastic tone. "Care to guess again?"

Jonathan's jaw dropped. This was not part of the plan. Perhaps he should pinch himself to make sure it wasn't a nightmare. "What are the Draconians doing here? They never get their hands dirty; hence the extermination order."

"Perhaps you'd care to inform them of that little detail?"

Out from behind the planet Terks, the Chantell marauders zoomed toward the Draconian dreadnaught. They swarmed, pelting it with little yellow bursts of energy.

Jonathan clenched his fists. "This is a problem."

Chapter 46

EVACUATION

I sabeau stood at a control console on the Center of Workmanship of the *Kaliptica*. Keeping one finger on a list of ship callsigns on her reader, she watched the time on her comm-band. "...Gamma 6, go. Gamma 7, go. Gamma 8, go."

In the center of the room, a hologram of the planet Terks hung in the air. The line of cruisers and their squadrons of Trident fighters were on one side of the planet along with the seven Korells. The three Euroo cruisers along with the convoy were on the other side of the planet. The *Aloriel* opened a hyperspace portal and flew through it. Close behind, the ships Isabeau had named each followed the *Aloriel* into the portal. Then the portal collapsed and vanished.

"Commander Isabeau," a handsome man in a fine suit called out. "The ship identifying as Gamma 8 reports that they 'missed the window'."

Isabeau hung her head a moment in frustration. Several stray strands of her black hair fell across her face. She blasted a hot puff of air, tossing them aside. Why did it have to be so difficult? The computer simulation never accounted for the delay time in activating a ship's thrusters. As a result, ships were missing the window before the hyperspace portals collapsed. The *Aloriel* had already opened its hyperspace portal and led in the first group of ships. Only the *Pentora* and the *Kaliptica* remained that could open hyperspace portals without the need for a hypergate. All the remaining ships of the convoy would need to be divided up between them. If all the ships couldn't get through in time before, how could they get all the stragglers through as well?

She quietly cursed under her breath and typed rapidly on her reader. She would have to adjust when she called for each ship to go. If she told them to go a few seconds early, that should compensate for the delay. "Okay, tell the *Pentora* to open her portal on my mark—"

"Cancel that command, Commsman," Vaynar said.

Isabeau flashed a confused look at him.

He pointed to the three-dimensional hologram of the battle scene. "A Draconian dreadnaught has just arrived. It doesn't look as if they've detected us yet, but their scanners are even better than the Scorpii. If we open a new portal, they'll definitely notice."

"So, we just sit here?" she asked.

"Hardly a productive use of our time, Commander Isabeau. I intend to get further instructions." Vaynar turned to his commsman. "Open up a transmission to Colonel Jonathan, on the *Saratoga*."

"As you wish, Sune."

Isabeau rolled her eyes. "With all due respect, Sune Vaynar, we don't have much time until those Korells recover."

"Your objection is noted. And may I remind you that our orders are to—"

An orange beam of energy sliced through the emptiness of space and cut into the hull of the *Pentora*. It exploded, hurdling large fragments in all directions. Vaynar stared at the holographic display in horror. "By the stars...they have found us regardless." The Korells were just peeking around the edge of the planet.

"We have to get out of weapons range," Isabeau explained. "Those Korells probably can't outrun us."

"I should think so," he said. "But we don't have enough fuel to run for very long. Those Chantell ships are supposed to occupy them for just this occasion."

Isabeau sighed. "They have their hands full with that dreadnaught."

"Ahead full," Vaynar ordered. "And signal the other ships in the convoy to follow. We shall put as much distance between us and the Scorpii as possible."

"Sune," the handsome gentleman said. "We have an incoming transmission from the Earthian ship calling itself *GSS Tresska*."

"On stage," Vaynar said.

The holographic image switched to a three-dimensional hologram of Captain Brumanhoff. "Greetings, comrades. I have contingency package to deliver to those Korells. However, it would be helpful for you to lead them to me. You scratch my back, I scratch yours, yes?"

Vaynar returned a look of bewilderment. "I beg your pardon?"

"Yes," Isabeau blurted out. "Sune Vaynar, we need to alter our flight path to intercept the *Tresska*."

"Steersman," he said. "Lay in a course for that Earthian ship."

"Indeed not, Sune. Their ship does not appear on our scanners."

Brumanhoff's eyes widened. "Oh, yes. We have stealth field activated. Bring your ship to course 117 by 010."

"Steersman, bring us to 117 by 010, increase speed to three-quarters."

"As you wish, Sune."

Deep in the underbelly of the *Tresska*, in the torpedo launch room, Corporal Kowalski stood in a line with the rest of his SEAL team. He flexed his fingers in anticipation. The years of training and the grueling hours of practice all led up to this moment.

In front of their line stood the Lieutenant, anxiously staring at a revolving light overhead. The overhead klaxon buzzed once and the revolving light flashed yellow.

"Just like we practiced it," the Lieutenant shouted. "Stick to your assigned targets unless I direct you otherwise. You each have a secondary target that we didn't plan for. So, to prevent stray shrapnel from flying around, do not—I repeat, do not—detonate until all charges are set. Your placement has to be exact to hit the reactor. The *Tresska's* stealth field will mask you from target lock but you still need to watch for stray fire."

He took a quick breath. "This is what we train for! You are the best of the best! The core of a SEAL is determination, stamina, and heart! The only *easy* day, was yesterday!"

The entire company of men shouted in unison, "Hoorah!" It echoed throughout the lower deck just as the klaxon blared again and the revolving light flashed red.

The SEALs clamped on their helmets and clamored to the torpedo tubes. Kowalski waited behind his teammates for his turn to enter the launch tube. Chief Gunner's Mate Rowland turned to the Lieutenant. "Lieutenant Greer, request authorization to launch the SEALs."

The Lieutenant enunciated each syllable, as though each was as important as the last. "You are authorized to launch the SEALs."

"Pressurize the tubes," Rowland said.

Kowalski returned his eyes forward and climbed feet first into the launch tube. The hatch sealed shut, making all as dark as night. He pressed a button around the base of his helmet and his interior helmet light turned on. A sound of hissing filled the silence, drowning out the thumping of his heart and his exhilarated breathing. He felt the intense weight of the air being pressurized for launch. He groaned, flexing his muscles against the pressure. Tube launches were never fun; that is, until the actual launch.

A clanking sound rumbled overhead and then a moment later the outer launch door blew open. Kowalski was shot out like a rocket. "Woooweee!" The hull of the *Tresska* flew past in an instant. He was soaring free like a human spaceship. He zoomed past floating debris toward the double-crescent-shaped battleship of the Scorpii. Kowalski ignited his thruster pack and adjusted his trajectory.

Jonesy, his unit leader, spoke over the comm. "Alpha team, this is Alpha Leader. Report when you have a visual on target one."

Kowalski reached up and pressed the two buttons around his neck. "Alpha Leader, Alpha four, I have a visual. Targeting computer identifies it as target one."

His other two teammates, Harris and Orland, also reported in. It was just like clockwork. The massive Scorpiian ship came ever closer. It was so much bigger up close than he had ever imagined. The sleek orange metal reflected the light of the distant sun. The bloody red glow of the engines gave an eerie look to the metal monstrosity.

His helmet's HUD calculated the range to target. It was almost time to deploy the mag-hook. He unclamped the launcher from his side and aimed it at the hull of the Korell. The shot didn't need to be perfect, but the more accurate the shot, the easier it would be to maneuver into place. The weird physics behind simulated inertia were too complicated for anyone but eggheads to understand. Something about the mix between the internal gravity field and the external propulsion field made the whole thing work. It was a logistical dance to stay holding onto the hull of the moving battleship.

His HUD flashed red numbers and a beeping sounded in his ear. It was game on. He aimed, adjusting for both lead and lag, and fired. The mag-hook fired, pulling a tether line behind it. It slammed up against the enemy hull and magnetized. Direct hit. He clamped the launcher to his belt and pressed the button to reel him in. Three other mag-hooks nailed the hull pretty close to center target.

Kowalski smiled. His was still the closest to perfect. He was the first to reel in and touch foot onto the hull of the speeding Korell. The shiny orange metal was a little slick. He would have to be careful. "Contact!" he hollered in triumph through the comm.

"Does that mean we should start calling you ambassador now?" Harris asked with a chuckle.

"Cut the chatter, Alpha two," Jonesy said. "Alpha three, mount your charge on this one. Alpha two, you'll mount yours on the next target."

"Hooyah," Orland said, stepping onto the orange hull of the metal giant.

"Watch your footing," Kowalski said.

Jonesy and Harris stepped onto the hull a moment later. Orland detached a large case from his back, holding onto the tether line with his other hand. Kowalski, with one hand on his tether, grabbed the other end of the large case and lowered it to the slick orange hull.

Jonesy tapped a few buttons on his arm, scanning the site for signs of reactor radiation. "Alpha four, half a meter toward you."

"Roger," Kowalski said, pulling it closer.

"Alpha two, secure the charge."

"Roger, Alpha leader," Harris said, pulling out a small space welder. He clicked it on. It sputtered with a bright light and began melting the charge to the surface of the enemy ship. Harris slackened his hold on his tether to reach further, completing the welding.

"The package is secured, Alpha Leader."

"Secure your tethers and head for target two."

"Roger."

Orland slipped, holding fast to his tether. He slammed down onto the hull knocking the detonation transmitter out of his hand. The little box flew past them like a handkerchief carried in a stormy wind.

"The detonator!"

Kowalski exchanged a horrified glance with Jonesy. In a flash, he pulled out his combat knife and cut his tether line. The huge Korell thundered past him into the distance. He looked forward and ignited his thruster pack. Scanning the scene before him, there was no sign of the little detonator box. He pressed a few buttons on his arm. He hit the wrong key. He grumbled a curse and keyed it in again. His HUD flashed up cycling through moving objects in front of him.

A single beep sounded in his ear. He glanced at the thruster fuel gauge. Almost depleted. His heart pounded. Without that detonator, they would have to wire another one to connect to that shape charge.

363

That would take too long. The Korell only needed two clean shots to destroy the Euroo cruisers. Without them, the convoy could never escape into hyperspace. They'd be stranded.

His heart raced and his breathing accelerated. The display on his helmet flashed yellow and sounded three beeps in his ear. Target acquired. It was the right size and heading in the right direction. It was impossible to know how fast it was traveling, it flew through the thruster wash of the Korell's engines. That probably propelled it quite a bit faster. He glanced back to his fuel gauge. Ten percent and falling.

The tiny object grew closer. He took a deep breath of relief. It was the detonator. Even though it was spinning, he could see the little red light on it. He was gaining on it, but would it be enough? He reached out his hand. It was still too far away. And to make matters worse, he was drifting to the left. He would need to compensate with a little thrust to the side. But not too much or he would veer too far away from it. He tapped the controls on his chest. The side thruster sputtered. That wasn't enough. He tapped it again. It sputtered again and popped an unexpected burst of thrust.

Kowalski cursed and hit the controls again, trying to correct his trajectory. It was no longer a simple game of catch-up, now he was playing ping pong with his side thrusters. His helmet beeped again. His fuel gauge was down to five percent and falling fast.

The Lieutenant's staticky voice spoke in his helmet. "SEAL teams, this is Big Charlie, return to base and detonate. I say again, return to base and detonate."

Oh great, no pressure. It was time for them to go boom and he was still chasing his detonator. The Sarge and the Lieutenant were right. The only easy day really was yesterday. With one hand, he tapped his side thrusters while reaching out with his other hand. Slowly the zig-zagging target grew ever nearer. Great white and yellow light illuminated behind him. *That would be the other targets going boom*, he thought.

His helmet beeped three times and his fuel gauge flashed red. The thrusters stopped responding. He was out of fuel. He reached out his hand one last time for the detonator. It twirled close to him, still inches out of his reach. Without any additional thrust, they were both traveling at the same speed. It hovered teasingly before him.

"There's still one left," the Lieutenant's voice said. "Who didn't detonate?"

Jonesy's voice responded. "Alpha team, sir. We lost one of the detonators; Kowalski went after it."

Kowalski reached as far as he could stretch his arm. It was still out of his reach. "No, no, no, no!" There had to be something he could do. Could he vent some oxygen? No, the controls were on his back and he couldn't even see what he was doing, let alone reach it. He had left his mag-hook behind when he cut his tether. There really wasn't anything he could do. His heart sank and his breathing shallowed. It couldn't end this way. It wasn't fair.

He reached out again, despite the lingering distance. Then a huge shock wave struck him on the back like someone hitting him with a bat. It knocked the wind out of him, shoving him forward. His fingers latched onto the detonator. He took in a deep breath, his heart pounding with excitement. He had the detonator in his hands. He finally had it. After a brief moment gazing at the little device in delight, he glanced back the way he had come. If six Korells blew, there were five more shock waves just like it on their way.

It was best to act fast. He flipped open the safety lid that covered the switch. The red light turned green. He eagerly pressed the button and glanced back at the small Korell in the distance. The deep panting of his breath was all that he could hear. Something was wrong. It didn't go boom. He pressed the button a few more times. Was he out of range? Did he just go through all that for nothing? Was the convoy going to be destroyed anyway?

He glanced back at the Scorpiian battleship, racing off to kill more ships. Then it exploded in a bright blue and white flash of light followed by a swarm of debris. *Oh, right*, he thought. *Time delay due to the distance.*

"Hoooorah!" he hollered into his comm. "Alpha four requesting a pickup!"

Chapter 47

THE BELTARES

F ox stood motionless once again in the Center of Workmanship of the *Calmao*. A heavy weight tugged at his heart. How could the Skorath refuse to help? There must be some mistake. They could not have understood. After all, resting on their posteriors for thousands of years probably required some time for the blood to circulate back to the brain. Maybe the word *ancient* didn't equate to powerful after all; maybe it just meant decrepit.

Fox spun around to face Xer. "What else have you got?"

Xer picked up his reader. "The transcript of the last senate convention. I haven't yet written an opinion for it, though."

"Send it!" Fox said, letting his irritation seethe. "There's got to be *something* those brainless geezers understand!"

Xer quickly punched keys on his console.

"Lieutenant Colonel Fox!" Diahlus said in a stern and horrified tone. "May I remind you that you are addressing my crew? Furthermore, the transmission is still open—they can hear your every word."

Fox took a deep breath and clenched his fists. Diahlus was right. Such conduct was unbecoming an officer of the Earth Navy, let alone speaking to allies. He breathed out, relaxing. "Forgive me, Diahlus. I am in the wrong. I let my feelings get in the way of my duty."

"Your apology is accepted on condition that such outbursts are discontinued," Diahlus said.

Fox nodded. "Understood." He turned to Xer. "Forgive me, Xer. I, uh...don't know what came over me."

Xer looked at him and nodded. "Accepted."

Fox turned back to the holographic image of the Skorath ship. It was such a waste. All that effort and time—precious time that could have been spent at the Colonel's side—was all for nothing. Now, instead of saving the Colonel and Isabel, he had missed his only chance to fight in a real battle alongside the Hero of Mesa Sol.

Fox again clenched his fists, irritation and rejection bubbling up. How could those ancient losers lead him on with the promise of help? Prophecy indeed. It was one thing to have failed to decipher it, but it was wholly unacceptable to be rejected by what was essentially a promise of support. Were there any words adequate to express just how appalling their behavior was?

Fox glared at the image of the Skorath ship and stabbed the air with his finger. "You are not worth another word, else I'd call you knave!"

"What are you doing?" Layna whispered with a pale face and worry in her eyes.

"Foul spoken coward, that thund'rest with thy tongue, and with thy weapon nothing dares perform!"

"Commsman, close the transmission at once!" Diahlus ordered, his hair blackening. "Lieutenant Colonel Fox, that behavior is completely unacceptable."

Fox took a deep breath and stood at attention. The military training ironed into him the instinct to know when he was being dressed down by a superior. It had been a long time since he had been called out in such a manner. "Understood, sir."

Diahlus stared at him for an eternal moment. "Fox, it grieves me to have to ask you to—"

The loudspeaker rumbled. "Prepare for the crossing, Beltares."

Fox glanced up at the overhead speakers. That was an unexpected response. "Beltares? What does that mean?" Maybe it was their language for knave?

"I'm more worried about what The Crossing means," Diahlus said. "Crossing into what?"

The whole ship began to shake and tremble. Diahlus clung to his chair while Fox and Layna tumbled to the floor.

Layna clung to Fox. "Crossing into the afterlife?"

What? Afterlife? Would the Skorath really attack them? A benevolent, wise, and ancient race would not callously attack after a few insults, would they?

"What is our status?" Diahlus called out over the cacophony, the chandelier swaying overhead.

"Skorath ship is emitting a large graviton wake."

Fox's eyes lit up. "Are they attacking us?"

Diahlus glared. "It would appear that not all civilized races take kindly to being called a coward."

Fox paled, his heart racing. What had he done? After coming all this way and finally communicating with the one alien race that could compete militarily with the Draconians, had he just ruined the opportunity? Well, they weren't exactly eager to help. But, still, it may not have been the wisest choice to antagonize them. The violent shaking of the ship increased. Fox tried to get to his feet but tumbled back down and landed atop Layna. She stared at him with a startled expression, her face only inches from his. Fox blushed. This was awkward.

"Lieutenant Colonel, I must protest," she said, her hair burning into an embarrassed burgundy.

"Sorry, ma'am," he said, rolling off her. His cheeks still burned, and he cringed all over. How was he supposed to avoid tension between them now? It wasn't on purpose; it was an accident. The rumbling of the ship was to blame. Fox ran his hand down his face. If shouting insults at the Skorath wasn't bad enough, now he may have committed a vile offense to a very proper people.

"Steersman," Diahlus called out. "Can you turn the ship out of the wake!"

"Indeed not, Brigadain. The magnitude of the field is too great!"

"Steersman, see if you can—"

Fox gasped for breath. His body became very heavy, his arms and legs pinned to the ground. Crewmen fell to the floor, unable to move. Small decorative prisms from the chandelier snapped and fell against the floor as if an invisible hand pushed them down.

"What's happening?" Layna said, struggling for breath. The delicate folds of her dress pressed to the floor.

Fox strained for another breath and suddenly pulled in an enormous breath. His arms and legs felt light again, able to move. The shuddering and shaking of the ship subsided, the chandelier gently swaying. The room filled with the groanings of people picking themselves up.

Fox stood and dusted off his uniform. He glanced down at Layna who was still recovering. Should he try to help her up? Would she accept his offer for help now? There was only one way to find out. He offered her his hand. To his delight, she accepted it. He helped her to her feet and turned partially away while she readjusted her dress and jewelry.

"Thank you, Lieutenant Colonel Fox."

"You're welcome," he said, not making eye contact. "And, uh...I'm terribly embarrassed by the, uh..." He gestured with his arms toward the floor where she was lying a moment ago.

She smiled gingerly and gently shook her head, her burgundy locks of hair swayed. "Think nothing of it. True, it was a startling occurrence of happenstance, but I do not hold it against your propriety in the least."

He looked at her and returned her smile.

"What happened?" Diahlus asked, rising to his feet.

"I am unsure, Brigadain," a woman answered.

"Get me a visual on stage, please."

"As you wish."

The gold circle in the center of the floor lit up and projected a holographic image of the *Calmao* and the surrounding space. The nebula was missing, and in its place was a large brown planet.

"Where in the stars are we?" Diahlus asked.

Fox stared at the planet with a dropped jaw. He had seen that planet so many times during the last six months that it could never be forgotten. "It's the planet Terks."

Chapter 48

FULFILLMENT

Ellyra stumbled trying to stay on her feet. Her cabin aboard the *Saratoga* jumbled around as if it was being tossed back and forth. She had never been in a battle before. Was combat always this bumpy? She took hold of a shelf that was welded to the wall, steadying her balance. Katheryn clung to the other side of it.

"Either they're havin' a lot of turbulence up there or things aren't going according to plan."

Ellyra sighed. "I do hope Jonathan is all right." The sentence escaped her lips before she could stop it. Why should she care what happened to him? He had deceived her and tried to use her. She was nothing more than a pawn in his master plan. Her eyes watered and her hair tingled. Why did this have to happen? In her ignorance, she had been happy. If knowing was, indeed, empowerment, then it was also pain.

A heavy weight tugged at her heart. Why did she have to care about it? Why was it so difficult to leave him behind? Why did her thoughts keep turning back to him? What was he to her now? She took a breath and knew. She loved him. Even though it was a hopeless and one-sided love, she still cared for him. The memory of him asleep under the blue glow of the stasis field came rushing back to her memory. When he was poisoned, she had almost lost him. She had wept for him and had stayed with him.

If she had to do it all over again, knowing now how deceitful he had been, she would not change anything—she could not change anything. Tears fell from her eyes. He was such a contradiction. His calculating mind and fascination with strategy made him the cold-hearted man she despised. Yet the loving smile and the gorgeous brown eyes that could look into her soul were nothing of the sort. His laugh and the way he looked at her were all so endearing. And that was the man she loved. How could these both be the same man?

Did it really matter? If he didn't love her, would her heart be of any value to him? If she was just a tool to be used, a strategy to play, could he ever love her in any meaningful way? More tears ran down her face. She squeezed her eyes shut. Why couldn't he have loved her?

"If you're that worried about him, ma'am, you can try calling him," Katheryn said.

Ellyra wiped away her tear lines with her free hand. "On this thing?" she asked, holding up her wrist with the comm-band.

Katheryn nodded. "If he's busy he might not be able to respond, but you can always give it a try."

"Would you show me how?"

"Sure, ma'am." Katheryn leaned over and looked at Ellyra's comm-band. "It looks like you have a message," she said, pointing to the small indicator light.

"Oh, that?" she said. "It's been there for days. How is it a message?"

The room rocked to one side and Ellyra clung to the shelf with white knuckles. Katheryn laughed. "This is one fine time for a tutorial."

A laugh bubbled up from within Ellyra and came out as a muffled giggle. She smiled. "Yes, I do suppose this is looking rather ridiculous."

Katheryn leaned over again and pointed to her comm-band. "You need to double-tap that symbol and it will bring up the message so you can read it."

Ellyra did as instructed and the screen on her comm-band showed a short, written message:

Timestamp: 04.36.21836

From: Terynn, Col. Jonathan

Hello gorgeous. I've been thinking about you. I just wish we could throw out all this planning and just run away together. I love you.

Ellyra's breathing halted. Goosebumps washed over her skin. Her hair tingled as it darkened into a wishful violet. Her heart pounded. *He wishes he could run away with me,* she thought. A deep breath forced its way into her lungs. Her eyes widened. There was at least a part of Jonathan that truly loved her. Her breathing accelerated. Could that be enough? If even just a part of Jonathan would love her, could that be enough?

"Is everything all right?" Katheryn asked.

Ellyra glanced at her with wide eyes, exhilaration building within. "Yes!" she declared, nodding. "Yes, it is." A smile spread across her face, beaming.

The overhead speaker clicked on. "All able-bodied personnel of rank not at a battle station, report to damage control. I say again, all able-bodied personnel of rank not currently at a battle station, report to damage control."

"Ma'am, I gotta go," Katheryn said, making her way to the door, clinging to whatever handholds she could find. "I'll check on you later."

Damage control, Ellyra thought. *The ship has been damaged.* How badly were they damaged? Was Jonathan injured? Would there be any guarantee she would see him again? Her heart raced as she made her way to the door, one handhold at a time. She needed to find Jonathan. She had nearly lost him once. Could she bear to lose him again? What if this was their last hour together? She had to get to the ship's command room. That is where Jonathan would be.

373

She exited the room, leaning hard against the wall for balance. Several men dashed back and forth, some carrying equipment. How could they keep their balance in all this? Perhaps the running helped? Ellyra waited for an opening between crewmen and dashed across the hallway. Surprisingly, the faster pace made the balance easier. She grabbed ahold of the stairway railing and climbed. Where was she even going? She hadn't ever been shown the command room of this ship before.

She stopped the first man that passed her down the stairs. "If you will excuse me, where might I find Colonel Jonathan Terynn?"

"He'll be on the bridge, ma'am," he replied, hustling past her down the stairs.

It seemed manners were far less common in a battle. Considering the circumstances, there would have to be some allowances. A man rushed up the stairs from below her and she held out her hand toward him. "If you would please, kind sir, where might I find the bridge?"

"What?" he said, leaning his ear toward her.

"The bridge. Where might I find it?"

He pointed up ahead and spoke louder than necessary. "Another two decks up, in the forward section."

"Thank you," she said, as he continued on his way.

Another large jolt of the ship left Ellyra clinging to the railing. Earthian ships must be crudely constructed if they can't even keep the floor stable. Such conditions were not dignified. She climbed, holding the railing with one hand and picking up the hem of her gown in the other. When she finally reached the top of the stairs, she ran down the narrow hallway in what hopefully was the correct direction. A large crash of metal echoed through the ship, jostling it. Ellyra fell forward and slid down the corridor.

Clinging to a doorway, she picked herself up, peering into the bridge. Jonathan and another uniformed man helped Cynthia back into her chair. Blood dripped from a fresh cut on Cynthia's forehead. She promptly fastened her safety strap and crossed her legs. On the view screen, the monstrous form of the Draconian dreadnaught loomed. It fired angry red beams of energy, slicing into ships and intercepting missiles. The small Chantell marauders circled it, pelting it with little yellow energy bolts.

"Skipper," Gordon said. "The *Azeltar* is powering up its energy shield."

"About ruddy time," Cynthia said, brushing some hair back into place. "Gordon, signal the other ships to retreat beneath the Greys' shield."

"Aye, Skipper."

"Skipper," Pierson said. "The *Azeltar* is powering up its quantumspace drive."

"The first brilliant thing I've heard today."

The ship began to shudder and quake. Ellyra clung to the doorway. Then the shaking abruptly stopped.

Cynthia huffed. "Confound the Greys! Why haven't they got us out of here yet?"

"Cindy," Jonathan said, "I need to talk with T'Kal."

"Gordon, open a ship-to-ship with the Greys."

"Opening a transmission with the Greys, aye Skipper."

A moment later, the screen flickered and displayed the bridge of the *Azeltar*. Thick white fog rolled across the floor with bright white lights overhead. T'Kal motioned with his hand as if in conversation as subtitles scrolled across the screen. GREETINGS, COLONEL TERYNN. IT IS GOOD TO SEE THAT YOU ARE ALL RIGHT.

"It's good to see you too, T'Kal," Jonathan said. "What's your status?"

More subtitles scrolled. OUR ENERGY SHIELD IS HOLDING FOR THE MOMENT, BUT IT IS STEADILY DRAINING.

"Can you get us out of here?"

T'Kal shook his head. UNFORTUNATELY, THE DREADNAUGHT IS EMITTING AN ANTIGRAVITON FIELD THAT IS DISRUPTING OUR QUANTUMSPACE DRIVE. WE ARE TARGETING THEIR EMITTERS BUT THEIR HULL IS EXTREMELY DENSE. THEIR HULL ARMOR HAS BEEN WEAKENED ONLY TWELVE PERCENT.

Jonathan wiped his brow and hung his head in thought. "How long will your shields hold out?"

Subtitles again scrolled across the bottom of the screen. NOT LONG ENOUGH TO CUT THROUGH THEIR ARMOR. WE ESTIMATE OUR SHIELD WILL BE AGAIN DEPLETED IN UNDER THIRTEEN MINUTES.

"Great! What else can go wrong?"

"Skipper," a woman called from the other end of the bridge. "Hyperspace portal opening dead ahead."

Cynthia glared at Jonathan.

He rolled his eyes. "Sorry, I'm honestly *not* trying to jinx us."

"On screen," Cynthia said.

Out of the wavy distortion, a second black Draconian dreadnaught emerged.

Ellyra gasped. "By the stars!"

Jonathan jogged over to her and took her in his arms. "I wish I could say it would all be okay."

"Oh, Jonathan...I have so much to say."

"Me too," he said, holding her tight.

The ship began to rattle and shake. Jonathan and Ellyra dropped to their hands and knees. The overhead lights flickered and a computer console blasted sparks in the air.

"Now what?" Cynthia asked in exasperation.

"Large gravimetric wake to our starboard!"

"On screen!"

Large dark blue waves emanated outward from a black spot in space. Then a large black ship faded into view. The bumpy dull black surface of the ship reflected very little light. It was very different from the hewn-rock look of the Draconian ships. This one had a mysterious elegance to its shape. Jonathan stared at it with wonder in his eyes.

"What is it?" Ellyra asked.

"The Skorath," he said, with a slight catch in his throat.

The pointed bow of the Skorath ship fanned open like a blossoming flower, revealing a large glowing purple ball. Electricity danced over the surface of the ball. It lit up in an instant and fired a thick purple beam of energy. It burrowed right through the side of the big black dreadnaught and continued out the other side. The Skorath ship pivoted effortlessly toward the second dreadnaught. It fired again, sending another thick purple beam of burning energy through its hull.

Fires erupted where the purple beams had cut. A cascade of explosions pounded throughout each of the dreadnaughts. They shattered in a final explosion, sending rocky debris washing harmlessly around the shield of the *Azeltar*, and raining down upon the planet Terks. The fan-shaped bow of the Skorath ship closed.

Jonathan and Ellyra climbed to their feet, silent in amazement. What had they just witnessed? The mighty Draconian dreadnaught, the final word in total power in the galaxy, had been destroyed. Two of them had been obliterated in seconds.

"They are real," Ellyra finally said.

The *Saratoga* began shaking once more. Jonathan pulled Ellyra close. She buried her face in his shirt. What was happening now? Ellyra and Jonathan collapsed to the floor, pinned down under a great weight. She gasped for breath. "Oh, Jonathan," was all she could say. A moment later, she felt light again and took in a huge breath. She could move her limbs again. She moaned as she moved them.

Jonathan pulled her to her feet once more. "Are you okay?"

"This is proving to be quite enough to cure me of my notions of adventure in space. What happened?"

He shook his head. "I don't know." He glanced over to the screen on the wall. It was dark, powered off. "Cindy, can we get a visual?"

"Gordon, fix my view screen."

"Working on it."

The screen blinked on and displayed a video image of a sky without any stars, covered by orange and blue hues. A gray planet loomed silently in the distance. A dim red sun burned far in the background.

Ellyra held onto Jonathan. "Where are we?"

He replied without taking his gaze from the screen. "I don't think we're in Kansas anymore."

Chapter 49

JUSTICE

Matt marched down the dimly lit halls of *Able Station* with urgency in his pace. His ribs complained with every step despite the pain medication. If only he could go faster. Lord Vaux was again on the station and this time Ross was not around to keep Cossette safe. It wasn't a guarantee that the vile squiddy was looking for blood, but there was also no guarantee that it wasn't.

Matt rounded a corner and then abruptly stopped. The hairs on the back of his neck stood on end. His hands chilled despite his black leather gloves. He straightened up his posture and planted an arrogant smile on his face. It was time to put on his show.

Matt turned around. "My dear Lord Vaux, how gracious of you to visit our humble establishment."

The stupid squiddy skittered toward him from the other hallway. Its grotesque form closed the distance with a calm pace. It stopped right up next to Matt. It hissed with an air of contempt.

"Lazy? Oh, don't be stupid," Matt said with a dismissive tone. "They're just keeping out of sight. After that mess you made with Ross, who could blame them?"

Lord Vaux squawked, pointing an accusatory tentacle at him. Matt suppressed the urge to huff. Of all the unmitigated gall; an invertebrate lecturing on the importance of a backbone. Matt forced a smile and bowed his head. "You are, of course, entirely correct. I shall get to work on that at once." He turned to leave but only took a few casual steps. The brainless squiddy always wanted the last word and never failed to add something in at the last moment.

Lord Vaux squealed and groaned.

Matt stopped and paled. His heart raced and his gloved palms sweated. This would have to be handled with care. He had already used up his best bravado on the squiddy after it killed Maren. Feigned ignorance would be the next best approach. But for it to be convincing, it needed to look casual. And that would be difficult if he couldn't reign in his emotional responses.

He took a deep breath, relaxed his muscles, and turned around. "Woman?" he asked, taking a few steps closer to the hideous waste of flesh.

Lord Vaux squawked and waved a tentacle around in description.

"Her name was Merin, you killed her for no reason some months ago."

Lord Vaux hissed, shaking its head.

Matt's heart pounded. He forced a casual posture. "A new one?"

Lord Vaux nodded, squawking.

It was time to show a little emotion. The complete absence of it would be suspicious. The trick was in knowing just how much to show and in what area. Additionally, knowing what emotional outbursts were tolerated was mandatory for this to work.

Matt placed his hands on his hips. "If Ross hired a woman, it would have been while I was on board the *Brah'Kerov.*" Matt narrowed his eyes and let a controlled amount of disdain follow his words. "But I can't ask him about that now, can I?"

High-pitched footsteps pattered on the floor at the end of the hall, followed by a gasp. It was Cossette. She stood frozen; her eyes locked with Lord Vaux. Its beady yellow eyes flared in recognition and it hissed.

"No!" Matt said, stepping in front of Lord Vaux. "It's a mistake—"

Lord Vaux shoved him to the wall and skittered down the hall, barreling after Cossette. Matt slumped to the floor, flinching in pain. His ribs throbbed and a sense of nausea climbed his throat. He gritted his teeth, forcing it back down.

Cossette stood still, wide-eyed and staring at the approaching monstrosity. As Lord Vaux drew close, she bolted back through the door from which she had come. Lord Vaux squealed and followed through the door. Matt rolled over to his hands and knees, panting for breath and cringing under the throbbing pain. What in the galaxy was that blasted woman doing wandering the halls? She knew Lord Vaux was aboard. She was smarter than that. Matt groaned, trying to get to one knee.

A burst of flames and debris erupted from the doorway they had disappeared through. The floor rumbled with the sound of the explosion. The doorway and part of the wall collapsed, with smoke billowing out.

Matt stared, dumbstruck. At that moment, there wasn't any pain in his ribs. There was no throbbing, and in fact, there wasn't any breathing either. There were no thoughts or words to form. There was only the sight of a burned-out and exploded hallway. And yet, something about the whole scene was familiar. Goosebumps coursed over his skin. He recognized it.

Heavy footsteps approached from behind, followed by a faint cackle. It was Jerry's signature laugh. "Well, well, Matt. I will be the first to admit, your accidents are a whole lot more convincing than mine." He helped Matt to his feet. "And yes, it was modified a little from your original outline."

Matt stared at Jerry, the anger building. Did Jerry put Cossette up to this? She could have been brutally killed. "You used Cossette as bait!"

"Matt," Cossette said, putting her hand on his shoulder.

Matt looked over his shoulder at her. He hadn't noticed her approach. Whatever her planned escape route was, it had been efficiently planned. Without thinking, he turned and took hold of her arms.

She produced a warm smile. "Your plan was excellent. I just needed to give that squiddy more motivation. Your notes indicated that Lord Vaux was more cunning than most. I wasn't convinced that simple curiosity was enough to overcome its suspicions."

What she said made sense. And out of all the accidents he planned out, this was the one he would have chosen. She was right about the lack of motivation. Even he was not convinced the spineless squiddy would have fallen for it. And he most certainly would not have approved of using Cossette as bait. And the most troubling thing was that she made the perfect bait. She was wise not to tell him about it.

"Why was I not informed?" he asked, keeping his tone neutral.

Jerry smirked. "Your natural reactions would be more convincing. And it would take less time editing the surveillance footage."

Natural reactions indeed. The stupid man had little confidence in his acting abilities. A failing that needed correcting. Matt backhanded Jerry, causing him to stumble backward.

Jerry cackled again. "I knew it would impress you."

"Your faith in my abilities is less than inspiring, my dear friend. But on the whole, you've both done an excellent job." He glanced down at the end of the hall. "Get the footage edited. I need to announce that a dreadful accident has occurred."

"We are back on track then?" Jerry asked.

"Hardly," Matt said, turning his attention back to Jerry. "The Scorpiian senator has just died. There will be a power struggle over not just this station, but over the senate seat as well."

"How long will that take?" Cossette asked.

"If last time was any indication," Matt explained. "We have a grueling seven months ahead of us. We'll be laying low, so to speak. Once the power vacuum has been filled and the dust settles, we'll be back on track." Matt held his side and began walking away.

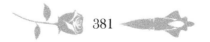 381

"Matt," she said, walking up to him. "I'm sorry I didn't tell you."

He sighed, looking down. "It's not that..."

"What then?" she asked, searching his eyes for understanding.

Matt stopped and pulled off a glove. He reached for her but halted. Something in the back of his mind protested. He hadn't touched another woman since Megan. Would he betray her if he reached out to another? *Such things shall have to work themselves out later,* he decided. He placed his hand on her cheek. She closed her eyes, leaning into his touch.

"I was afraid I would lose you," he said.

"I'm sorry, Matt."

"No need," he said in a soothing voice. Since when had his voice ever been soothing? Maybe it was something more than just the medication that had gotten into him. "It may take another five years," he explained. "But we'll stop wishing for things to be different, and start making them different."

Chapter 50

THE RACE OF PROPHECY

J onathan paced across the bridge of the *Saratoga*. It would have been nice to stay next to Ellyra. But with the sense of awkwardness swimming in the air, it just wasn't possible. The memory of her black hair and fierce eyes flooded his senses. The feelings that were so easy to put aside in the heat of the battle came barging into his idle thoughts. Why had she come to the bridge? She had seemed so resolutely antagonistic when he left her. Jonathan shook his head. War often brought soldiers together in a brotherhood that could not easily be understood. Could that have been what brought her to the bridge? He sneered at the thought. Someone to love and cherish was what he desired, not a companion to share war stories with.

Repairmen had been funneling onto the bridge, changing out circuit boards, and running diagnostics. The shooting may have stopped, but the battle wasn't complete until everything had been assessed. The effort marched on.

"What does Kansas mean?" Ellyra asked.

"Just an expression, duckie," Cynthia explained. "We're prone to saying things of that nature whenever we're gobsmacked."

"Cindy, has the Skorath ship answered?"

She swiveled around in her chair around. "No. And they haven't for the last twenty minutes. They don't appear to be talkative."

"Skipper, incoming transmission from the *Azeltar*."

Cynthia glanced back at Gordon a moment before returning her gaze to Jonathan. "But I believe I now know someone who is."

Jonathan smiled.

Cynthia swiveled her chair facing forward. "On screen, Gordon."

The large screen on the wall flickered and displayed a video image of the bridge of the *Azeltar*. T'Kal was out of his hovering chair and instead stood in the middle of the room. A thick fog rolled across the floor obscuring his feet. He motioned with his hands and subtitles scrolled across the screen. COLONEL TERYNN, IT WOULD BE WISE TO CONVENE AND DEBRIEF ON THE EVENTS WHICH HAVE UNFOLDED.

Jonathan nodded. "Agreed. And since we don't know the extent of the damage to each ship, let's meet in person. Is your teleporter operational?"

T'Kal nodded as more subtitles scrolled. IT IS, COLONEL. AND I WILL TAKE THE LIBERTY OF GATHERING TOGETHER YOUR COMMAND STAFF.

"Thanks, T'Kal. See you shortly. Terynn out."

The transmission ended. Cynthia unfastened her safety strap and stood, stretching. "When you've got yourself some answers, Jonathan, don't be in any rush to tell me. I intend to lie down with a hot cup of that dodgy import."

Jonathan shrugged. "Well, if it makes you feel any better, now that we're completely cut off from Earth, that has now become the best tea in the fleet."

She grimaced. "What have we been reduced to?"

A blinding white light flashed all around. Jonathan took in a startled breath. After a brief moment of dizziness, he opened his eyes. He stood on the bridge of the *Azeltar*. He glanced up at the precariously low ceiling. Somehow the room looked bigger on the screen than in person. He looked down toward his feet. What was with the fog, anyway?

"Greetings, Colonel. It is reassuring to see you in good health." T'Kal said into his mind.

"Likewise, T'Kal," he said strolling up to him.

In another blinding white flash, Isabeau appeared on the bridge. Her startled expression and wobbly posture meant he was not alone in that dizzy feeling. She looked up at him with relief in her smile.

"Jonathan!" She ran over and hugged him. She abruptly pulled away, blushing. "Sorry, Colonel, sir."

He smiled. "It's good to see you, too, Izzy. And don't mind the formalities right now. We have plenty to worry about already."

Another blinding flash of light brought Lucas. He strolled through the fog on the floor like he was taking a walk in the park. Why didn't he look affected by the dizziness? Lucas smiled. "Forgive me, Jonathan. My roommates and I couldn't help but overhear your thoughts. Not to go into boring details, but in short, they stimulated my inner ear during the transport."

"You couldn't help overhearing my thoughts?"

Lucas flushed. "I did not mean to pry; I'm still getting used to this whole partnership."

"That could have come in handy at the senate."

He shook his head. "Has to be up close."

In yet another blinding white flash of light, Fox appeared and stumbled. Isabeau's eyes lit up. "Fox!"

He smiled and gave a ridiculous bow. "Have I thought long to see this morning's face, and doth it give me such a sight as this?"

"We've missed you, too," Jonathan said as Fox approached. "How did you get here?"

"Long story," Fox said. "The short version is that I found the Skorath."

385

"So, you're responsible for bringing the cavalry? How did you ever sweet-talk them into helping?"

Fox stammered a moment for words. "Well, I...you see, um...I–I guess diplomacy just came naturally."

"Good work, Fox."

"Which reminds me," Fox said, turning to T'Kal. "Can you also bring Miss Layna from the *Calmao*? She's the literature expert who helped me find the Skorath."

"Are there any other individuals that would be appropriate to bring?"

"Yes," Jonathan said. "Please bring Diahlus Melquinn from the *Calmao*, along with my wife from the *Saratoga*."

The blinding white light flashed again, bringing Diahlus and Layna to the bridge. They each exchanged confused looks, surveying their surroundings. The light flashed again, bringing Ellyra.

"A little warning would have been appropriate," Diahlus said, looking at Fox.

"Diahlus," Ellyra said, rushing over to him. "I am so pleased to see you again."

"My dear," he replied, "the sight of you brings peace to these old eyes. I had feared I might never again see you."

Layna walked over to Fox and stood close to him. "Lieutenant Colonel Fox, where are we?"

"Oh, yes. Introductions. Miss Layna, may I introduce you to T'Kal, Supreme Commander of the Tumnei naval forces. Isabel, whom I work with, and the Colonel. Everyone, this is Miss Layna, who has been an enormous help in finding the Skorath."

Layna curtsied, her hair turning burgundy.

Isabeau tensed, glaring at Layna.

"On behalf of all of us," Jonathan said, "thank you for your help."

"The pleasure was all mine," she said.

Fox rubbed his hands together. "So, what do you think of the Skorath?"

"Tight-lipped and mysterious," Jonathan said.

"You mean they haven't said anything to you yet?"

 386

He shook his head.

"Colonel Terynn," T'Kal said in their minds. *"Sensor scans of the planet show there is a structure present with a stable oxygen atmosphere."*

"Well," Jonathan said, "since the Skorath aren't particularly talkative right now, maybe we can find some answers down there." He turned to T'Kal. "Can you teleport us inside the structure?"

He nodded, waving his hand in the air. A holographic keypad appeared. He punched several holographic keys. Then the blinding white light flashed yet again.

Jonathan blinked, steadying himself from the dizziness. They stood in a large dark room. Lights started turning on, slowly illuminating the room. Ornate carvings decorated three of the four large walls. The vaulted ceiling towered high overhead. Massive computer consoles littered the center of the room. Fox strolled into the center of the room, over to one of the computers.

"What are you doing?" Isabeau asked, almost in a whisper."

"Getting answers," he replied. "Care to join me?"

Jonathan and the others followed and surrounded a large control console. "Whoever used this computer had very big hands," Fox said, taking a seat on the bench. He fanned out his fingers over the palm-sized crystal plates. "I'm not much of a typist," he said, pressing some plates at random. Whenever he pressed one plate, it lit up. But when he pressed a second plate, they would both go dark.

Isabeau leaned over and pressed a few plates. Fox swatted her hand away. "I'm playing with it first."

She glared at him.

"...but I can share," he said, scooting over.

Isabeau slipped in beside him and began systematically pressing the plates. On one particular combination, both plates remained lit up. The wall at the front of the room grew bright, like a computer screen, and displayed a video image of a large alien with blue glassy eyes and a broad nose.

"You seem to be correct, Fox," Diahlus said. "They were indeed large."

The alien raised one hand. "Kalisahr Vendier, Lo'Kana. Jon tan'eer wilu ecba." The recording halted and the massive computer hummed and beeped. Then the recording continued. "...we never encountered anything like their kind before..."

Jonathan shot a glance at Isabeau. "How did you translate it?"

"I didn't," she said, shrugging. "It just sort of did that on its own."

The recording paused. Everyone looked back at Isabeau. She glanced back at the plates. "I don't think I touched anything."

The light in the room grew brighter as a brilliant white orb of light passed through the ceiling and floated down to chest height. The orb dissolved into sparkles of glimmering light that faded into the form of a woman dressed in glowing white robes. She took a few steps closer to the center of the room, casting shadows from the light she emitted.

Jonathan took a step closer to the woman. "Are you...?"

"Yes, Jonathan," she said. "I am Skorath."

"Your appearance is that of an Earthian," Ellyra said.

The woman turned to Ellyra. "It was meant to be a comforting appearance."

"May I inquire after your name?"

The woman smiled. "My name is unpronounceable on your tongue. You may refer to me as Vera."

"To guide or to instruct," Lucas said.

Vera smiled at Lucas. "You know the ancient tongue."

"Well, my roommates know a little, oddly enough."

Fox turned around to Layna. "I hope you're writing this all down."

Ellyra walked up to Vera with slow, timid steps. She gave her a formal hug, but her arms passed right through Vera as if she were a ghost. She glanced at Vera with a startled expression.

Vera gave a sad smile, extending her arms out. "I wish I could feel your embrace. What you see before you is but an echo, a projection."

"Then, may I ask where you are?"

Vera strolled over to the wall and waved her hand. The wall opened to reveal a window. Out in the starless sky of the orange and blue nebula, she pointed to the Skorath ship. "That is Vera. I am Skorath. I live in the waters of space."

"It's an honor to finally meet you," Jonathan said. "We have tried so hard to prepare for you. I'm afraid all our plans went out the airlock, though. We were hoping to meet you as allies instead of refugees."

She smiled and bowed to him. "Kalisahr Vendier, Beltares." She walked over to the computer at which Fox and Isabeau sat. She touched her ghostly hand to the console and the image on the screen flickered and began playing again.

"Kalisahr Vendier, little ones. I am General Elyin'Adar. You know as well as we do that the war goes not well in our favor. The Draconian armada has broken through our lines and destroyed our staging post on Quel'Sitar's moon. The nightmare we feared is now upon us. What the Draconians lack in power and technology, they make up for in determination and sheer numbers. We have never encountered anything like their kind before. In the last twelve years of this war, we have lost eighty-seven star systems to them. And now, with the loss of Quel'Sitar..." The alien looked down with sullen eyes. "My friends, I fear we are lost. Antares is lost."

Isabeau's eyes widened. "That's an Antaren."

Fox scratched the side of his head. "Not exactly what I had envisioned."

Elyin'Adar continued. "But make no mistake, little ones. This war is far from over. Our seeress tells us that in the generations to come, a new race will arise from a remote corner of the galaxy. They will have the power to do the impossible; they will frighten the Star of Draconia. Even the very heart of Draconia shall tremble before them."

Elyin'Adar took a breath. "You must hide beyond the reaches of the Draconian armada—we are unable to go where you can. Antares will die, nothing can change that now. But you must wait and watch for the new ones that will arise. And this is how you will know them: they will have the power to listen to what they do not hear. They shall say what they do not speak. And their name shall be called, young, interesting, unorthodox, the Will and the Way. And this shall be their sign:"

Elyin'Adar drew in the air with his massive finger. He drew straight across and then down. It looked as if he had drawn the top and side of a rectangle in the air. To Jonathan, it looked like the letter "F" without the middle line.

"Friends," Elyin'Adar again continued, "you had once asked us why we call you Skorath. In our tongue, it means the light at the end of the darkness. You have always been there to aid us in our darkest times. Now we need you to vanish into the shadows, to wait and to watch. Seek for the Beltares, the race of prophecy. Find them and bring them here, to take their place as heirs of Antares. I have hidden away what they will need. They will succeed where we could not. And in that sense, Antares *will* return." Elyin'Adar raised his hand in farewell. "Kalisahr Vendier, beloved Skorath."

Jonathan turned to Vera. "Beltares? Why did you call me Beltares?" He pointed to Lucas. "The Voonsu are the race of prophecy."

Vera shook her head with a graceful motion.

"What?" he asked in disbelief.

Ellyra put a hand on his shoulder. "Jonathan, do you not remember my first day on *Gamma Station*? You gave me a tour and we spoke of your Earthian expressions."

"Yes," he said, still puzzled.

"One of the things I said to you was that it was a wonder you could understand each other with all those expressions. You see, to someone unaccustomed to your way of speech, you seem to say what you do not speak."

"And to listen to what you do not hear," Diahlus said. "When we fought those two Scorpiian Harkons to save the Earthian frigate, you understood a message in how the ship appeared to come from Gamma Station when, in fact, it did not."

"I have often heard my father refer to the Earthians as a young and interesting race," Ellyra said. "And has not even Diahlus, here, referred to your strategies as unorthodox?"

"I did?" Diahlus asked.

Jonathan gave him a playful glare. "Yes, when you were complementing the spectacular results of this uncultured, arrogant, and impulsive ruffian."

"And the phrase you told Xer he should learn if he would learn anything from Earthians," Ellyra said.

Jonathan nodded. "Where there's a will, there's a way. But that could all be coincidental."

Fox blinked in realization, looking at Vera. "Is that why you spoke to me in metaphor? To see if I would talk that way?"

She nodded. "And then the sign," Vera said reaching her ghostly hand toward the shoulder patch on Jonathan's uniform. She pointed to the prominent shape which resembled the letter "F" without the middle line.

Jonathan glanced up with a look of confusion in his eyes. All the phrases and things that had been said were much more likely to be a coincidence. But that symbol—that very familiar symbol—was on every uniform and even on the flag of *Gamma Station*. It was such a common sight that it blended into obscurity. It was the Greek letter gamma.

He ran his fingers across his shoulder patch and then looked into Vera's golden eyes. "But...but we don't have a power that can frighten the Draconians."

She smiled. It was the kind of smile his mother would give him when he was missing something obvious. "The Draconians did not attack you because they were angry with you, but because they were afraid of you."

Jonathan blinked. A breath caught in his lungs. "Afraid? Of us?"

She nodded.

"How?" he asked in dismay.

She motioned to Fox. "The one that reminds me of Kalmeedes, gave us the answer." She looked back at Jonathan. "Do you remember your last senate convention?"

He nodded. "Yeah, the Scorpii were making a play to dictate everyone's energy output."

"You posed a very serious question," Lucas said. "You phrased it in a way that made it look like the Scorpii wanted to dominate the Draconians."

Fox shifted his glance between Jonathan and Lucas. "Boy, I missed some really good stuff."

"In all the time the Draconians have convened their senate," Vera explained. "There has never once been a race that could mold and shape the entire outcome of a convention with a few words. You hold no great influence, nor harness any technological might. Yet, you defeated an elder race with mere words. No one has ever seen such power in a young and deprived race."

"Is that why the Draconians became personally involved in the battle?" Ellyra asked.

"The dreadnaughts," Jonathan mumbled, the gears turning in his head. "That's why they sent them."

"And now," Vera said, "the others wish to meet you."

"Others?" Isabeau asked.

Vera nodded, pointing to the window where new Skorath ships were appearing. "We have waited for so long to meet you."

Numerous glowing orbs of light slowly descended through the ceiling, like the gentle falling of angelic snow. Layna grabbed ahold of Fox's arm, gazing up at the floating orbs of light. When each orb came down, it dissolved into the form of a man or woman. Each one would bow, giving the same greeting. "Kalisahr Vendier, Beltares." Ellyra placed her hand on her chest, watching the ever-increasing number of glowing orbs descending into the room.

Jonathan walked over to Vera, unnoticed. "I always knew the Senate was pointless. Why the Draconians ever entertained such a charade was always a mystery until now. They were looking for us, weren't they?"

Vera nodded.

Jonathan swallowed. "They knew about the prophecy too. And I'll bet they saw something in us that pointed to the prophecy."

"But they needed to make sure," she said.

"Dividing us up among the space stations," he said in conclusion. "By having the elder races study us, they could look for the other signs in the prophecy."

Vera smiled. "Your insight is a credit to your birthright."

"So, what happens now?"

"You must cease to be the Beltares and become the Antarens."

Jonathan took a deep breath. "I don't even know where to start."

"You must first become whole."

He stammered for words, confusion on his face. "What does that mean?"

"You must bind up that part of you which is in pain."

He huffed looking heavenward. If she was talking about faults, he had a million and one. It wasn't possible to be perfect. There had to be another explanation. "How do I find where I am broken?"

She took a step closer, her angelic face near his. She placed her ghostly hand to his cheek. He felt a warmth like the rays of sunshine. "A leg in pain will stumble. You already know where you stumble." She dropped her hand. "A broken cup can hold no water, Beltares."

Jonathan's eyes widened. He turned around and looked at Ellyra. Her contented light-blue hair swayed as she looked around in wonder, watching the falling orbs of light. The old enemy of awkwardness seeped into the air. How was he to redeem himself to her? In her eyes, he was a deceiver. And yet, she also saw him as an honest man. Truth was something that was supposed to set him free. Instead, it separated him from the woman he loved. This was where he stumbled. This was where there was pain. But, how could he win? This wasn't a battlefield with troops or starships to position. This was something entirely different. It was the realm of a woman's heart.

Something Ellyra had said to him months ago came flooding into his mind. She had said that the only difference between a commander and a politician was the weapon and the battlefield. Could the same be true of a commander and a man in love?

"Carpe diem," he whispered to himself.

He took a deep breath and walked over to Ellyra, soliciting her attention. He took her hands in his and gazed into her blue within blue eyes. "Ellyra, I am so very sorry, for how I treated you. I foolishly took no consideration for your feelings. I will not make that mistake again. Is there any way you can forgive me?"

Her eyes watered and her hair turned rose-red. She nodded, a tear breaking loose.

"There is something that needs to be said. Something I should have said a long time ago. Ellyra, daughter of Lord Areo of the house of El'Allel, I love you and I want you to be my 90. Will you be my wife?"

"Yes," she said, wrapping her arms around his neck. "With all my heart."

He leaned in and kissed her, letting the whole world fade into the background. He realized he had been wrong. He didn't need to see Earth to be complete; he needed her.

EPILOGUE

Isabeau scrolled through a digital checklist on her reader device. Most of them had been checked off, the rest would be soon. She slowly paced across the vast open room. The tapping sound of her high heel shoes echoed in the emptiness. She hadn't often worn heels, let alone a dress. It was one of the many delights that the evening's celebration afforded. Her only complaint was that the dress didn't have sleeves; it was the current Euroo fashion.

The door at the far end of the room slid open and Rana entered. She crossed over to Isabeau and handed her a pair of long gloves. "Here," she said. "These should fit you."

The elbow-length gloves felt soft and stretchy. She finally got to wear the lovely long gloves that she kept seeing the Euroo women wear. She eagerly slipped her arms into them. The ornate fabric hugged her skin and shone in the dim light. Wait, why was the light dim? Isabeau glanced at the ceiling. The room was still at half lights. She had been so worried about tonight's checklist that she had forgotten to turn on the rest of the lights.

"Vactu maral," she called out into the room. The lights obeyed her and the entire room lit up. It had taken over five months to translate the

Antaren computers and another six months to map out the basic Antaren language. It was helpful that Ambassador Lucas's Voonsu friends knew a little of the Antaren language.

Rebuilding the language was an ongoing project that she dearly wanted to get back to. Being officially assigned translation duties was a dream come true. It wasn't just translating one language into another; it was an actual study of a brand-new language. And, it sure beat space station traffic control any day.

"Oh, Rana," she said. "The gloves fit beautifully."

Rana returned half a smile. "I made sure they matched your gown."

Isabeau glanced down at the glimmering blue fabric, admiring how it looked.

"Just be sure to lift up the dress when you dance," Rana advised.

Isabeau shook her head. "Oh, I won't be dancing." Dancing was not something she was good at. Growing up in a military colony had given her very few opportunities to learn formal dances.

Rana set her hands on her hips. "You must," she said with an air of dismay. "It's tradition to dance the Mezonee."

"I don't really dance, Rana. I—"

Rana held up a silencing finger. "I shall put a remedy to that at once." She turned and marched across the room and out the door.

Isabeau rolled her eyes. Dancing just wasn't a priority. She looked back at her reader as a few people entered the large room. They were the event coordinators she had assigned. One checked the floral arrangements while the others managed a variety of last-minute arrangements.

Isabeau glanced back at her reader and checked off another item; the flowers were being attended to. When she heard footsteps approaching, she looked up. Chaplain Fiorelli walked up to her with a nervous look. "You going to be all right?" she asked. "You look a little nervous."

"I am nervous," he admitted. "The ceremony is easy but memorizing my lines in another language is challenging."

To hear Chaplain Fiorelli make an admission like that was surprising; he had the best pronunciation. Out of everyone she had been tutoring, he could speak the vowels so beautifully. It was pure joy to listen to the strong Antaren words roll off his tongue with such grace. During the rehearsals, she would close her eyes and just listen to him speak. It was like being transported back in time thousands of years. She could picture herself in the same room as Elyin'Adar.

She placed a comforting hand on his arm. "You have nothing to worry about. You speak Antaren so beautifully."

"But if I mix up my lines—"

"No one but the Skorath will be the wiser," she said with a friendly smile. "Trust me, whatever you do will be just fine."

He smiled and relaxed. "I'm glad you're here to talk some sense into me." He excused himself with a nod and headed to the front of the room.

Isabeau had scarcely glanced back at her reader before Rana had returned with Arkamenos at her side. "You shall find the Mezonee to be a simple dance," she explained.

"There isn't time to learn," Isabeau said in protest.

"Nonsense," she said. "We shall be brief."

If Rana was anything, she was relentlessly helpful. Arkamenos bowed and then offered Isabeau his hand. Rana held her reader and coached her on how to hold up her dress while she danced. As Rana counted, Arkamenos guided her by the hand through a promenade. Then they released their hands, turning in place. He took her other hand as they promenaded in the other direction. Rana was right, the dance did seem very simple to learn. There were some bows and curtsies, a simple spin, and a lot of simple footwork.

"This is fun," Isabeau said with a smile.

Arkamenos grinned. "That is the measure whereby you can affirm that you are dancing correctly."

At the conclusion, Arkamenos bowed to Isabeau and she curtsied. She turned around to the sound of Jonathan applauding her. He wore his dress black uniform but with a few modifications. To satisfy Rana's demands for Euroo tradition, he had added a red silk sash and a large scarlet-lined cape.

"You look as if the dance was made for you."

Isabeau blushed and retrieved her reader from Rana. "Sorry, Jonathan, I should be going over the checklist—"

"Now Izzy," he said, "you have triple-checked everything. Everyone has their assignments and instructions. It is now time to stand back and let the event unfold."

He was right. She did over-plan. But for such an occasion, she didn't want to let anything go wrong. After all, he was like the brother she was never allowed to have. Somehow, the evening needed to be perfect.

She shrugged sheepishly. "Okay, you have a point. I'll relax."

He grinned and turned to the long sidewall. "I think it's about time we open the window, don't you?"

"Ketu Shagall," she called out. In response, the wall parted like giant doors sliding apart. The parting wall revealed a window into space. The vast immensity of outer space, dotted with glimmering stars, caused everyone to pause what they were doing. A giant red star shone brightly in the distance. A small bright blue star was nestled in close to it. The window's radiation shielding allowed them to get close to the star. And with the luminance screen, they could look at the star in all its glory. The star looked close enough to reach out and grab it as she would an apple.

Ellyra walked into the room and stopped short, seeing the beautiful view. "Oh, Jonathan..." was all she could say.

Jonathan walked up to her and took her hand. "We don't yet know where the original Antarens came from, but this is the star my people call Antares."

"It would appear this breathtaking scene is what inspired the design of the new seal you have implemented."

"I thought it both fitting and symbolic."

Hundreds of bright orbs of light began descending into the room. Each one transformed into a man or a woman. One of them was Vera. She approached Jonathan and gave a slight bow. "Kalisahr Vendier, Beltares."

"Kalisahr Vendier, Vera," he replied. "Thank you for coming."

She nodded. "And thank you for allowing us to participate in your ceremony."

Ellyra smiled. "We would have it no other way."

Vera gave another slight bow and stepped aside. She joined a small group of Skorath that lined a straight path to where Chaplain Foireli stood. Jonathan took Ellyra's hand and led her down the aisle between the two rows of glowing Skorath. As they passed by, each gave a slight bow.

The large host of the mixed crew stood in rows to watch the ceremony. The front rows had been reserved for the shorter Tumnei crew. Isabeau fell into line and found herself beside Fox. Why did it have to be Fox? Lately, he hadn't been seen without that Layna lady at his side. At least she wasn't there at the moment; she had been selected to be one of Ellyra's maidens for the ceremony.

Jonathan gave a formal bow to Chaplain Fiorelli. "Kalisahr berikoof, 'ik sakal."

Chaplain Fiorelli cleared his throat and began speaking in a harmonic, fluid tone. "Presentum perelium ictu kalisahr, urectu fizim ma'ham..."

Isabeau closed her eyes, absorbing the rich sounds of the Antaren words. "Just listen to that pronunciation," she whispered.

"That's the problem," Fox whispered back.

Isabeau opened her eyes in alarm; she hadn't intended to speak aloud. Fox's dumbfounded expression told her what was wrong. She pursed her lips. "You didn't study the ceremony outline, did you?"

"Nope," he admitted in a whisper. "I figured it'd be Kalisahr Vendier and then a whole lot of English."

She smiled in amusement. "I'll translate for you." She turned back to watch the ceremony. "...as the twin celestial bodies of Antares embrace one another, so shall your temporal bodies embrace each other, becoming as a single solar light amidst the heavens..." Her voice caught in her throat. She sniffled. No matter how many times she heard those words, she still could not escape with dry eyes.

She wiped her eye and then continued, "...from the depths of tragedy to the heights of triumph, from the brightness of Antares to the darkness of solitude, standing together, immutable throughout the eternities..." She glanced at Fox. "And that last word simply makes the entire sentence a question."

Jonathan's voice echoed through the room. "Ferekoom 'al Satay'es."

Fox leaned in. "I guess that's Jonathan saying, I do?"

She bobbed her head in hesitation. "Well, yes and no. It literally means 'all that I am unto her'. But when used in this context, it denotes the formal acceptance of a pledge."

"Oh, so it's a very fancy way to say, I do."

She smiled. It was perhaps the best way to describe it.

Ellyra's voice then echoed through the room. "Ferekoom 'al Satay'er."

Slowly, step by step, Rana approached Jonathan. She curtsied, floating to the floor and rising back to her feet. She presented Jonathan with a long metal case. He took it and gave a slight bow to Rana. Opening the case, he presented it to Ellyra. Inside, lay two long dangly earrings. The shiny silver metal reflected hints of red and blue, the colors of the House of El'Allel. In the center of each, hung a glimmering white gem.

Ellyra sniffled and removed her stud earrings and exchanged them for the ones in the case. Jonathan handed the case back to Rana, who elegantly curtsied once more and walked back.

Chaplain Fiorelli removed the medallion that hung around his neck. The Antares stars were engraved in silver with red and blue ribbons. He walked up to Jonathan and Ellyra and wrapped their hands together with the ribbon, letting the medallion rest on top. "Brisnu 'al malad..."

Isabeau whispered, "...as the emblem of Antares binds them symbolically, so the Heavens bind them unto the eternities."

Chaplain Fiorelli backed up a few steps. "Priviku vak 'anin 'el Sahar 'vish Skorath."

Isabeau continued. "The Skorath will now pronounce their blessing."

Vera and a small group of Skorath encircled Ellyra and Jonathan, their glowing ghostly forms casting light on them. The Skorath dissolved into orbs of pure white light and circled around Ellyra and Jonathan. Their enchanting sounds didn't seem like words; it was as if they were singing. The angelic sound filled the room.

When the Skorath were done, they faded back into their human forms and stepped back. Chaplain Fiorelli removed the medallion from their hands and gave a short bow. "Kalisahr Vendier, Antarens."

All the Skorath in the room repeated, "Kalisahr Vendier, Antarens."

Jonathan kissed Ellyra and the tension in the air broke. People sauntered over to congratulate them. Isabeau turned back to Fox and stiffened. That Layna woman glided over to him with a bright smile, tugging on his arm like a giddy impatient schoolgirl. And yet she somehow managed to do it with an air of dignity. "Come, Fox. They will start the Mezonee soon."

Fox followed her to the center of the floor where lines were forming. Jonathan and Ellyra stood in the center. Arkamenos and Rana stood behind them along with many other couples. Isabeau stared at Fox. That was why learning to dance was a waste of time. Who she really wanted to dance with was occupied. Her heart sank. She needed to be somewhere else—anywhere else. She turned to leave but stopped short of bumping into Xer.

"Oh, forgive me," she said. "I didn't see you."

Xer bowed. "Quite all right, Commander Isabeau. I was just coming to see you."

"What can I do for you?"

"If your Commandership is not otherwise engaged, I should be delighted if you would honor me with this dance."

She looked into his intense grayish-blue within blue eyes. Why was he asking her to dance? From what Rana had told her, Xer was Ellyra's cousin and the next in line to lead her father's great house. There were plenty of Euroo women in elegant gowns who were much better dancers. It was crazy for him to choose her as a dance partner. Or was it the other way around? Maybe she was crazy for considering turning down a dance with a handsome Euroo aristocrat.

"Well...my dancing is...well, it's—"

"More than adequate for a dance such as this, I can assure you," he said with a smile, offering her his hand.

Isabeau blushed and curtsied. Her curtsy was rough at best. It would need a lot more practice. She took his gloved hand and he led her to one of the dancing lines. The music began to play. The symphony of instruments produced a melody that seemed to sway with the flourish of the ladies' dresses.

Isabeau concentrated on her feet as he led her down the promenade line, but she soon forgot her nervousness and smiled as they danced. Xer was a great dancer. It didn't matter how many times she missed a step or forgot a cue; he simply adapted to it and somehow made it look like it was part of the dance.

She giggled and smiled, letting herself enjoy the dance. It felt incredibly freeing. And, perhaps even more incredible, was that Xer's hair color had turned blond. He was enjoying the dance every bit as much as she was. It was disappointing when the music wound down to a close and the dance ended. Xer bowed and she curtsied once more to conclude the dance.

She took a breath, now conscious of the stiffness in her cheek muscles. Had she been smiling through the whole dance? Her eyes drifted past Xer until she met Fox's gaze. He had a strange look in his eyes. It didn't quite look like he had just remembered something. Rather, it looked a little more like he had just noticed something.

Appendix

CHANTELL

Skorath is rumor not. Chantell long ago lived.
Much exploring made. In far place, black ship
found. They Draconian enemies are. They in
great war fought. But they the war did lose.
Chantell wish in great war could have fought.
Chantell Skorath would have helped. War they
would have won. — Ambassador Trrrz'Kizits

DRACONIANS

All that is They Who Shall Not Be Named is forbidden. All technology, all stories and likeness, and all mention is illegal. Punishment shall be extermination. There will be no second chances. — Creus-Thanus

Benjamin Boekweg

EUROO

Much of what is referred to as Skorath has been lost to time. It has been conjectured by some, one Earthian in particular, that the ancient race of the aforementioned had visited our dear planet of Eurosia in our distant past. If such a claim could be substantiated, then all we know of as mythology might have sprouted in reality. And if that be the case, which of our mythological gods were real and which were the figments of our culture? — Ambassador Jonick Cora'Del

xii

SCORPII

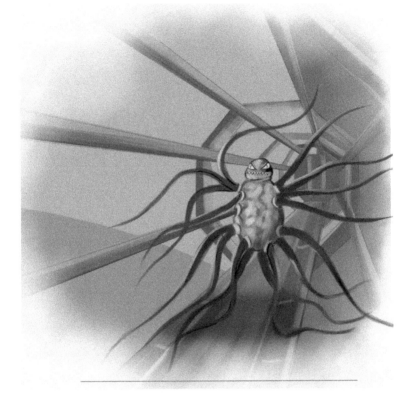

[Hiss], [squawk], [squeal], [grunt] – Lord Vaux

BENJAMIN BOEKWEG

SKORATH

*Speak of what is, and we shall tell of what has
been. The rain cannot precede the cloud; we
await the return of the Antarens. — Vera*

TUMNEI

*Much consideration has been taken regarding the
Skorath—much to our dismay in light of the decree of
the Draconians. To ascertain if these presumptions
are grounded in logic, more research would need to
be conducted. However, such research has been
forbidden. — Ambassador L'Por*

About the Author

BENJAMIN BOEKWEG

> *Some men see things as they are, and say why. I dream of things that never were, and say why not.* — Robert Kennedy

I was born a long time ago, in a galaxy far, far away...okay maybe not—but you've got to admit it would be pretty sweet to claim that! It would certainly make for a more interesting introduction. My name is Benjamin, and I love to tell stories of far away and the impossible. I enjoy a good sci-fi space opera or time travel story. My first introduction to fantasy was Brandon Sanderson, and I fell in love with his books. I simply love Sanderson's Rules of Magic.

Clean language? Why not? This is science fiction and fantasy; I can make up whatever words the characters use for "harsh language" and it doesn't have to offend me or my readers.

Buckle up; there's no Walmart where we're headed... My stories reside far outside the realm of normal modern life. They don't explore what we know, but what could be out there.

I believe the best stories are the ones that can send your emotions on a roller coaster and provide some humor as well.

Website: https://benjaminboekweg.com

Also by

Aberrant Star

Starfighter mechanic Vance Brewer never thought he wanted to leave the safety of his starcraft carrier. But when his secret is discovered, he quickly finds himself in a deadly struggle for survival. Now he must draw upon all his skills to defeat two invisible enemies; one is in his head, the other is stalking him...

The Last Wayfinder

I am outlawed and alone among the frontier planets. As a favor, I accepted a simple task to help a stranded 10-year-old girl. This special girl is not what she seems. Now the vile Corporation will stop at nothing to kill me to get her back and unlock her secret. Protecting her means confronting my past, which could be just as deadly. My very name attracts danger, for I am the last.

Ingram Content Group UK Ltd.
Milton Keynes UK
UKHW032238260423
420810UK00004BA/345

9 798986 144252